Case Study Designs in Music Therapy

Case Study Designs
in Music Therapy

Edited by David Aldridge

Jessica Kingsley *Publishers*
London and Philadelphia

First published in 2005
by Jessica Kingsley Publishers
116 Pentonville Road
London N1 9JB, UK
and
400 Market Street, Suite 400
Philadelphia, PA 19106, USA

www.jkp.com

Library of Congress Cataloging in Publication Data

Case study designs in music therapy / edited by David Aldridge.
    p. cm.
Includes bibliographical references.
 ISBN 1-84310-140-8 (pbk.)
 1. Music therapy--Research--Methodology. I. Aldridge, David, 1947-
ML3920.C327 2004
615.8'5154--dc21

                                        2003026466

British Library Cataloguing in Publication Data
A CIP catalogue record for this book is available from the British Library

ISBN 978 1 84310 140 6
eISBN 978 1 84642 000 9

This book is dedicated to Lutz Neugebauer,
Professor of Music Therapy, colleague and friend

Contents

CHAPTER I

A Story Told from Practice: The Reflective Inquirer in an Ecology of Ideas

David Aldridge

Language, before being a code or a depository of established meanings, is but a generalized style, a way of singing the world.

Maurice Merleau-Ponty quoted in Smith 1993, p.195

My colleague and I visited a man at his bedside in hospital. He was a participant in a research program and one of the treatment options was music therapy. As it was a controlled trial, he had given his permission to be part of the treatment group or the control group. Before the session started, he was given a questionnaire to complete.

We duly sang for him and his family. He and his wife talked about their life together, what songs they enjoyed singing, some from way back then, and we played some of those songs. They were also given a list of favourite songs chosen by other people in the hospital. Both identified songs from this list that they liked to hear and sing along with. Interspersed with these songs that we sang together were reminiscences about past events and a generous sprinkling of anxiety about the near future from the man and his wife. He had only just been admitted to the hospital and the first stage of the treatment was imminent that same evening. After we had sung, he asked, 'Was that the music therapy or the placebo?'

Now most therapists when they talk to their colleagues will use such vignettes from practice. When we talk to each other, we tell stories that work on different levels of meaning. The above anecdote is a commentary on the possibility of 'blinding' in clinical trials, music therapy placebos and the questionable quality of my singing. It also points to the advantage of songs that bring out reminiscences and topics for conversation.

While we present lectures in formalised styles and write papers according to given formats, when we get down to talking about what happens to each other, then we use stories. And these stories are about people, about 'cases' we have worked with. This does not turn people into objects, we give those cases names, albeit pseudonyms. Case is an abstraction for talking about the generic. A case may be a person, it may be a collection of illustrative examples, it may be a group. In some instances it may be an event, like the implementation of a new service, or it may be a situation.

In this book we will be reading how such stories are expanded into case studies which are formed into case study research designs. This is a broad spectrum of methods, as the reader will see from the varying chapters. At the heart of this approach is a move towards a formalised rigorous presentation of practice by practitioners thinking deeply about the meaning of their work and its implications for practice. But these ideas do not stand alone, we put them out to be used by others, just as others will influence our writing and our talk. They form, then, an ecology of ideas. Hence, we have stories that are told from practice by the reflective inquirer in an ecology of ideas.

The aim of this book is to show how we can formalise our studies to understand what we do and to communicate this to others. Together we can contribute to a body of knowledge. I do not assume that research will necessarily improve practice, nor that practitioners who do not use research are any less able than those who do. Simply, we have a variety of ways to do practice-based research and case study design is a flexible form that adapts itself well to what we do.

Staying close to practice

We need an approach to music therapy research that stays close to the practice of the individual clinician; that is, the musician as therapist. Each therapeutic situation is seemingly unique. Yet we compare our cases and share our knowledge with each other. Research methods are means for formalising our knowledge so that we can compare what we do.

What I will be arguing for in this chapter is a flexible structure that can be applied to clinical practice (D. Aldridge 1996). The practice is allowed to remain true to itself, although any research endeavour, by the nature of its reflexive scrutiny, alters practice. In doing research we ask questions of ourselves as clinicians, and when we involve our patients in the process, then they too will reflect about what is going on. Indeed, Robson now uses the term 'flexible designs' as opposed to fixed designs, and case studies are categorised by him as flexible designs in the qualitative tradition (Robson 2002, pp.176–184).

Rich empirical inquiry

Case study designs are research strategies based upon empirical investigation. A particular case is identified and located in context, which may be social, temporal or spatial. It is the bounding of the case in a context that makes the case study a 'case' study – the case may be a person, several persons, a group or a situation. Because the case itself is specific, and the context bounded, some authors contend that it is difficult to generalise from such research (Gomm, Hammersley and Foster 2000; Robson 2002; Stake 1995). However, it is the very context-related feature of case studies that make the approach important for music therapy. Case studies relate what is being studied to real life situations and allow us to use a multiplicity of variables. Selecting cases is central to this approach as this selection is, in effect, the 'population' to be studied. The nature of that selection will also colour the study; selection on theoretical grounds will offer a different view from when the population is determined solely by the situation at hand. In the qualitative research literature there is an emphasis on determining which sampling method is to be used. Many of us have to be content with the people that we meet in practice as the population of our sample and I would like to introduce the term 'reality sampling' here as an expression for choosing who, or what, is introduced into the case study.

The classic source of reference for case study research has been Yin's *Case Study Research* (Yin 1994), where he writes, 'A case study is an empirical inquiry that investigates a contemporary phenomenon within its real life context, especially when the boundaries between phenomenon and context are not clearly evident' (p.13). He goes on to say that there are opportunities for multiple sources of evidence and this comprehensive approach is beneficial in validating findings. We will see this use of multiple data in the following chapters where quantitative data is mixed with qualitative data to provide a rich source of material for interpretation.

Hammersley and Gomm (2000) say that the most important dimensions are those relating to the number of cases and the amount of detailed information. The fewer the cases that are investigated, the more comprehensive the information that can be gleaned. In Merriam's (1998) definition from education research, this comprehensiveness is reflected as '...an intensive, holistic description and analysis of a single instance, phenomenon or unit' related to field-oriented research (p.27).

What data are to be collected is the crucial focus of case designs. From an experimental perspective, where the data are fixed beforehand, then the data will be strictly controlled and the researcher will define the cases to be studied, as we will see in Tony Wigram's chapter. However, some researchers will construct cases out of naturally occurring situations, as we will see in Trygve Aasgaard's research relating to the life history of songs.

What is important is that case studies can incorporate multiple levels of analysis within a single study using mixed sets of quantitative and qualitative data (Eisenhardt 2002). We see this in Hanne Mette Ridder's study where she sings with late stage dementia patients, correlating physiological changes with behavioural observations. Such designs are flexible as they respond to the needs of both the patient and the researcher. As patients change, so does the therapy. To incorporate this aspect of music therapy practice, we need to include flexible designs that occur in naturalistic settings.

In-depth approaches encourage a rich source of data sources from tape recordings, questionnaires, interviews, photographs, letters and observations. In my suicidal behaviour study I collected material from newspaper reports over a given time frame, from observations in a psychiatric hospital ward, letters from women who had attempted suicide, questionnaires and observations from an admissions ward in a general hospital and videotaped recordings from a family therapy day clinic (Aldridge 1985, 1998a). When we have such rich studies we can begin to generate theories. Building theories from practice examples is a particular strength of the case study approach for the arts therapies in general (Higgins 1993).

Historical context

The folk-lore of case study methods suggests that these designs emerged from the practice of experimental psychology and psychoanalysis. Such a myth ignores the simple fact that human ideas have been conveyed in story form for centuries. 'Once upon a time …' until 'They lived happily ever after.' reflects this basic narrative form. Bruscia (1991) endorses this position in his book of case studies in music therapy when he writes in acknowledgement, 'To the individuals whose stories are told in these case studies'. When therapists of whatever therapeutic persuasion gather together their clinical discussions, they focus on cases; whether these be diverse, difficult or dangerous. Indeed, patient narratives are a valid form of health care research (Aldridge 2000b).

The origins of case study are nebulous, some authors citing a medical model (Robson 2002), others a sociological model from social worker's case histories (Hammersley and Gomm 2000) and yet others an ethnological perspective (Stake 1995). There appears to be a consensus that the early work of anthropologists and ethnographers promoted case study perspectives and that this was strengthened further by the Chicago School of Sociology (Chapoulie 2002; Horn 1998). Later researchers were also to develop the theme of human stories written as biographies from lived experience and these were to achieve an elaborated form in dramaturgical studies of people and the situations we find ourselves in. Indeed, it was Ervin Goffman's *The Presentation of Self in Everyday Life* (1959b) and a sequence of his other studies (1959a, 1961, 1990), which I read as a student, that was to have an influence on my own study of suicidal behaviour (Aldridge 1985, 1998a). Our patients tell us dramatic stories and these need to be reflected in the research that we do.

Making sense: the pursuit of 'meaning' in researching therapeutic realities

We are currently in an age of evidence based medicine. In music therapy we have been constantly challenged to provide a basis for what we do grounded in research results. To that end we have developed research traditions and provided a reasonable preliminary foundation that substantiates our work. This work is far from complete and, really, we have only just begun. While I have argued that we should indeed provide sound evidential basis for music therapy based on rigorous studies, we also need to consider what counts as evidence. This is not a new question and both general practice medicine and complementary medicine, now also appearing as integrative medicine, have also faced such a challenge (Aldridge 1988a, 1988b, 1991; Aldridge and Pietroni 1987a, 1987b).

Therapy occurs in a psychosocial context. Music therapy is a social activity. The way people respond in a therapeutic situation is determined by the way in which they understand that situation. By studying the way that people perform their symptoms in the context of their intimate relationships we glean valuable understanding of illness behaviour. Through real life case studies we have the virtue of continuing a close relationship with the natural social world of people of which we ourselves are part. The knowledge that we have of the world, and what counts as evidence, will not solely be gained from empirical sources but also from aesthetics, personal knowledge and ethical understanding. We have rich and diverse cultures and it is this rich diversity that we can utilise in understanding therapeutic practice.

Anecdotes as evidence

Music therapy is often dismissed as relying upon the anecdotal material of case reports, as if stories are unreliable. My argument is that stories are reliable and rich in information. We rely upon stories when we talk to each other, they are a common basis for communicating understandings in all cultures. What a case study does is offer a formal structure for these stories.

We are not alone in telling case stories. Detectives present cases and lawyers represent cases. Anthropologists and ethnographers develop narrative studies in exotic locations. Social workers, psychotherapists and counsellors all have their case study reports, often from not-so-exotic settings. Managers argue their case studies to improve situations. People who work with people are not only the luckiest people in the world, they are also hermeneutic people in the lived world; we abstract meanings from experience to inform each other as case studies. Although 'case study' itself is a catch-all term, the case study has regained stature in qualitative research and particularly amongst clinical practitioners.

While anecdotes may be considered bad science, they are the everyday stuff of clinical practice. People tell us their stories and expect to be heard. Stories have a structure and are told in a style that informs us too. It is not solely the content of a story, it is how it is told that convinces us of its validity. While questionnaires gather information about populations, and view the world from the perspective of the researcher, it is the interview that provides the condition for the patient to generate his or her meaningful story. The relationship is the context for the story and patients' stories may change according to the conditions in which they are related.

Anecdotes are the very stuff of social life and the fabric of communication in the healing encounter. As Miller writes, 'every time the experimental psychologist writes a research report in which anecdotal evidence has been assiduously avoided, the experimental scientist is generating anecdotal evidence for the consumption of his/her colleagues' (1998). The research report itself is an anecdotal report. Stories play an important role in the healing process. Testimony about what has occurred is an important consideration. Indeed, we have to trust each other in what we say. We are witnesses to what happens. This is the basis of human communication and is at the heart of therapeutic practice.

Case study design will take these stories as a basic foundation. These are then formalised according to the needs of the teller and the listener. This forming of clinical experience into a structured case study narrative provides the relationship of our experience to the broader context of professional practice. We need to build bridges to those with whom we want to communicate. That will at times necessitate using the instruments that belong to their discourse in finding appropriate forms for reporting experience. While music therapists could see clearly what was happening when Cochavit Elefant showed videotapes of her singing with the girls in her study, it was the formalised study based on identified baselines that brought her work to a broader audience of professionals, as we see in Chapter 7. Similarly,

the work of Hanne Mette Ridder has provided an elaborated basis for understanding communication with the elderly demented using a set of structured data
sources that other practitioners can relate to.

Understanding narrative forms

> The point of these therapies is not so much to cure the individual as to
> develop forms of viable meaning. (Gergen 1997)

When we each come to tell the stories of our lives they are not of the substance of
conventional research reports, nor of the quantified language of science. Our lives
are best described in the dynamic expressions of a lived language. The essence of
language is that of musical form which is the vehicle for the content of ideas
(Aldridge 1989a, 1989b).

For those of us involved in the Family Therapy movement, core texts had been
the books of Gregory Bateson (Bateson 1972, 1978). Everything became process,
system and ecology with the intention of stamping out nouns. We see this perspective in Christopher Small's book *Musicking* (1998) where he also references the
same discourse as I have done in my earlier work. What we do as individuals is
understood in the setting of our social activities and those settings are informed by
the individuals that comprise them. Research as process, the collection of data, the
outcomes of research and the ideas or theories we generate from that data have
meaning within a social context – our research milieu. What conventions exist for
researching are part of that ecology of the research and practice milieu of which we
partake. When I write of the various languages of research, I should, to stay true to
my roots, be writing about the languaging of research(ing).

When we classify, codify and conceptualise from experience we are taking the
classical approach to observation and experimentation. We see this in botany,
meteorology and astronomy. The world is grasped through our senses or instruments designed specifically for the purpose of observation. This is the mode of
explanation. It is a narrative born of convention and as such informs us by
belonging to a broader set of narratives. Within a scientific culture we have conventional forms within a repertoire of expressions.

However, whenever we seek the meaning of experience and wish to make that
meaning manifest we can turn to other modes of expression. This can be seen in the
process of story telling. My argument is that we need to extend our repertoire to
include varying conventions of research forms and that is the strength of case study
research.

Music and therapy

Research from a therapeutic perspective is not medical science in that it has no generalisable reference. The importance of such work is in its particular subjective and unconventional reference. While the aesthetic may appear to occupy a pole opposite to the scientific, I propose that a pluralist stance is necessary to express the life of human beings (D. Aldridge 2000a). Pluralism is being used here in the sense that no political, ideological, cultural or ethnic group is allowed to dominate the discussion. That is why the evidence-based medicine needs a counterbalance, not against the concept but to counter the idea that such a perspective is the only legitimate perspective to inform practice delivery.

The concept of pluralism is borrowed from theology. The basis of the understanding is that no one of us as human beings can begin to claim a full understanding of the divine, thus in all modesty we have to recognise that we have only parts of the picture. Surely the same goes for music therapy: no one group can claim hegemony, nor absolute understanding of the truth of what music therapy is. A challenge is for us all to come together and merge those various understandings. To do that we tell our varying stories in differing ways, all of which have their own validity. Whether they have a validity outside our own field of expertise depends upon how we negotiate that validity and which languages we encourage. One of these languages will surely be research and amongst its dialects will be those of case studies, amongst clinical trials and a rich variety of other methodological approaches.

Emphasising one authoritative base for music therapy research is suspicious. The quest for one superior model for empirical evaluation is the quest for disciplinary power and an attempt to marginalise other opinions. We have differing ways of languaging music therapy, as we have of musicking, but we can still respond to each other and find commonalities of understanding. These will be local rather than global.

What is important in a pluralistic approach is that we accept music therapy research with its various emphases: *music* therapy and music *therapy*. As research is a therapeutic approach, we must reach some accord with the principles of clinical research. As an aesthetic approach, we can find coherence with research within the arts. As a psycho-social approach, we can also call upon a broad repertoire of social science research strategies.

Forms of expressing ideas

Both art and science bring an appreciation of form and the expression of meaning and have their own conventions. Maps, traces and graphs are articulate forms of an inner reality. So are the objects of art. They exist as articulate forms; they have an internal structure which is given to perception. In expressive art sensory qualities are liberated from their usual meaning. While science requires the graph for regularity, art requires that forms are given a new embodiment; they can be set free to be recognised. In the studies presented in this book, we will find a variety of forms of expression, each of which adds further to our understanding.

What we need in clinical research is to facilitate the emergence of a discipline that seeks to discover what media are available for expressing this ecology of ideas which we see as a person, and with which we engage as a therapist or researcher to discern the meaning of change. These media may be as much artistic as they are scientific.

To work in this way is also to consider aesthetics; the essentials of pattern and form. For a research methodology in music therapy we cannot always revert to the questionnaire and a standard test. What we are challenged to develop is a way of presenting the work of art itself *as it appears in the context of therapy*. This is not to deny the value of the questionnaire and the standard test but to encourage an extension of our research repertoire to include other forms of assessment and presentation. The chapters from Gudrun Aldridge and Denise Grocke show two different formalised ways of telling clinical stories based upon two differing contexts of therapeutic practice. In this way, clinical practice influences the research narrative, just as the researchers' questions influence the form of presentation.

A praxis aesthetic

Originally aesthetics was the philosophical study of art but its meaning has been extended to the way in which we look at nature. I have extended this to say that it is also an attitude that we can take to assessing the products and processes of therapy. The aesthetic attitude is a style of perception that is not solely concerned with factual information but with the immediate qualities of the experience itself. In the aesthetic attitude we consider what the characteristic values of an aesthetically satisfying product are.

In a praxis aesthetic we are looking at the products of therapy. These are traces that we take for the therapy process. Music therapy demands such an approach. While music therapy may be submitted to scientific scrutiny from a medical perspective concerning its therapeutic aspects, it is also an 'art' therapy and can be considered from an aesthetic perspective. As the results of such research are produced from therapeutic practice and not as art objects, I use the term praxis aesthetic so that we can identify characteristic features that are pertinent to what is done in practice. There is a tension inherent in the concept of music therapy, as it brings two realms together: that of art as music and of art as therapy. When we come to research music therapy, and particularly when we come to justify the reasons for using music as therapy, then we need to consider what forms of assessment we are using.

When we come to interpret what takes place in music therapy we can rely, in part, upon artistic terms. For example, the music therapist talks about the patient's ability to maintain the logic of a sustained melodic line alone and this has significance for the development of the therapy as we will see in the chapter by Gudrun Aldridge. In the chapter by Denise Grocke, the case material is also presented through imagery and mandala drawings.

At the centre of therapeutic work in some music therapy practices is the creative art in performance or composition. It follows then that we use aesthetic means to attend to the meanings of such works of art. Works of art do not point out the meaning directly, they demonstrate it by recreating pattern in metaphorical shape or form. What we see is indicative and demands an interpretative approach, the *emic* qualities of ethnographic studies. Emic data require an interpretation by the researcher while data from systematic observations are classified as *etic*. This is inevitably a rough and ready distinction because the observations of naturally occurring phenomena also require interpretation, as we will see later.

From a modern scientific stance, the body is to be manipulated according to the processes of classification and normalisation. People are observed, classified and analysed as 'cases' in relation to their deviance from a given norm. Disease becomes a category like any other rather than the unique experience which it is. Merleau-Ponty (1968) calls this the 'second positivity', that is, we assume there is a normal human body against which any particular body can be measured.

In music therapy there is often no normal performed expression of the body against which we can judge others. Yet, somehow, we manage to judge what is an expected performance in the context of our relationships. We know and experience in a way that we communicate within our cultures. Discerning this knowing is at the basis of qualitative research. We expect people to perform themselves as unique works of art, thus 'cases' become objects not of comparison against a norm but of celebration. This is a fundamental difference of approach where cases are not seen as examples of potential or actual deviance but as unique.

Of course we compare, that is a natural activity of making sense, but it makes a difference whether we compare experiences to celebrate their richness of diversity or scrutinise them for pathology. Some case studies will be idiosyncratic and offer a unique perspective. Yet we incorporate these into our understandings because we, as readers, are not passive consumers of knowledge. We resonate with what we read, making associations between what we read and what we have experienced.

Therapy, treatment or care?

There is a tension inherent within music therapy research. It is *music* research, an aesthetic activity contextualised by a therapeutic situation. We can utilise a broad spectrum of musicological approaches. It is also a *therapy* research, albeit defined by its emphasis on music, and therefore subject to forms of therapeutic scrutiny. When we attempt to enter systems of health care delivery, then we must be aware of the conventions of legitimate research. But those conventions are not fixed. We can demand that they accommodate what we have to say if we argue our point articulately and rigorously, just as we must be prepared to offer appropriate research related to those conventions. Case study designs offer such formats. The task that we have before us is to explicate and negotiate those flexible conventions.

Advocacy and the evidence-based metaphor

The evidence-based medicine debate places case reports as 'mere opinion' along with recommendations from expert committees (Sackett, Rosenberg and Haynes 1996). Yet opinion is the common currency of our daily lives. Opinion is informed and that is what patients and colleagues expect from us. One of the sources of that opinion, but only one of the possible sources, will be clinical trials. The danger of an evidence-based approach is that evidence is restricted, and one of those restrictions is an elite opinion based upon a certain set of defined criteria. Hence my plea for pluralism.

Yet the concept of evidence is being used here as a legalistic metaphor rather than a scientific metaphor. In a courtroom, various forms of evidence will be produced where experts are invited as witnesses. It makes no sense to restrict the range of evidence. We have to establish the reliability of the witnesses and the basis of their expertise but not restrict the forms of evidence a priori. I am not advocating the use of dogma, nor opinions without reasoning, simply that there are various forms of reasoning. Case studies offer reasoning through perspectival forms as research practice conventions. Common to these forms is a focus on a specific theme, locating the evidence within bounded contexts, establishing the sources of the demonstrative material that we are using and arguing our conclusions only from the material that we have presented. This is simply sound research methodology, no matter from what methodological persuasion we come. The demonstrative evidence may be measurements, it may be recordings, it may be interviews or it may be questionnaires.

Whether or not we accept the validity of the witness is a political act. In the music therapy research debate we are arguing for wider inclusion in the service delivery of health care. Evidentiary material must have a broad base; if case studies are being refused under the guise of appropriate research then this has to be recognised as simple prejudice by those who determine what is 'appropriate'. The basis of many therapies is, in reality, 'case' based.

There has been a shift of interest in the concept of disability from an emphasis on biological impairment to the unique experiences of the sufferers. Similarly, we may argue that relevant outcomes are dependent upon what the sufferer has to say. Practitioners also relate outcomes in terms of a clinical narrative and both clinicians and patients have global vocabularies regarding functioning and coping (Bilsbury and Richman 2002). While evidence-based medicine emphasises quantification, it runs the risk of losing the vital elements of individual difference in particular contexts, which is what we see as clinicians. Change is the experience of qualities relating to stages of transition rather than being a sequence of symptom scores. Case studies allow us to include transitions as process and as events, as the important moments between the scores.

The greatest challenge of 'evidence' is how such evidence finds meaning in everyday practice. While we talk of music therapy, the actual practice is varied across a broad spectrum of practices and these themselves may vary across continents according to which model is being used. In psychotherapy research there has been an attempt to standardise treatment by offering treatment manuals for empirically validated treatments for specific client groups and particular problems (Beutler, Moleiro and Talebi 2002). The primary reason is to provide insurance administrators with selection criteria in choosing which services to provide.

In contrast, there is research demonstrating that it is common, global qualities related to expectation about treatment, the perceived charisma of the therapist and the relationship between therapist and client that are effective (Luborsky, Singer and Luborsky 1975).

A difficulty of evidence-based medicine, when it sponsors a treatment manual approach, is that the therapist is forced to follow a rigid treatment plan and those elements of spontaneity and creativity, that music therapy cherishes, are discarded. Furthermore, manual-based treatment will be based on treatments that are easily converted into manuals and these will tend to be both highly structured and short-term. This poses a skewed research cycle biased in favour of short-term, highly structured interventions, which promote more research studies because they are easier to organise as clinical trials and are of short duration. We are still left with the problem of converting these studies into clinical utility. Nurses have found the same problem in that 'best practice' requires not only comparable outcomes from evidence-based research but a knowledge of the context of service delivery that includes the patient and his or her community (Driever 2002).

Research as advocacy, the idea that burns

In the early sociological studies that used case study method, there was an element of advocacy that gained distance, and strength, by having a research base. These studies intended social reform, looking at the homeless (Andersen 1923) and the delinquent (Shaw 1930). In my study of suicidal behaviour, I was so annoyed by the crassness of medical arguments regarding what I was seeing before my eyes in practice, that I decided to do something about it. But rather than simply tell people they were wrong in their understandings of suicidal behaviour, I began a series of research studies that could say why those approaches were wrong and base that argument on a broad platform of evidence. The validity for that argument was that it occurred in an academic context of a doctoral thesis[1] – this was the ecology.

This process continues today with those doctoral candidates who study with me; they are advocates for their own ideas and for anomalies that they see in health care delivery, for patient groups that 'fall out' of the system or champions of music therapy practice. All I ask is that a small flame burns. This flame might only flicker sometimes but it can be fanned into the fire of research. There is inevitably a partiality in this process, in that by taking up causes, we open ourselves to bias. That is why I emphasise an ecological approach. We do not research alone, we have supervisors, sponsors and spouses. Our patients want to know what we are researching when they are part of research programs. Our institutions also have vested interests and the audiences for whom we are writing scrutinise us for our prejudice.

On the other hand, I question the believability of uninterested research lacking any vitality of knowledge. Like musicking, languaging and researching, knowledge is an activity and needs to be pursued vigorously as well as rigorously.

I would like, then, to present here some personal beliefs about research because researching is an activity that has to be lived fully. Doing research is not simply applying techniques of collecting data and devising formulae for analysing that data.

1. Music therapy research is evolutionary, at times revolutionary. Such research will influence practice to a limited extent. What we need to bear in mind is that theory and practice are shaped by social processes. Research is only one small, modest contribution amongst many that bring about change. I hope that I haven't dissuaded too many

---

1   Incidentally, the biggest difficulty was finding examiners to examine a qualitative study in 1985.

would-be researchers, or bruised the vanity of my professional colleagues by stating this.

2.   Varying traditions of thought: psychological, musical, medical, socio-
      logical, philosophical, influence how we do music therapy research.
      Each of those discourses will vie for legitimacy, and that legitimacy
      will be localised to places and times. These discourses too will be
      relativised by economic and cultural processes. Some institutions only
      support applied research performed by trained music therapists. This is
      a political decision, just as it would be if another institution fostered
      only theoretical music therapy studies by ethno-musicologists. Some
      centres say that they only support particular clinical studies that attract
      grant funding. Again, this is decision based not solely on 'scientific'
      grounds, it belongs to a cultural and fiscal ecology.

3.   Clinicians and health care providers are more likely to accept research
      findings if the results are about specific problems and the research is
      based in a naturalised setting. Research is of no use if it sits upon a
      library shelf. We have a broad variety of journals within music therapy
      to disseminate results. Furthermore, it is possible to publish music
      therapy research in other journals. Our potential readers' questions are
      always about how the research findings can be applied in daily
      practice.

4.   Bodies of music therapy knowledge are not universalisable but there
      are commonalities of practice. The more that I see music therapy
      research developing, then the fewer the opportunities for global state-
      ments about 'music therapy'. We could at best say 'music therapies'. In
      practice we need to look at specific approaches to recognised needs as
      identified by the communities in which we work. How we weave those
      localities of understandings into the cloak of knowledge is the basis of
      teaching, the ground of authoritative reviews and a good argument for
      symposia and conferences.

5.   The praxis knowledge of music therapy is fluid and fixed research
      models lose this fluidity of knowledge. Music therapy research based
      upon considerations of therapeutic relationship is less likely to be
      reactive to fixed response measures than it is to flexible patterns of
      response that adapt to changing circumstances.

6.   There are no universal criteria for judging music therapy research. We can, however, be specific about the purposes that research is expected to fulfil for identified client groups and music therapy initiatives.

7.   When resources are scarce we need to establish the applicability of our findings and a means for implementing those findings. This is a political decision.

8.   Research will be used when it is accepted as offering viable guidelines to practitioners that relates to their own knowledge of clinical change.

9.   The search for a list of validated treatments is a political agenda that attempts to legitimise one predominant form and disenfranchise others.

Health care delivery

What we also need to debate is the nature of therapy as treatment or care. If we claim that music therapy is a form of treatment, then we fall under the rules of evidence for establishing the efficacy of treatment. If however, therapy is a form of care, then the rules change, and we can speak more openly of qualities of care. Music therapy is an overarching term for a variety of practices in a plethora of clinical, educational and social fields. This makes it difficult to provide any definitive statements about 'music therapy'. We can take heart, however, as we only have to hear surgeons talking about psychiatrists to know that 'clinical medicine' is also a craft of diverse practices.

If an aim of health care initiatives is to improve service then we can learn from industry. Quality is improved by attending to the process of delivery where suppliers are in a close dialogue with consumers. This also reduces costs. Any new attempts to collect information must begin at this primary care interface between the practitioner and the patient, and the practitioner and his or her sources for referral. This would mean an emphasis on local networks according to local need (Aldridge 1990). However, we must first understand the complex process of health production before we can try to improve it, particularly in the field of chronic illness where many of us work. An understanding of health production must also be supplemented with measurement tools which represent the values of the producers at the work-face (practitioners), and the consumers with whom they meet (patients). Epidemiological methods can be developed to establish baselines from which the success of health care initiatives can be measured and outcomes can be monitored. One of the bases of epidemiology is the case study. From here we have our starting point. It is imperative that we develop a common language for

health outcomes that is understood by the consumers (patients), deliverers (practitioners) and providers (those who pay).

When we speak of health care we are not only concerned with economic
aspects of health, but the practice of 'caring'. It is this qualitative demand which
articulates the health care debate and stimulates the inclusion of music therapy into
health care delivery.

Health care, educational needs, social desires and political will

Meeting health care, educational and social needs is a matter of social strategy and
political will. Health is not an homogeneous concept, it is differentially understood. Educational and social needs are negotiated not written in tablets of stone.
Music therapy, like medicine, is not an isolated discipline but an agglomeration of
concepts taken from a variety of fields. These fields include the arts, the humanities
and the sciences.

The social understandings of health and education and how to practice
therapy are not fixed. Patients and health care professionals negotiate solutions to
health care needs from an extensive cultural repertoire of possibilities. This repertoire is composed of understandings from Western medicine, but also from folk or
traditional medicine and modern understandings of psychotherapies and creative
arts therapies. Similarly, professionals working in educational and social care
settings have varying agenda set within the communities in which they participate.
These repertoires too are varied.

However, there are factors common to a variety of health and educational
understandings. These understandings include promotion and prevention, health
maintenance and indications for treatment. Such factors are influenced by
economic strategies and cannot be divorced from considerations of community
welfare. Poor housing and poverty mock any talk of music therapy initiatives based
on consumer demand. There has to be a minimum level of income whereby people
are fed and housed before the luxury of health or educational choice can be
exercised.

A consumer-based health service will be pluralistic and integrative, offering
modern scientific medicine, complementary medicine and art therapy practices. If
health care is delivered as a commodity then we fall prey to perceiving health only
as a materialistic representation and only offer short-term solutions. If we consider
health as a process which can be actively promoted within the span of a person's
life by the allocation of appropriate resources, and that health can also be maintained by an appropriate life-style, then the expensive, but not inevitable, end
process of treatment may in some cases be avoided. This entails a long-term
strategy for health care. To plan a long-term co-ordinated strategy takes political

will and can only be accomplished by the active collaboration of those in health care delivery and consumption. Where therapy occurs, then consumers can be offered alternatives which fit the ecology of their own lives. Modern scientific medicine as it is delivered in primary health care will inevitably be at the core of such a pluralistic provision. What we have to do is to make the case for the inclusion of music therapy and this can be achieved through the case study approach that allows both empirical data and discursive arguments from that data applied to a broader ecological context.

The future delivery of health care will depend upon accurate information about the management of resources. To assess health care we will need accurate and appropriate tools of assessment. Case studies, in their traditional role of advocacy, play an important role in establishing practice models. We can use tools of assessment that relate to the management of resources while remaining true to the people we are trying to represent.

Case research designs

Case study methods are a part of a whole spectrum of research methods applied to the investigation of individual change in clinical practice. Such designs have the advantage of being adaptable to the clinical needs of the patient and the particular approach of the therapist. The designs are appropriate for the development of research hypotheses, testing those hypotheses in daily clinical practice and refining clinical techniques.

If systematically replicated, case studies can provide an ideal developmental collaborative research tool for uniting creative practitioners from differing back-grounds. From one study, we can generate ideas for new studies. In Tony Wigram's chapter we see an example of a cumulative study where hypotheses develop in a sequence of studies. Petra Kern demonstrates how a series of studies build up a powerful argument in support of her integrative approach. Those sceptical of case study methods can learn from Petra's methodology; she has been approached by various academic organisations to present her work to them because of its pragmatic appeal and the rigour of her research foundation.

Most appropriately, case studies allow for the assessment of individual development and significant incidents in the patient-therapist relationship. We see this in the traditional case study by Barbara Griessmeier where she tells us the story of Pedro as she accompanies him through his last eighteen months of life. In the case study by Trygve Aasgaard we see how he transforms this case study approach into a research study format. Both powerful studies are about the same therapeutic process, using songs with children with cancer, yet they each have differing structures.

In Denise Grocke's study we see exactly how musical choices are related to imagery during the course of therapy and how the therapeutic narrative unfolds.

Whereas single case experimental designs in medicine can ascertain significant change in a physiological variable leading to timely intervention, psychotherapy studies concentrate both on changes in the symptoms that the patient displays and interactive events in the ongoing process of therapy. We see this in Cochavit Elefant's study where, using multiple baselines, the process of learning is accommodated within the study design matching the process of research to the process of therapy.

Petra Kern uses a single-case design basis, cumulating a series of studies evaluating the effects of music therapy interventions in an interactive play setting. The practice interventions designed for the integration of young children diagnosed with autism spectrum disorder occur in the setting of an inclusive childcare program and are implemented in close collaboration with the children's teachers, and embedded in the ongoing classroom routines. Treatments' effects are evaluated using several single-case experimental designs, providing practitioners with a controlled experimental approach to the investigation of a single child under different circumstances, and the flexibility to adapt the intervention to the child's needs and the particular treatment approach. Such an approach offers immediate feedback about how the practice intervention is working.

Hanne Mette Ridder, in her work with dementia patients, offers a rich variety of data to support a developing argument. Again, her music therapy approach uses songs, but she is concerned with the ability to recognise communication amongst those who are said to be communicative. Through an elegant design, using quantitative and qualitative data, she establishes a basis for demonstrating that dialogue can indeed take place. Like Petra Kern, her therapy sessions are structured through songs. In these two studies, songs are not only part of the process but also provide structural elements within the therapy ritual.

Tony Wigram uses a cumulative design involving six studies where questions raised from practice are reframed as research hypotheses. Each completed study then raises questions that are answered in a following study. The results of each study contextualise the other studies, again bringing a rich set of related cumulative data. The lesson that we can learn from this is that we do not have to complete our research all in one action. We can have a research strategy that cumulates data. This strategy can also be shared by cooperating groups.

Jörg Fachner takes a mixed design exploring the relationship between physiological data and music perception establishing, like Hanne Mette Ridder, an important connection between physiological change and changes in consciousness or states of awareness.

Single case designs are particularly important for the creative arts therapies as they allow for a close analysis of the therapist-patient interaction. We can compare differing sets of data throughout a course of treatment. Personal change is considered within the patient, not by comparison with a group norm. A music therapist can, for example, treat a patient over the course of a year and compare his or her findings (changes in the music), both with colleagues in other creative arts disciplines (changes in painting or movement) and with colleagues from psychological disciplines (changes in mood rating scales or personality inventories). These findings can then be compared with the timing, and reasoning, behind varying therapeutic interventions. Such process research allows the therapists to see, or hear, how the emerging phenomena of therapeutic change are related to their therapeutic activities, hence the emphasis on single case designs for the promotion of theory building based on clinical practice and in generating data to support new models of intervention.

Applied studies

Case studies bring an important facet to clinical research – that of personal application. While clinical medicine demands the study of groups as its research convention, it accepts single cases as special examples drawing attention to anomalies in practice, alerting practitioners to matters of urgent attention (in the case of dangerous side-effects, for example), or as falsifiers of a particular theory. This process can be inverted; we can also propose that case studies propose theoretical insights (Yin 1994).

In the creative arts we are looking for methods which say what happens when we do our therapy, and the reasons for doing what we do. Ideally, as research practitioners, we would want to be so clear about what we were doing that another practitioner could try it in a similar situation. Such clarity of practice description leads to replication and is one way of conferring validity on what we do as individuals but also builds up the common research stock of our professional groups.

Case study formalises clinical stories. These designs take as their basis the clinical process where the illness is assessed and diagnosed, a treatment is prescribed, the patient or client is monitored during the application of that treatment, and the success of the treatment is then evaluated. Yet we do not stop there. We talk about our practice. We reflect upon what we have done and we talk to each other and our fellow practitioners from other therapeutic disciplines about what we have done and what this means – the reflective practitioner in a community of inquiry (Aldridge 1996).

In all these studies we see a personal commitment to a clinical practice, and strong opinions about the value of music therapy practice. These researchers are not neutral in their attitude to practice, nor distant to questions regarding that practice. We have pretended too long, in a perspective loaned from natural science, that somehow we can stand back from what we do. The reverse seems to be the case. Music therapy researchers are very much engaged with the implications of their work for patients, and for the professional groups to which they belong. What we need to develop is the ability to engage and disengage at the appropriate moments, to reflect upon our research recognising our own bias.

Bias need not be a negative aspect. Once recognised, we see how bias works. In England and Australia, there is a game called lawn bowls. To play the game, bowls have to be rolled to hit a target bowl. The nearest wins. Each bowl has an inbuilt weight in the side, so that if you attempt to roll it in a straight line, it will curve away in the direction of the weighted side. This enhances the game, in that it is possible to avoid your opponent's bowl by curving the path of your own bowl. This is the recognition of bias and its controlled usage.

Exactly the same goes for bias in research, we need to recognise our own bias and how that influences our work; that is, the process of reflexivity. Through such a process, and engagement in the research, we begin to understand the world itself. As we will read, the researcher is often the therapist, having to switch between modes of engagement and critical questioning.

Research has a variety of aims; one is the establishment of practice in a wider setting than our own personal circle, and to do this we have to recognise the dialects of other researchers and the languages of patients, practitioners and providers. What impresses me in reading these chapters is that most music therapists have a broader training background than music therapy alone and are almost inevitably polyglots in terms of practitioner languages.

All the studies here have a naturalistic setting. While research changes the emphasis within the setting, the setting itself is most important in terms of applicability. Similarly, we also have emphasis in these studies on pragmatic methodology in terms of what can be done in a situation given often limited material resources. However, as the reader will discover, the human resources are considerable and impressive. And this is what gives us heart to research further. While financial resources may become restricted, it is our inquiring minds and our very selves, with those whom we research and practice, that are important resources.

At the end of the day, data must be interpreted, and are thereby hermeneutic, they cannot stand alone. This is the qualitative aspect of the works in this book.

What we see here are practitioners looking for patterns in the data. These patterns depend upon the context, that ecology of ideas, of which the researcher is part. Quantitative data also help establish a context – low scores on a scale help us to assess severity and how to understand the importance of the intervention. It is the intermingling of appropriate sets of data that facilitate our understanding. What we need is a clear sense of design to understand how the data relate to each other such that patterns of understanding emerge. Subject and object influence each other mutually, we have a milieu of understandings that are performed in the world. Occasionally these are explicated as formal studies and printed as papers or book chapters, at other times they appear in lectures, at others in study group meetings or in the form of intimate and deep conversations. What is important is the dynamic of understanding and its various forms of explication. Case studies offer one such flexible form.

Coda

I will end this chapter, as it began, with a story. This story illustrates the unity of knowledge and how elusive it is to the ordinary intellect. It is told by Rumi, a thirteenth-century mystic from Afghanistan. We use the symbol of the elephant in our projects as a reminder of the partiality of our knowledge and the importance of including the knowledge of others when attempting to understand the elephant of therapy. In *World Tales*, Idries Shah (1991) recounts the story 'The Blind Ones and the Matter of the Elephant'.

There was a city where everyone was blind. A king, with a mighty elephant, camped nearby.

The people of the city were anxious to experience the elephant and some from among this blind community ran like fools to find it.

Of course they did not even know the form or shape of the elephant, so they groped around touching different parts of it.

Each person who touched a part thought he knew what an elephant was.

When they returned to the city, groups of people gathered around, each anxious to learn the experiences of those who had touched the elephant.

They asked about its shape and were told by the man whose hand had reached an ear that an elephant is a large, rough thing, wide and broad, like a rug.

The man who had felt the trunk said that an elephant is like a straight and hollow pipe, awful and destructive. Another, having touched its feet and legs, said that it is mighty and firm, like a pillar.

Each had a partial experience and based their description of the whole on the partial. All imagined something about the whole by surmising from an experience with the part. No mind knew all and thus knowledge is not the companion of the blind.

When we try and understand the phenomena of becoming sick and becoming well, and how music therapy plays a role in that process, then we can only recognise the partiality of our understandings. We can however bring together differing perceptions and by working together, with an acknowledgement of our mutual partiality, begin to understand what happens. That in turn will help us to bring others to such understandings. Indeed, part of that process will be our joining with 'others' such that our understandings expand and merge.

CHAPTER 2

Therapeutic Narrative Analysis as a Narrative Case Study Approach

Gudrun Aldridge

In this chapter I will present a way of analysing music therapy sessions suitable for case study approaches. This approach is based on my doctoral thesis looking at the development of melody in music therapy (G. Aldridge 2002). It is a retrospective approach, I look back on my therapy sessions with a patient trying to make sense of what happened using tape recordings of those sessions and my field notes. But I am not simply interested in understanding what I did, I want to know how those understandings influence what I do and what the patient does – that is, meaning and action together.

The difficulty facing most of us in our clinical work is how to analyse the piece of work that we have before us using a systematic procedure that has both therapeutic and clinical validity while remaining true to the art medium itself. If we wish to discover how a particular creative art therapy works, then it is of paramount importance to maintain a focus on the work using the material traces of that work. What we need to develop is a means of discerning at what level we are describing, or interpreting, the traces before us. This method is not bound to any particular music therapy orientation and can be applied to other creative therapy orientations. In music therapy research we may use recordings, transcriptions as musical scores, and transcriptions from interviews as texts.

The method being used here is called 'Therapeutic Narrative Analysis'. It is intended as a method for the creative arts therapies and has been developed from previous writings about therapy (D. Aldridge 1996; Aldridge and Aldridge 1992, 1996, 1999, 2002; G. Aldridge 1993, 1996, 2000). It is a constructivist form of research design, meanings are negotiated. At its heart it is hermeneutic; it is based on understanding the meaning of what happens to us in the process of therapy and how we make sense of the world. I refer here to 'us': researchers, therapists and patients.

I choose to use the concept of narrative here as this is a broad concept well-suited to research in the creative arts therapies. Central to the narrative methodology presented is the idea of *episodes* (Aldridge and Aldridge 1999; Harre and Secord 1971). An episode is an event, incident or sequence of events that forms part of a narrative. Taken from the Greek *epi* = in addition and *eisodios* = coming in, we have the notion that it is something that is added along the way (*eis* = in and *hodos* = way, road or manner). Thus, therapeutic narratives are composed of episodes and it is episodes that we will consider as the basic units for our research methodology. Narrative is the story that brings these events together. In this way, we can use a variety of textual materials: written reports, spoken stories, visual media, recorded materials and musical material in the telling of the story. The research part is the analysis of those materials that bring forth new therapeutic understandings, hence, Therapeutic Narrative Analysis. The 'case' is the development of a melody throughout a course of music therapy sessions.

The process of interpretation

What I want to emphasise is that when we consider the phenomena of music therapy as recordings or transcriptions, they are abstracted from that initial experience of therapy. Such abstraction is inevitable as soon as we try to explain the situation in which we are acting. If I were to play you a recording taken from a music therapy session, you would hear in the extract of music that I play an experience that is at one step removed from the original session. It is tape-recorded and has thereby lost some qualities, although within the limits of recording fidelity it stays true to the original experience. It is still auditory and in the realm of music.

Using the word 'music' has already made a statement about the sounds that we have heard. Even attributing the term music to the experience has separated it from random sounds or organised noise. We are in effect making the statement 'Construe these sounds you have heard as *music*', and we can also add that 'This *music* is in the context of music therapy'. Knowing the context is necessary for defining events.

When we chain understandings together to make a story or a case history, then we are composing a narrative account. When we begin to try and understand such narrative accounts then we are using a *hermeneutic* method of therapeutic narrative analysis.

Therapeutic Narrative Analysis as process

As an introduction I present an overview of phases in the research process. These phases will be elaborated later in the paper (see Table 2.1).

Table 2.1 The phases of Therapeutic Narrative Analysis	
Phase 1: Identify the narrative	Gather the material together that will form the narrative. This may be a case study, or it may be a series of case studies. It is the story that you wish to tell.
Phase 2: Define the ecology of ideas and settings	Explicate the theoretical ideas present in the literature or from your own standpoint. This is the initial locating of the research context in the wider perspective of current knowledge (Context 1).
	Define the setting in which the narrative occurred. This will include details of the place of practice, the demographic details of those involved and may include historical details (Context 2).
Phase 3: Identify the episodes and generate categories	Identify episodes that are crucial for analysis.
	Generate a set of constructs from that episodic material and identify categories for analysis.
Phase 4: Submit the episodes to analysis	Analyse the episodes according to their contents using the guiding framework of the constructs. At this stage it is possible to use a regulative rules based hypothesis.
	It is also possible to submit episodes for categorical confirmation to colleagues.
Phase 5: Explicate the research narrative	Synthesise interpretations based on therapeutic traces to form a therapeutic narrative.

Phase 1: Identify the narrative

Gather the material together that will form the narrative of the case study. It is the story you want to tell about what had happened in therapy. In this case, two patients had played melodies in their final sessions of therapy. In this chapter I will present how I developed the narrative of one of those melodies. Audio-taped recordings, as episodes, from previous therapy sessions with the same patient provided the material for analysis (G. Aldridge 2002). These episodes were also transcribed as musical scores, so that I had both recordings and scores and musical 'texts'.

Phase 2: Define the ecology of ideas and settings

Explicate the theoretical ideas present in the literature or from your own stand-point. This is the initial locating of the research context in the wider perspective of current knowledge (Context 1). While this may appear as a literature review, the intention is not to give an exhaustive account of all possible papers but to locate the study in an ecology of ideas. When writing such material, it is not always necessary to have the theory part at the beginning; as the study develops new material enfolds itself into the study. This enfolding of literature contexts into the study reflects the narrative process that we go through as researchers. As we discover new ideas from the material, we read what other authors have written. Ideas have their own story in a case study. When we study, we read and collect new material. Similarly, at the end of a study we are challenged to put our new findings either into a new theoretical construct or within an established landscape of thought. This can be reflected within the case study form.

Define the setting in which the narrative occurred. This will include details of the place of practice, the demographic details of those involved and may include historical details (Context 2). Contexts 1 and 2 are ecological explanations; the subjects of the research are placed in an ecology of ideas, times and situations (Aldridge 1985; G. Aldridge 1998; Bateson 1972, 1978).

Phase 3: Identify the episodes and generate categories

Identify episodes that are crucial for analysis. This is inevitably a subjective process but this process can be validated by giving the material to colleagues to see if they identify the same episodes. When we collect a wealth of case study material, we often cannot analyse it all. There has to be a discriminatory choice of what we will focus upon.

Generate a set of constructs from that episodic material and identify categories for analysis.

Phase 4: Submit the episodes to analysis

The episodes are then analysed according to their contents using the guiding framework of the constructs.

Phase 5: Explicate the research narrative

This is the completed narrative based on the understandings gleaned from the analysis of the episodes. We weave together the categories of understandings from the previous phases and this is the process of synthesis following analysis.

Getting at knowledge

One of the tasks of the researcher in a qualitative approach is to make tacit knowledge, as a therapist, available as a propositional knowledge. The purpose of some research is indeed to find out what we know. A conversational paradigm is used here to draw out how researchers understand their own work, and elicit the structure of those understandings that are not immediately apparent in everyday life (Aldridge and Aldridge 1996; G. Aldridge 1996). From this perspective such work is hermeneutic (Moustakas 1990), that is, it is concerned with the significance of human understandings and their interpretation.

A strength of qualitative research for music therapy is that it concerns itself with the interpretation of events as they occur in natural settings and, therefore, has a resonance with the very processes involved in music therapy as the therapist tries to understand his, or her, patient. It is important to note here that I am working from the premise that therapists invest their practice with an element of deep personal meaning. As the music semiologist Nattiez himself remarks, 'The musicologist's persona is present behind his or her own discourse' (Nattiez 1990, p.210).

There is a continuing debate about subjectivity and objectivity in research. Yet the very choice of these seemingly opposing poles is a diversion. We are indeed subjects reaching out to an objective world, but this separation is not apparent in music therapy. The music, as object in the world, is performed by the subjects. The lived body, from a Merleau-Pontyian perspective, is a lived context in a milieu that has no objective existence (Smith 1993). We reach out into a performed world.

It is also important to emphasise that talking about therapy is always at several steps removed from the actual activity in which we partake. Dancing, painting, singing, acting, doing therapy are different activities to talking about dancing, talking about singing, talking about painting and talking about doing therapy. We need to emphasise that there are also different levels of interpretation as we see in Figure 2.1 (D. Aldridge 1996).

Level 1: Experience

Here we have the phenomenon as it is experienced. This is what transpires in the therapy session. It lives and exists in the moment, and is only partially understood. It cannot be wholly reported. We can see, feel, smell, taste and hear what is happening. These are the individual expressive acts themselves as they are performed, painted or posed. We can capture these events onto a medium like videotape or audiotape, although these moments too are 'interpreted' through the use of the medium. We can take only a limited perspective from a camera angle, through the orientation of a microphone, and there is always a loss no matter how good the equipment is.

These are the raw data of our experience in practice before we begin to reflect upon them.

Level 3: Interpretation and discourse

When we explain what happens in terms of another system; that is, to interpret the musical activity into terms of academic psychology, psychotherapy or systems of medicine.

When we say what the relationship is between the musical activity and the process of healing then we are involved in interpretation.

Level 2: Revelation and description

When we talk about what happens in the therapeutic situation using the terms of our particular disciplines or therapeutic approach: rhythm, melody, harmony, timbre, phrasing.

Perceived as music, therefore demanding a description that is itself based on an implicit theory.

Level 1: Experience

The phenomenon as it is experienced.

Sound as it is perceived in the moment.

Figure 2.1 Levels of interpretation

Level 2: Revelation and description

We can talk about what happens in the therapeutic situation in the particular terms of our artistic disciplines. These descriptions are accessible to verification and they emerge into conscious with lexical labels. For example, we can talk about the particular notes and rhythms in music therapy and the particular colours and patterns in art. We play our recorded tapes or show our pictures and describe with words what has happened. This is the shared element of language that is available for systematic study, part of our common everyday discourse, and is what Nattiez (1990) would regard as the trace or the neutral level of understanding. Whereas level 1 would be 'sounds', this level 2 is already perceived as music, therefore demanding a description, which is itself based on a theory implicit to the listener. When we begin to score the music that we include in our narratives, the very process of scoring is an interpretation, the choice of symbols and time divisions, particularly related to improvisation, is an interpretation and belongs to a cultural context.

Level 3: Interpretation and discourse

When we come to explain what happens then we are involved in interpretation. We make interpretations of what is happening in the therapy; what the activities of therapist and patient mean.

A shared language

At the level of performance, what passes in the therapeutic session exists for itself. However, as therapists working together with patients we do need to talk to each other about what happens and what we do. We also need to talk with our patients about what has happened and understand how they make sense of the therapy. Knowing at which level we are talking will aid our discussion and prevent confusion. As a music therapist I need to find a basic shared language at level 2, which is based upon descriptions of the artistic process, yet not too far removed from the activity of therapy itself. This is the level where personal construings emerge as revelations, where we put a name to what is going on. It is a level of description. By doing so, we can then discern when the therapeutic process is being described at level 3, i.e. that of interpretation and inference. At this level we begin to find commonalities between individual discourses and these are the languages of the therapeutic discourses that we are trained in. This is a step forward on the road to establishing the meaning of events in clinical practice. There may indeed be further levels of interpretation. Take for example the various schools of psychoanalytic therapy, or the different humanistic approaches; each will have a varying interpretation system that may find some commonality at a meta-level of interpretation. This is not confined solely to qualitative research; clinical reports, assessment using standardised questionnaires and reference to statistics are formal systems of interpretation.

Nattiez (1990, pp.140–142) gives examples of varying relationships between the description of the music and the interpretations of meaning that those description hold for the researcher. These relationships can be translated into the music therapy situation, and the music therapy research approach. In Table 2.2 we see in situations III and V the inclusion of external interpretations of the therapeutic events that will include more than the music itself.

Note that Nattiez, as a musicologist, is willing to include in an analysis more than the musical events themselves. We have a similar situation in music therapy in

Table 2.2 The relationships between Nattiez's analytic situations and Aldridge's music therapy interpretations

Analytical situations after Nattiez	Music therapy interpretations	Levels of interpretation
	The music therapy session	**Level 1** The sounds themselves, the experience as itself, the performance as phenomena
I Immanent analysis, neutral ground of the music, the physical corpus being studied, the trace	The score as a description of musical events	**Level 2** Revelation and description, descriptions of what happens in the therapeutic situation
II Inductive poietics	The music therapy index of events	
III External poietics	Clinical reports from other practitioners, drawings from art therapists	
IV Inductive esthesics	Music therapy meanings, interpretations of therapeutic significance	**Level 3** Interpretation and discourse, relationship between the musical or clinical activity and the system of interpretations
V External esthesics	Sampling methods from psychology or expert assessment of chosen episodes as part of a research methodology	
VI A complex immanent analysis relating the neutral ground of the music to both the poietic and the esthesic	Therapeutic interpretation from a fixed point but intuitively used in the therapeutic explanation	

clinical settings where not only is the music available as a tape recording (situation I) enhanced by a commentary from the therapist (situation II), but there are also clinical reports available from other practitioners (III). What significance those descriptions and interpretations have for practice will then be assumed under situations IV and V, inductive and external aesthetics. In this way, a case history or report can be transformed into a case study by achieving a level of analysis and interpretation. I make the interpretation explicit and contextualise that interpretation either into my own personal understandings, as we will see later, or into the context of another discourse. The discourse here is the original Foucauldian sense of specific texts, and those texts are from Nattiez (1990) and D. Aldridge (1996).

Personal construct theory

The personal construct theory of George Kelly (1955), and the repertory grid method that is allied to it, were designed specifically to elicit such systems of meaning. This approach does not concern itself with identifying a normative pattern, rather it makes explicit idiosyncratic meanings. However, while each set of meanings is personal, and therefore unique, there is built into the theory awareness that we live in shared cultures and that we can share experiences and meanings with others. The personal construct theory method allows us to make our understandings, our construings, of the world clear to others so that we can identify shared meanings. As Kelly devised this conversational method for teaching situations, counselling and therapy, we can see the potential relevance for the creative arts therapies and for supervision. Indeed, Kelly regards human beings as having a scientific approach. He proposes that we develop ideas about the world as hypotheses and then test them out in practice. According to the experiences we have, we then revise our hypotheses in the light of what has happened. Our experiences shape, and are shaped by, our construings. Each situation offers the potential for an alternative construction of reality. The personal construct approach allows us to elicit meanings about specific natural settings as we have experienced, or can imagine, them.

The important factor in this method is that it allows the therapist to stay close to his or her practice and use the appropriate language related to that practice. What it offers is a means of validating subjectivity: we see how the therapist, as researcher, is basing his language in experience. Furthermore, it challenges the researcher to understand that descriptions are not neutral, and to understand the transition from description to interpretation.

Qualitative methods and, particularly, those proposed by Lincoln and Guba (Guba and Lincoln 1989; Lincoln and Guba 1985), present themselves as being constructivist. Therefore, there should be a historical link with Kelly's personal construct theory. However, nowhere in any of the major books related to qualitative research cited above do we find any reference to Kelly. It is only in Moustakas (Moustakas 1990) that we find a reference to Kelly in terms of 'immersion' where, during the collection of research data, the researcher as 'subject' is asked what he or she thinks is being done. While some commentators have found Kelly to be rather cognitive in his approach, this may be due to the way in which he is taught. A reading of Kelly himself stresses the application of beliefs about the world in practice, and that the words that are used to identify constructs are *not* the constructs themselves. He argues that we each of us have a personal belief system by which we actively interpret the world. We create and change the world along with our theories. While we may be charged with bringing those beliefs into the realm of words and conscious expression, it does not mean to say that those beliefs are verbal, or necessarily conscious. This is an important point for the music therapist who is often asked to translate his or her musical experiences and understandings into the realm of verbal expression. Knowing that some slippage occurs between these realms is an important stage in our understanding.

Making clear constructions of the world is important for establishing credibility. We can see how the world is constructed. As a therapist, I can reflect upon my own construction of the world of clinical practice. Such understandings are discovered when we talk to each other, this has been called the 'conversational paradigm' (Thomas and Harri-Augstein 1985). Each person has their own set of personal meanings that can be communicated, but these meanings can be shared with another person. In this way of working, the personal construing of the world is primary in evaluating the world and leans towards the narrative methods of qualitative research. Sharing those meanings with others must be negotiated and is, therefore, a social activity. To establish our credibility and trustworthiness as researchers, then we need to make explicit our understandings of the world in some form or other. The repertory grid approach is one such way of eliciting and presenting such understandings as a formal process or method.

The process of therapeutic narrative analysis

Phase 1 is where the materials to be studied are gathered together. Narratives have a structure, there are themes and plots that are played out in scenes and vignettes. This is where we collect the stuff of our story following the definition of our research question. In the tradition of qualitative research, this may be a stage in the process that is reiterated. We go through the same circular process, discerning if we have included all the material pertinent to the narrative. This means listening to the taped musical session over and over again. My experience is that the more that I listen, the more I begin to hear.

We may find as the story unfolds that other scenes need to be included. It is a stage of focusing effort and gathering together the case material to be used. The selection of material may also be influenced by Phase 2.

In *Phase 2* we locate our narrative amongst other stories being told. It is a contextual act where we locate the story in a particular culture of stories. Indeed, we may ask our readers to consider the therapeutic narrative from a particular methodological perspective, as ethnomethodology for example, or as ethnomusicology. Or we may locate that narrative in a theoretical framework like the traditions of psychotherapy and medicine. Others may want to base their stories in concrete data traces drawing concepts from published literature. This phase is where the content of the study is placed into context.

Influential theories may also influence the choice of case material. This is a process of theoretical sampling *not* random sampling. What is being presented here is a retrospective method.

The case presented in this chapter is linked to another study for my thesis. What I was trying to discern was how melodies develop during the process of therapy. This was a musicological interpretation of events and therefore the method and literature was primarily based on musical scores and musical analysis.

Phase 3 brings us to the stage of identifying the categories inherent in what we have collected together. It is a major step of abstraction. From the material that we have before us we need to select episodes that illustrate our focus of interest, in this case, melodic development.

This approach is a conceptual method and depends upon the researcher's ability to identify abstract categories. Abstraction, like interpretation, is a process, often invisible to the researcher, and itself based in a discourse. What we are looking for are recurrent patterns within the material, and then, as Bateson (1978) suggests, the pattern that connects those patterns.

We have to identify episodes and then elicit constructs from those episodes to define the categories for interpretation of the material.

Selection of episodes as punctuation

Social scientists have become interested in the way in which we select meaningful patterns of behaviour from the ceaseless stream of events occurring in daily life. This selective structuring has been referred to as *punctuation* (Bateson 1972). Other researchers refer to *frames* that are stable patterns of mutually co-ordinated activity, which set the scope of the dialogue (Fogel *et al.* 2002). These can be verbal or non-verbal.

To an outside observer, a series of communications can be viewed as an uninterrupted sequence of interchanges, but the participants themselves may introduce episodes of interchange which for them have clear beginnings and endings. Punctuation is seen as organising behavioural events and is vital to interaction. Culturally we share many conventions of punctuation that serve to organise common and important interactional transactions. We observe this when someone says 'He started the argument' or 'It first began when her work ended'.

The punctuation of events occurs as episodes that we identify. Harre and Secord (1971) define an episode as 'any part of human life, involving one or more people, in which some internal structure can be determined' (p.153). Although imprecise, this definition offers a tool for considering behaviour in that behaviour is located interpersonally and structured (Pearce, Cronen and Conklin 1979). Episodes can be described in ways that represent the process of construing, and that construing can occur at differing levels of meaning (Aldridge and Aldridge 1999).

The punctuation of events into episodes serves the same function as phrasing in musical time. We organise time to make sense in terms of the performed activity. Thus, if we are looking at videotaped material for examples of interaction with a particular quality, we will identify when that interaction begins and when it ends. We may of course identify differing categories of episode. How we choose to label those episodes is also a matter of construing.

Personally, episodes can be seen as patterns of meanings and behaviours in the minds of individuals. This is a privatised meaning that represents an individual's understanding of the forms of social interaction in which he or she is participating, or wishes to participate. In a study by Parker (1981), girls deliberately harming themselves describe what they do as similar to being alone and crying or getting drunk. This construing is quite different to a medical perspective that sees the activity as manipulative or as a cry for help.

Relationally, episodes may be construed as common patterns of actions that assume a reciprocal perspective (Aldridge and Dallos 1986; Dallos and Aldridge 1987). Such construings are developed through interaction. In the way that people live and play together they co-ordinate an understanding of what experience means. In therapy, when people are used to playing music together, they begin to construe their musical playing mutually. This mutual construing is musical, it is not necessarily verbal. Our challenge is to convert this musical construing of events into a lexical realm if we want to write about it. The basis of the research material will be audiotape or videotape material.

Culturally, episodes can also be patterns of meanings and behaviours that are socially sanctioned and that exist independently of any particular individual meaning. This is perhaps best seen by the 'cry for help' notion of distress. Such construings reflect the concept of significant symbols described by Mead (1934) that reflect public shared meanings. We would see such cultural construings in the way in which rituals such as marriages and funerals are understood, and ritualised ways of dealing with social events such as greetings, deference and leaving (Geertz 1957). These are seen in music therapy as formalised and ritualised greeting and leaving songs.

Eliciting constructs

The first step in this narrative analysis approach is to identify the episodes. The second step is to identify those episodes with names and then to compare those episodes and elicit constructs (see Aldridge and Aldridge 1996).

An advantage of this way of working, as Kelly himself proposed, is that it elicits verbal labels for constructs that may be pre-verbal. In terms of a researcher's understanding, and bias, the explications from a musico-therapeutic realm of experience into a verbal realm may be of benefit for practice, supervision and research (Aldridge and Aldridge 1996). The verbalisation of musical experiences is one step on the way to establishing credibility by getting the practitioner to say what she means in her own words. However, the strength of this approach is that the basis is the practice and here I worked with a non-verbal musical trace – recorded episodes of music.

There are two principal forms of data analysis and presentation. One is in the form of a focus analysis that shows a hierarchical conceptual structure of the constructs (see Figure 2.3). The other is in the form of a principal components analysis that shows a spatial conceptual structure of the data (see Figure 2.4). Each can be displayed graphically. Both offer ways of presenting the data for further analysis. The discussion of the graphical data with a colleague or supervisor is a part of the technique (Aldridge and Aldridge 1996). It is not a finished analysis in terms of unequivocal results. Like all methods of research, these results demand interpretation. Even statisticians have to interpret data.

I looked at the graphical displays of the constructs, Figures 2.3 and 2.4, and considered if this meant any sense to me in terms of my experience with the therapy. It is important to note here that such construings, and their interpretations, are always made in the words used by the therapist. An advantage of this method is that a phrase can also be used to represent the pole of a construct; for example, 'tendency for playing to become calm' (Figure 2.2). It was essential for me to use a natural language description as I was struggling to make explicit what I felt to be an understanding within me. Being pushed into using specific words can also push us into a premature categorisation that is not 'new'. This is the process of 're-search', looking again to find new understandings of experience. I could have used an existing therapeutic vocabulary from my own training background but, apart from this being imprecise, I knew there was another set of personal understandings ready to emerge.

The supervisor or consultant can then also suggest patterns that she recognises within the data that make sense for her too. This negotiating of a common sense is a part of the supervisory activity and the ground for establishing validity in a qualitative paradigm. It also encourages a dialogue where ideas can be challenged and confirmed. As researchers, we often have to work alone and it is important at times to enter a social world where our ideas begin to make sense for, and with, others.

It is possible to bundle the constructs together to form categories that are then labelled as 'intuition', 'decisiveness', 'action', 'relationship', 'expressivity' and 'contemplation' (see Figure 2.3). These were categories that I decided made sense in terms of the broader context of the therapeutic process. While they may have a generalised meaning from a context of a common vocabulary, looking at the personal construct grids they have a particularised meaning within my own vocabulary.

The computational analysis takes the values of the construct as they are assigned to the elements as if they are represented as points in space. The dimensions of that space are determined by the number of elements involved. The purpose of the analysis is to determine the relationship between the constructs as defined by the elemental space. The computation is looking for patterns in the data and organises the constructs and elements until patterns are found. What we see is how similar the constructs are when they are plotted in space. Two constructs that appear close together may be being used in the same way to understand the data. Other constructs may not be equivalent and will affect the whole of the data as a constellation. Indeed, the principal components analysis of the data presents such a stellar appearance (see Figure 2.4). Here the two principal components of the data are used as axes onto which the constructs are projected. This allows the researcher to gauge the major dimensions on which the experiences of clients are being construed. These two axes appear as horizontal and vertical dotted lines in Figure 2.4. We see how 'developing musical playing – lingers in musical playing' and 'leading – adapting' are located along this horizontal axis, while 'rhythmic playing – melodic playing' are constructs aligned near to the vertical axis. The task is then to put these constructs together as a concept by asking the therapist what these could mean when considered as a concept.

The focus analysis structures constructs and elements that are closest together in the dimensional space into a linear order. These are then sorted into matching rated scores and mapped according to their similarity (as percentages). Clusters of

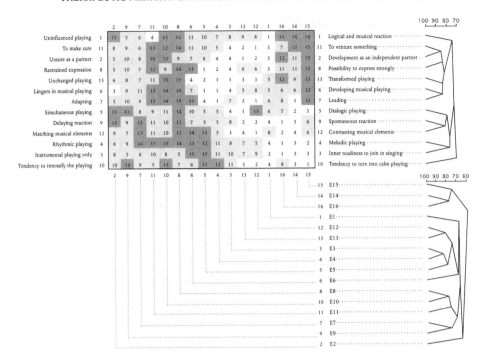

Figure 2.2 A Focus construct grid showing relationships between the therapy episodes and the constructs

constructs are then computed by selecting the most similar ratings and presented as a hierarchical tree diagram that shows the linkages between groups of constructs (see Figure 2.3). In the figures, similar constructs are arranged together so that we have a visual display, albeit two-dimensional, of how meanings are linked together.

The results of both forms of analysis are then discussed to see what sense emerges. At this stage, I looked for labels that would bundle constructs together, and these labels themselves represent constructs at a greater level of abstraction. These labels are a step in finding categories for use in analysing case material in qualitative research. There are analogies here with the process of category generation in grounded theory methods. For phenomenological research, such categories, once they have been articulated in this way, could be bracketed out of the analysis.

Phase 4 is the stage where the episodes are analysed in terms of the constructs and the overarching categories that have been generated. While I want to know how I construct the world as a therapist, I also need to know what the consequences of those meanings are when I play. I know the 'what' of meaning. I understand what this means to me as therapist. 'What happens next?' is the appropriate question to ask next.

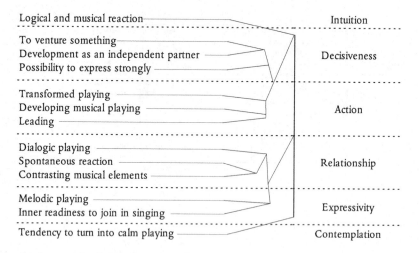

Figure 2.3 Constructs bundled together as categories

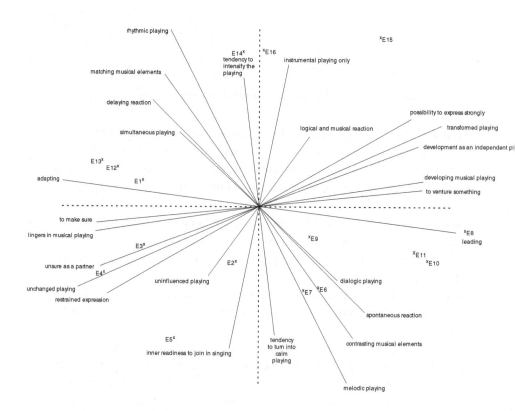

Figure 2.4 A principal components analysis of the episodes and constructs displayed graphically

Once I know how I construct a therapeutic event, I need to know what I did with this understanding in the therapy. This is a vital piece of knowledge because I am not solely concerned with understanding, I am also concerned with actions that have to take place in therapy. Furthermore, in the process of therapy, I need to know what the patient will do next and also interpret what this means for me. This gives me a chain of understandings and actions from my perspective of myself, as therapist, and of the patient. Of course, these interactive understandings are dynamic, they change during the play. In some way, this is at the heart of improvised therapy, what happens next is not fixed, there is always the possibility of something new happening.

This interplay of understanding and actions forms the narrative. Stories have plots, characters, meanings and events. So too with music therapy sessions; there is a plot, therapist and patients, meanings and musical exchanges. I combined my understandings of levels of interpretation and applied them to understanding the musical texts of my episodes. The benefit of this approach is that I could base my interpretation on a musical trace, originally the recorded sounds, and make that bridge to a lexical description using the constructs and the scores, showing how I arrived at the interpretation as it occurred in a specific context. I emphasise context here as the intention is not to make a generalised interpretation but a specific localised statement.

Phase 5 is the stage where the understandings are woven together to form the narrative based upon the categories discovered during the analysis. We see this in Figure 2.5 where categories generated from constructs and categories generated from episodes are taken to describe the development of a melody. Here the narrative structure is involved initially with episodes of communicating, integrating, leading and forming. It is the concept of integrating that then leads into the phase of independent playing that precedes the final completed melody.

Looking at the categories of constructs in their assignment to the course of therapy, I could also detect how the patient moves from one phase to another. This takes place in two cycles. In the first cycle the patient combines her intuition with decisiveness. This brings up the category of action. Decisiveness and action lead the patient to the categories of relationship and expressivity. Both influence each other. In combination they create a focal point within this first cycle. At the end of this cycle contemplation emerges as a new category.

In the second cycle all categories appear again in a condensed way. Here the patient is able to evoke what allows her to become an independent active musical partner. This cycle immediately turns into the melody which is carried by the categories intuition, decisiveness, action, relationship, expressivity and contemplation.

Figure 2.6 displays some musical examples underlying the described connections that lead towards the development of the melody in the last session. Example Ep. 3, 3–4 illustrates the interpersonal relationship between patient and therapist in the mutual shared swinging 6/8 metre which appears harmonious in the tonal framework of C minor. It results in expressivity which becomes apparent in the form of a fuller tonal expression in example Ep. 4, 13–14. Both examples are conducive to a close constellation of expressivity and relationship in Ep. 5, 5–6, whereby expressivity has a more direct reference to the patient's vocal expression, and relationship may be associated with its intramusical reference (joining of vocal and instrumental part in expression of C minor harmonic).

All three examples illustrate their position within the higher level of the second development phase (see Figure 2.6), which characterises the patient's integrative playing. It influences the subsequent therapy process and becomes obvious in its close constellation in the fourth phase, the content of which is defined by the development of musical parameters.

The category 'relationship' is visible in Ep. 8, 6–7 (see Figure 2.6) in the pattern of interaction alternating between patient and therapist. This interaction gradually intensifies and turns into a melodic form. It is this form to which the patient connects her emotional expression and which she produces in shaping the elements of dynamics, articulation and motivic continuation.

In example Ep. 10, 1–3 the patient deepens her expression with the help of the calm dialogue she initiated in her playing which evokes the interpersonal relationship. In this context expressivity refers to tonal relations, in particular to the melodic interval of the expressive major sixth. Both examples contribute to contemplation in Ep. 11, 26–29. The descending final motive reveals the inner composure and concentration on one element.

Conclusion

I understand the process of therapy by looking directly at what happens using material from therapeutic sessions. I have used the word 'traces' here as a general term referring to the material left behind as an indicator that something has happened – the recordings and the scores transcribed from those recordings. These traces are empirical data. How these events are described and interpreted as therapeutic process is the stuff of methodology. The interpretative process in qualitative research is referred to as hermeneutics. In this chapter I sketch a suitable methodology for eliciting understandings, how such understandings are constructed and how those understandings can be chained together as sequences of action.

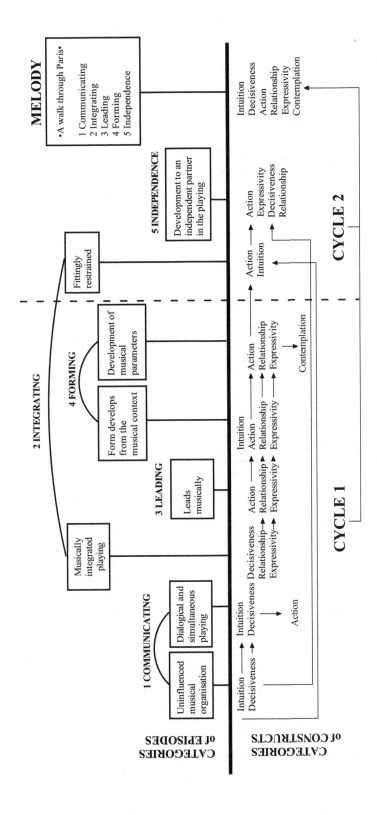

Figure 2.5 A therapeutic narrative analysis showing the development of a melody based upon the categories of constructs and the categories of episodes

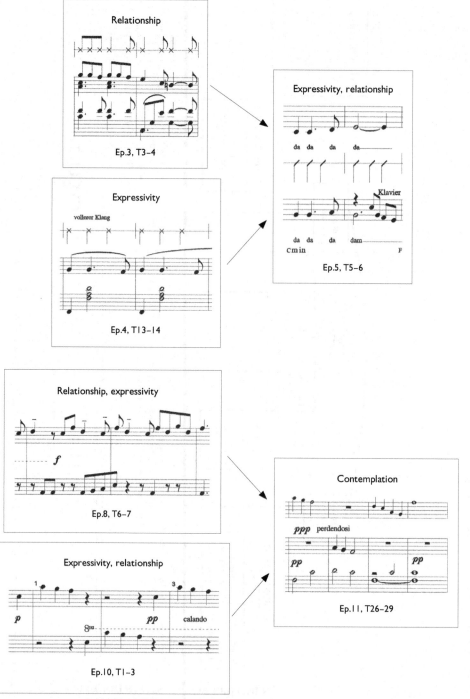

Figure 2.6 Examples of categories and their development within the first cycle

In the process of interpretation there are varying stages of abstraction, and we use differing sets of meanings. By using a constructivist approach I elicited meanings from events and saw how events were understood as a system of meanings. Those meanings are 'chained' together to understand the therapeutic process. This is a form of narrative analysis applied to the therapeutic process that we call 'Therapeutic Narrative Analysis' (Aldridge and Aldridge 2002).

Communication is dependent upon linking behaviours together. How those links are made and what they constitute is the basis of this form of research analysis. Narrative structures as case studies are based upon case histories. Events gain meaning in the way in which they are linked together. This level of formalised abstraction and explication of meaning changes the case history into a case study. Therapeutic Narrative Analysis elicits those links between events, the hermeneutic lies in the linking as much as in the events. Meaning has to be made, it is an activity. The same can be said of science, it is not static but is a dynamic process of understanding (D. Aldridge 2000b).

Central to the understandings is the concept of context. Culture itself is a context, and within a cultural context events gain different meanings. These nested forms of understandings within specific situations are given a formality here through constructs and categories. By explicating what happens from the traces of therapy, we begin to make the processes of therapy accessible to others and lend credibility to our accounts.

CHAPTER 3

'How Wonderful That I've Been Born – Otherwise You Would Have Missed Me Very Much!'

Barbara Griessmeier

During the last 20 years music therapy in palliative care has become a growing new field in the profession of music therapy. Since the first publications by Susan Munro, working as a pioneer in Canada in the early 1980s, many new posts have been created both in hospices and palliative care departments of general hospitals. Little has changed, however, in the general necessities of music therapy in this field. Working as a music therapist in palliative or hospice care requires a lot of flexibility as the patients' physical condition may vary greatly from day to day and the music therapy setting has to be adapted according to their individual needs. It is often difficult to keep to the security of a set day and time of sessions as patients may move from inpatient to outpatient services. Even the room the sessions take place in will not always be the same. Sometimes it is possible to use the privacy of a music therapy room but often it is necessary to meet patients either in their bedrooms or in common rooms, with other patients, visitors or staff being present, or even to see them at their homes.

The aims of music therapy in palliative care are not always easily determined. At times it is necessary to work towards certain goals like pain relief or relaxation. Often the music therapist can do nothing more than be an attentive companion, trying to support the patient in his desire to live as intensely as possible and at the same time help him to prepare for letting go everything he has ever cherished in his life. The dying process can be short and sudden, but is sometimes long and challenging, leading through different phases of hope, desperation, denial and acceptance.

Working in palliative care does not necessarily mean that we work with dying patients all the time. The definition of the word 'palliative' means that there is no possibility to heal any more, that the patient will eventually die, but not always in a short period of time. In general, palliative treatment starts from the moment when doctors have to admit that to their knowledge there is no remedy to a certain disease any more, and that the patient's condition will deteriorate. They will be able to alleviate pain and also to control the symptoms of a disease to a certain degree. But the end of all palliative treatment is inevitably death.

In the following case study of a ten-year-old boy suffering from leukaemia, I will describe how the different phases of a music therapy process follow the ups and downs of his medical career leading from hope and high expectation, at his first relapse, to his death, 18 months later.

To be a music therapist on a children's cancer unit means to be in constant contact with all phases of the disease. There are newly diagnosed children whose statistically relevant healing rate is considerably high. And there will always be children with relapses in different stages of treatment, those who are still under-going a treatment protocol, those who are subjects of rather experimental thera-peutic attempts and those who are in the dying process. But where exactly is the beginning of the dying process? Quite often the children stay in a kind of waiting state for a long period of time. Waiting for the tumour to grow, waiting for leukaemia cells to take over, waiting for new treatment regimes, waiting for a miracle. And the certainty that a child will not survive grows gradually in patients, staff and family. This process, of the growing knowledge of the coming death, can lead through very different stages of hope, denial and frustration in all involved.

Pedro's story

Pedro had first been diagnosed with leukaemia at the age of eight. He was born and raised in Portugal and his family had moved to Germany just one year prior to his illness. As his mother told me much later, he had health problems right from the beginning of his life in Germany. He had obvious constant pain and was diagnosed with some kind of rheumatic disorder before his leukaemia was finally discovered. Despite these problems he had adapted well to his new surroundings and made new friends at school.

Pedro's parents both had jobs. Pedro and his younger brother Carlos learned German very quickly. The family was well integrated into the Portuguese community in town and there were no financial or social strains in the family when Pedro was diagnosed as having leukaemia.

During his first intensive chemotherapy Pedro adapted well to the hospital situation. He was very grateful that finally his health problems could be treated and that he did not have pain any more. During his initial treatment I did not have any contact with Pedro. I would say hello to him every now and then, but he did not seem to be interested in music at all.

My first real contact with Pedro happened when his leukaemia returned about one and a half years after he was first diagnosed. This early relapse meant that his statistical survival rate had dropped to about 10–20 per cent and a bone marrow transplant was planned to secure the highest possible chances. For the next two years, we established a therapeutic relationship which was strongly expressed through music and which lead us through various stages of his disease from hope of survival to his death at the age of 12 years.

When I first met Pedro, then aged ten, after his relapse, he was disappointed and upset. He was angry that the first chemotherapy treatment obviously had not succeeded in destroying all his leukaemia cells, so that some of them were able to survive and had started to grow again. His mother was sad and did not talk much. Pedro seemed to adapt to the situation extraordinarily quickly again. He still knew most of the staff and was especially fond of the two occupational therapists in the hospital. He was very willing to continue with his studies with the help of hospital teachers. He loved to play with other children and was always ready to take part in various activities on the ward. He never saw the hospital as a terrible place and he pointed out very clearly that in Portuguese hospitals there would be nobody to take care of the children and to keep them occupied. He told me that the Portuguese word for 'hospital' was 'house of health' which he considered to be much more appropriate than the German word 'Krankenhaus', which means 'sick house'. So in his perception the hospital was not only a place for treatment of his disease, but also a place where he was nurtured and well taken care of.

So from Pedro's point of view, the main problem at this stage was the fact that he was isolated from his friends at school and from his normal life again. From my point of view, I knew that the forthcoming bone marrow transplant would be a situation of highest possible risk. Pedro's own bone marrow would be destroyed through high dose chemotherapy and total body irradiation, which would leave him without any blood building system and literally kill him, if his donor's bone marrow was not accepted by his body. Besides the fact that the transplant could be rejected, there was also the risk of various life threatening infections due to the lack of white blood cells, of Graft-versus-Host-Disease and of a relapse of his leukaemia despite bone marrow transplant. Fifty per cent of all children who undergo bone marrow transplant will die during the first year after the procedure for various reasons.

For Pedro and his family the bone marrow transplant at this stage was just another step in the treatment protocol. I think that his parents were quite aware of the risks and chances, but I am not sure if Pedro himself was able to understand the extent of the procedure. So my aim at this stage was to offer Pedro the possibility of a musical relationship he could use in different ways whenever he felt like it. As I knew from experience, the time in the bone marrow transplant isolation unit is usually a time of high expectations and hope on one hand, and fear of all kinds of negative physical sensations on the other hand. I hoped that Pedro might benefit from the possibility to express his feelings in a musical way to support him in times of hardship.

In three group sessions prior to his bone marrow transplant Pedro had told me that he loved music. He joined in songs and structured musical games very easily, and I was quite astonished how many German songs he had picked up in his 18 months at German school.

Music in the isolation unit

In preparation for the bone marrow transplant, I took Pedro to my music therapy room to find out what kind of music he was interested in. He was fascinated by the variety of instruments and tried the drum set, the gato drums and a keyboard. He immediately chose the keyboard and the gato drums to take into the isolation unit. In a second session he was interested in a pentatonic steeldrum and we started to play pentatonic dialogues with xylophone, steeldrum and piano. To my astonishment Pedro showed a rare sense of musical structures. The two of us seemed to be completely well balanced in our musical expression. He had a strong sense of dynamic and made it very clear that each piece came to a proper ending. I offered to tape one of our pieces and Pedro loved the idea. At the end of the session, Pedro said that there was hardly anything in his life he had enjoyed so much as this music session. I think that Pedro had discovered a musical desire that had been hidden so far.

During the following three weeks, we had ten music therapy sessions together. Pedro's general condition was surprisingly good during the time in the isolation unit. As neither a family donor nor an unrelated donor could be found, he finally received his mother's stem cells which could never be exactly the same genetically as his own, and therefore bore a higher risk of rejection. On the day before he received the stem cells, we discovered the possibilities of playing the keyboard together while he asked me about the transplantation. He wanted to know everything about the nature of the different cell types and made it very clear that he did not want to be excluded from the process. After a while, he asked me to teach him

'Jingle Bells' on the piano and started to sing the Portuguese version of it. He made his mother write the words down for me, thus starting a combination of German, English and Portuguese sing-along that we would come back to again much later.

I had the impression that Pedro not only needed the possibility of free improvisation but he also had a desire to learn some 'real' music. I taught him a simple piece using black keys only, playing a more elaborate piano part myself. Pedro loved this piece and was very proud of himself, as was his mother who was always present during sessions. I suggested taping the music for his father and brother who were not allowed to visit him. He immediately agreed to the idea and worked very hard as he would not tolerate any 'mistakes' on the tape.

In between the taping sessions Pedro came back to free musical dialogues on the gato drums but he did not seem to be comfortable with them. He told me that he structured his day in isolation according to certain television programmes and I got the impression that structure helped him to cope with the tension while waiting for his white blood cells to grow again.

When the first cells were to be seen in his blood count, Pedro wanted to play a very simple nursery rhyme on the keyboard, whose German words are 'All My Little Ducks'. I told Pedro that another patient had once converted the words of the song into 'All my doctors', and he wanted to know all about it. He made up two more verses saying 'all my doctors always say no, whenever I ask them if I can go home' and 'all my doctors always want blood, even when I'm asleep, then I get really angry'.

I think that with these words Pedro expressed some of his feelings towards the strict medical routine he had to stick to in order to get well again. Pedro then asked me if he could videotape the music as well as audiotape it. When I brought the camera into his room he wanted to tape not only the music but everything in the isolation room and send the tape to his grandparents in Portugal to show them how he was doing. I left the camera with him and he taped all his daily routine, commenting on everything in Portuguese. When we came to the song about the doctors he even translated the words into Portuguese. He found it quite hard to play the piano and sing simultaneously but eventually he managed and was very proud of himself.

Pedro's bone marrow transplant was successful. His bone marrow was working again, and he had sufficient white blood cells to leave the isolation unit without any side effects. I copied the videotape for him to send to his grandparents in Portugal.

The music during this first part of our music therapy relationship served two different aims. First, Pedro discovered that music was something he really liked and that he was able to experience new abilities in a situation when his general possibilities were extremely limited. Second, Pedro found a way to connect his newly found abilities with his family outside the isolation unit through the use of his mother tongue in the music. By taping the music both on audio and on video he presented himself not as a sick person but as somebody who was creative and alive despite a life threatening disease.

Interlude

About two months after the successful bone marrow transplant we learned that something had gone wrong: Pedro's general condition was still good but the analysis of his blood cells showed that Pedro's own cells had come back. His mother's cells were still there but their percentage was dropping in favour of Pedro's cells. At that time there were no leukaemia cells to be found but everybody knew that this would be only a question of time. Pedro himself did not seem to be as worried as his parents were but I am not sure if he really realised the meaning of this situation. The doctors did not know what to do – knowing that there was no other donor to be found the bone marrow transplant could not be repeated, so everybody was basically waiting for things to happen.

In this situation I considered it to be useful to keep the relationship with Pedro alive. I knew that there would be hardly any possibility Pedro would survive as soon as the leukaemia cells came back. I did not want to frighten him, so I just suggested that we could play some music together whenever he felt like it during his weekly visits to the outpatient clinic. During the following six months we had another ten sessions together. During this time Pedro was feeling well. He was still not allowed to meet other people, as he was still at high risk from infections. He had not been to school for more than a year, but continued his studies at home. He had a lot of support from his family, but the constant strain and fear had started to be present day and night.

Our first music therapy session after the bone marrow transplant took place in October. I brought the keyboard into Pedro's room, and we repeated everything we had been playing before. Pedro could still remember these pieces but after a while he sort of 'confessed' that he was not interested in the keyboard any more. He said that the music was boring and that he loved techno-music and everything that was fast and danceable. And he also confessed that he had always wanted to play the saxophone – and that he dreamt he would be playing for his family at Christmas.

This was a major challenge for me. I had played the clarinet for a short period of time 20 years ago – could I possibly try to get a real saxophone and teach Pedro? Or should I try another way to get him into contact with the kind of music he wanted? After we had listened to some saxophone CDs together I managed to borrow a saxophone for Pedro. He was able to produce a tone immediately and was absolutely happy to accomplish three different notes in the first session. Pedro was now very keen on playing and he told me that he practised with his brother's recorder at home as he had found out that the use of the fingers was the same with both instruments. By Christmas he was actually able to play his first Christmas carol.

As his medical situation had still not changed, the family decided to spend the Christmas holidays in Portugal together with their family. Pedro told me that his older cousin there was playing the saxophone as well and that he hoped to play together with him.

When Pedro came back from Portugal he seemed to be rather quiet. He said that he had enjoyed himself there – but something seemed to be different. Much later it became clear that Pedro would never see his country again and so maybe he was starting to be sad about the loss.

Pedro wanted to keep on playing but due to water damage in my room we could not use it for nearly two months. By March, the time of waiting came to an end. Pedro's leukaemia cells were back. Pedro was worried but his general condition was still fairly good. So he continued with his visits to the day clinic while the doctors tried to reduce the number of leukaemia cells with chemotherapy again. I did not see Pedro very often but he kept saying that he wanted to play music again.

Five months after our last session, we finally managed to meet again and we had a last saxophone session. Pedro still remembered everything he had learned before and was very proud of himself, as was his mother who was still present during the sessions. Weeks before, I had started to organise a saxophone teacher for Pedro as I realised that he was talented and needed better coaching than I could provide. But, after this last session, Pedro developed an infection in his lungs and would never be able to play again.

Music for Life and Death

Because of his chemotherapy Pedro had to come to the hospital again. During all the months of the 'waiting period', he had come for visits every now and then and had taken part in various activities like Halloween or Christmas parties. As the hospital surrounding had become Pedro's second home, he used this for social contacts with staff and other children. Pedro had always been very joyful and positive but, during this stay at the hospital, he started to show his sadness and his disappointment. He cried easily now but always tried not to bother his parents. As his German was much better than his parents', he often had to translate for them.

In June, six months before his death, our last phase of music therapy began, which would last for another 25 sessions. As Pedro could not play the saxophone any more, he said that he now wanted to play the drums. I began by playing some rock 'n' roll on the piano as Pedro said he loved fast music. He played together with me in a rhythmically proper way but was very shy and careful. He was disappointed that his music did not sound like 'on television' and said that he was missing the 'melody' – I tried to comfort him by saying that this would be a matter of practice (without being really sure about it).

In this first drum set session Pedro said he wanted to play the song 'Country Roads'. 'Country roads, take me home, to the place where I belong …' – these words seemed to become the motto of Pedro's last six months.

It became clear now that the chemotherapy was not successful in rejecting Pedro's leukaemia cells. On the team, we discussed his case thoroughly. It was obvious that Pedro's parents had to know – but should we tell Pedro himself that he would not get well again? Pedro needed daily infusions of antibiotics because of his lung infection – but should we offer another visit to Portugal for the family, so he could see his country again? In the meantime his parents had arranged other family members to come over from Portugal to see Pedro. One of the first visitors was his saxophone-playing cousin, a young man of about 20 who spent his summer holidays in Germany. He came to see Pedro at the hospital and we had the first of many 'family-music-sessions' together. The young man not only played the saxophone but also the drums. I encouraged Pedro's younger brother Carlos to join in the session as well, as I had the impression that every effort uniting the scattered family members was most important.

So we agreed to play blues together – the saxophone playing cousin, Pedro and his brother at various drums, and me playing the piano. It was quite difficult for me as the family had turned to speaking Portuguese completely, while Pedro's mother was videotaping the whole session with her own camera. The two boys were absolutely delighted, especially Carlos, who was dancing and hopping around with his face glowing with joy and laughter.

On the next day we had agreed that the consultant would talk to Pedro's parents alone, without Pedro, to give them the chance to ask any questions they wanted without having to hold back in front of their son.

When I went to ask Pedro if he wanted to play again he was lying in his bed crying while watching television. Obviously the doctor had just told him that he wanted to talk to his parents and Pedro had realised that something unusual was going on. I sat down in front of him (with the telly at my back) and asked him why he was crying? And he said that he felt excluded and that he needed to know every-thing that was going on because he was sick and not his parents. He also said that he was fed up with everything and just wanted to got home and live a normal life again.

When I turned round to have a look at the telly my heart sank. In the middle of a film there was a funeral service going on! I asked Pedro about it, but he did not know who had died. Instead he started to talk about death and dying and the funerals he had attended. He assured me that all his family members had died very old, except for a little cousin who was killed in a car accident. He asked me if one could possibly believe that this little girl would be in Hell now? And how can children die at all? And what is the difference between Heaven and Hell? I tried to share my doubts about the strict Catholic point of view without offending his strong religious belief. And even if I was shocked about the coincidence of the subject of the doctor's message to his parents and the funeral on the television at the same time, I was glad to be there at exactly the right moment to be able to listen to Pedro's fears and anxieties.

We had another session with Pedro's cousin while the doctor was talking to his parents with the help of an interpreter. Pedro's parents understood the situation very well and agreed to palliative treatment in order to try to control Pedro's symptoms. At the same time, Pedro enjoyed the music again and in the following weeks we had a number of very lively and joyful sessions. Pedro had started to bring his favourite CDs and play together with the music. My role was just to be there, maybe to contain the situation, and play with a small tambourine (because I felt a bit lost doing nothing). Pedro always wanted his mother to be present – maybe he realised that I was looking for another opportunity to talk to him again in private? Whenever possible, Pedro's brother would join the sessions and one after another of his various Portuguese family members turned up. Pedro always wanted them to listen to him, to see him in his joy in the middle of his dying process.

Over the weeks Pedro developed a very good rhythmical feeling. I did not teach him any technical details but he tried to listen to his CDs very carefully and copy the rhythms from there. He was becoming more and more creative, and despite of his ongoing lung infection, and his deteriorating health, he played for an hour and sang without difficulties.

The music he chose was partly from the charts, like 'I.O.' or 'La Bamba', and partly from a 'Mallorca' CD with a German type of beer-party music. The titles of these songs all represented a way of life he could certainly not take part in any more but that expressed his desire to live, to be lively, joyful and creative. With titles like 'Life is Life', 'There is One Thing Nobody Can Take Away from Me: It's the Joy of Being Alive', 'I Am the Greatest' and so on, Pedro showed all his relatives who had come to say goodbye to him that he was not going to die yet.

When Carlos was present he always started to dance to his brother's music – in the same way as in the video clips on television. Carlos loved these sessions as it was one of the rare occasions when he could be together with his brother in a normal way, without being constantly reminded of his illness.

Being aware of the real treasure these sessions would be for his family later I suggested videotaping them again and again. When I once said to the boys that they would be able to remember these sessions now and in eternity, and that they might want to watch the tape with their grandchildren (which was silly of me) Carlos smiled at me and said 'But maybe we won't become grandfathers because we die before …', thus telling me that he as well had a subconscious understanding of the situation.

Every now and then I introduced some technique exercises to give Pedro the possibility of a broader repertoire for playing. He was very eager to try them but often found it very hard. By the middle of October, we had come to some exercises with 'Oh, When the Saints go Marching in' using a drums method. Pedro loved the song. When his grandmother from Portugal came to visit together with her brother, Pedro wanted the two of them to listen to him again. His grandmother did not seem to be interested in music from the pop music charts but started to cry when we played 'Oh, When the Saints'. It turned out that the old women had often sung this song in Portuguese at her church at home. On the last day of her visit, she came again together with Pedro's father and the three of them joined together in a very lively performance of a Portuguese song, while Pedro was constantly working on the improvement of his technique on the drums.

By the end of October Pedro again had pneumonia and had to be admitted to hospital. He had difficulties with breathing but wanted to play music again. On this particular day another patient, a seven-year-old girl, was dying in the room next to Pedro's. Her history had been very similar to Pedro's. She had also had a relapse of her leukaemia after a bone marrow transplant and Pedro knew her quite well. The two of them had spent many hours in the day clinic together during the last couple of months and she was now dying from severe pneumonia. Hours before, she had fallen into unconsciousness and her breathing was quite irregular. The nurses had switched of the monitoring system so that her parents could concentrate on their daughter and not watch the figures dropping on the monitor. And Pedro wanted to play music. I felt very uncomfortable, as I went in and out of the girl's room, sitting with her parents and wondering if I should play something for her without really daring to do so.

So I finally asked Pedro if he wanted to go to my music room – but he said that he would prefer to stay in bed as every movement was painful for him. What kind of music could be appropriate in this situation, when one of his friends was dying next door and he himself was not too far from his own death? After all the hours of playing joyfully on his drumset? Remembering 'Oh, When the Saints', I asked him if he would like to sing today. He agreed immediately and told me about his grandmother who knew the song from her local choir. Pedro's mother brought her Portuguese hymn book and showed me the words: 'ressuscito, alleluja', 'he is risen, alleluja'. With a little fruit shaker Pedro was able to take over the rhythm part with minimal movements that were not painful for him. Despite his breathing problems he started to sing 'Oh, When the Saints' in German, English and Portuguese. The words of the song are very much orientated towards life after death and I'm sure Pedro sang them not only for his friend but also for himself. The situation was very moving; Pedro's mother and I both knew about the girl next door dying, but Pedro made it possible for us to bear the situation with dignity.

The day after the girl's death Pedro wanted to continue with spirituals. He told me about all the songs he had learned at religious education at school, like 'Kum Ba Yah, My Lord', 'Laudato si', 'Swing Low, Sweet Chariot'. He was arguing with his mother who often was not able to fit the Portuguese words into the music and he told me about the Portuguese Christian community that he often visited. His faith seemed to be strong and unbroken.

Pedro recovered from his lung infection and on the day before Halloween he asked me for a tape recorder and microphone as he wanted to tape scary sounds to frighten the nurses at night. But he also made a tape for his favourite occupational therapist, where he made a kind of love song for her, describing why she was so wonderful.

At Halloween, we had a party on the ward. As a matter of coincidence it was one of the children's birthdays as well and we sang the most popular German birthday song to him:

'How wonderful that you've been born, we would have missed you very much'.

And there was Pedro, his face painted in scary green, with a bright red curly wig on his bald head, an enormous fake safety pin through his nose and 'blood' dribbling from his mouth. With his clear voice he sang:

'How wonderful that *I've* been born, you would have missed me very much...', his face glowing with excitement!

In November there was a big charity concert with about 20 different chart bands for children with cancer. As the hospital got free tickets, we agreed on the team the Pedro should come, even if he was still in high danger of infection. But in his situation it seemed useless to protect him completely from infection as he would be dying soon anyway. Pedro was absolutely thrilled by the idea. He had never been to a live concert before and all his favourite bands would be there! A television programme asked us if one of the kids would be ready for an interview and Pedro said how happy he was and how nice it was of all the musicians to encourage children with cancer. He even was invited backstage to meet his favourite boygroup, B3.

After the concert Pedro's general condition started to deteriorate. He had repeated severe pain attacks. We had one last drumset session together with another uncle and his father, where he played his favourite songs for the last time. It was very important for him that this uncle took a copy of all the videos we ever made back to Portugal. So I spent hours copying music sessions but also tapes of family meetings. Obviously Pedro wanted to be sure that his family could remember him in his happy times.

By the end of November Pedro was not feeling well any more. He had to come to the day clinic more often and did not want to get out of bed. One day he wanted me to sing for him. So I sang all the Portuguese spirituals together with his father. Pedro closed his eyes and looked very relaxed despite his pain. His mother could not tolerate the situation and left the room.

Pedro's health was deteriorating by now. We tried to let him stay at home as much as possible, so he only came for blood transfusions. Before Christmas we agreed on the team that somebody should start with home visits to support the family in the dying process. I asked Pedro if he wanted me to come and see him at home – and he made it very urgent that I came before Christmas. So on Friday night before Christmas, after a full day at the hospital, I drove to Pedro's home. He was sitting on the sofa and asked me to sing Christmas carols with him. Carlos and his parents joined in and we sang through all the boys' favourite German and Portuguese Christmas carols. His father seemed to enjoy it very much and Pedro was looking forward to his grandmother's visit after Christmas.

For me the situation was hard to bear: I knew that this would be the last Christmas the family could spend together with Pedro, and I kept wondering how they would ever be able to celebrate without him? When we had tea together Pedro did not speak at all. He made sure that his mother gave me a Christmas present, and was silent for the rest of the time.

The next day Pedro experienced a cerebral fit and was brought to hospital again. He could spend Christmas at home but his condition had changed dramatically. He had difficulty walking and speaking and seemed to be very slow in his reactions. When I saw him again after the Christmas holidays, he was able to tell me that he had a fit and that he was not feeling well. He did not want any music. As he did not drink enough any more, we decided that we had to discuss openly with his parents where he should die. We offered home nursing, as Pedro would need infusions. His parents were very reluctant and his mother especially wanted us to ask Pedro.

Pedro was sleeping most of the time and when he first understood that he would have to go to hospital he was crying. We offered that he could have infusions at home but after a few hours Pedro made it clear that he did not want any nurses he did not know to visit him at home but wanted to be in hospital. The situation seemed to be more relaxed after the decision was made. Pedro was now sleeping most of the time, he needed an oxygen mask to breath. Many friends of the family came to visit but the general atmosphere was supportive and not invasive.

I thought about the kind of music that would be appropriate in this last stage and came across Portuguese translations of songs of Taize with very comforting words. I showed them to his father, and together we sang a few of them while other members of the community listened. Pedro recognised me once again and said, in Portuguese, 'I know you – you are the music lady ...'.

Pedro died two days after his last admission to hospital in early January. He died peacefully with his parents present in the room. His family organised a service in the hospital for him before they took his body to Portugal, where he is buried.

Conclusion

For Pedro music therapy played an important role during the last two years of his life, starting from his early relapse until his death. In about 50 sessions, Pedro discovered a love for music he had not known before. The music he used changed during this time and served different purposes.

First, Pedro used the keyboard and free improvisations to keep himself occupied during the time in the isolation unit but also to make sure he would still be connected with his family outside the hospital.

Second, Pedro wanted to learn to play the saxophone as a very extraordinary instrument during the time between his bone marrow transplant and his second relapse, identifying with his older cousin who was his great idol in the family.

Third, Pedro started to play the drums when his lung infection prevented him from playing the saxophone, thus expressing his joy of being alive and at the same time inviting all his family members to celebrate life together with him.

And as a last means Pedro used spirituals and gospel songs to express his knowledge of his coming death and to prepare himself for life after death.

Reflecting on these two last years with Pedro, I am full of admiration at how this boy managed to fulfil his utmost needs with the help of music, the need to be connected with his family and with his roots, and at the same time prepare himself for life after death.

Pedro never talked to me again about this subject directly after the scene with the funeral service on television but I'm sure he was able to express himself in the way he wanted – to live and enjoy life as long as possible despite his limitations, and to die in dignity when his time had come.

And I am sure that nobody who ever met him will ever be able to forget how wonderful it was that he's been living with us.

CHAPTER 4

Song Creations by Children with Cancer – Process and Meaning

Trygve Aasgaard

This chapter presents one example of how music therapy related social phenomena can be explored and interpreted through a case study, or more specifically, through a multiple instrumental case study. The project's title refers to the songs five children with leukaemia, aplastic anaemia or myelodysplasia made while they were treated in paediatric cancer wards in Oslo, Norway during the late 1990s.

Two questions constitute point of departure for the research process:

1.   What happens when the songs are created, performed and used?

2.   What do creating, performing and using those songs mean to the child?

Secondary questions are: How, where and when are the songs made, performed and used? Who are the participants in the song activities? What characterises the texts (lyrics) and music? What are the relationships between the song activities and health? Question 1 refers to the descriptive side of the study: actions/events (= 'process'). Question 2 refers to the constructed themes based on the descriptive material (= 'meaning'). The two main questions are seen as interrelated. Human processes gain their meaning (signification) from their contexts. 'Meaning' is related to what the studied songs/song activities might mean to the child in the paediatric oncology ward context. The interplay between the child and other song-participants, listeners (audience) included, is therefore highlighted.

Rationale

This project was conducted in order to learn more about the 'lives' of songs created in music therapy practice and possible relationships between song creations and health aspects in the lives of young patients with malignant diseases. The shared fate of 'children with cancer' is that of facing a life-threatening medical condition, a long-lasting treatment usually producing a number of unpleasant and partly dangerous side effects. These factors, in addition to the inevitable isolation and hospitalisation, influence many aspects related to the young patients' health such as 'social relationships' and 'self-concepts', 'hopes' and 'joys', and bring about various restrictions in the patients' possibilities of action (von Plessen 1995).

'Making songs' is one of many music related activities for the young cancer patients. I have experienced that song-texts made by these children often focused on the good and funny things in life rather than the miseries of being sick and hospitalised. I never proposed particular themes and did not take part in the creative process before the patient presented me with some oral or written material. My certainty as to 'what is a song' started to waver when I experienced how the child patients talked about and used their own songs: the 'content' of the song seemed occasionally to be less important for the sick child than the song-related skills and activities.

Music neither heals cancer nor prolongs life. Many cancer families' life situations seem to be more or less continuously tough and strenuous. No musical involvement can take away the many problems related to disease and treatment. But I soon 'discovered' that, even if such patients were seriously marked by their illness, they very much appreciated having the possibilities of living out their normal and healthy sides. Parents I met shared this common interest with their children as patients, and these experiences led to this study of song-related activities focusing *health* (promotion) and the interplay between the individual patient and her or his *environment* or *ecological context* (see Bruscia 1998).

Research on patients' own songs

'Song creation'[1] is probably the most common compositional technique in music therapy practice today (Maranto 1993, p.697). Research projects on song creations are limited in number (Johnson 1978, 1981; Haines 1989; Amir 1990;

---

1   The term 'song creations' encompasses related terms like 'song-writing' and 'composition'.

O'Callaghan 1996). Even if the majority of the case studies describing song creations hardly deserve research status, several of them present both thorough and well reflected accounts – sometimes also of new appliances/new techniques in song creative processes or of new groups of patients involved. But music therapy literature has, until now, said little about the songs' fate after they have once been created. I wanted to record the events where songs were created and developed, performed and used. Which method was the most suitable to trace, describe and make sense of such phenomena?

A multiple, instrumental case study

The interpretive paradigm guiding the actions of this researcher is based on Egon Guba and Yvonna Lincoln's 'constructivist paradigm', originally discussed under the heading 'naturalistic inquiry' (Lincoln and Guba 1985; Guba and Lincoln 1998). It gives no meaning to study the 19 song creations as they *'really* are', because 'reality' is only understood (or constructed) subjectively and is therefore always relative. As our constructions are alterable, our 'realities' will change. 'Truth' is not absolute, but a result of more or less sophisticated or informed constructions (Bruscia 1995; Guba and Lincoln 1998). The qualitative researcher faces the difficult task of interpreting and transforming multi-faceted song-related processes and meanings into words – a study of 'culture' (and not 'nature') that is not intended to reach final conclusions nor absolute answers.

There are several reasons why a qualitative, not quantitative, research method is applied in this project. Neither processes, nor meanings, can be properly measured, only described and interpreted. The low number of songs and song-makers present no sufficient material for statistical analysis but this material is well suited for in-depth interpretative analysis of meanings and processes. The naturalistic settings (where variables cannot be well controlled) do not 'produce' data suitable for analysis of causal relationships between selected variables but are ideal for developing dialogues with subjects and multi-voiced texts. If the creative song activities had been evaluated in relation to the subjects' medical progress, survival rates or even with Quality of Life scores, quantitative methods would certainly have been necessary. All these relationships are interesting but beyond the scope of this investigation which is, first of all, directed to gain new knowledge about the life histories of songs and related meanings.

Five young patients have made between one and ten songs each during hospitalisation (see Table 4.1). The chosen method of research needs to be well tailored to organising multiple sources of information in an interpretative, naturalistic study of phenomena over time; that is, 'who does what, where, when and with whom?'

Case studies are well suited to get hold of each song-history in the light of the changing life situation of the patient-song-maker where the contemporary and near history perspectives are closely interwoven.

Brian	**Henry**	**Hannah**	**Mary**	**René**
'School Song' 'All the Girls' 'Doctors are Kind' 'Love'	'We Must Wait and See' 'On the Outside'	'Ba, Ba Blood Corpuscle' 'Hair Poem'	'It's Boring to Stay in Hospital' 'If I were the King' 'Emil's Bone Marrow' 'Nurse' 'I'm Bored' 'Friends' 'My Hat' 'The Tango Song' 'Randi Took a Shower' 'A Suspiciously Cheerful Lady'	'School Holidays in Isolation Room Number 9'

Table 4.1 The collected songs made by each child while in hospital (all names are fictitious)

It would of course have been possible to concentrate this study on one particular case, for example 'Mary's song' or a music therapy case history of 'Mary'. The case is thus given (or pre-selected); the researcher has an intrinsic interest in the case and performs an intrinsic case study (Stake 1995, p.3).

The present project, however, started with a specific interest in studying the lives of songs made by/with children with life threatening illnesses and what such song activities might mean to the child and other people involved. Through studying different songs made by different children I believe I can gain an even better insight to these questions – the present case study is therefore both an instrumental case study and a collective case study (Stake 1995, p.3–4).

I employ different cases to obtain multi-faceted study material. The presentation of the 19 songs' life histories may be read as 19 intrinsic case descriptions. When the song histories are further analysed for particular themes, particular elements are focused on in order to understand what the song (activities) mean to those people involved. Each of the cases can be understood as instrumental for learning about the theme 'song creations', and some cases will be better in this respect than others. Understanding 'song creations' in music therapy practice is of limited interest if not linked to particular persons and contexts. Stake's distinction between intrinsic or instrumental case studies may not be absolute. I even believe that a field-focused researcher, during the process of gaining understanding, oscillates his attention between outside and inside (of the case), foreground and background, between an exceptional entity and a general theme.

In the present study the case can be understood both as 'patient' and 'song' ('creation'): each of the 19 life histories of songs can be read as one case, the history of each of the five patients' song-related activities can also be termed one case. A song qualifies to be termed a bounded system because a song (history) has a reasonable definite beginning, if perhaps not a definite end (in time). The song (related) phenomena also take place in a certain hospital setting and involve certain people. A young patient is the point of departure for those phenomena, but it is not initially known which other persons will become involved. It is not, however, possible to study a territory, a political event, a song or a patient 'as such' – one needs to have some conceptions as to which aspects one wants to focus on. On the other hand is it not given beforehand what exactly constitutes a case empirically/theoretically – the boundaries between phenomenon and context are often not clearly evident. This explorative aspect related to what the case 'turns out to be' might also add new knowledge to how we understand music and music therapy.

I picked out a limited number of child patients who had already made one or more songs. At the time this study commenced, I knew several young patients who were song makers but eventually I chose as cases (all) the songs that five children had made alone or in collaboration with me or other persons during their many months of hospitalisation. The five children were old or new patients at the time of the start of study in 1997. Three had been discharged from hospital but returned for shorter re-admissions (or day visits for routine medical checks). One child was still an inpatient and one girl had just arrived in the cancer ward for a bone marrow transplant.

The five children were all treated for malignant blood disorders, such as acute lymphatic leukaemia, acute myelogenic leukaemia, aplastic anaemia and myelodysplasia. There are two reasons for choosing patients with these disorders: their medical conditions/treatments were potentially life threatening and they had to go through hospitalisation (including various degrees of isolation) for many months. My goal has not been to obtain new knowledge about particular illnesses, but to better understand creative work and interplay by children who share (if nothing else) a dangerous disease/treatment and a long hospital stay. No particular disease indicates that a sufferer has special need for making songs. No particular disease indicates what kinds of songs/song activities are likely to emerge from music therapy involvement.

According to Lincoln and Guba (referred to in Bruscia 1995, p.407), sampling (understood here as selection of cases) has two main objectives: 1. in order to achieve a holistic understanding, the researcher must look for maximum variation in cases of participants; 2. the researcher must endeavour to find cases or participants who will shed more light on whatever ideas or constructs are emerging from the data which require further exploration. One criterion for selecting just these patients' songs was the variety in ages of the children when their hospital song creations started: Henry was four years old, Hannah and Mary were seven, René was 13, and Brian was 15. The patients have not been thought of as representing particular age groups, they simply represent themselves as younger or older children. Another criterion for selection has been that these five children, at least once, seemingly *liked* to make songs; they had actually all made songs on their own initiative. Henry and Hannah made two songs each, Brian made four songs and Mary made ten songs. René made only one song in hospital but she was hospitalised for a shorter time than the other four children. There is no average paediatric cancer patient (as there is no average song). A child who participates in song creations is neither typical nor untypical in relation to anything. Participation in song-creative activities only indicates that the child has had the strength and interest for doing so at a given time. Comparisons between 'song-makers' and patients who have not made songs are outside the scope of this study.

Data sources

From a constructivist's stance one neither 'collects' nor 'gathers' data (as though data are just 'out there' waiting to be discovered or harvested). Mason (1998) states clearly that a researcher's information about the social world cannot be a completely neutral process and therefore speaks of 'generating' data. To 'utilise' data is also an expression that is meaningful in this process of generating data – indicating that the researcher bases his further constructions on certain data. 'Data sources' just denote the building stones for the researcher's constructions. The researcher's preliminary understanding of what is 'a song' determines where he looks for evidence and what may be regarded as evidence.

Table 4.2 Major sources of data applied in the 19 songs' life-histories

Documentation/Archival records

Case/progress reports

Diary/logbook from a mother/music therapist/ students

Letters from patients

Public newspapers

School magazine

Audio/video/photo

Interviews

Focused interviews/spontaneous conversations with patients, parents, primary nurses, enrolled nurses, (paediatric) oncologists, welfare nurses, hospital (preschool) teachers, home school teachers, physiotherapists, special school music therapists.

Observation

Participant observer of song-related events in various hospital sites and in patients homes (as 'natural inquiry')

Physical artefacts

Written texts and/or music

Cassette/CD/video made by or with clients as a product related to the song creations

Each of the different data sources has its own strengths and weaknesses as to the way in which it represents reliable data and calls for different skills on the part of the researcher (see Table 4.2). Every song history is constructed with a framework of documentary materials, some that exist prior to the act of research upon them, some that are generated for or through the process of research, some that are generated by the researcher, and some that are generated by other people. The life histories of these songs deal with events that occur both inside and outside scheduled music therapy sessions. As far more people than the patient and the music therapist are involved as song-makers, performers or as audience, their expressed stories, experiences and reflections provide basic data about both processes and meaning. In qualitative case studies interviews are usually the principal source for gaining access to multiple views, this closely relates to the ontological stance of 'multiple realities'.

I have been performing formal interviews in addition to having entered spontaneous conversations with the people encountered – not totally by chance and aimlessly – but in order to shed new light on the songs' lives. Both the researcher and the interviewee might actually be led into new knowledge, self-understanding and reflections through these encounters.

The five children who are the main persons in this study actually represented five different points of departure for selecting interviewees in order to obtain detailed ('thick') enough descriptions of the life histories of the 19 songs. The family situations of the patients were rather diverse. Songs that had many participants (related to creating, performing and listening) understandably provided a broader base for commentaries than songs that were primarily a more closed 'family affair'.

Sometimes interviewees told me about song activities involving, for example, a home schoolteacher that I had never met. A telephone call to this person could provide valuable information about a song's life after the patient-song-maker had gone home. Sometimes hospital personnel whom I had not interviewed approached me and spontaneously shared with me their stories or comments related to a song's life or provided relevant contextual information.

I decided at an early stage not to interview the five child patients separately. There were several reasons for this. I had worked closely and over time with all the children and had recorded their comments as the songs were created, performed and used. I also had a strong feeling that these children had already told me all they wanted to say about the songs (but they were sometimes present and commented on their songs during interviews with their parents). When song-histories acquired more chapters added weeks, months and even years after the actual interviews took place, it was partly because many conversations continued as a result of encounters between the families and the music therapist even after the patients had finished treatment and returned home. After a regular post-treatment medical check, a child sometimes stayed in hospital longer simply to take part in musical activities. Music therapy activities (more or less related to the song creations) also continued with three of the children after they had returned home.

In the study of the 19 songs, the researcher is both participant and observer. He never enters the 'sites' of the song activities simply for observation purposes and he can only write what he believes he sees and hears. For some topics the researcher has no other way of gathering data but 'being there' himself. It is probably more difficult for an external researcher to carry out a 'site'-investigation in this study than in a study primarily focusing on scheduled sessions in a music therapy room. The 'site' in this study changes from the isolation room to the patient's home, from one hospital to another, and from a scheduled session to a spontaneous song-event in a hospital entrance hall. As we are dealing with very sick children and families in crisis situations, there are also ethical questions related to who should be allowed into the patients' space for the purpose of conducting research. Making and recording numerous observations over time in (mostly) familiar milieus is no guarantee against bias, but possibly a prerequisite for insightful records of song phenomena over time. A possible bias due to my own manipulation of events is, to a certain extent, controlled through other people's observations (interviewees, a mother's logbook, video recordings, etc).

Artefacts in relation to music therapy have, as far as I know, been very little explored until now. This researcher's evaluation of 'physical objects' as data sources has also changed during the years of studying these 19 song creations. While the music therapist's interest initially focused on the making and the live performances of a song, he soon discovered that the patients (families) showed an interest in and used the written sheets with song and melody. For example, a nurse hung a song sheet on her refrigerator door at home (and the young song maker noticed this on a visit). Another song sheet was presented to the kindergarten at the patient's return from hospital. Cassettes with a hospital song were copied by parents and used as Christmas gifts. One patient was particularly interested in having her picture on a CD cover and was highly praised by her classmates for her cool-looking song product.

Case presentation

Each individual song history (case) is presented with specific contextual information and with references to the original 'text and music' (see Figure 4.1) and various audio documents. The first song history of each of the five patients contains basic biographic (including diagnostic) information (see Table 4.3 for an example). For practical reasons this is not repeated for each new song. As the project takes place in natural settings, these provide both a condition and a soundboard for the song-histories. Describing the central sites and the general music therapeutic work that goes on there will provide the reader with a necessary basis (and probably also unnecessary prejudice) for studying the individual songs. The crossover between general music therapy and the specific song creations in these milieus is made far more distinct here than in the actual music therapy practice. The researcher is also a key instrument of data collection. He has, according to good qualitative research traditions, spent extensive time in the field and describes this with an 'insider' perspective (Creswell 1998, p.16). It will be somewhat artificial to pretend that he does not carry with him his total understanding (at the time) and all his previous experiences from the very start of a research project.

Paediatric wards in two metropolitan university hospitals constitute the basic arenas for this project. The music therapist/researcher has initiated and developed the music therapy service in both wards. When this study was commenced, I thought of the 'sites' as the two hospitals only. I soon discovered that the songs, in some cases, 'moved out' of the wards and the hospitals. Some of these sites I did not know or visit personally but I received information about songs being (re-)created or performed in various patients' homes, in kindergartens, hospitals/schools and

Text written down by stepfather

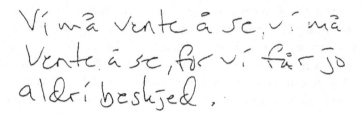

Figure 4.1 Text and music of Henry's song 'We Must Wait'

Table 4.3 The history (case) of Henry's song no. 2: 'We must wait' (Norwegian: 'Vi må vente')

Time and context	Events	Commentaries	
		Interviewes	*Music therapist*
Henry (five years old) has survived months of intensive treatment (including weeks with respirator treatment) because of a number of life-threatening conditions that developed during his scheduled treatment for his acute lymphatic leukaemia (ALL): brain-thrombosis, pneumonia and pneumothorax.	Henry and his stepfather are sitting together and waiting for 'narcosis'. It is time for a bone marrow aspiration. Nothing has happened and staff cannot explain the delay. The stepfather says: 'We must wait and see, we must wait and see.' Henry answers: '"cause we surely will be told something'. But as time passes, the last words are changed to: '"cause we are never told anything' ... or in a less literal translation: 'we get no information'.	*Stepfather:* 'This was a period when we got very little information. We were sitting there waiting indefinitely. So we had to take some initiatives ourselves. [...] (This time) I suddenly realised the rhythm of the words (we were saying to each other) ... Henry liked it too.'	It was thus a complete little poem, easily remembered and easily understood by anyone who has been a long-term hospital patient. The 'instant' melody was simple and (hopefully) sounded nice on its own; the song was performed with a strong offbeat. When I received this text by Henry, I felt strongly that he expected this new song of his to be another success. And he was right: all children and relatives present laughed during the first performance, and at the 'encore' almost everyone joined in singing. This is probably one aspect of hospital life that is not funny at all.
18 months after admission Henry is three-quarters of the way through the scheduled treatment of his leukaemic disease. Some weeks are spent at home (more or less isolated) and then Henry must move to the paediatric department for some time. His general condition is as normal as can be expected (that means: good and bad periods related to times and types of medication, unwanted infections, and social circumstances).	In Norwegian this text has a strong, consistent rhythm. The last words in the two lines also rhyme ('se' and 'beskjed'). The stepfather writes down the little rhyme and some days later Henry gives the small piece of paper to me during a musical hour. English translation (by the music therapist): *We must wait, wait and see/ We must wait, wait and see/ 'cause they never tell nothing to me.* I make a melody immediately, do not change a word, and present the new song for patients, relatives and staff. Afterwards the melody is written down. Henry gets a copy.	*Mother:* 'We [sic] who are hospital patients ought to have medals for simply waiting! We were really never told anything. And you have to nag, and nag, and nag persistently. And the longer you are there, the more you learn (about these things).' *Preschool teacher:* 'This is a very basic way of expressing their experiences. [...] But it's probably first of all the stepfather who is waiting and feeling he is never told anything. Very often the children think waiting is ok, because they make the most of time and do many pleasant things. Sometimes, at any rate, Henry was always clever at utilizing every possible activity offered at the (ward) playroom.'	

Continued on next page

Table 4.3 (cont.) The history (case) of Henry's song number 2: 'We must wait' (Norwegian: 'Vi må vente')

Time and context	Events	Commentaries	
		Interviewees	*Music therapist*
Half a year after discharge (about one year after the song was created) Henry is back in his old kindergarten.	Henry's mother says that Henry brought the 'We Must Wait' song with him when he returned to the kindergarten. There his song sheet was copied, and performed.	Henry (answering a journalist asking, 'What did the others (in the kindergarten) think of your song?'): 'They shouted with joy and things like that … and they said: "This must be celebrated"'.	He was probably referring to the happy reception he received when he returned. But the song was at least something *he* brought back to his 'old friends'. The mother had told me that Henry was seemingly quite proud when he was presented his song.
One and a half years after discharge Henry is a schoolboy now. He is getting on quite well, both mentally and physically and appears to be basically happy and healthy. His major problem is slight attention deficit at times. He also runs home from school when he does not like it there. Every second month he is controlled at the local hospital, and every half year he has a major check at the National Hospital.	Henry is at the National Hospital for a medical check. One Tuesday morning, ten minutes after the start of the paediatric department's musical hour, he joins the singsong. More than 30 people are present. Solemnly he presents me with a necklace he has just made (mostly by his own effort) at the ward playroom. We sing 'We Must Wait'. Big applause, a deep bow from the author. After the session he reminds me that I once talked about making a CD with songs by children with cancer. (He is right!) He would actually like to have both his songs recorded, preferably by a choir, Henry says. I promise to do something and keep him informed. Perhaps Henry would like to sing his songs himself on a tape/CD? His mother stands smiling in the background. The hospital AV Services makes a video recording of this event (one part of a film featuring the hospital paediatric department). The next week a young cancer patient, 'Terry' (eight), tells me that he knows Henry's song well. He has been singing it since he learned it a week ago. We make a recording with Terry singing 'We Must Wait'. Henry's other song 'On the Outside' is being recorded with my daughter, Fransiska, as a soloist, and the cassette is sent to Henry and Terry. Four days later, I receive a letter written by Henry and his mother. Now he is ready for a recording with himself singing, but only if I will sing together with him. A 'final' recording is made in Henry's home. The mother, the little sister, and the stepfather are present. A journalist and a photographer from a daily newspaper, Verdens Gang, are there too. They have interviewed the family about their child cancer experiences.	Henry (in a letter) about the cassette with other children singing his songs: 'The cassette was cool.' Terry's *father* (half a year afterwards): 'He plays the cassette ever so often.' Henry (after he had sung his two songs, and the performance had been recorded, I asked him if he had made any *new* songs recently): 'I will, I will, but have no skill.' (He said it in a kind of '*sprech-gesang*' style.)	Very often, when this song was performed 'in public' at the paediatric department, parents (and new staff) commented the 'short' / 'clear'/'true' 'message' of the song. I came to believe that many hospital children and their relatives were quite familiar with the situation that was described. But very often the humour in the song (and in the performing) became more underlined in the comments than the actual problem. Henry had clearly appreciated that other children sang his song. Terry said it was nice to sing and record Henry's song and send it to him. I had never before thought of letting patients perform each other's songs like this. In Norwegian, Henry's spontaneous answer is this: 'Jeg vil, jeg vil, men får det ikke til.' By employing a nice rhyme to express that he does not manage to make songs, this cryptic answer gives some indication that he, at least, can play with words.

Time and context	Events	Commentaries
		Music therapist
Two and a half years after discharge	Henry is back in hospital for a new check up; he appears to be as healthy and happy as ever. After being most active during the musical hour session, he tells me that he is now singing this song in a new way. With a strong voice he sings for me and other persons present (while sitting high up on the back of a bronze horse sculpture in the entrance hall): English translation (by the music therapist): *We must wait, wait and see.* *We must wait, wait and see,* *'cause I never get any jel-ly!*	In Norwegian 'gelé' ('jelly') rhymes with 'se' ('see'). I believe this development of his old song was one way of communicating with me: he was still a song-maker! I was not sure to what degree this was just a whim, or if Henry had thought about it for a while. However, he looked most contented and confident as he was singing.

even in a television programme. During the years of the present study, individual music therapy was never officially prescribed for a particular patient, nor offered as a standard part of a treatment regime in either of the two hospitals. Establishing individual music therapy agreements has been somewhat casual, often with patients or relatives taking the initiative regarding (what I like to call) prospective musical collaboration. Nurses, medical staff or teachers have often asked the music therapist to see a patient, but further appointments have been on a strictly voluntary basis from the patient/family and the music therapist's own assessment.

Analysis and interpretation

Organising and sorting the data in the 'hyper-text' song-tables (exemplified on the three previous pages) have not been conceptually neutral procedures; even my original research questions suggest that song creations, at least understood as music therapy phenomena, have social meanings and can be understood as (social) processes. My role as a researcher includes understanding lay interpretations as well as developing relevant theoretical reflections about the song phenomena. As time passes, the time-distance from the actual song creations increases. Interpretative conclusions by this researcher are not necessarily more true than those of other investigators (professional or not) studying the same material; proposing well-founded answers and prolific new questions are, however, major (and sufficient) goals here. I have commenced transforming data long before making the final 'song tables'; one piece of information, for example, an excerpt from an interview, is actually a written interpretation of what somebody wanted to share from her memory about earlier events and experiences with the interviewer.

Five different strategies have been applied in the continually interdependent manoeuvres of analysis and interpretation: to highlight and display specific constructions (or 'findings'); to compare cases; to extend the analysis; to orientate in the direction of a theory; and to connect with personal experience (see Wolcott 1994, pp.23–48). The different interpretative acts result in new constructs.

The 'geography' of the songs

As 'ecological context' or 'environment' constitutes one basis for understanding the song phenomena in this multiple case study, knowing the 'geography' of the individual songs is necessary in order to understand the process of making and performing. The first highlighted feature is therefore an overview of sites (*where* do the song activities take place?), persons (*who* participates?) and times (*when* and for *how long* were the songs developed and performed?). The life histories of these songs go beyond scheduled music therapy sessions in some 'music room' or in the patient's own hospital room. Songs are not just made and performed in a contextual vacuum, the locality of these activities is a type of data that cannot be overlooked in a study of meanings (see Table 4.4).

Table 4.4 Locations: where the songs have been created and performed	
Song maker's hospital room	Brian's song nos. 1, 3; Mary's song nos. 1, 2, 3, 4, 7, 10; René's song no. 1
Isolation room	Brian's song no. 2; Hannah's song nos. 1, 2; Mary's song nos. 1, 2, 5, 6, 7, 8, 9; René's song no. 1
Hospital common rooms	Brian's song nos. 1, 2, 3, 4; Henry's song nos. 1, 2; Hannah's song no. 1; Mary's song nos. 1, 4, 7
Hospital school	Brian's song nos. 1, 3, 4; René's song no. 1
Song maker's home	Henry's song nos. 1, 2; Hannah's song nos. 1, 2; Mary's song nos. 1, 3, 8; René's song no. 1
Other patient's home	Henry's song no. 2
Home school or kindergarten	Brian's song no. 3; Henry's song no. 2; Hannah's song nos. 1, 2; Mary's song nos. 1, 3, 10; René's song no. 1
Public television	Mary's song no. 10
Two hospitals	Mary's song nos. 1, 5, 6; René's song no. 1

Songs fly easily from one part of the hospital to another, to other hospitals and to the 'outside world'. Some patterns, as to the individual children, can also be seen in this table, which, however, does not show how often a song has been performed (or attended to) or the 'length' of a song's life.

The participants are not only a young patient and a music therapist. Figure 4.2 shows potential participants (in addition to the patient) and audiences in three different 'areas': 1. people within the 'inner circle' of the patient in hospital; 2. people within the bigger hospital environment; 3. people remaining outside, or 'beyond', the hospital environment. A song can directly reach audiences far away from the patient's isolated existence when a CD is sent by post to classmates, for example.

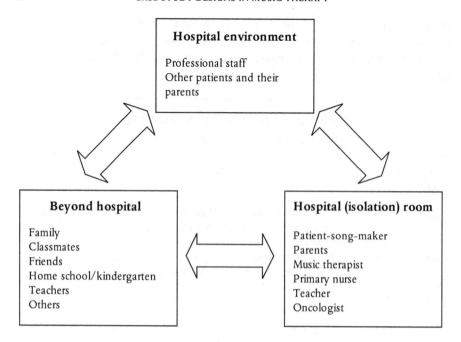

Figure 4.2 Potential song-participants and audiences in three major areas (the arrows indicate where a song can 'move' between these areas)

Each of the 19 songs can be viewed in this framework. The patient moves between the three areas and so, often, does the song. Some songs have been used or played for many different people in all three arenas. Other songs have only been known by the near family and patient (and the music therapist) and have hardly been performed outside the isolation room, for instance. The more people involved, the more difficult it is to get an accurate (or total) overview of where, who and when the song-activities have taken place.

Each of the 19 songs' 'length of life' seems related first to the patient's own involvement and interest, and second to which other persons are taking part in the musicking. The more people are involved, the more opportunities for renewed interest and 'uses' of the song. (I also guess some of the songs were remembered and performed long after the completion of this project.)

Detrimental for *any* song's life is the combination of the song's qualitative aspects, it's 'promotion' and various contextual aspects. These song cases tell of very different life spans of the individual songs, but in all the cases the song has been performed more than once. In other words, each song's life history goes further than the song's 'creation'. Some songs had seemingly short but 'intense' lives, not exceeding two or three months. Some songs have perhaps not been performed more than once or twice after their creation. Other songs, however, have been performed for and by a number of different persons in many different situations, in different places within or beyond the hospital environment.

The history of Henry's song no. 2 (presented in Tables 4.3a, b, and c) covers a period of three years! The history of Mary's first song, 'A Suspiciously Cheerful Lady', covers a period of one year and three months. During this period many persons were involved in performing, recreating or responding to this song: Mary's parents, her little brother, nurses, medical staff, a physiotherapist, her home school teacher and school mates, a hospital choir, a ward rock band, etc. After one and a half years in hospital she played the song on a keyboard together with a singing music therapist on a popular television programme.

Not all of these 19 songs proved suitable for performance in different settings nor for audiences outside the patient's room. Others may have had the potential for a long life but the patient's interest in the song (or in presenting it to others) did not last long. Some songs were performed instrumentally by the song-maker after the interest for singing (the text) had ceased. In some cases the children have been in charge of the creative process from start to finish, other cases tell of parents or teachers who have certainly inspired the five children and of co-operative creative work.

Meanings related to the 19 songs

The therapeutic value of the 19 songs in this study is not dependent on the number of performances or life-length but to what *meanings* the song (activities) seem to have. Even if some important features appear only once, my focus of study shifts now from the single event or observation to comparing and looking for relationships, and from studying the individual song to studying what the selected themes imply for each of the five young patients. Such comparative investigations may disclose a variety and nuances – probably more so than within a study based on one case, either understood as one song or one child – and may lead to more informed and sophisticated (re-)constructions.

After a long period of considering the song cases and several attempts of 'lumping together' what I believed were instances with common features, I constructed three major themes: *expression, achievement* and *pleasure*. These thematic boxes seemed sufficiently different and inclusive to encompass the majority of meaningful aspects that I see in the life histories of the 19 songs. They are, however, not mutually exclusive; some statements can be understood as both 'the one and the other'. The chosen themes are seemingly also inter-related and can be seen as three interchangeable sets of lenses (fitting the same frame, however) for studying the songs.

Expression

This is a meaning category employed in relation to what the song (text and music) is believed to 'say' or 'express'. As the child-authors/composers/performers themselves have not been asked what they want to 'express' through their creative work, 'outsiders' perspectives' (not the least that of the music therapist researcher) mark the interpretations. We know, however, something about the stated intentions for making some of the songs. I do not believe there is any direct correspondence between the artists' (here: song-maker's/composer's) emotions and listeners' reactions. But because 'expression' is (perhaps) better studied as an interplay of giving and receiving, rather than as 'one-way communication', I have been interested in reactions, comments and opinions about expressive phenomena related to the songs.

The many themes within the 19 lyrics show that these five young song-makers chose to make songs referring to life in hospital as well as to the world beyond (see Table 4.5). Some texts are seemingly accounts of autobiographical experiences, telling a story in present tense, singular; in other texts references to the author are absent. Various persons may be presented through their proper names or e.g. as 'nurses'; 'doctors', or 'girls'. When a text also provides quite clear cues as to location, any informed reader will understand that it is written by a sick child. Other texts give no such cues.

A change of focus from 'content' to 'form' and 'style' reveals different lyrical modes of expression within the song material. The 19 songs' life histories show no formal tendencies as to how the young authors have presented their various themes. This study brings forward little information about the text makers' eventual stylistic considerations. But any text (whether it be written or just spoken/sung) always appears in a certain form/style – important features that are essential for how the song is interpreted. I am aware of the possible danger of 'explanation overkill' when discussing these songs' formal poetic features as means of expression. On the other hand such elements can not be completely overlooked either: in some of the songs the young poets' own *ways* of saying something certainly has a decisive expressive function. Patients or parents seldom discussed writing techniques with me.

The original written lyrics (16 of a total of 19) have the shape of prose, verse or various hybrids thereof. In some cases I have very gently edited the texts received from the five young patients: dividing a prose text into verses, repeating a line or repeating the complete text. Any alteration may influence listeners'/reader's

Table 4.5 Lyrics: major categories

Themes related to the 'Hospital world'*

Procedures	Treatment / symptoms / physiology	Psycho-social themes
Mary's song no. 1: a diagnostic blood test?	*Brian's song no. 2*: his 'growing' bone marrow	*Brian's song no. 2*: isolation; *no. 4*: musical activities
	Hannah's song no. 1: loss of hair; *no. 2*: waiting for more blood corpuscles	*Henry's song no. 2*: waiting without information
	Mary's song no. 3: eating and farting; *no. 8*: praising her new bone marrow; *no. 10*: nausea	*Mary's song no. 2*: an interrupted meal; *no. 5*: friendship (with the primary nurse) and common funny activities (not hospital related); *no. 6*: being bored, but helped by the primary nurse; *no. 7*: nurses' properties
		René's song no. 1: staying in hospital during school holidays

Themes not related to the 'Hospital world'*

Other themes	'Nonsense' (?)
Brian's song no. 1: love – courtship; *no. 3*: various girls	*Henry's song no. 1*: rhyming or neologisms
Mary's song no. 4: a dancing hat; *no. 9*: life on the seas and a feared pirate	*Mary's songs nos. 3 and 5*: also have such elements
René's song no. 1: characteristic features of her classmates	

* *'Hospital world' here means: related to sickness, symptoms, treatment, care and hospitalisation*

interpretation of what a song expresses. I have, however, aimed not to bring in any new elements but simply to make the text as 'sing-able' as possible within the boundaries of the original point of departure. Very few words have been altered, left out or added.

The texts often have distinctive metric elements and are often based on end-rhymes and repetitive elements. Some texts have borrowed ideas and words from other texts, but can still tell something of the children's preferred styles. Hannah's first song is marked by her mother's ingenious transformation of a well known, innocent children's poem to a new poem about hair-loss. When Hannah is improvising her next song, she uses the same trick. The point of departure is 'Ba, Ba, Blacksheep' (loved by children in many countries); Hannah's version also starts with 'Ba, ba'. She is, however, not addressing a little lamb this time, but her own, demanding, new blood corpuscles:

> *Ba, ba blood corpuscles*
> *You are far too few!*
> *Yes, yes, we'll increase,*
> *but smile and laugh must you!*
> *One pair to my arm,*
> *One pair to my head,*
> *and two pairs of whites*
> *to stomach and legs.*

(English translation by Trygve Aasgaard)

Humour is a prominent feature of many of the songs; indeed all the five young patients have made one or more songs with humorous qualities. The song creators express humour through lyrics, music and through particular ways of performing the song. Humorous features can be interpreted as aims, means, content or form in these songs. Some texts deal with a serious and/or (probably) 'uncomfortable' topic but combine the account of misery with slapstick and presenting one or more 'fools'.

Humour is iconoclastic whenever it tackles the mighty and powerful. René presents all her classmates, the majority described as being rather idiotic or clumsy, before she laconically finishes: 'And here (in the isolation room) I am during my school holiday(s)'. She does not say that she wishes to return to those stupid classmates as soon as possible. Ironic humour is a prominent feature of the songs: what is said, expresses satirical, critical intentions or the opposite of what is (probably) meant. A related kind of irony is created in both of Hannah's songs because of sudden and surprising text changes from innocent (nursery) rhymes to references related to treatment and care. Serious themes indeed, presented with very little seriousness. This stylistic manipulation of both serious themes and familiar forms of presentation creates an expressive message containing several possible meanings; a rather sardonic ambiguity that is not just funny but also resonant with the sound of tragedy.

A second type of humour is found in the 'coarse' texts applying indecent words or descriptions. I name this category 'naughty humour'. Fifteen-year-old

Brian's third song tells about a girl who is standing 'on the top of a table' pulling down 'her roller blind' ('her underpants'). Mary's little brother's version of 'A Suspiciously Cheerful Lady' changes the described battle about an injection to a 'farting battle' (Aasgaard, 2000). Some other songs open the door to a fantastic and playful world having few or no 'real life' references.

Neologisms that sound funny are typical traits of Henry's song no. 1. He composes new words by putting together well-known words in completely illogical relations, like 'a nose-tip-toe' and 'a peep-peep-toot-toot'. Mary's song no. 4 describes a talking and dancing hat: This is free floating fantasy. Song no. 5 tells about 'friends saying please, pull out my teeth'. Even if rhyming has first priority here, the result can be interpreted as slightly amusing because of the rather accidental 'meanings' rising from the rhymes (as can also be studied in Henry's new 'waiting for jelly' version of his song no. 2, Table 4.3). These songs exemplify children's various initiatives of using particular types of humour – what comes 'from the outside', as therapy, as the initiation to make songs and practical assistance.

One cannot escape the question of what music is able to express and I asked myself 'How do musical elements influence the expressive sides of the 19 songs?' Some of these songs have a melody/musical arrangement described as 'innocent' or 'happy'. The combination with a dramatic song-text (as wanted by the young patients) was seemingly fostering songs with an ambivalent 'message'. Other amusing, 'non-sense' texts seemed to be strengthened (as to being 'funny') through a 'merry' melody. Only one of the 19 melodies, made in company with the child, was experienced as sad and gloomy.

The 19 life-histories of the songs show that the music therapist has made melodies/arrangements to 14 of the texts (some with minor suggestions/contributions from patients/parents). One melody has been made by a patient; another by music therapy students; two texts have, from the very start, been based on and made with well-known melodies in mind, and one melody (and lyrics) is an almost exact copy of another song. Musical features, not the least those features which are performance related, are far more inconstant than the song words.

The music therapy perspective becomes evident through a broad approach to expression that also bears in mind data related to the actual performances and recordings. Humour, actually a bag with many different expressive tricks, is more prominent in these 19 songs than depressive, scornful or openly angry voices, even when the dark sides of cancer and hospitalisation are dealt with. This tendency can also be observed in the music. Even when the lyrical theme can be understood as rather gloomy, the preferred musical style is usually light and gay. But there are no rules as to textual-musical relationships within these 19 songs. 'Expression' is not a static element of each song, rather a bundle of tightly woven elements experienced differently by different persons at different times.

Achievement

'Achievement' is a meaning category employed when the child is being praised for her/his work (production/ product/performance) related to the songs and/or has finished a piece of work related to the song. It is probable that the child experiences this as positive (appearing to be contented and/or verbally acknowledging a 'success' or a skill related to the song and/or is positively interested to make more songs). The participants in this study were engaged in non-obligatory creative activities resulting in certain products or outcomes (different versions of 'finished' songs/song performances). To some extent one might say that the child itself sets the goals and also decides when she/he has reached those goals. To achieve something positively through the song activities relates to the patient's own endeavour; the song becoming a token of surplus activity of the child's own choice. What we see is an operationalisation of the humanistic credo of music therapy introduced by Even Ruud in 1979 and since quoted by many: 'to increase people's possibilities of action'. The children were not *always* dependent on other people's comments, not even (!) the music therapist's positive or negative sayings about their 'oeuvres'.

The concept of 'achievement' has undoubtedly a core of meaning inseparable from a person's action(s) – what the person is actually doing; that is, reaching a set goal or demonstrating a skill or an ability to do something special. But, considering the song creations, 'achievement' is also closely related to what the action results in, such as a 'funny' song, a 'tough' song, or to possible physical products. Those products may include a piece of paper with written text and music, an audiotape or a compact disc recording (see Table 4.6).

'Achievement' probably does not mean exactly the same to each of the five child patients in this study. One might claim that every song creation represents some kind of achievement, but I have chosen to use the term only when I have information about particular phenomena that, in all likelihood, tell about 'achievement' in the meaning described above.

There are continua between the solitary and co-operative creative actions and (even) between 'actions' and 'products'. Having created a song on one's own is, in some cases, a bigger achievement than collaborating with other persons or having been 'helped'. In other cases, accomplishing something together with a loved, or admired, other person is an equally important source of achievement. Throughout the history of one song, the achievement 'point of gravity' may vary along the

Table 4.6 Song-phenomena (in four song cases) related to 'achievement'

Brian Song no. 3

Action: Having participated in the making of a song, collaborating with a 'pop star'.

Product: A song-text and a video with a tough, rude, pop-style profile.

Henry Song no. 2

Action: Having participated in the making of a song that people in hospital took interest in and/or performed; a song that other children inside and outside hospital could sing.

Product: A written, funny, song; an audiotape with another child singing; an audiotape with Henry singing his song.

Hannah Song no. 2

Action: Having made a song on her own.

Product: Memorised personal, funny song; audiotape with Hannah singing.

Mary Song no. 1

Action: a) Having made a text on her own (later to become a song) that people inside the hospital(s), her classmates and little brother took interest in. b) Performing (singing/playing) her song to various audiences.

Product: A personal and funny song text; an audiotape with music therapist singing; audiotape with Mary singing; an audiotape with a hospital choir singing; video of TV performance.

René Song no. 1

Action: Having participated in the making (text, music and singing) of her own song.

Product: Written personal and rude text; CD with René singing and with a 'cool' cover.

continuum of independence and along the continuum between the creative act and its outcome.

Comparing what the children in this study have done that is labelled as an 'achievement' reveals a continuum between dependent and independent actions within the song creative processes (see Figure 4.3). When the child is, for example, making a song text on his or her own initiative and without any assistance, we can call this action 'independent' as well as 'individual'. 'Working together', however, is certainly not equivalent with 'dependency'. As this study is focusing processes and meanings related to song creations, I find it just as interesting to look at how people work together (co-operate) as to consider degrees of dependency. In the 19 song stories we see a multitude of modes of co-operation. But the young patients also develop and/or exhibit individual skills and may take pride in doing things 'alone'.

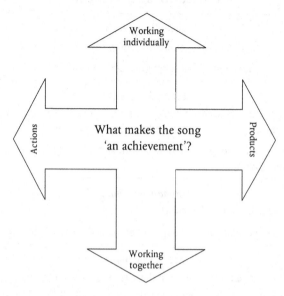

Figure 4.3 Continua of 'achievement' related to the songs

To be able to make something that can be sung might be a big achievement in itself; potential song-makers might be satisfied with simply having made 'a song'. The children in this study, except for Henry, had unquestionably intentions of making special kinds of songs. Which features of a song the song-makers considered to be particularly important differed from song to song and from time to time. Some of the song-features mentioned by the song-makers were rhythm, lyrics, melody and physical objects (related to the song's representation). Sometimes the song-makers have clearly expressed what kind of song they intended to create; sometimes specific aims have been added during the song's life; finally, some songs simply 'happen' without any discussions or comments about how it should be. Melodic lines, rhythm and harmony may be experienced as tightly interwoven and not easily understood or talked about as separate entities. On the other hand a 'bad' melody, the 'wrong' rhythm, etc, will make the song uninteresting or unfit to use: pragmatically speaking, a 'non song'. General opinions about simply good or bad songs are not difficult to obtain from the children. Even if the children have had nothing to do with the musical side of the song, it is spoken of as 'my' (and not 'our') song. This is partly because of the 'superiority' of the text and partly because of the 'interwoven-ness' of the song elements.

All the young song-makers in this study got copies of the song-melodies/arrangements including the child's (or parent's) original lyrics. A song sheet could, for example, be put on the wall above the hospital bed, at the ward staff room door or on the refrigerator door in the home of one of the nurses who knew a patient well. As a rule, audiotapes with the song sketch or the finished song were also copied and given to the child. Such objects could of course be useful when the child (or the family) were presenting the song oeuvres for others or simply for performance reasons. The music sheets or tapes were objects that the children sometimes seemed to be proud of. When I got hold of a compact disc recorder and mentioned to René that her song could be presented on a compact disc, she commenced talking about the cover and a possible picture of herself on it. This became some sort of an 'aha' experience to me. The tapes had never been supplied with nice looking covers, but this patient taught me that covers matter!

I believe the joint experience of reaching a successful result boosted the confidence of both the child, the parents and music therapist – a phenomenon perhaps not very unlike that of many successful treatment processes in the hospital setting dependent on the hard work and co-operation between doctor, nurse, patient, relatives, etc. What is special with creating songs is the focus of man as a cultural, creative being. Musicking, and indeed having made one's own song, is surplus activity, a demonstration of not just being alive, but of *living.* The 19 songs in this study were not more … or less … necessary for life than the making of a song anywhere outside hospital. When we are employing the word 'achievement' in relation to 'hospital-songs', we are also expressing an attitude to the general usefulness of art in man's life.

Pleasure

'Pleasure' is employed as a meaning category when the song activities result in various agreeable/enjoyable (and similar) experiences. Naming a category pleasure is an attempt to stop and reflect on certain aspects of the song histories that notably are related to the 'here and now' and direct experiences from or, more correctly, within the musicking. Such experiences are not automatically positive or pleasurable. But as far as I can read from the song histories, song participants become thrilled, delighted, amused (etc) in very different song 'situations' (see Table 4.7). To achieve something desirable or to express something successfully through a song, as described earlier, can without doubt also be pleasurable experiences. When used as a category here, 'pleasure' is specifically reserved for what is very different from 'business' (understood as goal-directed purposeful activities).

Table 4.7 Collocation of song phenomena (in four cases) related to 'pleasure'
Brian Song no. 3 Making a spicy pop-song and collaborating with a real 'popstar'.
Henry Song no. 2 Creating (together with stepfather) an amusing text from a 'boring' point of departure. Later eagerly performing the song and making a new verse. Appreciating that other patients (etc) learn to sing and laugh at his song.
Hannah Song no. 2 Moments of fun when playing with words (the no. 1 text is turning an unpleasant situation upside-down). Song creation/performance as family entertainment. Agreeable expectation of song creative activities to take place with the music therapist. Playing eagerly (on various instruments) melodies on return home.
Mary Song no. 1 Song development and performances as family entertainment, possibly alleviating a frightening procedure. Appreciating other persons who perform/praise her song when too weak to sing herself. Mary later performs song as an ironic drama (the text is joking with an unpleasant situation). Playing eagerly the melody on various instruments.
René Song no. 1 Song creation as family entertainment. 'Fooling' René's various classmates and appreciating them praising her song product (a cool CD). Making the CD with her own song was the best experience from the time of bone marrow transplantation, she says.

Positive emotions can be caused by any welcomed experience. The two previously described categories, 'expression' and 'achievement', are far from fixed and eternal elements related to the song creations. 'Pleasure' is an even less stable phenomenon, and this quality must be kept in mind when investigating processes and meanings.

I find nowhere in the 19 song histories testimonies of patients or relatives having fun continuously, nor of pleasurable experiences directly exceeding the actual time of song involvement. These cases present, first and foremost, examples of pleasurable elements occurring during different phases of the actual song activities. I interpret the accompanying expressed eagerness, the frequent smiles, and the children's endurance as tokens of this interest. The mentioned activities of playing and rhyming with words, making nonsense-words, making texts of one's own choice or making text and melody simultaneously, seem all to be pleasure-related. To perform one's own song (sing or play) and to watch other persons learning to sing and performing this song were potentially pleasurable experiences for the song-maker.

Some song cases indicate that to expect doing, or experiencing something nice, adds pleasurable moments in these patients' lives. 'Expectancy' is perhaps an underestimated component of music therapy. To expect pleasurable events, and to recall them, are two sides of the same coin. When the act of recalling or waiting for music therapy activities is linked with a pleasant memory or an expectation of something nice to happen, the symptoms-sickness-diagnosis-treatment-outcome panorama fades for a while and a different focus of mind is temporarily substituted. I understand this ability of providing good memories and creating pleasurable expectations as important spin-offs from the actual song activities. Perhaps there is a resemblance between pleasurable moments and 'time-outs' in sports: short periods where the players can 'recharge their batteries' to restore power for the rest of the game.

The song-related musicking does certainly not abolish the displeasures of disease, treatment and hospitalisation. But many moments of just a little sweetness are perhaps significant helpers as to maintaining contact with the good life during very hard times.

Many of the songs are initially, or eventually, made and performed with some kind of expressed goal. The creative interactions seem, however, to be more marked by playfulness rather than by goal-directedness. Play releases tension, fosters excitement and enjoyment and is outside the realm of practical/material purposes (Claussen 1997). But play is no abstract thought, rather ways of being in touch with 'living' life.

'Musicking' is *per se* social! Even if musicking is not always pleasurable, the 19 song histories tell that joy and happy moods may also be contagious and easily spread from one person to another. I do not proclaim this as a general rule but the present case materials exemplify that hospital and home environments may be 'infected' by an aggregation of pleasurable experiences from song-related musicking. Having fun together or doing something meaningful together seems, in many cases, to be more pleasurable than solitary entertainment.

All the five young song makers have been involved with various socially pleasurable activities related to their song creations. It is unlikely that music therapy restricted to sessions with the music therapist alone could possibly provide as much fun! This study also shows many examples of parents who throw themselves into the playfulness, the childishness, sometimes even the naughtiness that the song creative activities invite to.

Parents sincerely wish to contribute towards a pleasurable emotional climate in the sickroom, specified by Mary's father as being an unwritten law in the ward. A wish to escape momentarily from a harsh, rational life world might be just as vivid for a parent as for their patient daughter or son. The song stories are not comprehensive enough to obtain detailed knowledge about parents' possible pleasures from being involved in playful activities. But the eagerness and the readiness I believe I have sensed amongst parents indicate that the play-aspect of the songs is, at least, dearly appreciated. Several of the 19 song histories demonstrate playful communication between patients, parents and hospital staff: hedonistic common play outside any treatment plans.

Final discussion

How can we interpret the phenomena categorised under the labels 'expression', 'achievement' and 'pleasure' in relation to health? Or, to be more specific; what are the relationships between those phenomena and 'well being' and 'ability' – understood as major subjective health elements (Nordenfelt 1987)? This question may be answered through a two-step procedure. First, by considering the three categories in relationship to social roles and the environmental aspects thereof and then by considering the three specified roles in relationship to health.

The five children are indeed individual personalities who experienced treatment and hospitalisation differently. However, they all experienced a common situation, being seriously ill and isolated. To various degrees they were stripped of their personal attributes and strength – appearing mainly as 'a patient': a person who suffers and waits patiently for better times to come. This is the role of the Homo Patiens, and I use this metaphor because the children's sick stories show that both 'well being' and 'ability' were diminished or at stake for long periods with restricted (temporarily lost or weakened) active social roles.

The current study gives many examples of song events where seriously ill patients develop various social roles and where the musicking seems to have had the 'power' to expand patients' role repertoire. All cases present sick children who are 'given' roles as artists and whose songs are understood and handled as pieces of art (and not only as therapeutic testimonies). But we also see sick children who 'take' new roles – roles far from that of being just 'a being who suffers' or 'a patient'. Very sick children show in these cases what Goffman calls '…an active *engagement* or spontaneous involvement in the role activity at hand' (Goffman 1997, p.36).

One feature of the song histories is that the song phenomena do not develop solely through interactions between patients and the music therapist. Song-participants may be the patient's relatives and/or other people in the hospital milieu and beyond, each person with her or his own set of expectations and with different roles in relation to the sick child and the song creations. The concept of 'role expansion' gets a wider meaning here and indicates a music therapy practice with ecological consequences for more than the sick child (see Bruscia 1998, p.230). Indeed, many parts of the hospital environment have temporarily been marked by these song activities. Song-related creative involvement and antici- pation can influence boring routines and long days, even outside the working hours of the music therapist.

What then are the roles related to 'expression', 'achievement' and 'pleasure'? The song stories present sick children and others who 'enter' (and 'leave') various roles for shorter or longer periods, but the present project has neither studied how long these role-changes have lasted nor what might have been the possible long-term 'effects' thereof. Through creative song activities patients have been assisted to communicate with persons with whom they want to share something – inside or outside of the isolation/patient room. Songs have been media for com- municating thoughts and experiences, but have also been developed and shared as gifts or as tokens of creative skills. Song performances have functioned as the patients' voice in (and from) the hospital environment at times when they have not been able to sing or do much else themselves. The Homo Communicans challenges isolation and communicative obstacles – in these cases patients' own songs have served as important communicative channels. Several other persons within the patients' families and various other persons in the hospital milieu have been partic- ipants in the song-communicative activities. The five patients' own songs have therefore fostered communication (and indeed dialogues rather than monologues) within the paediatric oncology ward and between the ward and the 'world outside'.

The life histories of the 19 songs present sick children who have developed skills that have no direct links to coping with health problems or the tricky part of the patient role. Each of the five patients has acted as a Homo Faber (a being who creates/produces) – even during really hard times when discomfort and fatigue might seem overwhelming. Through music therapy the children have got a tool to make something they (and indeed also their parents) appreciated and were proud of. They appeared not only as creative persons, but also as persons having success- fully achieved certain skills and as persons enjoying the outcomes thereof.

Strict treatment protocols, an environment marked by high tech devices and procedures, and tight time schedules combined with periods of 'nothing', have not been elements favouring playfulness and fun. Homo Rationalis must have a dominant role within the hospital premises and the five main characters in this project, as well as their parents, did seemingly all conform to the rational values within the hospital culture – values far from those related to play. Sometimes, however, the being that plays, Homo Ludens, entered the 'stage'; and 'stages' varied from a big hospital entrance hall to a small room in the isolation unit.

Many of the songs have been made and performed (initially or eventually) with some kind of expressed goal. The creative interactions seemed, however, to have been more marked by playfulness than by goal-directedness. Hospital environments changed, for a minute or for half an hour, to arenas focused on leisure where elements of fun and laughter were prominent.

Various combinations of 'well-being' and 'ability' are distinct features of the (social) roles suggested above. I therefore call these roles health related. The 19 life histories of songs demonstrate the children's ability to express themselves and to communicate, their ability to create and to show others their various song-related skills and, not least, their ability to have fun and to enjoy some good things in life, even if many other life-aspects were rather unfavourable. 'I perform, therefore I am' is being loudly signalled from these cases (D. Aldridge 2000a, p.13). These children have all been creatively present in their own life during a difficult time.

The roles I have related to the three main themes in the 19 life histories of songs are all ways of performing health. Aldridge calls health '...a performed activity; a performance that takes place with others and, while dependent upon the body, incorporates mind and spirit' (D. Aldridge 2000, p.13). When the five children were assisted to create and perform their own songs, these elements of music therapy added new elements of health in their lives and environments during the long and complicated process of being treated for serious blood disorders.

CHAPTER 5

A Case Study in the Bonny Method of Guided Imagery and Music (BMGIM)

Denise Grocke

The Bonny Method of Guided Imagery and Music (hereafter BMGIM) is one method among various forms of music psychotherapy. It differs from other music therapy methods in that there is a prescribed format for the session and there are specific music programs that the BMGIM therapist uses. BMGIM has been described in many publications (Bonny 2002; Clark 2002; Erdonmez Grocke 2001; Goldberg 1995) and only the outline of BMGIM will be presented here.

The BMGIM session comprises four segments:

1.   The 'prelude' or preliminary discussion. The client discusses any issues or concerns and together with the therapist decides on the main issue to be explored in the session (for example, personal issues, relationship difficulties or issues relating to clinical pathology).

2.   The induction. The client lies down on a relaxation mat (or comfortable chair), with eyes closed, and the therapist provides a relaxation induction that is individually tailored to the client's level of energy, and to the main issue for the session. At the end of the relaxation induction the therapist provides a focus image, which is also related to the issue of the session.

3.   The music and imagery segment, in which the BMGIM therapist chooses the music program of approximately 30–45 minutes duration. As the music plays, the client's experiences and images are relayed verbally to the therapist. The therapist asks questions (interventions) which are designed to bring the client closer to the imagery and to

encourage the client to notice any feelings or emotions that are associated with the image. The therapist also takes a written transcript of the imagery sequence.

4. At the end of the music the therapist helps the client bring the imagery to a close, and the client is re-orientated to a non-altered state of consciousness. The client is encouraged to make connections between the imagery in its symbolic form in relation to daily life issues. This processing is done through verbal discussion, free drawing, mandala drawings or sculpting with clay.

Clients have a range of experiences in BMGIM, as we see in Table 5.1, that are associated with a rich variety of imagery.

Table 5.1 Categories of experience in BMGIM	
Visual experiences	Colours, shapes, fragments of scenes, complete scenes, figures, people, animals, birds, water (lakes, streams, oceans, or pools)
Memories: childhood memories	Memories of significant events, significant people, and feelings in the client's life are explored through reminiscences
Emotions and feelings	The full gamut of possible feelings like sadness, happiness, joy, sorrow, fear, anger, and surprise
Body sensations	Parts of the body may feel lighter, or heavier; parts of the body may become numb and feel split off from the body; there may be feelings of floating or falling; sensations of spinning, or feelings that the body is changing in some way
Body movements	The client may make expressive movements of the body in relation to the imagery being experienced, e.g. hands create a shape, arms reach up in response to an image, fists or legs pound on the mat in reaction to feelings of anger
Somatic imagery	Changes within the internal organs of the body may be experienced, e.g. pain felt in the chest or heart, exploring an internal organ for its shape and colour, a surge of energy felt through the entire body
Altered auditory experiences	There may be an altered auditory perception of the music: the music comes from far away; the music is very close; one particular instrument stands out (which can also be transference to music)

Continued on next page

Table 5.1 continued

Associations with the music and transference to the music	Memories of when the music was heard last, memories of playing the music; the music is being played especially for the person; the person is actually playing the music being heard
Abstract imagery	Mists, fog, geometrical shapes, clouds, etc
Spiritual experiences	Being drawn toward a light; a spiritual person: a monk, priest, woman in flowing robes; being in a cathedral; feeling a presence very close
Transpersonal experiences	The body becoming smaller, or larger, change felt deep in the body (cells changing, parts of body changing shape)
Archetypal figures from legendary stories may appear	King Arthur, Robin Hood, the Vikings, Aboriginal man/woman, a witch, Merlin, etc
Dialogue	Significant figures from the client's life may appear in the imagery and often have a message, so that dialogue may occur, e.g. with parental figures; aspects of self may be symbolised in human form (a baby or adult figure), or significant companions (e.g. an albatross or an eagle) and dialogue may occur with these aspects
Aspects of the shadow or anima or animus	Aspects of the shadow frequently appear in the image of a person of the same gender, aspects of the anima/animus in images of a person of the opposite gender
Symbolic shapes and images	A long tunnel, a black hole, seed opening: these shapes or images can be symbolic of moments of change or transition; symbolic images such as an ancient book or the trident shape often have specific meaning to the client

Source: Erdonmez Grocke (2001/1999)

The BMGIM music programs

Each of the music programs (of 30–40 minutes) incorporates selections from the Western classical music repertoire. A movement of a larger work may be programmed alongside a work of another composer or another stylistic period.

Each music program is designed to have a beginning piece that stimulates imagery, a middle selection to deepen the experience emotionally and a final selection that returns the client to a normal emotional state. Bonny designed 18 music programs but currently there are 66 in use (Bruscia and Grocke 2002, pp.555–591) developed by other BMGIM therapists.

The BMGIM therapist chooses the music program for the client based on the issue for exploration, the mood of the client and level of physical and emotional energy on the day. The therapist, therefore, needs to know the music programs intimately. The Bonny programs are grouped according to the relative needs of the client and also the client's experience of BMGIM as a therapeutic method. Some programs are considered 'diagnostic programs'. This means that they are frequently chosen for the client's first session, to encourage the client to engage imagery, and also for the therapist to make an assessment about the client's ability to use the method productively as therapy.

Following the initial assessment session, the therapist may subsequently choose music programs referred to as 'working programs'. This term implies that the music is more demanding in mood and intensity.

A third group of programs may be used for clients who have experienced BMGIM over many sessions. They are able to use strong music to enhance their experiences, while maintaining the ability to close the imagery at the end of the music and return to a non-altered state of consciousness.

A fourth type of program has been devised for specific emotional needs: for example, Grieving (devised by Linda Keiser Mardis) and Affect Release, programmed by Bonny, which comprises music for the release of anger and other strong emotions, such as triumph and celebration (Bruscia and Grocke 2002).

Choosing a music program for a session

The therapist chooses a music program either to match the mood of the client or to match the issue that the client talks about during the discussion segment of the session. Sometimes the therapist may change the music program if it does not support the client's imagery experience, on other occasions the therapist might spontaneously program all of the music selections.

The mandala

In the integration phase of the BMGIM session the client is encouraged to draw a mandala. The mandala is a circle shape that is 'an archetypal symbol representing wholeness' (Bush 1992). In discussing the meaning of the mandala, the therapist and client consider the colours, shapes and forms that might be symbolic of the images that emerged during the music.

The BMGIM therapist may note whether the client's drawing is within the circle, or extends beyond it, and how much of the circle is filled with images. In viewing the mandala the therapist generally draws on the theories of Kellogg (1978), an art therapist who worked with Helen Bonny at the Baltimore Psychiatric Centre (Clark 2002).

Overview of types of case studies in BMGIM

When writing a case study in BMGIM, the therapist/author is faced with a large amount of material that must be organised and reduced into some structure for publication. Data from BMGIM sessions comprise:

- the therapist's notes taken during the preliminary discussion, which may include details of the client's dreams
- the choice of music program and salient features of the music selections
- the written transcript of the music and imagery session including the client's imagery, feelings, dialogue, and other experiences
- a sketch of the drawn mandala, and interpretations of meaning
- the therapist's reflections, written after the client has left the session.

The biggest challenge in writing a BMGIM case study therefore is not what to put in to the case study, but what to leave out.

There are various kinds of case studies in BMGIM:

- the individual case study
- collective case study
- negative case study
- heuristic case study.

The individual case study

Much of the early research in BMGIM came from single (individual) case studies. In advanced level training (level 3), the Association for Music and Imagery (AMI) in the USA requires a case study of a minimum ten sessions in BMGIM. Many of these case studies are published in the *Journal of AMI* and are written from the author/therapist's perspective. The author/therapist must organise the information to show the client's development through an analysis of key images, symbolic changes in key images, or in recurring patterns of imagery sequences, or through transformation of imagery or emotional responses.

The typical structure of an individual case study in BMGIM is:

- background of the client's history and presenting issues
- goals for the series of BMGIM therapy
- synopsis of the sessions identifying choice of music, key imagery and mandala
- interpretation of the symbolic and metaphoric meaning of the imagery and mandala
- outcomes of the therapy in relation to the client's issues or goals.

An example of an individual case study in BMGIM that traces changes in key images is Pickett's (1992) case study of a woman with multiple addictions (an eating disorder and addiction to prescribed medication). Pickett traced key images (the wall, the addict, the talking loaf of bread and the dead tree) that related to the client's therapeutic process. She identified various parts of the client's personality which emerged during the therapy, and concluded that the client was better able to 'directly confront her feelings' (p.66). This impacted positively on the client's ability to develop meaningful social relationships, which had been one of the goals of therapy.

Individual case studies also draw on interpretations from theories allied to BMGIM, including the theories of Jung and Gestalt. For example, in Borling's (1992) study of a woman survivor of childhood abuse, he provides a summary of the 17 sessions given to the client, identifying physical, embodied responses as the most common experiences of the client. Borling then discusses the outcomes of the therapy from three different frameworks: Bradshaw's Inner Child, Grof's Basic Perinatal Matrices and Kellogg's Mari Card Test. He found that when he placed the client's progress in BMGIM alongside the three frameworks, it confirmed that she was at the same point on each of the three paradigms.

Jungian archetypes appeared in Erdonmez' (1995) case study of five BMGIM sessions with a woman in the terminal stages of motor neurone disease. The archetypal images included a wise old man, a wise woman in the image of a crone and other significant images of transition (the snake and the tortoise).

Collective case studies

The collective case study describes several clients who have an aspect of common need, where the commonalities between the clients are noted and identified.

An example of a collective case study is Clark's (1995) study of four clients, in which she traced the similarities between the clients as applied to the Hero's Journey (Campbell 1968). The stages of the Hero's Journey typically include: the call to adventure; meeting supernatural aid; crossing the threshold of adventure; trials and tasks; reaching the nadir; receiving the boon (prize); the return and crossing of the return threshold. Clark illustrates each of these stages through the imagery of the four clients.

Bruscia's (1992) collective study of 20 men diagnosed with the AIDS virus, categorised the clients' experiences over a total 250 sessions. He found that for each client the healing process began with visits from the other side – that is, a visitation within the imagery of a significant person who was deceased. The experiences commonly found in BMGIM sessions of gay men carrying the AIDS virus included 'getting out of limbo', healing relationships, finding forgiveness, putting anger aside and embracing life and death.

Negative case study

It is unusual in music therapy to find a case study that describes the therapeutic intervention as contraindicated. Clarkson (1994), however, described the difficulties she encountered when using BMGIM with a client in a hypomanic episode, where BMGIM tended to aggravate the client's confusion. Negative case studies are important in building a knowledge base of conditions and disorders that are contraindicated.

Heuristic case studies

Most case studies in BMGIM are written by the therapist, who inevitably imposes a biased view on the outcome of therapy. Heuristic case studies allow the client to describe their experience, thereby providing an unbiased account of the relative value of the therapy. Several heuristic case studies of BMGIM appear in Hibben's *Inside Music Therapy* (1999). Authors have used narrative to describe their experience from their own perspective (Buell 1999; Caughman 1999; Isenberg-Grzeda 1999; Newell 1999; Schulberg 1999).

Challenges in writing a case study in BMGIM

One approach to writing a case study in BMGIM is to organise the session information into themes, or phases of therapy. Decisions have to be made about how much of the imagery is included, how much information to give about the music chosen for the sessions, and how many of the mandalas are reproduced in order to provide the necessary flow to the writing of the case study.

In the case study that follows, there were a number of issues that required decisions:

- The case material was spread over 56 BMGIM sessions. It was impossible therefore to include information on each and every session.

- The client, a graduate in English literature, had imagery that was saturated in meaning and significance, and only some interpretations could be included.

- The client worked through an impressive number of issues in her life, and these were grouped into four phases of therapy.

- The client drew many mandalas – sometimes two to three in each session, as well as five to seven during the week between sessions. Only a few mandalas are reproduced in the case study.

As therapist I chose music selections that resonated with the different personalities that appeared in the client's therapy work, and I often chose the music in order for a specific personality to be brought forth.

Case study: Samantha

Background history

At the time of referral, Samantha was 36 years old. She had referred herself for therapy following a weekend workshop on 'Music Without Stress', during which the author had spoken about music therapy approaches in the treatment of performer anxiety. Several music therapy methods were described, including the Bonny Method of Guided Imagery and Music (BMGIM). Samantha had performed on the piano during the weekend workshop showing a high level of anxiety. She commenced therapy with the author one week after the workshop weekend.

Samantha was born in a country town and described her childhood as a time of confusion. She recalled instances of physical and emotional abuse by both parents. Her father brought into the family unit an explosive, uncontrolled aggression. Her mother was also physically and emotionally abusive to the children, frequently strapping them and shouting at them. As a young woman Samantha had gained a Bachelor of Arts degree, majoring in English literature and languages.

She has one sister who is two years younger and she described their relationship as close, claiming that her sister knew her better than herself. Samantha had worked as a high school teacher and then set up her own practice as a piano teacher. She was married but, by choice, had no children.

At the start of therapy, Samantha identified difficulties with performer anxiety in that she often could not remember details of her piano performances, and felt very anxious before, during and after performances. These symptoms are consistent with a 'dissociative' reaction consistent with a childhood marred by physical and emotional abuse (DSM-IV).

Samantha had good insight into her problems, and was highly intelligent. She also had a delightful sense of humour and enjoyed playing on words.

Initial assessment

At the first session she mentioned that she would be sitting an advanced level piano examination in two weeks time. It seemed contraindicated to commence therapy work until after the examination and I mentioned to her in the first session that she might like to purchase mandala materials and express her feelings and anxieties over the next two weeks through drawing. I explained that a circle should be drawn in the centre of the page as a reference point, and the drawing could be contained within the circle, or extend beyond it.

The second session occurred after the piano examination, which Samantha described as a disaster. She had argued with the examiner and had little memory of her playing. She was very anxious about how she would face her friends and piano students (and their parents) if she failed. She had drawn seven mandalas during the week, and the last of these depicted death (Figure 5.1).

Figure 5.1

Session 3, following the examination was the assessment session. I considered several options for Samantha, and decided on a short three-minute piece of music to see how she might work with imagery. The music was 'Lullaby' from James Galway's 'Songs from the Seashore'. Samantha was seated in a comfortable chair, and a short relaxation induction was given focusing on her breathing, followed by the focus image of a scene by the seaside.

Immediately Samantha pictured an albatross. Her eyes flickered open and stayed open for the remainder of the imagery. The albatross had a child on its back, and they were flying out to sea. There was a girl on the edge of the cliff, waving goodbye to them. The albatross was white with black tips on the wings, and the child on its back felt wonderful, and free. The girl on the cliff felt sad – she wanted the bird and the child to come back, but she knew they wouldn't.

In the discussion about the imagery, Samantha recognised she was all three of the images – the albatross, child and girl. The albatross was serene, strong, and knew in which direction to fly. The child enjoyed herself, but the girl felt sad to say goodbye. In this session Samantha showed that she understood the symbolic nature of the imagery, and was able to identify her 'self' in several roles.

A week after this session Samantha learned that she had failed her piano examination; her self-esteem was very low and she was depressed.

The initial goals I set for therapy were to:

- build her ego boundaries, through affirmation of her feelings and acceptance of her changing emotional state
- build a defence system through identifying strong supportive and integrative images
- build trust in the therapist and the process of therapy
- build trust in what Samantha felt to be 'real', to trust her thoughts as valid and credible, and to trust and identify her feelings
- strengthen her decision-making ability
- be less anxious in her music performance.

Phase 1 – sessions 1–10: Finding a face

A contract was made for ten sessions in BMGIM and these were given over a twelve-week period. Over the ten sessions, Samantha made significant progress. Initially her imagery showed a lot of free associations, or 'stream of consciousness' where images come and go very fast. The imagery at the end of session 4 was of her heart being wide open and a fairy sewing it up with gauze bandages. The vulnerability of this image depicted in the mandala (see Figure 5.2), was interesting given

that the music program concluded with the 'Pachelbel Canon', normally a very sta-
bilising work. However the memory of a special event caused her heart to open out
and this induced the vulnerability. In the mandala, the centre of the circle is empty,
and the stick figure lies precariously over the top, as if she was barely holding on to
reality.

Figure 5.2

In sessions 5, 6 and 7, much of her imagery was connected with archetypal figures
– King Arthur and his knights (representing positive, masculine hero figures), the
Queen of Light (the positive feminine figure), Merlin (the magical masculine),
Cassandra (the visionary feminine) and Lancelot and Guenevere (the lovers) (see
Table 5.2 for further information on the archetypes).

Having established her archetypal supports, she was able to break free from her
family in session 7. In the imagery (during Debussy's 'Afternoon of the Faun') she
left her husband locked up in an asylum while she played with a cheetah in the
forest. She returned to knock down the walls of the asylum and free her husband.
She concluded the session (during Vaughan-Williams 'Greensleeves') by reading
him a story. In this session Samantha made her first venture into independence,
locking her husband away, but then returning to him and assuming a parenting
role in reading him a story.

In the imagery of session 8, Samantha started building a new house for herself
and her music (during Britten's 'Sentimental Serenade', from the *Simple Symphony*).
This indicated that she was developing a stronger home for her creativity in music,
particularly in composing. In real life she had just finished composing a short
piano piece for children and the work had been performed on radio. This was a significant event for her, as her husband and male piano teacher were present, and she
felt very affirmed by these two positive male figures in her life.

Table 5.2 Key archetypal figures

Arthur	King at the age of 15 having successfully drawn the sword Excalibur from a rock. He formed the Knights of the Round Table, and performed awesome feats on the battle-field. He was slain by Mordred, and taken to Glastonbury where it is thought he is buried (Bullfinch's Mythology 1964).
Cassandra	Daughter of Queen Hecuba, she had the power of visioning. Her visions, including the fall of Troy were, however, never believed and she was ridiculed and thought to be insane (Bullfinch's Mythology 1964).
St Gabriel	It was Gabriel who announced to the prophets the coming of the Messiah. Gabriel is the archangel of communication – the Messenger. He is usually depicted as a young archangel, with a lily, kneeling and holding a scroll with 'Ave Maria' written upon it (White 1991).
Guenevere	Queen to Arthur, but pious and thought to be afraid of open places. She was Lancelot's lover and the two were disgraced (Bullfinch's Mythology 1964).
Lancelot	Knight, and lover of Guenevere (Bullfinch's Mythology 1964).
Medea	Daughter of the Colchian King Aestes. Through Medea's sorcery Jason was given strength to confront the fire-breathing bulls which protected the Golden Fleece. Jason then took the Golden Fleece to Pelias. Medea used her sorceress arts for both good and bad. She killed her own father, then also her children, set fire to the palace, and escaped in a serpent-drawn chariot (Grimal 1986).
Merlin	The wizard had the power to transform himself into any shape or form he pleased. He was the favourite counsellor to Uther Pendragon and King Arthur, and is chiefly represented as a magician (Bullfinch's Mythology 1964).
Mordred	A traitor to King Arthur, responsible for Arthur's death (Bullfinch's Mythology 1964).
Oedipus	The legend of Oedipus was that at birth he was marked by a curse. The oracle predicted that he would kill his father and marry his mother. Oedipus was fostered out to Polybus, and a series of events threw his true identity into confusion. The term Oedipal complex coined by Freud described males who were jealously bonded to their mothers and so were in conflict with their fathers (Grimal 1986).
St Michael	The chief of the archangels, Michael is said to intercede for the human race. He is the Protector, and deals with the devil. He conducts the soul to Heaven. He is the patron saint of battle and is depicted in full armour, with a sword and a pair of scales (to weigh souls). He stands over, or fights, a dragon or devil (White 1991).

In session 9 she again drew on the strength of archetypal figures (Oedipus and Medea), but these were the negative counterparts of the earlier archetypes. In legend, it was predicted that Oedipus would kill his father in order to marry his mother (Grimal 1986), hence Freud's coining of the term the Oedipal conflict. In legend Medea was the destructive feminine, often depicted with snakes in her hair, who devoured her own children (Grimal 1986).

Session 10 was a pivotal session. She described an abuse scene in which there was a black ogre, and she associated the ogre with her father. The ogre was 'the size of the inside of me' she said. Samantha was confused as to who was the child, 'him or me', and whether she was 'in the body of the ogre or the child in the shadow'. When she focused on the child in the shadow she felt terror. She confronted the ogre (in the imagery) and directed him to 'stand back'. As the ogre stepped back she had an image of a white egg and the beginning of new growth. Session 10 ended with the very powerful statement 'I feel I have a face for the first time.' The mandala was drawn with brilliant yellow rays radiating from the circle. The eyes, nose and smile were in bright green. The mandala is in stark contrast to the vulnerable mandala of session 4 (the stick figure). It is important to note that the face sits in the centre of the circle – an indication of the image being in the core of the self (Figure 5.3).

Figure 5.3

Samantha made significant gains in her personal growth over sessions 1–10. Drawing on the strength of the archetypal figures (Arthur, Merlin, Cassandra and the Queen of Light), she began to separate herself from the influence of others, e.g. her husband, and the black ogre (whom she later identified as her father).

The positive gains in the BMGIM sessions were reflected in her life, and she was particularly proud of her composition being played on the radio.

Phase 2 – sessions 11–18: Childhood memories: the emergence of Anita, the Inner Child

The second series of BMGIM sessions brought to the surface a number of memories around childhood, and the healing of traumatic events.

In session 11, Samantha's imagery was a childhood memory of her parents fighting and her fear as a child listening to them. 'Mother cried all day, and fights would start at dinner,' she said. She spoke of her ambivalence towards her mother – of hating her, but not wanting to lose her – and she expressed this ambivalence through tears. She had images of jagged glass in her chest and a fear of being injured. She recalled how her father was an irresponsible driver, driving on the wrong side of the road into oncoming traffic, then at the last minute swerving away. She often thought he wanted to kill all of them.

The music chosen for this session was the program 'Grieving', comprising slow movements of instrumental concertos (oboe, guitar and violin). Frequently a client projects feelings and emotion on to the solo instrument, as if that instrument is speaking for them. The orchestra is supporting the solo instrument, and this enables the client to disclose more intimate feelings and memories. In Samantha's session she was able to speak about her feelings toward her mother, and her fear of her father's behaviour.

In session 12, I gave her an image of material to protect her body on which she could focus. Samantha's material was gauze, which was 'sticking to burns – pale yellow cloth, like shrouds – I can't get mummy off – I'm mummified', she said. To the music of Haydn's 'Cello Concerto' (slow movement) Samantha then experienced images of death – of being eaten by worms, eaten down to the bone 'so you are clean, you're dead'. She then imaged herself as a skeleton in a coffin (during Sibelius' 'The Swan of Tuonela'), decaying, and the earth as warm. St Michael (the patron saint of the battle) and St Gabriel (the messenger) appeared. At this point a vocal selection, the 'Bachianas Brasileiros' of Villa-Lobos was playing. In response to the female soprano voice, Samantha called out 'Who are you?' As the voice continued to sing, she answered herself 'A grieving little girl'. I asked if she wanted to give the little girl a name and she responded, 'Anita', her Inner Child.

The mandala from this session shows a small child in foetal position flanked by the two archangels (Figure 5.4). The contrast in size between Anita and the archangels indicates the degree to which the Inner Child needed protection.

Following a very intense session like this one, the client often feels very vulnerable in the next session and may even question the worth of the therapy and the therapist.

In session 13 Samantha explored her ambivalence to female figures and her transference to the therapist. To the author she said 'I'm scared you'll be horrid, scared you'll be kind.' During the Vaughan-Williams 'Prelude on Rhosymedre', she said 'Only half of me is in the room.' She then expressed positive transference to the author 'I can bring all my differences here – they'll be honoured – it feels nice to be a woman here.' The transference statement occurred during Berlioz' 'Shepherd's Farewell' from *The Childhood of Christ*. It is written for four voices, in chorale-like style, and it is likely that the very supportive nature of this music enhanced the positive transference.

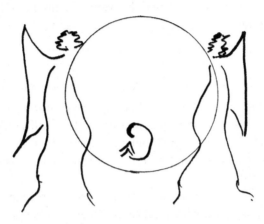

Figure 5.4

Session 14 was another powerful session in which Samantha experienced memories of her grandmother, Nana. She remembered that Nana bought lovely dresses of red velvet and that Nana had died in her (Samantha's) bed. At this point Samantha wept for her. She recalled that, on the day of Nana's funeral, she was sent to a music theory examination and she never cried for her. She said 'I wish Nana had been my mother.'

At the end of the session I suggested she try to obtain photos of her Nana. These were not easy to obtain as Samantha's mother had them hidden away, but Samantha arrived at the next session with hundreds of photos in a supermarket bag. She up-ended the bag on the floor of the session room and photos spilled out. She then picked the photos up one at a time, saying 'Look, this is me when …'. This session, and the three that followed, were emotionally very powerful as Samantha began to discover positive events in her childhood. Carefully, she arranged the photos chronologically into three separate photo albums. She then returned the albums to her mother. This was a turning point in her relationship with her mother, as if she had put the family history into some kind of order that she could now share with her mother.

In session 18, the true personality of Anita emerged in the imagery. She was making a cubby house (tree house) and had a lot of life energy and was fun. Anita was also angry, marching to the next door neighbour's house and throwing her in the river. During the playing of Bach's 'Prelude' and 'Fugue in D Minor', she said, 'Bach was a grump – why did you write those Preludes and Fugues? He drives me crazy, like wolves running around eating children for breakfast!' This indicated Samantha's sense of humour, which appeared from time to time throughout the BMGIM sessions. Her personal growth between sessions 11 and 18 indicated a balance of facing traumatic childhood memories, grief for her Nana, and playful images.

Phase 3 – sessions 19–24: Inner development – the sub-personalities

In sessions 19–24, three sub-personalities appeared. In Gestalt theory this is recognised as a means of identifying split-off parts of self (Yontef and Simkin 1989). The objective of therapy is to integrate the parts so that the client has a sense of an integrated self and in BMGIM this is achieved by inviting the different aspects of self to dialogue.

Session 19 was a significant session because the second sub-personality appeared. She was a figure whom Samantha named 'Faiblesse' (a French word meaning 'weak'). She drew the figure of Faiblesse as a stick figure lying precariously over the top curve of the mandala circle, similar to the mandala shown in Figure 5.2.

In session 20, the Inner Child Anita (who had a lot of energy) met Faiblesse for the first time, but initially didn't like her. Faiblesse was a wooden doll, with pins in her joints, and she couldn't dance. However, during Debussy's 'L'Apres Midi d'un Faun' Anita poured water on Faiblesse to get her to move and she floated on water. Samantha describes Faiblesse as creative, 'She dances, she writes music and is gentle … she also needs space and is one of the fairy folk.' In many respects Faiblesse represented the true identity of Samantha.

In session 21, I started to match certain pieces of music with Anita and Faiblesse. Faiblesse liked harp music (Pierne's *Concertstucke* for harp and orchestra, in particular). Anita enjoyed the playful 'La Calinda' from Delius' *Koanga Suite*. But, during the playing of '*La Calinda*', the third sub-personality, Carmen, the flamenco dancer, appeared. Samantha described Carmen as sexual – 'She likes the men.' She had similar energy to Anita, the Inner Child, so Anita enjoyed meeting Carmen. During the flute music at the end of the music program, the fourth sub-personality, Higher Self, appeared.

In the post-music discussion, Samantha linked the four sub-personalities to the appropriate periods of her life:

- Anita – the playful child
- Faiblesse – the pre-sexual adolescent
- Carmen – the sexual adult
- Higher Self – the spiritual self.

It was close to the time when Samantha was to sit the next piano examination and she creatively linked the four personalities to the four pieces of music to be played at examination. She consciously drew on the personality while playing the piece.

In session 22 she reflected on the positive feminine figures in her life once again. She said artistic women are a mixture of strength and vulnerability, and concluded about herself 'I am worth knowing.' This was a highly significant comment, indicating her stronger sense of ego and self-respect.

The imagery in session 23 was of Anita being afraid of her father. Her mother couldn't protect her, and Anita couldn't protect her mother from her father. During Holst's 'Mars' from the *Planets Suite* Anita entered her parent's bedroom, smashing them with a big stick. Anita became sad because now she was homeless. However, her anger returned and she cut off their heads, minced them up and fed them to the fish.

In the following session Samantha showed her vulnerability. This is consistent with a session following expression of anger and destruction. Anita was in her cubby house and she couldn't trust anyone. I changed the music to Handel's *Lute and Harp Concerto* (slow movement) and Faiblesse appeared, then Carmen. Carmen could protect them and urged Faiblesse to 'get up'. Symbolically, Carmen (representing sexuality) was energising the adolescent identity, Faiblesse, in order to strengthen her ego. Since Faiblesse was the closest representation of Samantha herself, this strengthening of her own ego was preparing her for the major challenge ahead – that of sitting the piano examination.

After discussion: Samantha linked the sub-personalities to the four elements:

- Carmen – fire
- Anita – earth
- Higher Self – water
- Faiblesse – air.

The mandala drawn in this session clearly illustrated the integration of the four personalities, held together by the web, in the lower right corner (Figure 5.5). The web is the integrating form as its filigree reaches into the other three quadrants.

Higher Self   Carmen

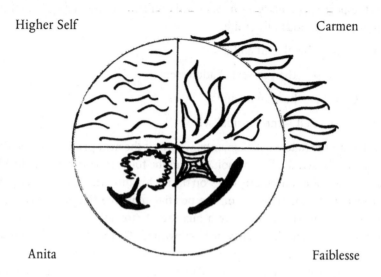

Anita   Faiblesse

Figure 5.5

The mandala was drawn on black and featured blue in the upper left quadrant (representing Higher Self), and red and yellow fire in the upper right quadrant (representing Carmen). In the lower left (representing Anita) the form is of a tree with a very long root, with colours of emerald green and brown. The lower right quadrant (representing Faiblesse) shows the form of the web, with a strong band of yellow forming a very clearly defined boundary.

The long root of the tree and the thick band under the web are indications of a stronger ego boundary, which was one of the main goals of therapy.

The day after session 24, Samantha sat her advanced piano exam. She telephoned the author after the event and described it in every detail. A week later she learned she had achieved an 'A' grade. This was just one year after the disastrous exam in which she recalled nothing. It was clear that the integrating work done through BMGIM had reduced her anxiety to the point that she could remain *in* the experience and recall what had occurred.

The sub-personalities

The Inner Child, Anita, appeared first. Initially she was bent over and weeping (sessions 12 and 13). Then she appeared as adventurous and angry (sessions 17, 18 and 23). The adventurous Inner Child was not a naughty child. She liked making mud pies and mashing bananas. The angry Inner Child, however was physically aggressive, kicking her friend next door into the river and, in session 19, smashing her parents in their bedroom, cutting off their heads, mincing them up and feeding them to the fish (session 23). This imagery had a profound healing effect on Samantha, and given that session 23 was just one week before her piano examination, it is likely that the effect was cathartic, ridding her of repressed energy around the anger and allowing the energy to be available for her piano examination. The degree of anger expressed was quite remarkable in light of Samantha's vulnerability in previous sessions.

Faiblesse appeared in session 19. Initially she was like a doll, a puppet who was held together with pins (similar to a Pinocchio figure). Faiblesse needed water that was poured on her from Anita (session 20) and help from Higher Self, before she could take form. Finally she needed the directive from Carmen to 'Get up, Faiblesse' (session 24). Faiblesse is the creative artistic personality and she is the piano performer. Only when Faiblesse took form could Samantha stay in the experience of playing the piano to the point where she remembered all aspects of the piano examination, and achieved a grading of 'A'.

Higher Self appeared in session 20. She did not play a major role in the imagery, other than representing the spiritual part of self. In some respects Higher Self seemed to grow out of the Queen of Light from the earlier series. It is interesting that at Samantha's stage of dealing with memories of childhood abuse, she was strengthening the ego. It may have been too early for her to explore the higher realms of spirituality through transcendental imagery. Her out-of-body experiences needed to be contained, rather than encouraged. It is not surprising therefore that Higher Self had a minor role in the integration of self.

Carmen was the last of the sub-personalities to appear (session 21). She came from the music of Delius, 'La Calinda' from the *Koanga Suite*. This music has a Spanish rhythm with the effective use of tambourines and dance rhythms to suggest the Spanish influence. Carmen appeared in red, orange and yellow, the colours of fire, and it is this fire that Faiblesse needed in order to perform at the piano examination.

From a Gestalt perspective, Samantha accepted and understood the importance of the sub-personalities being in dialogue. She named each personality easily and she assigned roles for them, according to:

- periods of her life
- the four elements
- the four piano pieces to be played at the examination.

Phase 4 – sessions 25–56: relationship with the masculine – the fifth sub-personality

The next phase of sessions related to Samantha's relationships with masculine figures in her life.

In session 25, Faiblesse was dancing, but didn't have much sense of her body. She was too frightened to feel passion. Samantha's imagery shifted to thoughts of childhood and that her father was absent emotionally from the family.

In session 26 the Inner Child (Anita) was hiding under the couch. She wanted to be free of burdens – thinking of children's stories, of crystals and transformations. She remembered how her father was proud of her intellectual achievements and that he had said 'I've been proud of you all along.' In this session Samantha started to recall the positive aspects of her father. This laid the ground for the next session in which very positive images of the masculine appeared.

Faiblesse was dancing an arabesque and a person was holding her. She wanted to push this person off, but she also wanted a male companion – 'Another half of myself – I have a feeling of not being complete.' The male person danced with Faiblesse, lifting her up, 'She does the twirling, he does the lifting,' said Samantha. I asked if there was a name for the male dancer. 'August', she said, and then listed his characteristics: 'He's very physical, deep-chested, got a round bum, strong thighs, sculptured face, sensitive and intense, and he is wise!'

In the next session, further attributes of August appeared. He was a gourmet cook and he prepared a special meal (here he represents the nurturing, sustaining masculine). He also formed a positive relationship with Anita. He played with her in her cubby house and taught her to dance. Symbolically the sub-personalities were strengthening her ego even further by drawing on the masculine animus. August, Anita and Carmen already showed positive energy, while Faiblesse (the true self) was drawing on their strength by dancing with August and being fed by him.

At this point in Samantha's therapy, she was dealing with several aspects of the masculine. This was reflected in events happening in her day-to-day life. She had a very positive relationship with her male piano teacher and was developing a closer, more intimate relationship with her husband. Her memories of her father too, were more positive.

Session 30 was another pivotal session. I used the Transitions program comprising a segment of Strauss' 'Ein Heldenleben' ('A Hero's Life'). August was rollerblading in the street and then dancing with Faiblesse. Faiblesse felt sad and in much pain – there were five shards of glass in her chest. August helped remove these but there was a lot of blood. If August could siphon the blood out there would be a large hole. I asked 'What does she need for the large hole?' Samantha responded 'A new heart.' Together August and Faiblesse created a new heart made out of patchwork, ribbon, lace and purple silk. Faiblesse placed the shards of glass on an altar together with the blackened old heart that was full of fear. I asked her about the new heart. 'It's complete in itself,' she said. This was a profound session and deeply moving. Samantha had effectively given herself a new heart, a new core of herself, which had grown out of all the previous sessions. Faiblesse had grown significantly stronger so that this open-heart surgery could take place. And she was ably assisted by the internalised masculine – August.

In this last phase of therapy, Samantha dealt with issues in the day-to-day world, teaching students and starting a new business.

Her father-in-law was hospitalised for a cancerous tumour and Samantha and her husband needed to care of her mother-in-law. They moved in with the mother-in-law, which raised old issues of being under parental control. At her parents-in-law's place, she had no power, no identity, and this was a very stressful time for her. Old issues resurfaced and were worked through (issues tend to be cyclic in long-term therapy). The final resolution to the situation came when Samantha decided to move back home on her own, leaving her husband staying with his parents. She functioned independently at home until the husband returned.

During this time she learnt to accept the parents for who they were and learnt to appreciate her own independence. Towards the end of the year, she commented that she wanted to finish therapy.

In our final session, Samantha asked for the music associated with each of the sub-personalities. I was not sure this would be a good idea. A final BMGIM session should be a discussion session where there is an integration and reflection on the advances made during therapy. However, Samantha insisted that she wanted to hear each piece for the last time. Anita and Carmen enjoyed their pieces but when it came to Faiblesse, Samantha started to weep, saying 'Faiblesse was born here, in this room, on this mat.'

There could be no more powerful statement to summarise the effect of BMGIM in her life. BMGIM allowed her to explore different aspects of herself – the playful adventurous inner child, the sexual woman and the spiritual woman. Faiblesse, who was the closest to her true self, had developed from a stick figure identity to a passionate dancer who enjoyed the close contact with the male dancer August, her internalised masculine. Samantha had created an integrated sense of self through identifying the different personalities and by creating a place where these parts could grow creatively and unite.

CHAPTER 6

The Use of Single Case Designs in an Interactive Play Setting

Petra Kern

Phillip learns to greet his peers, and Ben stops crying during the morning arrival time in their childcare program when singing a greeting song. Andy washes his hands and participates in cleaning up when using songs. And Eric and Lucas, as well as Phillip and Ben, start to interact with their peers on the childcare playground using the instruments in the Music Hut when singing their songs. Do music therapy interventions really have this power and positive outcome in inclusive preschool settings?

This chapter describes a series of studies evaluating the effects of music therapy interventions in an interactive play setting by using single-case experimental designs. It will be illustrated by interventions designed for the integration of young children diagnosed with autism spectrum disorder in an inclusive childcare program. The interventions were developed and implemented in close collaboration with the children's teachers, and embedded in the ongoing classroom routines. The effects of the treatments were evaluated using several single-case experimental designs: an ABAB withdrawal design, an alternating treatment design, and a multiple baseline design. This research methodology provides music therapists in early intervention with a controlled experimental approach to the investigation of a single child under different circumstances, and the flexibility to adapt the intervention to the child's needs and the particular treatment approach. Experimental control is achieved within the child, meaning each child serves as his or her own control by comparing the child's performance across two or more conditions over time (Alberto and Troutman 1995; D. Aldridge 1996; Barlow and Hayes 1984; Hanser 1995; Holcombe, Wolery and Gast 1994;

Kazdin 1982; Wolery, Baily and Sugai 1988). 'Single-case designs highlight individual change in daily clinical practice and allow the practitioner to relate those changes to therapeutic interventions' (Aldridge 1994, p.335).

Single-case experimental designs are commonly used across different professions in early intervention and are a scientifically accepted and valid method (e.g. Stile 1988). Such designs are not unknown to music therapists and quite prevalent in the literature (e.g. Gregory 2002; Nicholas and Boyle 1983). However, only a few music therapists engaged in early intervention research using single-case experimental designs (e.g. Harding and Ballard 1982; Kern and Wolery 2001). The use of single-case experimental designs has potential benefits in proving the quality of our work and in acquiring new knowledge that can be used for improving the children's and families' quality of life. It also increases our credibility among other professions and establishes music therapy as a widely recognised health service in early intervention.

Early intervention and inclusion

Given the importance of early intervention and inclusion, there is an increasing trend in enrolling young children with autism in childcare programs. A number of university based model programs demonstrate the effectiveness of individualised strategies for the inclusion of young children with autism spectrum disorder (Handleman and Harris 2001; National Research Council 2001). However, there are tremendous differences in the educational and therapeutic approaches used in these models. One of the recent models is the 'Center-Based Early Intervention Demonstration Project for Young Children with Autism', conceptualised and developed by Wolery *et al.* (2001). This model was embedded in the childcare program of the Frank Porter Graham (FPG) Child Development Institute. The childcare program enrols about eighty children from six weeks of age to five years old and approximately a third of the children have disabilities. The Autism Project's goals were 1. to develop a model for serving children with autism in inclusive child care classes; 2. to provide individualised support and assistance for families; and 3. to train others to use the model. The design of the Autism Project was a co-operative venture between the FPG Child Development Institute and Division TEACCH of the University of North Carolina at Chapel Hill, USA. This project was funded by the Early Intervention Program of the State of North Carolina.

Two components were important to the project. First, the classroom component that involves the inclusion of two- and three-year-old children with autism, use of individualised and structured teaching, establishment of predictable routines and schedules, and the use of integrated therapy. Second, the family support component that includes regular communication and home visits, and adherence to family centred practices. The following intervention studies were conducted in this context and were designed to incorporate many of the concepts inherent in these two components. The interventions were done in inclusive classrooms using the integrated therapy approach.

Inclusive classes are those in which children with and without disabilities are enrolled and in which the needs of both types of children are addressed. In an integrated therapy model, therapists work with the individual child or a group of children within the ongoing classroom routines or as a consultant to the classroom teachers. The goal for the therapist and teacher is to collaborate on the best approach to meet the child's identified needs. The rationale for this procedure is threefold: 1. to minimize stigma and isolation; 2. to capitalise on children's naturally occurring learning opportunities; and 3. to increase the number of experiences that promote learning (McWilliam 1996; Wolery and Wilbers 1994).

The music therapy interventions were designed and implemented using a 'collaborative consulting' model. This model suggests that the music therapist (consultant) and teachers engage equally in:

1. defining the problem

2. identifying the goals of intervention

3. planning the intervention

4. providing training for teachers on the use of therapeutic techniques

5. supporting the teachers during implementation

6. engaging in follow-ups (Bruder 1996; Buysse *et al.* 1994).

Specific goals, strategies and procedures of the music therapy interventions were individualised for each target child with autism. Because predictable routines, structured teaching and visual cues are effective ways of allowing children with autism to improve their skills and use their strength to act independently in childcare routines (e.g. Bryan and Gast 2000; Treatment and Education of Autism and Related Communication Handicapped Children (TEACCH) 2003a; Trillingsgaard 1999; Quill 2001), those elements were taken into consideration in the intervention's design.

From intervention to research

In an inclusive and interactive play setting, children with autism and their families face many joyful but also challenging moments. Along with the defining deficits in social skills, language/communication skills, sensory responses and repetitive and restricted behaviours, children with autism often have difficulties making transitions, following multiple step tasks and engaging and interacting with peers in large undefined environments and unstructured play situations (National Research Council 2001; TEACCH 2003b; Williams 1999).

The following experiments feature five children with autism, their teachers, caregivers and classroom peers mastering these problematic situations within the childcare day through individually designed interventions based on music therapy principles. As described by many authors, music therapy has potential benefits for children with autism. Music can support positive social interaction, facilitate verbal and non-verbal communication, enhance success-oriented opportunities for achievement and mastery, and music is often a relative strength for children with autism (e.g. Aldridge, Gustorff and Neugebauer 1996; Alvin and Warwick 1991; American Association of Music Therapy (AMTA) 2003; Gottschewski 2001; National Autistic Society (NAS) 2003; Thaut 1988; Warwick 1995).

The targeted children were diagnosed with autism spectrum disorder, using the Psychoeducational Profile-Revised (PEP-R), (Schopler *et al.* 1990), the Autism Diagnostic Observation Schedule (ADOS) (Lord *et al.* 1999), clinical observation and parent interview.

All experimental sessions occurred in the classroom and playground of the FPG childcare program where the philosophy followed guidelines for developmentally appropriate practice (Bredekamp and Copple 1997). The classrooms and playground were structured in different play areas which contained corresponding toys and materials (Harms, Clifford and Cryer 1998).

The children were identified for the studies by suggestions from their classroom teachers, parents and therapists based on 1. the diagnosis of Autism Spectrum Disorder; 2. Individual Education Plan (IEP) goals; and 3. interest and response to music. In experiments I and III classroom peers with and without disabilities participated voluntarily and were similar in chronological age to each child. Classroom teachers participated in all studies, and the children's primary caregiver participated in experiment I.

The purpose of these studies was to evaluate the effectiveness of music therapy interventions designed for young children with autism to 1. address problematic routines; 2. evaluate the effects of songs on children's functioning; 3. increase peer interactions; and 4. evaluate having teachers rather than the music therapists implement the intervention. 'There are many methods; finding the appropriate method to answer the question that we are asking is the central issue' (D. Aldridge 1998b, p.149). To this end each study requested a specific single-case experimental design to answer the stated research questions, as described in more detail below.

Experiment I: Morning greeting routine

The childcare day is filled with transitions between activities and routines within the classroom, as well as to and from the preschool setting. For many children with and without disabilities, the morning arrival time is one of the most crucial transitions (Alger 1984; Baker 1992). There are a number of strategies including the use of routines (Trillingsgaard 1999; Wakeford 2002), visual cues (Bryan and Gast 2000; Dettmer *et al.* 2000; Quill 2001), and songs (Cole-Currens 1993; Williams 1999) developed to support children with autism making successful transitions. 'Hello' and 'Goodbye' songs are common practice in music therapy and are often used to establish a predictable routine and to structure the session through a clear beginning and end (Bailey 1984; Hughes *et al.* 1990; Schmidt 1984). While there is empirical support for each of these strategies used for transitioning, no studies were conducted with young children with autism in the context of an interactive play setting.

The purpose of this part of the study was to evaluate the effectiveness of unique greeting songs and a routine developed to increase the independent performance of two young boys with autism, during the morning arrival time in their preschool. The evaluation of the intervention's effects was guided by the following research questions: 1. Does the use of an individually composed song sung by the teachers increase appropriate independent performance during the morning arrival routine of young children with autism? 2. Can classroom teachers learn to use the principles important to music therapy in a particular routine? and 3. Does the song increase interaction of peers with the target child?

Participants

The target children in this study are Phillip and Ben (n=2), both three years of age. Phillip was functionally non-verbal and used Picture Exchange Communication Symbols (PECS) (Bondy and Frost 1984), to communicate. Ben also used PECS, but he started to develop some functional speech. The difficulty Phillip exhibited during the morning arrival time was characterised by: refusing to enter the classroom, slamming the door, escaping, lying on the floor or screaming. Phillip's peer interaction was mostly negative. He was a large boy and sometimes used aggression (e.g. pushing, hitting, screaming) to start interactions with peers, or was physically too rough. Peers seemed to be afraid of him and often preferred not to play with him. The difficulty Ben had during the morning greeting time transition was characterised by: holding on to his caretaker, whining to intensive crying or screaming for a long period of time, ignoring the efforts of classroom teacher in greeting and play offers, stiffening his body, hitting or biting. Ben had a lack of interest in peers and a limited understanding of social rules or conventions. Peers seemed not to take notice of him. Neither child engaged in play unless supported by the teachers. Both children showed a great interest in music and seemed to be nurtured by certain musical pieces.

Materials and staff development activities

The major medium for mastering the greeting routine was a unique song composed for each target child. The songs were individualised and matched each child's temperament and the demands of the morning greeting routine musically. The children's rhythm and movement in walking, their vocalisation and their dynamic appearance were the cues translated into rhythm, melody and harmony. The form and lyrics of the songs focused on each step of the routine and were composed as follows:

1. The teacher/peers greet the target child.

2. The target child greets a person in the classroom.

3. The target child greets a second person in the classroom.

4. The target child says 'Goodbye' to the caregiver and the caregiver leaves the classroom.

5. The target child engages with a toy or material found in the classroom.

The five steps were presented in a musical AAABA form. As an example the song composed for Ben is outlined in Figure 6.1. The 'A' parts of the AAABA form reflected steps 1, 2, 3 and 5, as procedures happening in the classroom. To emphasise the detachment from the caregiver, the melody and feeling of the song changed in the B part. Social interaction was supported by greeting at least two peers through the song, and by handing over the picture symbol. Additional Individual Education Plan (IEP) goals included verbalisation for Ben and choice-making for both children. Choice-making was practised by choosing two different peers to greet, a toy to play with, and a weather condition at certain points of the songs. Verbalisation was practised by saying or singing 'hello' and 'goodbye' to a person or naming the greeted person. As a visual cue, Phillip and Ben used a 10 x 10 cm square laminated picture communication symbol showing a

Figure 6.1 Transcript of 'Song for Ben', addressing the demands of the morning greeting routine, social interaction and specific IEP goals

stick figure waving and the word 'Hello' placed above. The primary caregivers were included in the intervention by participating in singing, greeting peers and teachers and waving goodbye.

Additionally, each song was recorded on a practice CD (compact disc) and handed out along with a song transcription to the teachers and caregivers during staff development activities. Initially, teachers, caregivers and the music therapist discussed the intervention procedure, how the intervention would fit into existing classroom routines and how data would be collected. The songs were introduced to the teachers individually, and to the whole class during circle time prior to the actual study intervention. Specific instructions were given verbally and modelled to teachers and caregivers on how to greet the targeted children and support them to greet and interact with peers. The teachers were asked to include more than two peers in the greeting routine if peers showed an interest in participating. During and after the intervention consultation was offered.

Experimental design

An ABAB withdrawal design for Phillip, and a modified version (condition C) of this design (ABCAC withdrawal design) for Ben was used to evaluate the effects of the individually composed greeting songs sung by the classroom teachers, the caregivers and peers. In an ABAB withdrawal design, experimental control is established through comparing baseline performance (condition A) with intervention performance (condition B). If a difference in the data patterns exists each time the conditions change, and if those differences are replicated across conditions, then experimental control is achieved. Specifically, if there is a stable pattern of data in baseline and a change (e.g. change in level, trend or both) in the data pattern when the intervention is introduced, followed by a counter-therapeutic change when the baseline condition is reintroduced, and another therapeutic change when the intervention is reintroduced, then the investigator can conclude the changes are related to the intervention. This is considered to be a powerful demonstration of the effectiveness on an intervention because it limits threats to internal validity (Aldridge 1994; D. Aldridge 1996; Hanser 1995; Holcombe *et al.* 1994; Kazdin 1982; Wolery *et al.* 1988). Data collection occurred over two months for Phillip and over three months for Ben.

Procedure

Experimental sessions occurred every morning as soon as Phillip or Ben and their caregivers entered the classroom. The child had already put his personal belongings in his cubby outside the classroom and picked up the picture communication symbol.

The baseline phase (condition A) followed the five steps of the morning greeting routine. First, the teachers and peers greeted the child (step 1). Second, the child greeted a teacher or peer by handing over the picture symbol, and/or saying the greeted person's name (step 2). Third, the subject greeted a second teacher or peer by handing over the picture symbol, and/or saying the greeted person's name (step 3). Fourth, the subject said or waved 'goodbye' to the caregiver and the caregiver left the classroom (step 4). Fifth, the teachers encouraged the child to find a toy or material with which to play or engage (step 5).

In the intervention phase (condition B), the conditions were similar to the baseline phase. The only change was the introduction of each target child's unique song. The song, was sung during each step of the routine. That is, for step 1, the teacher sang the first verse of the song. Thus as the routine progressed, so did the song.

A modified intervention phase (condition C) was introduced for Ben, because his performance did not improve significantly with the introduction of the song. Finally teachers and the music therapist conducted an error analysis and the goodbye section was omitted.

The teachers used a system of least prompts (Wolery 1992; Doyle *et al.* 1990) both to give the targeted child time to respond independently to each step of the greeting routine, and to ensure that the child completed each step of the greeting routine.

The following five categories of the target child's behaviours were coded for each of the five steps of the greeting routine on a specially developed data sheet: 1. independent response; 2. prompted response; 3. no response; 4. error; and 5. inappropriate behaviour. After clinical observation of an increasing number of peers greeting Phillip, a measure was added to capture the number of classroom peers greeting Ben independently. In addition, field notes were taken. Data were collected live during the morning arrival time, over two months for Phillip and over three months for Ben. Reliability checks were carried out on an average of 22% of total observations within each phase and for each child. Inter-observer agreement ranged from 75% to 100%, with a mean of 94%.

Results

The results of the morning greeting intervention show that during baseline intervention (A phase) Phillip had a low level of independent performance (M=33.3%). Phillip entered the classroom independently and found a toy with which to play. With the introduction of the song (B phase), he steadily became more independent

(<u>M</u>=54%). A withdrawal of the intervention immediately decreased Phillip's performance (<u>M</u>=46.7%). Reintroducing the song increased his independence once again to an even higher level (<u>M</u>=77.8%). On the last day of intervention Phillip performed all five steps of the routine by himself.

During baseline (A phase) Ben had only one independent response, which was entering the classroom (<u>M</u>=23.3%). The implementation of the song (B phase) did not change his performance significantly (<u>M</u>=30%). When the intervention was modified by eliminating the goodbye part (C phase), the number of Ben's independent actions increased significantly and immediately (<u>M</u>=60%). Ben entered the room independently and greeted two peers. After withdrawing the song, Ben's independent behaviour decreased (<u>M</u>=40%). Reintroducing the modified intervention, Ben exhibited a high level of independent performance (<u>M</u>=80%).

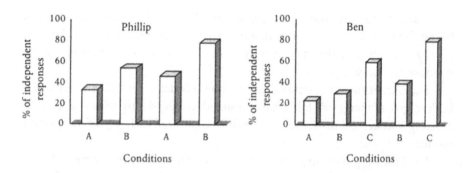

Figure 6.2 Mean (<u>M</u>%) of independent responses for Phillip and Ben during the morning greeting routine in each condition of the study

My field notes showed me that Phillip's peer interaction increased. On many days more than two peers asked for a turn to say 'Hello' to Phillip. Especially peers who were afraid of Phillip before the music therapy intervention came forward and interacted with him through the song.

The mother of one of Phillip's peers said, that prior to the study, her child was intimidated by Phillip's inappropriate behaviour at greeting time. With the implementation of the song, her child would run to school hoping to arrive before Phillip so that he could participate in Phillip's greeting routine. Phillip seemed to be less frustrated when transitioning from home to school. He often smiled during the morning greeting time routine and approached his peers independently for greeting. Though he was still physically too rough at times, his intentions were good, which was accepted by peers. The data collected on Ben's classroom peers confirmed the observations made during the intervention with Phillip. The number of peers greeting Ben changed from no greeting during baseline condition to at least two peers greeting him during arrival time. Neither the changes made to the intervention, nor the withdrawal of the intervention, returned the peer's behaviour to baseline conditions. Peers gave positive comments regarding Ben's behaviours such as 'He doesn't cry any more!' or 'He did a good job!' Ben started the day in the childcare centre without crying or screaming. On many days he entered the classroom with a smile on his face, jumped up and down, and vocalised while looking for a peer to greet. Further, Ben's verbal skills increased. During the morning greeting routine, he learned to verbalise peer's names and engaged in singing parts of the song during the childcare day. Ben preferred playing a floor drum or a hand drum that was offered to him as a toy to play with for the last step of the routine. Peers often joined in playing the drum and Ben's teachers facilitated the ongoing peer interaction.

Experiment II: Multiple step tasks

Another example of how single-case study experimental designs can be applied to evaluate the effects of interventions in interactive play settings is demonstrated in the following study.

The childcare day is not only filled with daily transitions, there are also many routines which are repeated on a daily time schedule. Some of these routines, such as hand-washing and cleaning up, include following a sequence of multiple steps. One of the identifying characteristics of autism is that 'A child with autism typically has significant difficulty organising and sequencing information and with attending to relevant information consistently' (Boswell and Gray 2003, p.1). Therefore following the multiple steps required in certain routines and staying focused on the task may be a significant challenge for them. To this end strategies similar to those for transitioning were developed to support children with autism to manage the multiple step tasks successfully.

Research and clinical applications show that songs can transmit and be used to help a child to memorise a sequence of information (Aasgaard 1999; Enoch 2001; Gervin 1991; Gfeller 1983; Jellison and Miller 1982; McGuire 2001; Wolfe and Hom 1993). Therefore using songs with young children with autism may be a successful approach to accomplishing multiple step tasks. Donna Williams, herself diagnosed with autism, says: 'If the person comes to sing known tunes, verbally, or mentally, songs can be a good way to carry along a sort of "map" by which to trigger the sequence of steps involved in doing something' (Williams 1999, p.299). While there is empirical support for using these strategies for multiple step tasks, no studies were conducted in comparing the effectiveness of strategies used for proper hand-washing skills and cleaning up for young children with autism in the context of an inclusive childcare program. The specific research questions were as follows: 1. Does the use of songs increase independent performance for a young child with autism during multiple step tasks? 2. Is the use of songs more effective in improving skills to manage multiple step tasks than the verbal presentation of the sequence? and 3. Can a classroom teacher learn basic principles of music therapy and implement song interventions in classroom routines?

Participant

The participant in this study, Andy, is a three-year-old boy with a strength in early academic concepts and, clearly, in music. However, his communication was limited and he needed assistance with managing several daily activities. He used a Picture Communication System and other visual cues. Andy also had some difficulty attending to language unless it involved a familiar song or physical routine. He seemed to love to sing and dance to music and fill in words of songs, if singing was paused. His classroom teacher described him in the following way: 'Andy really responds well to music. He makes eye contact with me as soon as I start a melody. Singing songs with him during major transitions in the classroom helps him to understand what to do next.' She also noticed that Andy would stiffen his legs and body, flap his arms, whine, try to escape and avoid transition if she just used words in the same situations. He transitioned easily when the routine was sung to him, but did not engage the same multiple step tasks independently.

Materials and staff development activities

The teacher used transition objects to cue Andy to engage in each multiple step task. For hand-washing a bottle of soap was shown to Andy. Additionally drawings of the hand-washing procedures (Fanjul and Ball 1995) were attached to the wall behind the sink. For cleaning up, the toy in use by Andy functioned as a cue.

For hand-washing the teachers used the familiar tune 'Row Your Boat' (American Traditional). This song was already in use for rubbing Andy's hands. The lyrics were expanded by including the following seven steps in the lyrics: 1. Turn the water on; 2. Wet your hands; 3. Get the soap; 4. Wash your hands; 5. Rinse your hands; 6. Turn water off; and 7. Dry your hands.

The pre-composed song 'Clean up!' from Barney & Friends (1992) was used for cleaning up toys and materials after play activities. This song was already implemented in the classroom routine. The lyrics of the song did not describe the steps of cleaning up or define how many things needed to be put away. In the already established classroom routine Andy was expected to follow six steps which were: 1. Get up; 2. Pick up something; 3. Put it away; 4. Pick up something; 5. Put it away; and 6. Go where directed by his teacher.

Prior to the study, the classroom teacher was informed about methods of data collection. Specific instructions regarding how to involve and prompt the child during the intervention were discussed and worked out in collaboration with the teacher.

Experimental design

An alternating treatment design was used to evaluate the effectiveness of two different interventions (songs versus spoken word) in a single subject. With the alternating treatment design two or more interventions rapidly alternate in a systematic order. The number of observation days for each intervention should occur equally. The different effects of the interventions can be observed by comparing the subject's performance under each of the conditions. If a consistent difference in the trend and/or level of data occurs, superiority of one treatment over another is demonstrated. The advantage of this single-subject research design is the rapid comparison of the efficacy between two interventions (Alberto and Troutman 1995; Barlow and Hayes 1984; Holcombe et al. 1994). In Experiment II a song intervention (condition A) was compared to a lyric intervention (condition B).

Procedure

Experimental sessions occurred daily before breakfast for hand-washing and shortly before circle time for toy clean up.

In the song intervention (condition A), Andy was prompted with a bottle of soap to transition to the sink for hand-washing. Data collection started as soon as Andy was ready to manipulate the handle to turn the water on. The classroom teacher started to sing about the first step of the hand-washing procedure followed by the other verses. For cleaning up Andy was prompted with the toy/material in use during free play. Data collection started as soon as the teacher started to sing the clean up song. While singing the song twice, Andy was expected to master the six steps of the routine.

The lyric intervention (condition B) was similar to the song intervention. The same transition objects and steps for each task were used. The only change between the song intervention and lyric intervention was the withdrawal of the song. Each single step of the routine was spoken twice.

Six categories of behaviour were coded for each of the steps of the multiple step task on a specially developed data sheet: 1. Did it; 2. Did not do it; 3. Did it with prompts; 4. Negative verbalisation Yes/No; 5. Escapes; and 6. Skipped the part. Data were collected live over two months. Reliability checks were carried out on an average of 40.7% of total observations within each phase and for each task. Inter-rater agreement ranged from 79.2% to 100% with a mean of 97.2%.

Results

The results of the multiple step task, 'Hand-washing', show that Andy's independent performance increased during both conditions. Prior to the intervention Andy only soaped his hands with the help of his teacher. Learning the other remaining steps occurred by implementing the routine. Particularly in the beginning of the intervention the song intervention produced greater independent performance ($\underline{M}$=66%) than the lyric intervention ($\underline{M}$=57.1%). Field notes indicate that Andy learned each step of the hand-washing routine, even when he didn't practise them every day.

The results of the multiple step task 'Clean up!' showed that the song clearly resulted in higher independent performance during the multiple steps involved in cleaning up than did verbal prompting. In all of the sessions Andy completed four steps of the six-step routine independently.

The song intervention produced greater independent performance ($\underline{M}$=66.6%) than the lyric intervention ($\underline{M}$=36.7%). It should be noticed that step 1 ('Get up!') and 6 ('Go where directed by his teacher') were almost never asked from him. Therefore, Andy accomplished all steps his teacher expected him to for cleaning up when singing to him. Overall, singing the songs was more effective than using just the lyrics (Figure 6.3).

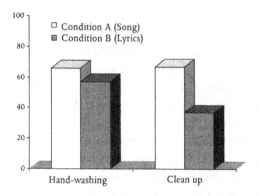

Figure 6.3 Mean ($\underline{M}$%) of Andy's independent steps during the hand-washing and clean up procedure in each condition of the study

Experiment III: Peer interaction on playgrounds

The single case study method can also be used effectively in a multiple baseline design. The following study exemplifies this research method. One of the characteristics of children with autism is their severe delay in understanding social relationships and communication, which often results in a lack of peer interaction. Therefore one of the major therapeutic objectives is to increase the children's interaction in the context of the environment and among their peers (e.g. National Research Council 2001). It is recommended practice for preschool programs to give children a daily opportunity to spend large blocks of time in outdoor play (Bredekamp and Copple 1997). Playgrounds are often large, unorganised spaces and not meaningful for children with autism. Thus, playground time is often seen as unstructured play time with no established play routine. In a free play setting where no predictable play routines are established, it is very difficult, if not impossible, for children with autism to join in the fast pace of play and play styles of their typically developing peers.

Playgrounds also need to be viewed as a therapeutic context, just as classrooms are, especially in early childhood settings using an integrated therapeutic approach. Predictable play routines and play activities which support the children's interests and strengths need to be identified and established to ensure the time spent on childcare playgrounds promotes the development of children with autism (Nabors *et al.* 2001). The purpose of this study was to evaluate the effects of a musical adaptation of a childcare playground and an individually designed intervention based on music therapy principles, to increase peer interaction of four young children with autism spectrum disorder in the playground. The target children had a lack of interest in peers or had few strategies for initiating or responding to interaction. The intervention was implemented by the classroom teachers and subsequently by classroom peers using peer-mediated strategies.

The specific research questions that were asked for this experiment were as follows: 1. Will the musical adaptation of a playground (Music Hut) increase the peer interaction of young children with autism on playgrounds? 2. Does the use of an individually composed song sung by the teachers and peers increase positive peer interaction on the playground for young children with autism? 3. Can classroom teachers learn the principles important to music therapy to increase peer interaction on the playground for young children with autism? 4. Will peers participate and model tasks?

Participants

Phillip and Ben from experiment I, as well as Eric and Lucas, participated in this study (n=4). The boys were enrolled in three different classrooms. At this time Phillip and Ben attended the same class. Detailed information of the characteristics of each target child appear in Table 6.1.

	Table 6.1 Summary of characteristics for each target child participating in Experiment III		
Name and chronological age	*Developmental information*	*Playground behaviour*	*Musical preferences and behaviours*
Eric 3 years and 4 months	Used objects and non-speech sounds to communicate Good imitation skills Short attention span for play Minimal interaction with peers	Motor activities such as riding a tricycle, digging in the sandbox, running around Interested in peer's activity, inappropriate interaction with peers, few initiations from peers	Vocalisation to songs and own activities Motivated engagement in rhythm and music activities Preference for rhythm-based music
Ben 4 years	Three-word phrases and gestures, not directed to others to communicate Imitation of words, sounds, and motor actions, when directly modelled Deficits in constructive and pretend play activities Engagement in repetitive patterns Minimal interest in peers	Ran aimlessly around, walked along the 'Sound Path' Sang familiar songs and spun around in repetitive patterns Lay in the sandbox, or talked to bunny in hutch Rare interaction with peers, no initiations form peers	Vocalisation to songs and own activity Video and computer games including music Musical activities such as singing, dancing, drumming Preference for soft and mellow music Accomplishment of tasks when accompanied with familiar songs

Continued on next page

Table 6.1 continued

Name and chronological age	Developmental information	Playground behaviour	Musical preferences and behaviours
Phillip 4 years 9 months	Two-word phrases, gestures, and non-speech sounds to communicate Imitation sounds and cues Deficits in range of interests and play skills Engagement in repetitive patterns Interest in peers, inappropriate interaction with peers	Wandered aimlessly around Engaged in respective patterns such as flapping his arms, spinning a leaf or stick Sat absently on a bench, or rode tricycle, when prompted by adults Interested in peers, inappropriate interaction, peers give him negative role or avoid him	Musical activities such as singing and dancing Playing the drum, which functioned as reward Preference for rhythm
Lucas 3 years 9 months	Objects and gestures to communicate Short attention span for play, only with maximal adult help Engagement frequently in repetitive patterns Interest in peers, minimal or inappropriate interaction with peers	Motor activities such as following moving objects Engaged in repetitive patterns such as spinning objects Minimal or negative peer interaction, is scared of peers, negative role among peers	Play activities accompanied by vocalisation Music combined with movement and fast changing sequences Responded well to rhythms and imitation of his vocalisation

In addition, the classroom peers (n=32) with and without disabilities, ages two to five, participated in the study voluntarily. Thus, two peers for each targeted child were formally trained as peer helpers. These 'peer buddies' consisted of typically developing children and a boy diagnosed as having high-functioning autism. The teachers (n=6) participated and implemented the intervention based on their schedule.

Material and staff development activities

An outdoor music centre (Music Hut), designed to expand the musical opportunities and therapeutic playground activities of young children, especially those with autism, was created (Kern, Marlette and Snyder 2002). A Chinese Wind Gong, six drums in different sizes, a cymbal, a Mini Cabasa, three Sound Tubes with different lengths, a Marching Drum and an Ocean Drum were located on a 10" x 8" wheelchair-accessible hardwood deck and attached to wooden beams, steel arches and Plexiglas walls. Design and construction met the guidelines of playground safety regulations (U.S. Consumer Product Safety Commission 1997) and was both functional and visually pleasing.

A unique song for each subject, matching the children's temperament and current abilities musically was composed. The intention of each song was to increase positive peer interaction and to engage in meaningful play during outdoor activities. The content of the songs focused on these general goals and embedded several IEP goals, developed by the child care program's interdisciplinary team. For instance, the song 'Phillip's Groove', outlined in Figure 6.4 started with the targeted child's two word phrase 'I want', and included his IEP goals as shown in Table 6.2.

Table 6.2 Overview of Phillip's IEP goals incorporated in the song 'Phillip's Groove'

IEP Goals	Song
Improvement in verbal skills and sign language	Sing the lyrics of the song, signing 'All done!', 'Goodbye', and 'Thank you
Make choices	Choose an instrument in the Music Hut
Name peers and self	Inclusion of peers and Phillip's name in the lyrics of the song
Wait for turns	
Use appropriate body contact	Peer plays four measures, Phillip plays four measures afterwards or vice versa
	Give hugs for 'Goodbye'

A CD recording of each song with a sing-along and a song transcription was handed out to the teachers and the families of the 'peer buddies.'

Training and consultation was similar to experiment I, and included hands-on training in the Music Hut for teachers.

Figure 6.4 Transcript of the song 'Phillip's Groove', addressing social interaction and specific IEP goals

Experimental design

A multiple baseline design replicated across four children was used to evaluate the effects of adapting the playground (condition B), the teacher-mediated intervention (condition C), and subsequently the peer-mediated intervention (condition D). In this design an intervention is applied to the same target behaviours across children who share common relevant characteristics. The first step is to identify the target behaviour which is shared by all subjects. This target behaviour becomes the baseline.

Experimental control is established by collecting baselines for each subject until a sufficient stability is exhibited (a stable pattern or constant trend, and a minimum of three data points). Then the intervention is applied to one subject while the baseline conditions are continued with the other individuals. If stability is achieved during treatment for the first subject, the intervention is applied to the second individual. This procedure is repeated at staggered times for all remaining subjects and for all conditions. The treatment effects can be seen clearly in comparison to the baseline condition and/or in contrast to other applied conditions. Because the intervention is replicated across several subjects at staggered times, it is very unlikely that external factors cause the response change. One advantage of this single-case experimental design is that replication and experimental control can be achieved without withdrawal of treatment (D. Aldridge 1994, 1996; Hanser 1995; Holcombe *et al.* 1994; Kazdin 1982). Data collection occurred over eight months.

Procedure

Experimental sessions occurred once daily during the morning outdoor play. The study procedure involved four sequentially implemented conditions:

- Baseline (condition A): The subjects' naturally occurring positive peer interactions on the playground were observed prior to the availability of the Music Hut. Data collection started as soon as the target children entered the playground.

- Adaptation of the playground (condition B): The subjects' interactions with peers were observed following availability of the Music Hut to document any changes related to the new materials only. When entering the playground, teachers walked the subject to the Music Hut, gave him a drum stick and said 'Play in the Music Hut.' The data collection started as soon as the subject entered the Music Hut.

- Teacher-mediated intervention (condition C): The unique song was sung in the Music Hut by the teachers with the subjects and peer volunteers. Teachers trained the formally selected peers to mediate the intervention in condition D. When entering the playground, the teacher walked the subject and at least one peer to the Music Hut and prepared them verbally for the activity. As soon as they entered the Music Hut the teacher started singing the specific song, initiated and encouraged the children to play the instruments, modelled the content of each song, and continued to play for ten minutes.

- Peer-mediated intervention (condition D): the same song was sung by the formally selected peers and subjects in the Music Hut. The teacher's support was gradually withdrawn. The goal was to have the peer-buddy and subject interact and play with one another independently. The procedure was similar to that in the intervention phase C. The only change was that the teacher's support was gradually withdrawn by first, reducing physical prompts, second, verbal prompts, and finally just giving prompts when necessary.

Categories of behaviours were coded in each condition for both peers and the target children on a specially developed data sheet: 1. Initiates interaction; 2. Positive peer interaction; and 3. Stays in the Music Hut. In addition, the subjects' play and engagement with materials and equipment were coded, as well as the teacher's support for positive peer interaction. In conditions C and D the teacher's and peer's performances in implementing the intervention was coded as well. Field notes were taken by the author. The categories were coded through direct observation of a ten-minute videotaped segment using a fifteen-second momentary time sampling recording procedure. Data collection occurred over eight months. Reliability checks were carried out on an average of 36.8% of total observations within each phase and for each child. Inter-observer agreement across all conditions and children ranged from 93.8% to 99.8%, with a mean of 98.2%.

Results

The results of this study indicated that during the baseline condition (condition A) target children had few positive peer interactions on the playground (Eric $\underline{M}$=5.9%; Ben $\underline{M}$=1.4%; Phillip $\underline{M}$=4.1%; Lucas $\underline{M}$=1.5%). The design and adaptation of the playground equipment itself (condition B) didn't improve their social interaction significantly (Eric $\underline{M}$=16.7%; Ben $\underline{M}$=2.7%; Phillip $\underline{M}$=6.3%; Lucas $\underline{M}$=2.5%), but facilitated involvement and the motivation to interact with peers and engage in meaningful play. However, the introduction of the teacher-mediated intervention (condition C) resulted, for all children, in a significant and immediate increase in positive peer interaction (Eric $\underline{M}$=48.8%; Ben $\underline{M}$=77.5%; Phillip $\underline{M}$=77.4%; Lucas $\underline{M}$=61.0%). With only one exception, a high level of the teacher's ability to implement the intervention within the day-care routine was observed ($\underline{M}$=84%). In condition D, peers participated and facilitated the intervention on a high level ($\underline{M}$=85.3%). Peer interaction decreased during the peer-mediated intervention, but was still significantly higher than during the baseline condition and the adaptation on the playground phase (Eric $\underline{M}$=N/A; Ben $\underline{M}$=17.3%; Phillip $\underline{M}$=21.9%; Lucas $\underline{M}$=24.1%). (Classroom demands and schedules did not allow the implementation of condition D for Eric.)

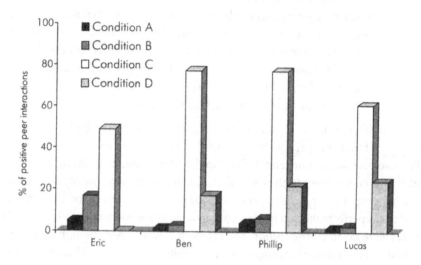

Figure 6.5 Mean ($\underline{M}$%) of positive peer interaction for each target child by each condition of the peer interaction on playground study

The effects of the intervention were also illustrated by the following field notes. The intervention significantly enhanced the children's quality of peer interaction, and frequency and duration of play. Additionally, the targeted children accomplished IEP goals such as improving communication and sign language, increasing choice-making, turn taking, imitation skills and using appropriate body contact. Crucial aspects of experiment III were the motivation of the formally selected helpers to participate in daily activity repetition over a long period of time, and the interpretation of the subject's uneven pattern of behaviour and communication style. A minimum of ongoing adult support in interpreting the meaning of the actions of children with autism, as well as verbal cues and reinforcement, were necessary to facilitate positive peer interaction. This replicates and broadens earlier studies which have pointed out that typically developing children and their partners with special needs may require adult support to successfully interact with each other (e.g. Nabors *et al.* 2001; Quill 2001). Some of the peers showed motivation by asking to record the unique songs on a CD in order to share it with their families. After the study, one class recorded their songs and a CD was handed out to each participating child.

The positive outcome of this study is also indicated by the reports of the target children's classroom teachers. One teacher commented:

> I had a wonderful time working with Phillip in the Music Hut. This was a fun and effective intervention. The best part for me was having Phillip look up at me with his big brown eyes in wonder while I sang to him.

Families shared the song recordings with their extended family, which validates the social impact of the intervention and music itself (Aasgaard 1999; Ricciarelli 2003). The parents of Ben's 'peer buddy' Carmen responded:

> We believe your work with the kids is a tremendous success. When Carmen first notified us that she was going to record a CD, we said, 'Carmen, what are you talking about?' She responded, 'We are going to record a CD with Petra.' You should have seen the joy that was exuberating from her. After we heard the CD, we thought WOW, these kids did a great job and how wonderful it was that you and the teachers explained to the kids what the instruments were and how to play them. We were so at awe that we made copies of the CD and gave them to our parents and close relatives. Everyone enjoyed them and said how great the CD was. Every now and then when I talk with my parents they recite some of the songs on the CD, 'play the cymbals, play the cymbals'. We all just laugh and reflect on how well this song was sung on the CD and how the kids seemed to enjoy it so much. I feel that the songs and the instruments were more than just singing and playing but were also a lesson on how to work together and how music is for everyone. We definitely appreciate what it has done for Carmen. Thanks.

Discussion

The purpose of this chapter was to demonstrate that single-case experimental designs can be used to evaluate the effectiveness of interventions based on music therapy principles implemented by a teacher in interactive play settings. The results of the studies show that this research methodology precisely answered the specific research questions. However, there are natural limitations of single-case experimental designs, including a limited number of participants. In order to understand the generalizability of the interventions, replications with multiple participants is warranted. But replication and generalisation of these findings might be difficult. These interventions are only implemented if the skills are useful to the individual children in the instructional environment, and there are significant variables among individuals. Other findings, as noted in the field notes or comments of teacher and parents, remain unassessed.

The interventions addressed challenging moments for children with autism (morning greeting routine, multiple step tasks, peer interaction on the playground) within an interactive play setting. Phillip, Ben, Andy, Eric and Lucas improved their independent performance in situations that were troublesome for them prior to the intervention. The individualised songs, the staff development activity and the peer-mediated strategies were effective techniques to accomplish the goals and also changed peer behaviour towards the targeted children positively.

From the positive outcomes of the interventions provided in Experiment III, we can conclude that classroom teachers were successful in implementing the interventions. Even when teachers did not previously know the songs, had no formal musical training or experiences with music therapy interventions, they were able to implement these interventions. This replicates and extends earlier studies showing that teachers implemented other therapeutic interventions successfully (e.g. Wilcox and Shannon 1996; Wolery 2002) and supports the Division of Early Childhood (DEC) recommendation that interventions should be embedded in ongoing classroom routines (Sandal et al. 2000). However, ongoing consultation and feedback in the form of reassurance, support and problem solving from a trained music therapist were necessary.

When using an integrated therapy approach, it is vital to establish a functional relationship between the teacher and therapist. The teacher and therapist play equal parts and share equal responsibility for implementing the music therapy intervention successfully (McWilliam 1996). It is the music therapist's responsibility to provide and share professional knowledge with the teachers to meet the needs of the child. In consultative methods, it is important to: respect the teacher's individual working style; keep the focus on the goals and tasks; be flexible and spontaneous both in scheduling and implementing interventions; communicate clearly and frequently; and provide enthusiasm and motivation. It is very important to take the teachers' fears and concerns about singing and playing instruments seriously and let the music become a natural activity within classroom routines.

The gathering and interpretation of my data made me consider several aspects of designing and implementing the interventions. It really surprised me how easily the children picked up the songs, which made me think of my song-writing and what it is in the music that draws the children's attention. I learned that simple melodies following the speech melody, with a driving rhythm as in 'Phillip's Groove', as many of the Nordoff-Robbins children's play-songs do (Robbins and Nordoff 1962; Robbins and Robbins 1998), work best with young children. Since in preschool settings most of the songs are sung without any instrumental accompaniment, it makes me wonder what the impact of the harmony is. Do the children and teacher internalise the harmony and hear it when singing a tune, or is it simply the melody which sticks with them? What influence do the musical expression of tunes and other musical elements have? Can Elefant's (2001) findings on this topic for girls with Rett syndrome be applied to children with other special needs and to typically developing children? Those are questions that definitely need more evaluation. However, the children's enthusiasm in being part of the project, their individual input and uninhibited and honest response added a lot to the quality of the experiments.

Working in an interactive play setting where integrated therapy is practised definitely changed my view and way of providing music therapy services. My understanding of improvisation improved not only on a musical level, but also with the environment (indoors–outdoors), availability of material and equipment, constantly changing numbers of children and staff participation. The continuously changing conditions of classroom demands and dynamics, and the spontaneous interactions with families, require great flexibility. Additionally, I find it beneficial to collaborate with interdisciplinary team members. It allows me to extend my knowledge and it is very inspiring to accomplish the ultimate goal to find the right treatment for the needs of the child in the moment and the environment. Clearly, integrated therapy has its limitations and is not the only way to provide services in early intervention. However, it is definitely an effective way of providing treatment and allows for the delivery of music therapy service in early intervention. More studies providing evidence that music therapy interventions can be implemented as embedded strategies in interactive play settings are needed. If music therapy consultation and training works, music therapy may play a future role in tele-health services (Wakeford 2002; TelAbility 2003) in training, consulting, and supervision in rural areas, where children with special needs lack music therapy services.

Conclusions

Single-case experimental designs are particularly useful for evaluating the effects of therapy on individual clients. The basic assumptions underlying these designs are 1. that repeated and careful measurement occurs multiple times in each experimental condition; 2. the participant serves as his/her own control allowing the independent variable to be evaluated within the participant; and 3. replication within or across participants is used to evaluate whether a functional relationship exists between the intervention and the participants' measured performance. In this way these designs allow music therapists to evaluate their clinical practice, including their consultation with other professionals, and to ask important questions about the practices and principles of music therapy in a quantitative and experimental way.

The use of this research methodology produced valuable outcomes for future treatments of children with autism in interactive play settings and demonstrated the importance of music therapy in early intervention. The experiments demonstrated that music therapy strategies can be effective in increasing the independent performance of children with autism during childcare routines. Individualised songs are an effective tool and are easy to use for teachers and children with and without special needs. Music therapists play a valuable role in consulting with and training classroom teachers to implement interventions based on music therapy principles in ongoing childcare routines. The interventions provided a valuable step towards inclusion, both for children and their families. Overall music therapy can enhance services for young children with autism and should be routinely considered as a treatment option. The information gained by using single-case experimental designs may help to improve future integrated therapeutic services for young children with autism and their families.

CHAPTER 7

The Use of Single Case Designs in Testing a Specific Hypothesis

Cochavit Elefant

If a man will begin with certainties, he shall end in doubts; but if he will be content to begin with doubts he shall end in certainties.

Sir Francis Bacon (1561–1626)[1]

Hypothesis is defined by *Webster's Seventh New Collegiate Dictionary* (1976) as 'a tentative assumption made in order to draw out and test its logical or empirical consequences'. The word actually has two meanings: on the one hand, the basic origin of the word is Greek hypotithenai meaning 'to put under', and on the other, it implies insufficient evidence to provide more than a tentative explanation. Thus it seems that hypothesis is both the base (which is under) of an inquiry and the drive to seek and provide evidence for assumptions.

A more general definition of the term hypothesis is '... an idea that can serve as a premise or supposition to organize certain facts thereby guide observations' (Robson 2002, p.548). It seems that there is general consent on the role and importance of the hypothesis as the primary building block of a research project. Decuir (1995) argues that the statement of the hypothesis 'can be a helpful step in the organization of the project' (p.240). Robson (2002) quotes Manstread and Semin (1988) as saying that the '...strategies and tactics you select in carrying out a piece

---

1   Sir Francis Bacon in *The Columbia World of Quotation* (1996) Robert Andrews, Mary Biggs and Michael Sidel (eds.). New York: Columbia University Press, quotation no. 5135.

of research depend very much on the type of research question you are trying to answer' (p.80).

Rudestam and Newton (1992) also state that 'the key to evaluating a complete study is whether the selected method is rigorous and appropriate to the research question' (p.23).

For the reader to accompany me through my thinking and decision making process for my research, I will begin by revealing some aspects of Rett syndrome.

What is Rett syndrome?

Rett syndrome is a neurological disorder mainly affecting females and found in a variety of racial and ethnic groups worldwide. It was first described by Dr Andreas Rett (Rett 1966) and received worldwide recognition following a paper by Dr Bengt Hagberg and colleagues (Hagberg *et al.* 1983).

Childhood development in females with Rett syndrome proceeds in an apparently normal fashion during pregnancy and over the first 6–18 months, at which point development comes to a halt, they regress and lose many, if not most, of their acquired skills (Graham 1995).

Thereafter there is a rapid deterioration and loss of acquired speech and purposeful hand use and they may exhibit one or more stereotyped hand movements (Ishikawa *et al.* 1978; Weiss 1996). The repetitive hand movements appear involuntary and occur during most of their periods of wakefulness. Deceleration of head growth and jerky body movements of the trunk and limbs accompany the developmental deterioration in individuals with Rett syndrome. Many girls begin walking within the normal age-range, while others show significant delays. Some begin walking and may lose this skill, while others will continue walking throughout their lives (International Rett Syndrome Association (IRSA) 1997) with a broad base gait and side-swaying movements of the shoulders (Kerr and Stephenson 1986). Other physical problems, such as seizures, scoliosis and breathing abnormalities may appear (IRSA 1997, 2000). Apraxia (dyspraxia), the inability to program the body to perform motor acts, is the most fundamental and severely handicapping aspect of Rett syndrome. It can interfere with all body movement, including eye gaze and speech, making it difficult for individuals with Rett syndrome to express their needs.

The prevalence among different countries ranges from 1:10,000–15,000 (Hagberg 1985; Kerr and Stephenson 1985) to 1:22,800 females (Kozinetz *et al.* 1993). It is considered a frequent cause of neurological dysfunction in females, accounted as the second most common cause for severe mental retardation in females after Down's syndrome (Ellaway and Christodoulou 2001).

To date there is no known remedy that can repair the neurological damage caused by the genetic fault of Rett syndrome. No medical solutions have succeeded in alleviating symptoms connected to Rett syndrome during pre-, peri- or postnatal periods and no subsequent medical treatment can improve the physical condition nor the functional abilities in this population. Therefore different types of remedial therapy are likely to be more important for any potential improvement, and even the slowing of deterioration. Some researchers believe that knowledgeable therapy might change the course of the condition (Jacobsen, Viken and von Tetchner 2001).

Music therapy is one, if not the most, potent therapeutic intervention method for Rett syndrome. Dr Rett recommended music therapy as early as 1982 in treating individuals with Rett syndrome. He believed it evokes positive response in girls and adults (Rett 1982). Reports show how music-making promotes and motivates a desire to interact and communicate with surroundings, as well as developing cognitive, affective, sensori-motor and physical skills (Allan 1991; Coleman 1987; Elefant 2001; Elefant and Lotan 1998; Hadsell and Coleman 1988; Hill 1997; Kerr 1992; Lindberg 1991; Merker, Bergstrom-Isacsson and Witt Engerstrom 2001; Merker and Wallin 2001; Montague 1988; Takehisa and Takehisa-Silvestri, n.d; Wesecky 1986; Wigram 1991, 1995, 1996; Wigram and Cass 1996).

Having addressed here some elements of this intriguing syndrome, I will continue by revealing the thinking procedure through which my initial idea turned into a mature form of a research study.

My personal perspective: moving from a general idea to a complete research project

When I first began thinking about my PhD it was clear to me that my project would be concerned with Rett syndrome. As a clinical music therapist working for many years with cognitively impaired individuals at educational settings, females with Rett syndrome always captivated me. Underneath the cold, rigid and, sometimes, pessimistic definition of severe and profound mental retardation, I have met enchanting souls who drew me into their world. Now, after 15 years of working with these individuals I had a chance of making a difference that might go beyond the here and now. I thought of my project as a tool to achieve a purpose and not just as an end goal.

Hence, the next step was to decide what specific area of difficulty characterised Rett syndrome, which I was going to focus on. Individuals with Rett syndrome display difficulties in physical, emotional, behavioural, cognitive, educational and communicative areas and most of these regions can be treated through music therapy. Due to my experience in speech therapy and to my desire of wanting the research intervention to end by leaving the participants with a usable functional tool, I decided to focus on the area of communication, which had previously been reported in the literature as being pre-intentional (Woodyatt and Ozanne 1993, 1994).

The decision led to the forming of the main research question:

Can songs in music therapy enhance communication in girls with Rett syndrome?

After contemplating this challenging question, it was clear that dividing it into sub-questions would focus my research on the core issue:

1.   Are girls with Rett syndrome able to make intentional choices?

2.   Are girls with Rett syndrome able to learn and sustain learning over time?

3.   Do girls with Rett syndrome reveal consistent preferences through choices they make?

4.   How do girls with Rett syndrome demonstrate emotional and commu-nicative behaviours?

After forming the research questions, it was time to think of a coherent and scientific way of answering them. To do this I needed a research design.

The research design

A single-case, multiple-probe design was used to evaluate individual choice of, and response to, familiar and unfamiliar songs. This method of research is a form of multiple baseline design, which enables several comparisons of behaviours, responses and musical elements to be made within each case. The experimental investigation is within treatment of the individual case (Barlow and Hersen 1984; Cooper, Heron and Heward 1987; Kazdin 1982; Kratochwill 1992).

The efficacy and value of single-case design in quantitative and qualitative research has become increasingly recognised in recent years. Single-case research design appears to have originated within quasi-experimental investigation and applied behaviour analysis (ABA). It has developed and its usefulness has become apparent within a variety of professional fields, such as: clinical psychology, special education, social work and research on communication disorders (Kratochwill 1992; Rosal 1989). It is one of 'a whole spectrum of case-study research methods applied to the investigation of individual change in clinical practice' (D. Aldridge 1996, p.111).

Repeated measurements are taken over an extended period of time in a 'time series design' single-case study, under precise and standardised conditions (Barlow and Hersen 1984; Kratochwill 1992; Sevcik, Romski and Adamson 1999). There are several approaches in single-case design, some of which rely on establishing baseline measurements. In order to evaluate change over time, a number of new baselines may be taken in a multiple baseline design.

The research model chosen for this study was a multiple probe (a variant of multiple-baseline design), a form of single-case design, which is highly flexible, enabling the analysis of the effects of the independent variable across multiple behaviours, settings and/or subjects (Cooper *et al.* 1987). Multiple-baseline design relies on the examination of performance across several different baselines in order to draw inferences or interpretations regarding the effect of treatment. The effects are demonstrated by introducing the intervention following baselines at different points in time (Kazdin 1982).

When a specific behaviour has achieved a stable and pre-determined level of response under the treatment condition, or reached a pre-established criterion, the independent variable is applied to the next behaviour under investigation. If this second behaviour changes, in the same manner as behaviour one, replication of the independent variable's effect has been achieved. After behaviour two has reached the pre-determined level, the independent variable is then applied to behaviour three. For the multiple-baseline design to achieve rigour as a research method, several replications are recommended (Cooper *et al.* 1987; Kazdin 1982).

During the initial period of observation, termed the 'baseline' (Barlow and Hersen 1984; Cooper *et al.* 1987), repeated measurements of identified target behaviours are made. Separate baselines are taken on selected behaviours in a particular case. A baseline establishes the current level of performance from which it becomes feasible to predict future performance or measure change. The purpose of the baseline measurement is to obtain a standard measure at a point in time of the efficacy of an intervention (D. Aldridge 1996; Barlow and Hersen 1984; Kazdin 1982). It demonstrates the effect of the intervention by showing that behaviour changes only when the intervention is applied (Kazdin 1982). The baseline must demonstrate stability and consistency before the intervention is introduced (Barlow and Hersen 1984; Cooper *et al.* 1987). In this research study separate baseline measures were taken each time a new set of songs was to be introduced.

The treatment was applied (in this case) after a stable response level to picture symbols of songs had been confirmed by means of baseline measurements. The time needed to establish a stable baseline depended on the behaviour of each participant, and ranged from four to five sessions.

The multiple-probe design used in this research is particularly appropriate when evaluating the effects of instruction on skill sequences (Barlow and Hersen 1984; Cooper *et al.* 1987) and in testing for possible learning effects that may occur during treatment. If baseline control is applied during the intervention period, there will be interruption of the intervention. With the population under investigation here, an interruption can easily destabilise or disrupt carefully established learning processes. Therefore periodical assessment (in the form of probes) is used, which enables the researcher to evaluate learning process over time. Probes, used as assessment for baseline or maintenance, are measured throughout the intervention at regular intervals (Barlow and Hersen 1984; Kazdin 1982). The probe provides the basis for determining whether behaviour change has occurred when intervention is applied, when compared to baseline measurements taken prior to intervention, or acts as an assessment of a maintained skill or response (maintenance probe) for determining internalisation of a learned behaviour or response.

The data that emerges from such single-case design research is typically analysed by means of graphs that present results visually and/or by descriptive statistics. In this study, 'Effect Size' calculations were applied (Coe 2000) in addition to graphic and descriptive statistics that describe change over time, to establish any effects resulting from intervention as compared with baseline levels of behaviours.

Participants

Rett syndrome is rare in incidence and the recruitment and randomisation of subjects to an experimental group relies on the availability of a large population from whom random selection can be made. This study was undertaken at a centre in Israel with an exceptionally large population of girls with Rett syndrome. Seven girls, ranging in age from four to ten, participated in this study (see Table 7.1). All the girls have been diagnosed with Rett syndrome according to guidelines established by the 'Rett Syndrome Diagnostic Criteria Work Group' (1988, revised by the International Rett Syndrome Association (IRSA) 1997). Six girls were in stage III, the 'plateau stage', of whom two were not ambulant. One girl was in stage IV, the 'late motor deterioration stage'. The girls' cognitive abilities were not evaluated, as standardised tools for measuring sequential and simultaneous processing of information, in order to determine intelligence levels in these girls as compared to other children of the same chronological age, cannot measure such severely handicapped individuals. Most test instruments, such as the WISC or the

Table 7.1 Participant personal information

Name	Age (years)	Onset of regression	Ambulatory	Stage	Epilepsy	Verbal skills	Duration of pre-research MT (years)
Aviv	9.10	20 months	Yes	III	No	No	4.5
Elisheva	8.2	18 months	Yes	III	No	No	1
Hilla	10.2	24 months	Yes	III	No	Few words	4.5
Meirav	9.8	12 months	Yes	III	Yes	No	4.5
Rachel	6.5	18 months	No	III	No	No	1
Tali	4.8	12 months	No	III	No	No	1
Talia	10.7	18 months	No	IV	Yes	No	4.5

Kauffman ABC, rely in part on verbal skills and good enough hand skills, both of which are significantly impaired or absent in this population.

Setting and material

The study was conducted by myself, the special education centre's music therapist.

Two chairs were placed in the music therapy room (one for the participant and the other for the researcher) facing each other. A set of cards containing Picture Communication Symbols (PCS) (Mayer-Johnson 1981) was prepared on a 10 x 10 cm card. The set of cards contained references to the songs with the title words written above the graphic picture symbol. A second set of cards contained only orthographies (Hebrew words) for the song title and these were displayed on 10 x 5 cm cards. A small piece of Velcro tape was attached to the back of each card so that it could be easily secured to and removed from a 50 x 30 cm communication board (made of a piece of tapestry). Hebrew is read right to left, so the order of presentation of the visual symbols on the communication board was always right to left.

The researcher used a guitar to accompany her singing and the typical style of accompaniment was chord strumming. There were a total of 18 different songs (independent variables) in the study. Some of them were familiar and some were unfamiliar to the participants. The songs were divided into three 'sets', a total of six songs in each set (four familiar and two unfamiliar songs in a set). The songs were either traditional children's songs or songs the investigator had written. All songs had been translated into Hebrew. The content of the songs covered a number of subjects, including animals, body-parts, food items and transportation. All the songs were short with a very simple repeated verse format with contrasts in phrases built into the style of the songs.

The dependent variables that were collected are behaviours presented by the participants during the course of all trials. These were determined after reviewing the literature on the topic of non-verbal communication (Sigafoos 2000; Sigafoos *et al.* 2000a) and careful preliminary observation of a few music therapy sessions. The following behaviours were analysed:

- intentional choices of songs by indicating and re-indicating picture symbols or orthographies that identified the songs
- response time
- song preferences
- affective responses (smiles, laughs, movements, etc)
- expressive vocalisation
- intentional speech
- eye contact
- the presence or absence of stereotypical hand movements.

Procedure

The trials incorporated choice-making with familiar and unfamiliar children's songs. During intervention trials, once the girls had made their choice, the investigator sang the songs. The sessions were held three mornings per week and each lasted between 20 and 30 minutes. The duration of the study was five months and included baseline, intervention and maintenance trials. During the following three months an additional three maintenance trials were administered.

The participants chose one symbol out of groups of either two or four presented symbols. Consistency and reliability of choice-making ability was established in pre-baseline tests undertaken in preparation for the main study. Five girls were found to be able to choose effectively from a choice of two stimuli. Two girls demonstrated the ability to choose from a selection of four stimuli on presentation and I decided to use four symbols, or orthographies, with these more able girls as they had to develop more discrimination in choosing from a choice of four. Hypothetically, development of choice-making by the presentation of more complex stimuli in these two girls would demonstrate more complex learning ability.

The purpose of the baseline measurement was to determine the current level of the participants' performance and to measure abilities to choose at a point in time that could later be compared with the intervention, in order to determine the efficacy of the intervention.

The investigator asked each participant to indicate a song (represented by picture symbols) out of two or four possible choices. This choice indication was made through movement of the girl's hand, nose, head or eye gaze, according to her preference and ability. Once the preferred song was chosen, the order of the symbols was randomly changed out of sight. The communication board was then re-presented with the symbols in different positions, and the girl was asked to choose again to confirm her original choice. The purpose of this was to verify that her choice was intentional and specific. The intervention had a structural hierarchy of prompting. Each part contained five steps in a hierarchy progression. The steps were graded from the most independent choice making (with no physical cues or assistance) to the least independent, where physical prompting and cues were utilised. Only the first two steps (1–2) were counted as independent choice-making and were included in the final data results. The three other steps (3–5) had prompting and could not be viewed as independent choice-making and therefore, this data was not eligible for inclusion as a confirmed choice. The lapse time between each step was 15 seconds.

Figure 7.1 illustrates through a flow chart how the various steps in the choice-making procedure were followed through, and decisions were taken at each point in the process. Immediately following her confirmation, the song was sung to her during intervention and maintenance.

Each participant had a total of six trials to choose from in each session and could hear up to six songs. The participant heard the song only when she had confirmed her choice, completing stage I and stage II of the procedure, as defined above.

The criterion for moving onto the second and then third set of songs was pre-defined. It was determined so that the length of time showed stability in the intervention. The participant moved onto the next set of songs after she had successfully chosen songs and confirmed her choice of a specific song in five out of six trials in total. These choices had to be made in three out of four sessions to demonstrate consistency and reliability.

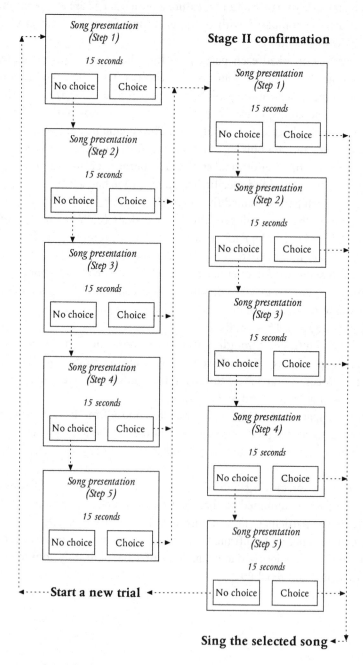

Figure 7.1 Song selection flow chart

Baseline measurement was established with each girl (typically four to five sessions) before the intervention was applied. All three sets of songs were presented in one session for the baseline. Once the intervention had been introduced, starting with songs in set 1, 'probe measurement' was taken every fourth session. This continued during the second and third sets of songs as they were presented. The probe technique continued not only as measuring baseline, but also as measuring maintenance of skills with sets that were completed (Figure 7.2).

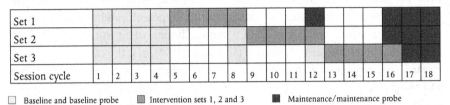

Set 1																		
Set 2																		
Set 3																		
Session cycle	1	2	3	4	5	6	7	8	9	10	11	12	13	14	15	16	17	18

☐ Baseline and baseline probe   ▨ Intervention sets 1, 2 and 3   ■ Maintenance/maintenance probe

Figure 7.2 Research design, a schematic display

The intervention ended when each girl had fulfilled the criterion with the completion of all three sets of songs. The investigator did not know beforehand the duration time of the intervention, as each participant was to complete all three sets at her own individual pace. When the intervention was completed the maintenance procedure was applied.

The Follow-up Maintenance Probe Sessions (FMPS) were applied three times, during the weeks after the trials had been completed, once the criterion of all three sets was achieved. It was determined before the study commenced. The first FMPS were implemented two weeks after termination of the intervention trials; the second, four weeks after the first maintenance trial (six weeks after termination of the intervention trials) and the third six weeks after the second maintenance trial (12 weeks after termination of the intervention trials). Therefore the total time between the end of the intervention phase and the final completion of the study was three months.

Data collecting

All sessions in the study were videotaped continuously throughout each session by two cameras. Both cameras were set in operation before the participant entered the therapy room to prevent their use influencing the participants' behaviour. The participant was seated at her chair and had a short acclimatistion period of two minutes after entering the room. At that time the researcher sat down opposite the participant, conversing with her and responding to her mood (Hartman 1984). The video material was viewed and data was collected and transferred into observational sheets as well. The data was analysed through several tools (observational sheets) and the results where collected.

Validity

Validity has not received much attention in observational research and has been considered 'inherently valid insofar as they are based on direct sampling of behavior and they require minimal inference on the part of observers' (Hartman 1984, p.129). Although each of the traditional types of validity is relevant to observation systems, content validity is especially important in the initial development of a behaviour coding system (Hartman 1984), as is the case in the present research. All variables assumed to be relevant to indicate behaviours were gathered and categorised. The fields and categories designated in the forms used during the research were evaluated by the researcher and by two other experts in the area of communication, mental retardation and Rett syndrome to ensure content validity.

Reliability

The present study was aimed at observing and measuring different behaviours as indicators of intentional choice-making and communicational abilities during music therapy sessions. Since observational instruments require periodic assessments to ensure intervention effectiveness (Hartman 1984) and in order to collect the data needed in a reliable fashion, records (videotaping) were collected continuously.

The videotapes were observed and analysed by three different observers at different times, using the video recording protocol as a mutual reference point, thus controlling possible biases (Hartman 1984).

Intra-observer reliability

In order to establish intra-rater reliability the researcher (one of the observers) observed the video materials and her results were compared with her notes taken at the time of the trial sessions.

Inter-observer reliability

The researcher and two independent evaluators measured choice-making. Inter-observer reliability was included in the design. Samples of video-recorded trials were randomly selected and both independent observers separately scored results on prepared forms to evaluate intentional choice-making. This process was carried out after, and separately from, the researcher's own scoring of video material. Agreement between observers of intentional choice-making was established using a randomly selected 20 per cent of the data.

The behaviour and the cases in the study were repeated for subjects during the trials, with consistent procedures and responses, indicating that the study can be replicated with good expectations of reliability in the method, while nevertheless still allowing for individual differences in presentations of songs.

Data analysis

All material in the study was videotaped and collected into observational data sheets. All data was viewed for intra-observer reliability both for dependent and independent reliability and resulted in 100 per cent accuracy. To ensure inter-observer reliability, 20 per cent of the data was randomly selected, observed and scored by an independent observer (a music therapist), which found 96 per cent inter-observer agreement with the researcher in the dependent variable reliability and 99 per cent inter-observer agreement in the independent variable reliability.

Results

Although this chapter's main focus is on the research design, I will add a short overview of the research findings, and then return to the main issue.

All participants in this study revealed lack of intentional choice-making during the baseline period (when no songs were sung), whereas when the intervention period was introduced (followed by periods of maintenance probes), they revealed a strong ability to choose songs then confirming their choice, demonstrating intentional choice-making. It is also apparent from the findings that these abilities are improving over time. Further investigation is warranted to determine whether these very positive results would generalise to the wider population.

The results suggest that music, and songs in particular, have an important role in revealing such potential in a population that until not long ago was thought of as uneducable, and with pre-intentional communication.

Considering the way this study was undertaken, these results also suggest that an attentive co-operative child, a good rapport between child and researcher, a familiar situation and strong motivational factors will facilitate such positive outcomes.

Response times decreased: the participants needed longer response time (up to 90 seconds) during the first three to four sessions, and thereafter their response time dropped to 15 seconds or less.

The reduction in response time was due to proper and meaningful interest (and as a result a proper response) achieved when a strong motivational factor such as music (songs) was used.

The findings suggest that with every intervention employed with this population a preliminary intensive acclimatisation period is needed (in this study three times per week over a two to three week period) before the achievement of a basic skill level for learning.

The participants demonstrated learning skills within the first set of songs and between the sets, showing a reduction of trials needed to reach the pre-established criterion. Learning was maintained throughout intervention and during maintenance, three months after the research had ended.

The research findings demonstrated that females with Rett syndrome as a group have discrete musical preferences (in this case song preference) and each child had clear individual likes and dislikes. Analysis of the song structure and its musical and non-musical elements revealed that there were very specific elements to the songs that attracted the participants. The preferred songs were typically familiar to the participants, had faster tempo than the less preferred songs, had tempo variability within the songs and included different vocal sounds and musical surprises.

This finding is important when trying to establish a child's individual preference to build a proper motivational factor list to ensure cooperation of the child in any activity calling for active participation.

An analysis of emotional, communicative and pathological behaviours at a qualitative level showed that there was an emergence of different types of response in certain types of songs and during baseline. Some positive responses were evident, which then tailed off accordingly when the songs were repeated too frequently.

The participants demonstrated various emotional, communicative and pathological responses that might be interpreted as understandable messages. Some behaviours were frequent and exhibited by all participants, while others were unique and personal.

The findings show that it is important to identify emotional responses and different behaviours that can be interpreted as communicative attempts by a familiar figure to the person, such as a caregiver or a family member. Recognition of these behaviours and understanding their intended meaning will increase shared understanding.

Overall, the participants were effectively choosing songs, responding appropriately to songs, demonstrating anticipation of elements and events in the songs and responding within normal response times (demonstrating learning skills), and the effects over time were significant in all cases.

Discussion of research design

The study investigated whether children's songs in music therapy enhanced communication skills in girls with Rett syndrome. A single-case, multiple-probe (multiple-baseline) design was applied to answer the research questions.

Multiple-probe, single-case design is not commonly used in music therapy research, and a discussion on this particular design and its adaptation in clinical research in music therapy, and specifically in the Rett syndrome population, is relevant to evaluate its reliability, validity and usefulness in its application here.

The multiple-probe design is commonly used in naturalistic environments such as classrooms with a population of people with developmental disability (Bambara *et al.* 1995; Hetzroni, Rubin and Konkiol 2002; Hetzroni and Schanin 1998; Hetzroni and Shalem 1998; Hughes, Pitkin and Lorden 1998; Nozaki and Mochizuki 1995; Sevcik *et al.* 1999). Multiple-probe, single-case design has also been used in studies attempting to establish communication in girls with Rett syndrome (Hetzroni *et al.* 2002; Koppenhaver *et al.* 2001; Sigafoos, Laurie and Pennell 1995, 1996).

The multiple-probe design, as a time-series design, is particularly appropriate when evaluating the effects of learning and its process, and this was one of the goals set forth for this study. The intermittent measurement (baseline probe) provided evidence of whether behaviour change had occurred prior to the intervention. This method analyses the interaction of the independent variable in treatment and control conditions, and enabled the researcher to identify both appropriate responses and learning over time when comparing results in the sequences of related sets of songs (Cooper *et al.* 1987). The design is a flexible one, enabling analysis of the effects of the independent variable across multiple behaviours and/or cases without withdrawing the treatment. The typical multiple-baseline design uses a very long baseline throughout the research, therefore interjecting probes during, in between and following the end of intervention sessions, at equal intervals, was found more appropriate in order to prevent interruption of the learning process and for the population under investigation.

The fact that the participants in this study demonstrated impatience during baseline and baseline probe sessions, manifested by 'protest behaviours' (such as: crying, shouting, pushing away picture symbols, closing eyes or turning their heads away), justified the use of multiple-probe design (over multiple baseline design).

An additional cause for employing multiple-probe design rather than the multiple-baseline design is that the Rett syndrome population typically has poor attention span and their ability to take part in a session longer than 30 minutes might be limited. During the research, the participants became exhausted when the baseline probes were applied to the sessions. These were done with limited frequency (every fourth session), whereas if the multiple-baseline design had been used, these baseline probes would have been applied throughout each session, possibly affecting the participants to a more serious degree in terms of their co-operation and hence affecting their performance potential.

Previous researchers have suggested that intentional communication with individuals with Rett syndrome should be investigated through multiple case studies. As this type of design allows for description and differentiation of intentional skills, group design may not be sensitive enough to the individual differences (Woodyatt and Ozanne 1993, 1994). The present study found the multiple-probe design to be most appropriate in collecting and enabling analysis of data concerning a Rett population's ability to communicate and use intentional choice making. This design has been found sensitive enough to differentiate individual abilities and variables.

In comparison to previous studies (Sigafoos *et al.* 1995; Hughes *et al.* 1998), which employed only one or two stimuli per trial (these were normally the actual objects rather than picture symbols), the present study used up to four stimuli picture symbols rather than objects. The evidence from this research supports the hypothesis that females with Rett syndrome can be presented and challenged with communicative demands more than had been previously anticipated. It could be suggested that the particular attraction of songs and music could demonstrate a higher potential for communication in the wider population of females with Rett syndrome, if further research studies repeat replicable findings.

Sigafoos *et al.* (1996) discussed the limitations of their research design in terms of the lack of maintenance and generalisation. In this study the first of these limitations was addressed by intermittently administering maintenance probes, after the intervention of each set was terminated. Maintenance sessions were applied at the end of the investigation as well. The maintenance sessions were performed after two week, four week and six week intervals, and have summed up to a total of three months after the investigation was terminated. Adding maintenance sessions to the end of the research (as suggested by Sigafoos *et al.* 1996) was found most important in establishing the process of learning and its sustainability over time.

Single-case design is a suitable design for the therapist, as it stays close to the practice of the therapist (D. Aldridge 1996). The present study, a single-case design, had the flavour of therapy sessions. It took place in a natural environment, in a known setting, and in a situation familiar to the participants and the researcher. When taking into account the difficulty the Rett syndrome population has in acclimatising to new places, people and situations, it was believed that the success they demonstrated was as a result of the familiar setting, familiar therapist and familiar materials. The familiar situation may have reduced the effects of unexplainable influencing variables, and enabled the participants to focus on the task, freeing the researcher to focus on the goals of the research.

It also has to be argued that the familiarity of this situation might have contributed to the effect of the treatment, and one should not assume that the same effect could be achieved in different circumstances. A new therapist, or a change in the songs presented or even a new setting could influence the effect of treatment. The present study had a concept of process behind it so that the participants could benefit from the actual learning experience with the intention of later applying it to other situations during their daily lives.

Some ethical issues of the design should be considered in future studies. During baseline, when no songs were sung in response to the participants' choice-making, the participants on occasions seemed confused, upset, bored or angry. During the interventions, a song followed the participants' choice immediately. They became frequently puzzled and confused, when baseline probes (with no music) were introduced during intervention. These baseline probes may have provoked a feeling of failure, as they were being sustained concurrently with the interventions and the process of the intervention was disrupted at the periodic probe measures throughout the intervention. Sessions became very long and dissatisfying during baseline when no music was applied. They also became very long when baseline probes were applied in the intervention sessions, as well as during maintenance sessions, when all three sets were used. However, this was due to the fact that this researcher decided to include three sets and eighteen songs (six songs in each set) in order to be certain that intentional choice-making was not a coincidence in one or two sets, but in three sets with different songs. On the other hand, the negative effect of the baseline probes was inevitable, and this fortifies the efficacy of the intervention.

It is recommended that in order to avoid long baselines and sessions, fewer songs or sets may be administered in future research, providing a larger sample is used.

Conclusion

The present study found the multiple-probe design (a research tool not frequently used in music therapy) to be most appropriate in collecting and allowing systematic analysis effects over time. This design has also proved to be efficient in determining the ability of the participants (females with Rett syndrome) to acquire and sustain choice-making skills. Moreover, this design has been found sensitive enough to differentiate individual abilities and variables and was especially suited for evaluating whether ability was sustained following periods of no intervention. It is my view that the flexibility of this design makes it susceptible to music therapy situations both in research and as a practical tool to organise and measure intervention with children with developmental disabilities.

This chapter summarises a research project process from its initial stage of forming the basic hypothesis until its completion. The reader can relate to the materials through different perspectives. It could be conceived as a description of a project in the making, serving as an example for future researchers. On the other hand, a therapist looking to cross the lines into the realm of research can find some helpful hints and pointers in the above writings. A third possibility is that someone interested in Rett syndrome (or in developmental disabilities as a whole) might find this chapter a starting point towards an organised intervention program. All the above possibilities are welcome in the hope that other children might gain from the knowledge that has been collected by so many devoted practitioners and researchers and summarised by myself.

CHAPTER 8

Music and Sound Vibration: Testing Hypotheses as a Series of Case Studies

Tony Wigram

Research is a process of discovery. The knowledge gained from one study quite typically presents a new set of questions that need to be addressed in consequent studies. The process is continuous. Each study becomes a new link in a chain of knowledge building that is aimed at defining and refining our scientific framework for academic study. Music therapy researchers typically focus on applied research. Questions or hypotheses that drive their research arise out of assumptions (or even gut feelings) in clinical work where experience over many years has revealed apparently consistent and reliable effects of therapy. Music therapy research is frequently built upon the findings and conclusions from a series of clinical anecdotes, examples or reports. Consequently, the formulation and exploration of aspects of clinical work relating to specific questions has provided the main motivation for investigation.

This chapter is concerned with just such a series of experiments, undertaken for a doctoral thesis (Wigram 1996), that were founded on assumptions, clinical experiences and anecdotal reports or research findings previously documented in the field of vibroacoustics (Chesky 1992; Chesky and Michel 1991; Lehikoinen 1988; Madsen, Standley and Gregory 1991; Skille 1982, 1986, 1989a, 1989b, 1992; Skille and Wigram 1995; Wigram and Weekes 1989; Wigram 1993, 1995).

The author had been working for several years in a large long-stay hospital for people with severe learning disability and multiple handicaps, using music primarily as an active and interactive tool within the improvisational model of music therapy typical in Europe. The potential for using vibroacoustic therapy as a receptive tool was ripe for exploration and this chapter will document the sequence of studies that were undertaken, defining them as a series of case examples where the findings from one study raised questions leading to the subsequent studies.

Research into vibroacoustic therapy began after a period of pioneer development when clinicians and other professionals exploring the effects of music vibration and sound vibration reported positive effects on a variety of physical disabilities and psychological problems. Music was already being used effectively in medical procedures (Dileo 1999; Spintge 1982; Spintge and Droh 1982; Standley 1995) and evidence had been presented documenting reductions in pain (Brown, Chen and Dworkin 1991; Chesky 1992; Chesky and Michel 1991; Curtis 1986), stress (Maranto 1994) and to meet emotional needs (Bonny 1976; Clark 1991; Goldberg 1995). Vibroacoustic (VA) therapy as developed in Norway and England is a treatment where a combination of relaxing music and pulsed, sinusoidal low frequency tones ranging from 25Hz–75Hz is transmitted through bass speakers built into a bed or chair, upon which a patient sits or lies, usually supine. This method was developed during the early 1980s by Olav Skille, a Norwegian headteacher of a school for children with multiple handicaps.

The anecdotal evidence from Skille's clinical trials reported a variety of beneficial effects on muscle-tone, heartrate and general well-being (Skille 1989). He documented a number of reports on his clinical experiences with a wide variety of mental and physical disabilities or disorders. As well as describing the physically relaxing effects of vibrational sound therapy on children and adolescents with high muscle-tone and severe spasticity, he also explored its effects on people with pulmonary disorders such as asthma, cystic fibrosis, pulmonary emphysema, general physical ailments such as ulcers, poor circulation and post-operative convalescence and even psychological disorders with somatic effects such as insomnia, anxiety, self-injurious behaviour, autism, depression and stress (Skille 1992).

The original foundation for some of the research studies described in this chapter was Skille's anecdotal reports of the relaxant effect of vibrational stimuli on people with high muscle-tone and spasticity, and suggestions from his experiments that different frequencies have resonant effects on different parts of the body (Skille 1982, 1989a, 1989b, 1992). This formed the main inspiration for the sequence of studies that are presented here as a series of 'case examples'. Both direct and related research from other fields provided some theoretical support and credence to VA therapy as a potentially effective intervention for some disorders or illnesses. Standley (1991) found that finger temperature (an indication of deeper relaxation) increased significantly in the presence of vibrotactile and auditory stimuli. Darrow and Gohl (1989) reported that children with hearing impairments identified rhythmic changes more successfully when auditory stimuli were paired with vibratory stimuli than when they were presented alone.

There were also results which showed no particular benefit. Madsen, Standley and Gregory (1991) found no significant differences between groups in physical behaviour in trials of college students, and no significant changes were found in subjects' respiration, pulse or behaviourally observed relaxation in another study by Pujol (1994). Therefore, as Hodges had already reported in a review of more than 21 studies, we find inconsistent and contradictory results when looking at the effects of music generally on physiological parameters (Hodges 1980).

The theoretical foundation for research into the effects of music vibration and sound vibration is underpinned by general research on the effects of vibration, low frequency sound and infrasound. A substantial amount of work had already been undertaken in collating this material between 1983 and 1985 by the Forsvarets Materiel Verk (FMV) of the Swedish Defence Material Administration, who established an inclusive bibliography and summary of articles on low frequency sound and infrasound (Forsvarets Materiel Verk 1985). Many of the research studies documented work exploring the physical effects of vibration (Berglund and Berglund 1970; Hagbarth and Eklund 1968; Wedell and Cummings 1938). Specific applications of vibration for its use as a tool in physiotherapy were underpinned by the work of Stillman (1970) who advocated the use of vibratory motor simulation and promoted the development of vibratory massage. This was further developed by Carrington (1980) and Boakes (1990) in the fields of physiotherapy and occupational therapy. Boakes looked in particular at the effects on muscle physiology via muscle receptors and advocated that vibration within the range of 20Hz–50Hz causes an inhibition of muscle impulses, so inducing muscles with degrees of spasticity to relax. She further describes the effects of vibrational frequencies within the range of 50Hz–100Hz as stimulating most tonic vibratory reflex impulses, inducing muscles to contract and therefore causing antagonist muscles to relax, which is of great benefit to those who have spasticity.

Therefore, research in the fields of vibration and in the applied clinical use of vibration supported the potential for sound generated vibration as a treatment. In addition, research on the effects of infrasound and low frequency sound had been undertaken on a very wide scale, looking at its influence on the environment, in everyday situations, and the potential problems it can cause where very high levels were recorded (Bryan and Tempest 1972; Englund et al. 1978; Møller 1984; Von Gierke and Nixon 1976). Griffin (1983) reported the negative effects of low frequency vibration as a general discomfort and annoyance, interference with activities and potential to produce motion sickness. Many of the studies undertaken on the effects of vibration, low frequency sound and infrasound had explored and reported discomfort and detrimental effects. Consequently, the application of sound as a 'treatment' to alleviate or reduce physical problems or disabilities had not been considered until the early 1980s when some of the pioneers began to use sound vibration as a physical treatment (Chesky 1992; Chesky and Michel 1991; Skille 1992; Wigram 1993, 1995). At the same time, a small number of pioneers in the fields of physiotherapy and occupational therapy were applying whole body vibration using mechanical stimuli, also for the purposes of reducing muscle-tone (Boakes 1990).

A combination of low frequency sound vibration used together with different forms of music was seen as a new approach with potential for a wide field of application, once efficacy and effectiveness could be demonstrated. Current practice, following such research, shows that VA therapy is a systematic form of intervention requiring a therapeutic relationship between therapist and patient, and involves musical experiences, thus meeting Bruscia's (1998) criteria for definition as a form of music therapy. Comprehensive reviews describing the equipment to be used, treatment indications and contraindications, and collected clinical reports and research studies can be found in Hooper (2001), Wigram (1997b) and Wigram and Dileo (1997a, 1997b). The anecdotal results from empirical investigations in the early to middle 1980s led to a series of experimental studies.

Table 8.1 shows the sequence of studies that were undertaken in order, defining the area of investigation, the subjects that were involved in the study and briefly, the method that was used.

VA therapy for people with multiple handicaps

This first study focuses on the effect of VA therapy in reducing muscle-tone in patients with spasticity. Cerebral palsy is caused as a result of an injury to a part of the brain before it is fully developed. The three main types of cerebral palsy are spasticity, athetosis and ataxia. The patients in this study suffer from spastic disorders. People with spasticity have different levels of muscle spasm, causing a rigidity of the muscles. A spasm is an involuntary and sometimes painful contraction of the muscle, muscle group or of the muscle wall of a hollow organ. Spasms of the whole body are referred to as convulsions, painful spasms of muscles or limbs as cramp, and those in the stomach and abdomen as colic. In cerebral palsied patients the most common form of spasm is a tonic spasm involving a firm strong contraction causing rigidity in the muscles.

Table 8.1 Six experimental studies in VA therapy with clinical and non-clinical subjects		
Study	*n=*	*Research focus and method*
1	10	A study investigating reduction in muscle-tone, blood pressure and heartrate in patients with high muscle-tone, quadriplegic cerebral palsy and severe learning difficulties. Comparison of treatment with placebo conditions in a within-subjects, repeated measures design.
2	27	A follow-up study investigating reduction in muscle-tone, blood pressure and heartrate in patients with high muscle-tone, quadriplegic cerebral palsy and severe learning difficulties. Comparison of treatment with placebo and control conditions in a within-subjects, repeated measures design.
3	39	A study investigating non-clinical subjects reported perception of a sensation of vibration in their bodies when presented with ten different low frequency tones between 20Hz–70Hz.
4	52	A follow-up study investigating non-clinical subjects' reported perception of a sensation of vibration in their bodies when presented with 20 different low frequency tones between 20Hz–70Hz.
5	60	A study investigating changes in non-clinical subjects' level of arousal, heartrate and blood pressure to VA therapy when compared with a placebo and control conditions, employing a between groups design.
6	60	A study investigating changes in non-clinical subjects' level of arousal, heartrate and blood pressure to three different rates of amplitude modulation of a 40Hz sinusoidal tone, and a constant tone, employing a between groups design.

Source: Wigram (1996)

Patients with spasticity are usually found to have:

1. a loss of control and differentiation of fine voluntary movements

2. suppression of normal associated movements

3. presence of certain normal associated movements

4. hypertonus of the 'clasp knife' type, with a following build-up of resistance to passive movement (stretch reflex)

5. exaggerated tendon reflexes and possible clones of the other joints

6. depression of superficial reflexes.

More typically, in spastic patients, we find an increase in flexor tone and this is often greater than extensor tone. Imbalances in the strength of muscles lead to contracture of spastic muscles, and weakness resulting from disuse of their opponents (Jones 1975).

Research into the effects of background music to assist relaxation in cerebral palsied adults with spasticity shows significantly improved decreases in muscle tension (Scartelli 1982). A placebo group of patients receiving EMG Bio-Feedback alone showed a mean decrease of 32.5% in muscle tension, whereas a treatment group receiving EMG Bio-Feedback training together with sedative background music demonstrated a mean decrease of 65%.

Study 1

For this first study, a repeated measures within-subjects design was used. Ten subjects were selected to take part in the experiment, which tested the hypothesis that sedative music, in combination with a pulsed low frequency sinusoidal tone of 44Hz, would have a greater effect in reducing muscle-tone in cerebral palsied subjects than sedative music alone. The two experimental conditions were a 30 minute treatment on the vibroacoustic unit, which consisted of a tape of sedative music, and a pulsed 44Hz low frequency sinusoidal tone (condition A), and the same sedative music presented without the pulsed, low frequency tone (condition B).

The 44Hz low frequency sinusoidal tone acted as an independent variable. Each subject undertook six trials in each condition, randomly ordered. The subjects undertook two trials each week over a period of six weeks. Changes in range of movement were measured on spinal mobility and limb flexion and extension using a centimetre ruler/measure to record the range of movement before and after each trial. The experiment was designed as a within-subjects study with single blind evaluation. The experiment evaluated the influence of VA therapy treatment consisting of relaxing music and a pulsed, sinusoidal low frequency tone, compared with the same music played through the vibroacoustic unit without a pulsed sinusoidal low frequency tone.

The subjects were three male and seven female subjects resident in a large hospital for people with moderate to severe learning disability. Ages ranged from 28 to 77 years (Mean 44.2, S.D. 12.39), and they were all diagnosed as profoundly handicapped. All had measurably high muscle-tone that affected each of them in differing ways, although there were some affected muscle groups that were shared in common by all. The most common problems were flexor-spasm in their arms and legs, and adductor-spasm causing difficulties in separation of the legs, which in turn can lead to 'scissoring' of the legs.

The equipment used in this experiment was purpose-built. The frame of a sprung bed was used, and two 18 inch speakers were mounted in boxes underneath the springs, with the cones directed upwards. The speaker boxes contained two inch by eight inch ports for acoustic balance, and the cone of each speaker was approximately two inches below the springs of the bed so that the subject would be lying within two inches of the surface of the speakers.

The speakers were so positioned in the bed that, when the subject lay on the bed, one speaker was placed under the thoracic and upper abdominal area of their body and the other speaker was placed under the lower thighs, knees and upper calves. On top of the springs was a single polythene sheet (as a precaution against incontinence), and on top of this was a half-inch pile sheepskin rug.

The speakers were powered by an Amba-414 purpose built amplifier. The maximum potential output from the amplifier was 80 watts per channel (RMS). A vibroacoustic stimulus of relaxing music combined with a pulsed, sinusoidal, low frequency sound wave, and the music in condition B was played through a Technics RS-T11 stereo cassette deck.

Intensity and tone controls on the amplifier were graded numerically. In the procedure of this experiment, the controls of master volume and bass volume were consistently set at the same point. When the subjects were treated with low frequency sounds and music, the bass and master volume was set at +7 on the numerical scale. When the clients were treated with music alone, the master volume was set at +7, and the bass and treble tone controls were set at zero ensuring that an equal balance of tone and equivalent volume was maintained in the music-only condition. The subjects were treated horizontally, and the speakers were set into the bed with the cones facing up. The equipment was isolated electrically, and recordings were used so the style of music, intensity of the low frequency tone and general intensity of the music were all constant for each trial.

A marker pen was used to mark points on the subjects' bodies for measurement, and a conventional cloth tape-measure with centimetre markings was used to record the range of movement before and after each trial. The music used in both conditions was 'Crystal Caverns' by Daniel Kobialka. This music is described as 'New Age', and is tonal, melodic and harmonic non-pulsed music produced on a synthesizer. The piece lasted 30 minutes, and a 44Hz sinusoidal tone, pulsing at a speed of approximately eight seconds peak to peak was recorded from a function generator with the music on the tape.

Table 8.2 defines the nine measures that were used to evaluate improvement in range of movement. Due to differences between subjects, not all nine measures were used for each subject, as can be seen in Table 8.3.

Trial number	Measurement	Purpose of measurement
Table 8.2 Physical measurements taken before and after each trial		
1	The extreme point of the left shoulder to the extreme point of the right shoulder	To measure rounded shoulders
2	The extreme point of the right shoulder to the right radial artery	To measure extension of the right arm
3	The extreme point of the left shoulder to the left radial artery	To measure extension of the left arm
4	The right elbow to the right seventh rib	To measure raising the right elbow from the body
5	The left elbow to the left seventh rib	To measure raising the left elbow from the body
6	The tip of the nose to the navel	To measure degree of kyphosis
7	The right side greater trochanter to the right side lateral malleolus	To measure extension of the right leg
8	The left side greater trochanter to the left side lateral malleolus	To measure extension of the left leg
9	The centre base of the right patella to the centre base of the left patella	To measure abduction of the hips.

Baseline measurements were taken of the minimum range of movement. Then measurements were taken of the degree of extension for each of these movements before and after each trial. Each subject had a different set of measurements, although there were some measurements that were common to many of the subjects. The measurements were normalised into percentages, and a calculation then made of the subject's percentage improvement in range of movement in each of the conditions.

Before and after each trial an independent evaluator (who was not present during the trial) measured the maximum possible extended range between each of the two marked points in each measurement (blind evaluation).

Measures	1	2	3	4	5	6	7	8	9	Means
Table 8.3 Mean scores of increased or decreased range of movement within minimum and maximum ranges, shown as percentage scores for both conditions										
Score 1:										
Condition 1		+8	+3				+5	+4	+14	+7
Condition 2		−4	−1				−6	−1	−4	−3
Score 2:										
Condition 1		+15	+23						+27	+22
Condition 2		−5	−2						−2	−3
Score 3:										
Condition 1		+11	+15				+22	+5		+13
Condition 2		+0.5	−1				+5	0		+1
Score 4:										
Condition 1		+16	+21	+27					+11	+19
Condition 2		−13	−3	−0.5					+0.5	−4
Score 5:										
Condition 1	+4			+16	+25					+15
Condition 2	−8			+7	+10					+3
Score 6:										
Condition 1			+1				+1	+2	+26	+7
Condition 2			+3				+0.5	+1	+5	+2
Score 7:										
Condition 1		+11	+1					+1		+5
Condition 2		+4	+1					+2		+2
Score 8:										
Condition 1		+20	+10							+15
Condition 2		+2	+5							+4
Score 9:										
Condition 1	+32	+22	+9				+9	+12	+31	+19
Condition 2	0	−0.5	+0.5				+6	+0.5	−1	+1
Score 10:										
Condition 1			+3			+27	+5	+21	+17	+11
Condition 2			+2			+16	−0.5	+1	+3	+4

Table 8.3 gives the mean scores in percentages of increases or decreases in range of movement within a minimum and maximum range. In the box on the extreme right are the means of all the measurement means for each subject. The means of all the scores of the subjects are shown in the box in the bottom right hand corner of the table, and show a 13% improvement in their range of movement in the treatment condition and 1% improvement in the placebo condition. A Wilcoxon Matched-Pairs Signed-Ranks test on the mean percentage improvement in range of movement within the subjects comparing the treatment and placebo conditions found a significant difference between conditions ($P = 0.0051$) indicating that the treatment achieved significantly greater range of movement in the subjects than did the placebo.

This result appeared to support the anecdotal findings of Skille and others, and provided some evidence of the effects of vibroacoustic therapy in reducing muscle-tone, albeit with a small group of subjects (Wigram 1995; Wigram, McNaught and Cain 1997). From the point of view of the clinicians involved in day to day treatment of these clients, it demonstrated that the influence of low frequency sound was significant and led to a discussion about the value of VA therapy as an independent and effective treatment, given that the population from whom the subjects for these trials were recruited typically need regular and intensive therapy. This, in turn, raised questions about the relative efficacy of VA Therapy when compared with other treatments (physiotherapy, music and movement) that were designed to achieve a similar outcome – namely the improvement (or at least main-tenance) of range of movement in clients with spasticity, and the prevention of the onset of fixed flexion deformities. Therefore, the next 'case' in this sequence of experimental studies is where another, quite different form of treatment, Music and Movement Based Physiotherapy (MMBP) was included as a third condition. Here, active movement to live music is the treatment modality by which range of movement is maintained.

Study 2

A second research hypothesis was formulated, following on from the first exper-iment:

> VA therapy would have a significantly greater effect in improving range of movement than music and movement or a placebo.

> MMBP treatment would have a significantly greater effect in improving range of movement than a placebo.

The movement and music treatment used in this second case was developed over many years (Wigram and Weekes 1983, 1985). Clinical experience has already suggested that patients respond positively to MMBP treatment, and it has benefits for the health and well being of the patients. However, undertaking such treatments is very labour intensive, and the patients need a daily or twice daily session in order to prevent the onset of fixed flexion deformities that come as a result of lack of movement and increasing contracture both in muscle activity and joint movements.

Each subject was given only one trial in each condition, with the intention of reducing or eliminating bias due to inconsistent development of patient/therapist relationships between the subjects and the staff involved in the trials. However, in order to take into consideration the fact that unfamiliarity with the treatment being administered might play an important role, three more trials were held in both the VA therapy treatment condition and the placebo condition with a randomly selected group of patients from the test group. This experiment employed a repeated measures design across three experimental conditions (the two experimental conditions already described above (A and B) and thirty minutes of MMBP (condition C).

In all the three conditions the subjects were treated lying down, either on a bed, or on a mat on the floor. The MMBP treatment session was conducted by music therapists, physiotherapists, teachers and therapy/education assistants on a one-to-one basis with the subjects. The subjects were treated on mats on the floor and the music was created live on the piano for each session. The same music was used for each of the exercises, and for consistently the same amount of time.

Measurements were taken before and after each trial of the subjects' range of movement. Evaluators were blind as to whether the subjects were receiving VA therapy (condition A) or a placebo treatment (condition B). They were not blind during the MMBP trials (condition C), and were aware the subjects were receiving this form of treatment. An element of bias was inevitably present for the evaluators in making their measurements before and after the MMBP trials. The additional trials were undertaken using ten subjects, randomly selected from the group of twenty-seven. Each subject was given an additional three trials of VA therapy (condition A) and three trials of the placebo treatment (condition B). Measurements were carried out in the same way as in the other trials. Fourteen male and thirteen female subjects resident in a large hospital for the mentally handicapped were chosen to take part in the trials. The subjects' ages ranged from 24 to 68 years and their level of functioning ranged from severely to profoundly handicapped. All the subjects had high muscle-tone which affected each of them in individually differing ways, although there were some affected muscle groups that were shared by all of the subjects.

The mean age of the male subjects was 46 and the mean age of the female subjects 39. The mean age of the 28 subjects was 41.04 (S.D. 13.01). The VA therapy equipment, music, low-frequency stimulus and measuring equipment used in these trials were the same as was used in the experiments described in the previous chapter. In all three conditions, measurements were taken measuring range of movement in limbs and hips of the subjects before and after each trial using the same procedures as in the first experiment. The MMBP consisted of a fixed sequence of movements working through the body. The type of movement, duration, and style of music used is described in Table 8.4.

Table 8.4 Music and Movement Based Physiotherapy programme

Movement	Time of movement	Music played
Spinal rotation (right)	3	'Can't Help Lovin' Dat Man' from *Showboat*
Hip extension (right)	2	Main theme from *The Godfather*
Shoulder girdle (supine)	4	'Humoresque' by Dvorak (fast then slow)
Arms – right arm	3	'Mary, Mary, Quite Contrary'
Left arm	3	'Mary, Mary, Quite Contrary'
Short break (3 minutes)		
Spinal rotation (left)		'Can't Help Lovin' Dat Man' from *Showboat*
Hip extension (left)	3	Main theme from *The Godfather*
Bouncy legs (supine)	2	'Can-Can' from *Orpheus in the Underworld*
Flexion and extension of legs (supine)	4	'Edelweiss' from *The Sound of Music*
Abduction (supine)	4	'Over the Sea to Skye', folk traditional

Subjects were treated in groups of approximately six to seven at a time. It was recognised that this was different from the individual trials in conditions A and B, and would add additional influencing variables.

Table 8.5 shows the means from measurements taken for each subject, and the changes in their range of movement in percentages over the three experimental conditions. In the right column the condition in which the greatest improvement that was achieved by each subject is indicated. This showed that 12 subjects improved most in condition A, 4 subjects in condition B and 11 subjects in condition C.

Subject	Condition A (VA therapy)	Condition B (placebo)	Condition C (MMBP)	Optimum condition
1	+2.50	−1.37	+1.02	A
2	+1.11	+3.40	+10.58	C
3	+9.00	−4.67	+3.64	A
4	−5.16	−0.90	+5.89	C
5	+2.47	+5.21	−4.15	B
6	+14.31	+9.61	+13.46	A
7	+10.63	+27.65	+63.82	C
8	+4.17	+22.82	+11.07	B
9	+10.93	−0.59	+12.10	C
10	+4.43	+7.92	+7.25	B
11	0.00	−3.12	+10.93	C
12	+2.37	+6.48	+3.88	B
13	+9.09	+12.38	+26.96	C
14	+17.84	+7.86	+18.50	C
15	+19.76	+5.55	+14.80	A
16	+1.46	−4.82	+4.60	C

Table 8.5 Mean percentage improvements of change in range of movement

Continued on next page

Table 8.5 continued

Subject	Condition A (VA therapy)	Condition B (placebo)	Condition C (MMBP)	Optimum condition
17	−5.21	+1.84	+13.39	C
18	+4.17	−5.41	−9.93	A
19	+17.58	0.00	+3.29	A
20	+9.83	+9.07	+9.08	A
21	+8.95	−3.52	+4.42	A
22	+8.40	−2.06	+4.24	A
23	+9.29	+5.93	−0.15	A
24	+9.96	+2.08	+0.49	A
25	+31.47	+23.00	+20.49	A
26	+12.48	+0.99	+15.24	C
27	+3.44	−34.48	+6.89	C

Table 8.6 reveals the mean percentage improvement and standard deviations for all the subjects in all three conditions. A Friedman 2-Way Anova found no overall difference between conditions (P=0.1054). To look at comparisons between the conditions, orthogonal planned comparisons were undertaken by partitioning the Friedman Chi square comparing condition A with condition C, and condition A and C with condition B. No significant difference was found between VA therapy (condition A) and MMBP treatment (condition C) (Chi squared=0.1, ns). A significant difference was found when comparing the two treatment conditions combined (A + C) with the placebo condition (B) (Chi squared=5.3, p 0.05). There was a significantly greater range of movement in the subjects following the treatment conditions than was achieved in the placebo condition. In the additional trials that were undertaken with ten randomly selected subjects from the sample, a significant difference was found when comparing the mean scores from three additional VA therapy trials (A) with three additional placebo trials (B) (Wilcoxon non-parametric signed-ranks test P=0.0051). The subjects had consistently greater range of movement when treated with VA therapy than when they were given the placebo treatment.

Table 8.6 Mean percentage improvement in range of movement in all three conditions (and standard deviations)			
Condition	VA therapy (A)	Placebo (B)	MMBP (C)
Mean improvement (S.D.)	+7.95% (7.88)	+3.36% (11.45)	+9.26%(13.86)

This outcome was interesting as the results did not support the hypothesis that VA therapy would have a greater effect in improving range of movement when compared with MMBP treatment, although both treatment conditions proved significantly more effective than the placebo. So in clinical application, this second 'case' helped place the value of VA therapy when compared with another, quite different treatment. Approaching this from a clinical perspective, one can understand that there is no one treatment that works better than all others for each and every client.

Having established the value of VA therapy in the first case, this second case illustrates the differences one finds in individual response, and the importance of recognising that. Knowledge of this population suggests that while some respond better to active treatment, and appear uneasy and less responsive to a receptive and non-interactional intervention, for others the opposite is true. So the fund of research evidence supporting VA therapy, and placing it in context is already growing. This study also revealed that both MMBP treatment and VA therapy achieve significantly larger improvements in range of movement than a placebo treatment, and the additional trials confirmed that VA therapy was consistently and significantly more effective than a placebo, suggesting the importance of familiarity with treatment (which was not evaluated with MMBP).

Perceived location of sensations of vibration in the body in non-clinical subjects

Questions emerged concerning the way people experience the sensation of vibration in their body and if the population of clients with severe spasticity to varying degrees in their body might be differentially affected by different frequencies, how this would influence intervention programs. Early reports had indicated that when subjected to low frequency sound, people felt localised resonant vibrational effects in different areas in their body (Skille 1982). Some anecdotal reports on infrasonic and low frequency vibration had located this sensation of vibration in the solar plexus, the stomach and the abdomen (Teirich 1959), while other reports had indicated that sensations of vibration from frequencies between 30Hz and 80Hz were perceived in different parts of the body when the frequencies were changed, explaining this through the principles of sympathetic resonance (Skille 1982; Skille and Wigram 1995; Yamada *et al.* 1983).

Dependent on the density and structure of a solid mass, it will resonate to different frequencies. In so far as the body is a mass consisting of 70% water, but with different densities depending on bone structure, cavities and the variety of soft and hard tissue, one would expect sympathetic resonance to sound to be variable. In much the same way as an operatic soprano singing a high-pitched note can shatter a wine glass, frequencies are felt as a vibration on the surface of the body and inside the body. It is this effect of internal vibration that is believed to be important and significant in the application of VA therapy. If specific frequencies can be used in the application of treatment to certain parts of the body which may be affected in a pathological way, the treatment becomes more applicable in targeting specific problems.

The new question that now needed addressing, and takes us on to the third and fourth 'cases' in this research process, was whether within a very small frequency band of 20Hz–70Hz, there were differences in the location of a sensation of resonant vibration in the body, and any consistency in subjects perception of those sensations.

Study 3

For this third case, the following hypotheses were then generated:

- Low frequency sinusoidal tones between 20Hz and 70Hz played for a period of ten to twelve seconds, will be felt as a resonant vibration in different parts of the human body.

- The sensation of vibration will be consistently felt in the same place in the body when a frequency is played more than once.

A total of 14 male and 25 female subjects (n=39) were recruited from professional people working in the hospital ranging in age from 21 to 37, and each subject had a short 10-minute trial in which a range of frequencies were presented to them through the speakers of a vibroacoustic bed on which they were lying. The equipment used was the same as that described in the first two cases.

A sequence of pure sinusoidal tones between 20Hz and 70Hz were generated in a specific order which was kept constant for each subject. The order of the frequencies presented was as follows: 40, 50, 60, 70, 50, 40, 30, 20, 40. Subjects verbally identified where they felt the stimulus in their bodies, and these were subsequently coded into nine general sites: feet – calves – thighs – sacrum – lumbar – thoracic – cervical – shoulder – head. Each frequency was played for 12 seconds, during which time the subject was asked to identify where they felt the sensation of vibration. Volume controls on the equipment were preset to the same point for all trials.

Table 8.7 shows the localised sensation of vibration of these different frequencies when body sites are grouped together. Each time 40Hz was played this frequency was felt in the legs, calves and thighs. 30Hz shared a similar effect. As the frequency moved up through 50Hz, 60Hz and 70Hz, so the subjects consistently indicated the location of the sensation of vibration was further up their body, with typical experiences of 60Hz being felt in the thoracic region, and 70Hz in the upper chest and head. There appeared to be some consistency in the sensation of vibration felt at 30Hz and 40Hz.

Table 8.7 Location of sensation of vibration in percentages for each frequency in the trials

Frequency	Presentation	Localised area	%
40Hz	1	Calves, thighs	77
50Hz	1	Thighs, sacrum and lumbar	61.5
60Hz	1	Sacrum, lumbar and thoracic	66.6
70Hz	1	Lumbar, thoracic, cervical and shoulder	69.2
50Hz	2	Thighs, sacrum, lumbar	59
40Hz	2	Calves, thighs	77
30Hz	1	Calves, thighs	74.3
20Hz	1	Calves, thighs, sacrum, lumbar	79
40Hz	3	Calves, thighs	77

The results here seem consistent, and there were quite a high proportion of subjects reporting sensations to specific frequencies in consistently the same place. However, the method of presentation was somewhat crude and the single sequence of frequencies not comprehensive. Due to the variability present in these trials, it seemed a good idea to repeat the experiment in a more comprehensive way to explore the reporting of not just one location of the sensation in vibration but maybe a secondary site where vibration is felt.

Study 4

Given a more complex and extensive presentation of frequencies, the following hypotheses were generated:

- A high proportion of subjects will feel a sensation of vibration to the same frequencies in the same areas of their body.

- When frequencies are presented a number of times, subjects will consistently locate a sensation of vibration to that frequency in the same area of their body.

Each subject in these trials received four presentations of 30Hz, 40Hz, 50Hz and 60Hz, and two presentations of 20Hz and 70Hz. Each subject undertook a trial which lasted 10 minutes, during which the total number of 20 frequencies were presented to them and they were asked to identify where they felt the strongest sensation of vibration in their body.

This time, 26 male and 26 female subjects (n=52) ranging in age from 19 to 60 were recruited from staff and students at Harperbury Hospital, England. They all attended for one trial and were randomly assigned to two groups, with equal numbers of male and female subjects in each group. Four different sequences of frequencies between 20Hz and 70Hz were recorded on audiotape presented in a random order. Group 1 received Sequence 1, followed after a pause of ten seconds by Sequence 2. Group 2 received Sequence 3, followed after a ten-second pause by Sequence 4. The sequences of frequencies that were used will be described in the next section. Forms were devised for each sequence in which the following areas of the body were defined: feet – ankles – calves – knees – thighs – sacrum – lumbar – thoracic – shoulders – neck – head – arms – hands.

It was anticipated that subjects might not only identify a primary area where they felt the vibration but would also experience secondary areas in the body where they also felt a sensation of vibration. The sequence of frequencies were placed on the x-axis, and the areas of the body on the y-axis. When the subject reported a primary sensation of vibration, a '1' was placed in the box corresponding to the frequency and the part of the body the subject identified. When asked to identify a secondary site, a '2' was placed in the relevant box. In the event that the subject described a general sensation of vibration, a wavy line was drawn down the column to cover all these areas. In the event the client reported no sensation of vibration, the column was left blank. At the bottom of the form a dislike box was included, and during the course of the trials the subjects were asked to indicate which frequencies they disliked, and this was recorded in these boxes. The form also recorded data on the gender, date of birth, weight and height of the subjects.

The data collected in this study revealed that subjects can experience a sensation of vibration in their body, and can describe the area where they experience the stronger sensations of vibration. The most effective way of presenting the substantial amount of data was to tabulate the number of subjects reporting a sensation of vibration in each part of their body for each frequency and look for consistency of the perception of vibration between subjects, and within subjects. During the trials, a total of 13 body sites were listed on the form in order to record as accurately as possible where subjects identified a sensation of vibration.

Table 8.8 Mean scores for primary sites in percentages						
	20Hz	*30Hz*	*40Hz*	*50Hz*	*60Hz*	*70Hz*
No effect	1.9	2.4	1.4	1.9	1.9	3.8
Feet	8.6	1.8	0.5	2.4	4.3	3.8
Ankles	6.7	7.7	1.4	0.5	3.3	1.0
Calves	5.7	10.0	20.2	7.7	6.3	2.9
Knees	7.7	5.7	9.6	10.6	3.8	1.9
Thighs	7.7	12.0	15.4	12.5	6.2	7.7
Sacrum/pelvis	4.1	13.4	8.5	17.3	5.3	2.9
Lumbar/abdomen	7.7	10.5	7.2	16.6	11.0	8.6
Thoracic	1.0	5.3	7.6	7.2	19.7	12.5
Shoulders	3.8	10.5	4.2	5.3	7.2	11.5
Neck	1.9	2.4	2.3	0.0	4.3	11.5
Head	1.9	7.2	8.6	5.8	11.0	19.2
Arms	1.0	0.0	0.5	0.0	0.5	1.9
Hands	2.9	1.0	0.5	1.4	2.4	1.9
General effect	17.4	10.5	12.5	10.6	12.5	3.9

Table 8.8. shows in percentages the number of subjects describing a primary sensation of vibration distributed over the 13 sites on the body in mean scores from the six presented frequencies. This reveals that there is considerable variability in

response. Analysis of the raw data revealed that this variability is present both between subjects and also within individual subjects. When grouping body sites together into general areas however, more consistent results emerge.

Table 8.9 Mean scores of the sensation of vibration of frequencies in primary sites in grouped body locations in percentages

	20Hz	30Hz	40Hz	50Hz	60Hz	70Hz
No effect	2	3	1	3	1	5
Legs	36	39	47	33	24	16
Sacrum/abdomen	31	23	16	34	16	12
Chest/head	9	23	22	18	43	55
Arms/hands	4	1	1	1	3	4
General effect	18	11	13	11	13	8

Table 8.9 shows the mean scores of the frequencies felt as sensations of vibration in primary sites. Grouping therefore gives a clearer summary of where the majority of subjects experienced a perceived sensation of vibration. The results, when analysing reports of a sensation of vibration in a secondary site, reveal equal inconsistency, and a much higher percentage of subjects report no effect when asked to identify a secondary site, as presented in Table 8.10.

Gathering data from subjects on frequencies they disliked produced some quite interesting results (Table 8.11).

While 30Hz–60Hz appear to be disliked by quite small percentages of the group of subjects, 20Hz and particularly 70Hz found a greater percentage reporting irritation or dislike of these frequencies. This factor had never before been evaluated in any way either by the pioneers of VA therapy, or by subsequent researchers, and reminds us that one cannot make assumptions about treatment effects unless one takes the trouble to ask. This issue could be generalised to other methods and techniques used in music therapy, where dislike of treatment may cause negative outcomes.

The first of these two studies supported the theory of a localised sensation of vibration, while the evidence from the second study indicates that while similar groupings occurred as in the first study, when a greater number of body sites were used to monitor the sensation of vibration, there was a more general and incon-

Table 8.10 Mean scores for secondary sites in percentages						
	20Hz	*30Hz*	*40Hz*	*50Hz*	*60Hz*	*70Hz*
No effect	45.0	36.5	31.2	38.5	33.1	27.9
Feet	2.9	4.8	1.4	2.9	5.2	5.8
Ankles	3.8	5.3	6.7	0.5	2.5	1.9
Calves	2.9	5.3	12.0	6.7	2.8	1.0
Knees	5.8	6.2	10.6	2.9	4.2	1.0
Thighs	7.7	4.3	6.2	9.1	5.2	2.9
Sacrum/pelvis	6.7	7.7	5.3	10.6	2.5	5.8
Lumbar/abdomen	5.8	4.8	6.8	6.5	6.6	3.9
Thoracic	1.0	4.9	1.0	4.8	11.0	12.5
Shoulders	4.8	7.7	7.2	6.7	11.0	9.6
Neck	2.9	2.9	3.9	2.4	3.4	9.6
Head	3.0	3.8	2.5	1.8	7.7	12.5
Arms	0.0	0.5	0.5	1.4	1.0	1.9
Hands	1.0	1.0	1.9	1.5	1.0	2.7
General effect	6.7	4.3	2.8	3.8	2.8	1.0

sistent effect. Reports from clinical treatment using VA therapy have previously documented the relaxing and beneficial effects of the low frequency sinusoidal tone used and subjects have frequently reported a sensation of localised vibration. These two studies examined this phenomenon particularly with reference to the question of whether there is a consistent and reliable local sensation of vibration that varies depending on the frequency used within a range from 20Hz to 70Hz. Skille (1986) has suggested that there is a localised sensation of vibration, similar to the principles of resonant vibration, which for any given frequency in the above range can be consistently felt by people in specific areas of their body. In his clinical reports he has sought to identify this and link it to effective frequencies for treating specific pathological conditions.

Frequency presented	Number of presentations in total	Number of subjects who expressed dislike	% scores of disliked frequency
20 Hz	104	20	19.2
30 Hz	208	18	8.7
40 Hz	208	14	6.7
50 Hz	208	16	7.7
60 Hz	208	24	11.5
70 Hz	104	30	28.9

Table 8.11 Results of self-reported dislike of frequencies between 20Hz and 70Hz

Effects of VA therapy compared with a placebo treatment and a control on arousal, blood pressure and heartrate in non-clinical subjects

Having explored this aspect of the influence of different low frequencies on non-clinical subjects, and found that some assumptions made by the pioneers and clinicians did not give consistent results, further questions regarding the effect of VA therapy when compared with placebo or control conditions arose, leading to two further case examples in this sequence of research studies.

The effect of VA therapy as a relaxant was found in the first two studies, and there are many reports of its value in reducing arousal, heartrate and blood pressure (Chesky 1992; Raudsik 1997; Skille 1992; Standley 1991; Wigram 1997a). As many of the clients or patients who had formed target populations for VA therapy were non-verbal, and sometimes multi-handicapped, a study on normal, non-clinical subjects was necessary to answer specific questions about the effect of the treatment, and the method of application.

Study 5

The next case example took a group of 30 male and 30 female naive subjects (n=60), recruited from the staff of a large hospital, and also staff and students from a university. They were randomly assigned to three groups. As a between groups design, this experiment was set up to measure whether 30 minute treatments of VA therapy, administered in a quiet, contained environment conducive to relaxation (Group A), would have a significantly greater effect in achieving changes in both physiological and mental states in non-clinical subjects than a normal resting period of the same time, either with a treatment of relaxing music (Group B), or with no treatment at all (Group C). The music given to both group A and B was relaxing, gentle 'New Age' music ('Crystal Caverns' by Daniel Kobialka) in group A with a 44Hz pulsed tone.

The hypotheses for the experiments in this chapter were that arousal levels, hedonic tone, blood pressure and heartrate would be reduced by VA therapy, when compared with a treatment of relaxing music and a control condition. Mood, arousal levels, blood pressure and heartrate were recorded before and after each trial. The subjects in each group only had one trial. The UWIST-Mood Adjective Check List was used. It is a 24-item adjective checklist which requires the subjects to score on a 1–4 scale, ranging through Definitely – Slightly – Slightly not – Definitely not (Matthews, Jones and Chamberlain 1990). The adjectives are selected to indicate positive (+) or negative (-) aspects of energetic arousal (EA), general arousal (GA), tension arousal (TA) and hedonic tone (HT).

Table 8.12 shows the results of an Analysis of Variance of energetic arousal, general arousal and tension arousal which reveals significant differences between groups. In the measurements of hedonic tone, although the differences were in the expected direction, no significant difference between groups was found.

Table 8.12 Analyses of Variance of EA, GA, TA and HT

	DF between groups	DF within groups	F ratio	F prob
EA	2	57	8.6125	.0005
GA	2	57	11.3147	.0001
TA	2	57	4.8992	.0109
HT	2	57	1.1974	.3094

Table 8.13 shows the results of orthogonal planned comparisons that were undertaken to assess whether VA therapy differed from music alone and whether the two conditions combined differed from the control. Scores in the group receiving VA therapy reduced by more than those receiving music alone, and those two condi-

tions combined reduced by more than those in the control condition in general arousal, energetic arousal and tension arousal. Hedonic tone scores revealed no significant differences between groups. A planned comparison showed that the groups receiving VA therapy and music alone had significantly reduced heartrates compared with the control group (Table 8.14).

Table 8.13 Planned comparisons of EA, GA, TA and HT			
	DF	*F Ratio*	*P (1 tail)*
Energetic arousal: Group 1 vs Group 2	1,57	3.7	< .05
Energetic arousal: Group 1 and Group 2 vs Group 3	1,57	14.0	< .001
General arousal: Group 1 vs Group 2	1,57	7.5	< .01
General arousal: Group 1 and Group 2 vs Group 3	1,57	16.1	< .001
Tension arousal: Group 1 vs Group 2	1,57	4.7	< .05
Tension arousal: Group 1 and Group 2 vs Group 3	1,57	6.9	< .01
Hedonic tone: Group 1 vs Group 2	1,57	0.9	N.S.
Hedonic tone: Group 1 and Group 2 vs Group 3	1,57	1.5	N.S.

Table 8.14 presents data from the repeated measurement of heartrate averaged every five minutes. Heartrate decreased by different amounts in the three groups. Heartrate was measured at seven points during the treatment, and there was evidence of a general decline in heartrate over time, $F(6,342)= 7.3$, P .0001. There was a significant difference in the rate of decline in heartrate across the groups, $F(12,342)=2.04$, P=.02 for the group by time interaction.

An important aspect of this study is that it provides evidence of the effect of VA therapy in the form of self-reporting from subjects which is untypical of previous studies. Anecdotal results from previous trials had shown reductions in blood pressure (Saluveer and Tamm 1989; Skille 1989a). However, these trials were undertaken without a control group or a treatment of relaxing music and only measured the results of reductions in blood pressure during treatment. This experiment measured reductions in blood pressure and heartrate when comparing VA therapy with a relaxing music treatment and comparing VA therapy combined with music alone with a control group, and showed no significant difference between conditions, although the results were in the expected direction. The one

Table 8.14 Means and standard deviations **of heartrate over seven measures**			
Heartrate *measure*	*Group 1 (Treatment)* *mean (S.D.)*	*Group 2 (Music alone)* *mean (S.D.)*	*Group 3 (Control 1)* *mean (S.D.)*
1	72.7 (7.63)	72.3 (13.17)	75.3 (10.10)
2	70.7 (7.41)	70.8 (12.07)	73.9 (10.54)
3	69.7 (7.06)	70.6 (11.22)	74.0 (10.88)
4	68.9 (7.04)	70.2 (12.28)	72.4 (10.67)
5	66.3 (6.00)	69.7 (12.76)	70.7 (13.13)
6	65.2 (6.48)	69.8 (12.23)	73.7 (11.10)
7	64.5 (5.67)	69.8 (12.42)	73.6 (11.26)

significant difference found between groups in physiological change was a reduction in heartrate in the treatment and music alone groups combined compared with the control group. The physical effect of the treatment appears to be significant, which may have an influence on state of mind. Because the effect of pulsed sinusoidal low frequency tones together with music affected their physical state, the subjects reported effects in their scores in the UWIST-MACL of the adjectives, which reflected a reduction in energy, tension and general arousal indicating both a physiological change and also a psychological awareness of that change.

Effects of three different rates of amplitude modulation and a constant tone on arousal, hedonic tone, blood pressure, heartrate and liking in non-clinical subjects

Finally, another assumption in the modality of the treatment was questioned. Skille had devised VA therapy software of relaxing music combined with a pulsed, sinusoidal low frequency tone. However no argument had been presented to support the speed of pulse of this low frequency tone, or indeed if it was beneficial that it was pulsed at all. So a question emerged for the last case that addressed whether the speed of the low frequency pulse (peak to peak), amplitude modulation, or indeed whether the tone was pulsed or constant, had a significant influence on the mood, blood pressure, heartrate and general enjoyment of the vibroacoustic stimuli.

Study 6

For this experiment, music was excluded as part of the stimuli in any of the conditions. Anecdotal reports found that there seemed to be some consensus that a slower speed of the pulsed tone was more relaxing and interfered less with any fixed or variable tempo there might be in the recorded music used in the treatment. Many of the tapes made in Norway during the developmental period had pulse speeds between two and eight seconds. This was felt to be too fast by some of the people who tried the system, and interfered both with relaxation, and the music.

Hypotheses were formulated that:

- there would be significant differences in arousal level and hedonic tone, reductions in blood pressure and heartrate

- there would be greater liking for slower pulse speeds between subjects receiving varied rates of amplitude modulation of a 44 Hz tone (0.17, 0.10, 0.07) and a constant tone.

A further 30 male and 30 female subjects (n=60) were recruited, and randomly assigned to one of the four conditions (groups). A single trial of 15 minutes was undertaken, before and after which the subjects completed the UWIST-MACL and their blood pressure and heartrate were recorded.

Table 8.15 Analyses of Variance of changes in mood, physiological measures, relaxation and like/dislike

	Degrees of freedom between groups	Degrees of freedom within groups	F ratio	F value
Energetic arousal	3	56	0.39	N.S.
General arousal	3	56	0.17	N.S.
Tension arousal	3	56	0.27	N.S.
Hedonic tone	3	56	1.72	N.S.
Systolic blood pressure	3	56	0.75	N.S.
Diastolic blood pressure	3	56	0.40	N.S.
Heartrate	3	56	1.20	N.S.
Relaxation	3	56	0.54	N.S.
Like/dislike	3	56	2.28	N.S.

The Analysis of Variance in Table 8.15 of energetic arousal, general arousal, tension arousal and hedonic tone of the UWIST-MACL revealed no significant differences between groups. Analyses of Variance of blood pressure, pulse and degree of reported relaxation measured before and after the trials also indicated no significant differences between groups. There was no significant difference between groups on the scores they recorded for liking or disliking the stimuli. There was no suggestion of any difference between age groups, or between male and female subjects.

Discussion

The series of studies described above are clearly and primarily quantitative in nature. They are described here as a series of 'case examples' in order to show a process where one study elicited questions that led to another study and then another study. Previous vibroacoustic therapy studies purported to alleviate many different symptoms, physical problems and psychological disorders, and the field was open to abuse and could even be accused of having a 'cure all' profile. These studies, presented above as a cumulative case study, were designed to answer specific questions and began to answer relevant and specific questions. So, in conclusion, we find the value of vibroacoustic therapy is that it influences both psychological and physiological activity. While it is undoubtedly an enjoyable form of treatment, with very few side effects reported so far, one has to accept that the placebo effect can be very influential. Where music itself is considered a 'placebo' in VA therapy (given that pulsed sinusoidal low frequency tones are the primary stimulus of treatment), it is important to establish both the influence and effect of the treatment of vibroacoustic therapy when compared with music on its own or no intervention.

The studies described have undoubted limitations, and caution should be exercised in interpreting the results of the trials considering the small sample groups involved, particularly in the clinical studies on high muscle-tone. However, the value of considering the evidence from a series of studies, as described above, is the process by which one can integrate information collected independently and better formulate a theory of treatment. These studies have shown us that arousal levels are clearly influenced and reduced, and physical effects do include reduced muscle activity and slower heartrate. The applicability of that will not simply be confined to populations of clients with cerebral palsy, in particular severe spasticity, they can also be applied to other populations for whom anxiety, high arousal levels and stress provoke problems in daily living and somatic health.

CHAPTER 9

Music Therapy with the Elderly: Complementary Data as a Rich Approach to Understanding Communication

Hanne Mette Ridder

I do not make an appointment with Mr B telling him to come to the music therapy room at 10am. It would make no sense to him. Instead, I go out to look for him at the unit where 24 residents, who need gerontopsychiatric care, live. I find him trying to push a big trolley with laundry. He is often occupied with pushing around big things and big furniture. It might have something to do with his former job as a truck driver. He has no success in moving the trolley, as it is either stuck or locked, and when I take his hand and ask him to come with me, he follows me to the music therapy room. He does not say anything, and when we enter the room he spots the songbooks on a table and starts moving them about and some of them fall to the floor. I guide him to sit down in a sofa. Our first individual music therapy session is about to begin. The video camera in the corner is already recording and I press the button on the heartrate monitor that will register his heartrate during the session.

Mr B is participating in the music therapy because he fitted certain predetermined referral criteria. He suffers a primary degenerative dementia (Alzheimer's disease), he is at level 6 (of 7) on the functional assessment staging (Reisberg 1988), he has no history of psychiatric illness or drug/alcohol dependency, he has not participated in individual music therapy before, he shows agitated behaviour (as defined by Cohen-Mansfield et al. 1989), and his family signed consent.

Mr B and five other residents fitted the inclusion criteria for this study. In these criteria, it was not formulated that the participant would be expected to benefit from music activities, nor that he or she liked music or singing. As a matter of fact, Mr B never sings and it is not expected that he 'participates actively' in the music therapy by joining me in the songs, for example.

Having worked clinically for five years with persons suffering from dementia, I have a very strong feeling that singing well-known songs in a therapeutic setting has positive effects on this group of patients who have suffered severe losses: loss of cognitive abilities and loss in their social lives. But the problem is how to *describe* these benefits and positive effects as these participants do communicate, albeit not in a direct way, that they are relating to what is going on in the therapy. The focus of the research therefore was on strategies that made it possible to *describe* effects of the music therapy, instead of trying to *prove* these effects. This is why I chose to carry out research to see what happens and document the effects of music therapy.

In the following pages I want to describe a smaller part of this case study research where I included quantitative measures and looked for patterns in the analyses of both quantitative and qualitative data. This complementary data was used later to match theories of communication, environmental attention (D. Aldridge 1996) and arousal.

Quantitative/qualitative data or paradigms

A music therapy session with Mr B lasts about 25 minutes and when I measure his heartrate during sessions I include quantitative data. I do not want to confuse the use of quantitative data and the use of a 'quantitative research design'. In the 1990s there was an explosion of interest in qualitative research (Robson 2002, p.xii), and in the debates on qualitative versus quantitative research strategies these were defined as two different research paradigms.

In her book *Videnskap og kommunikasjon (Science and Communication)* Professor Nerheim (1995), who is professor at University of Tromsoe in Norway, discusses paradigms, models and communicative strategies in health care theory of science. She describes health care science – based on, e.g. medicine, psychiatry, nursing and physiotherapy – as strongly related to the theory of natural science. But additionally she describes a bio-psycho-social or holistic model of comprehension having an increasing influence on theory of care. The concepts of sickness and health are here to be understood in *open systems*. In *closed systems* it is possible to carry out research under strict laboratory conditions. In open systems Robson says:

...we have to accept that we are dealing with tendencies and probabilities... People, information and all other aspects of the situation are likely to change in ways that may or may not have anything to do with the focus of our investigation. (Robson 2002, p.40)

If health care science defines sickness and health as aspects in open systems – where the patients interact with their surroundings – and show different strategies of how to cope with health and sickness, an understanding, not only of the *truth*, but also of the *meaning* of these aspects is needed. In order to understand meaning 'health care science needs hermeneutics (the art of understanding)' (Nerheim 1995, p.15). The point I want to stress from Nerheim's work is that she sees hermeneutics go beyond its traditional role as 1. a 'helping discipline' to other branches of learning; she sees hermeneutics as 2. 'independent' forms of methodology and as 3. 'basic science' (ibid., p.15).

In order to leave the 'paradigm wars' (Robson 2002, p.43) between positivists (quantitative researchers) and constructionists (hermeneutic, qualitative researchers) we can adopt a pragmatic stance. In pragmatism, truth is 'what works', which means that both quantitative and qualitative approaches are possible in mixed-method studies. In this view quantitative and qualitative approaches are 'degraded' to research instruments on the same footing, and not defined as two diametrically opposite world views or paradigms. This makes it possible to work with both strategies with a focus on finding the right tool to answer the research questions, instead of modulating questions so they fit a certain, pre-decided method; '…it is far more relevant to establish the focus of the research question first, before deciding on an appropriate research method' (Wigram, Pedersen and Bonde 2002, p.225).

When Nerheim (1995) distinguishes between helping disciplines, independent methodologies and basic science, I find it important to establish that thorough, profound and even radical research includes and discusses perspectives from other works and other disciplines where it is relevant to the research question. Large-scale outcome studies must basically rely on or refer to research that clearly describes details or categories. Basic science concerning Alzheimer's disease is, for example, based on foundation research that in implicit or explicit ways is connected to Alois Alzheimer's case descriptions of Auguste Deter (Alzheimer 1907) and Johann F. (Alzheimer 1911), case descriptions based on data from Alzheimer's notes and observations, as well as elaborate descriptions of neurological findings at autopsy. These observations on a single person are basic to further research. If an understanding of the fieldwork, of nuances, details and differences, is not included in a large-scale quantitative work, this might twist the 'truth' found as a result of the work. I consider quantitative work as weak if it is not based, at least in the theoretical understanding, on qualitative understandings or hermeneutic approaches that are closely bound to the field (to persons, their specific needs, their responding and acting, clinical approaches, theory of care, etc), and an understanding of variables that we try to isolate and control in closed systems in randomised controlled trials. I see hermeneutic approaches as basic to quantitative work, and therefore absolutely necessary when new research fields are developed, if research has to 'make sense' and bring 'meaning'. Qualitative data and subjective approaches can stand on their own as conclusive evidence, when research meets criteria for validity and reliability, and might also enrich the methodology by including quantitative data.

Open systems and retrospection

When Mr B is seen as a person in an open system, his acts and expressions are seen as his way of communicating. He interacts with his surroundings and is influenced by variables such as health, season, weather, contact with relatives, friends, health care professionals. In a hermeneutic analysis, we might focus on para-linguistic expressions (e.g. tone of voice, prosodic contour of the short sentences he might express, emphasis on certain words and pacing, pausing and timing in his expressions) or non-verbal expressions (e.g. gesture, posture and facial expression). When we consider these dimensions and qualities of communication it makes the research complex and suggests reflection and retrospection in the process of collecting data, compared to a process method that is predictable.

> In open systems, we can well be in a position to explain some event after it has occurred even though we were not able to predict it. In closed systems, explanation and prediction are symmetrical; if we can explain, we can predict, and vice versa. But in open systems, the actual configurations of structures and processes are constantly changing, making definite prediction impossible. This means that while the future cannot be predicted, the past can be explained by establishing the particular configuration which was in existence. (Robson 2002, p.41)

This reflects an existentialistic understanding where we understand in retrospect, as the Danish philosopher Søren Kierkegaard, 1843, formulates it, 'Det er ganske sandt, hvad filosofien siger, at *livet må forstås baglæns*. Men derover glemmer man den anden sætning: at *det må leves forlæns*' (Thielst 1994). In short: life must be lived forwards, but understood backwards. The collection of observation data and the process of understanding these in retrospect are methods that we see in hermeneutics and in phenomenology, as well as in research strategies such as case study research, in ethnography and in grounded theory. These research strategies are described as flexible designs by Robson (2002), who distinguishes between the terms 'fixed' and 'flexible' designs. These terms are not substitutes for the terms qualitative and quantitative, but in a pragmatic way reflect an understanding that integrates or co-ordinates both terms.

Fixed designs

In fixed designs, a tight pre-specification of data collection and data processing is needed. This demands thorough preliminary work and has the advantage that the amount of data is reduced to manageable levels right from the beginning. Data are often converted to quantities, which make them optimal for statistical analyses. Traditional fixed design research strategies are experimental or non-experimental with random selection of individuals from a known population and with control of variables. Single-case experimental designs are fixed designs too. Here the single subjects function as their own control in a non-intervention period (A, or baseline) compared to an intervention period (B). To this A-B design might be added a post-intervention baseline condition (A-B-A) and even a second intervention phase (A-B-A-B). In multiple-baseline designs dependent variables are measured across settings, across behaviours and/or across participants.

Fixed designs are often referred to as quantitative designs, which is logical, as they mainly use quantitative data. But in a pragmatic understanding of research it is possible to include qualitative data in the design. This makes the label fixed design seem more suitable.

Flexible designs

Flexible designs are often referred to as qualitative designs, but as it is possible to incorporate quantitative data it seems more suitable to label these designs flexible designs. These evolve during data collection, which moves the thorough and systematic burden of work to take place *after* the data collection in the process of data reduction. The data might have various forms, often transcribed words from interviews or observations, that become manageable when focus is put on certain phenomena or when data are sorted in codes or categories. Rather than relying on previously defined tools and instruments as in fixed designs, flexible designs involve the 'researcher-as-instrument' (Robson 2002, p.167). The researcher is not defined as being 'objective' and might function as a practitioner with tacit knowledge about the researched context and material. Case studies, where the data collection might be based on multiple sources consisting of, e.g. documents, archival records, interviews, observations and physical artefacts, is an example of a traditional flexible design strategy (Robson 2002, p.88).

Case study approaches in gerontology

In music therapy in gerontology case studies and single subject designs are used as the most common type of evidence. Out of the 75 studies exploring issues of music and dementia (see Ridder 2002), about a third of the studies (32%) use a descriptive case approach. A majority (almost 60%) of the studies use a fixed design, of which 74% use a fixed single subject design.

Sixty per cent of the descriptive case approaches use documented case studies integrating data based on neurological tests, music transcriptions or 'objective' clinical assessment. These studies are: G. Aldridge 2000; Baumgartner 1997; Beatty, Zavadil and Bailly 1988, 1994; Bolger and Judson 1984; Brust 1980; Clair 1991; Clair and Bernstein 1990; Crystal, Grober and Masur 1989; Eeg 2001; Fitzgerald-Cloutier 1993; Munk-Madsen 2000; Polk and Kertesz 1993; and Tomaino 2000. The remaining 40% of the descriptive case approaches use anecdotal case reports. There is a wide range of anecdotal case reports, from documented case studies to extensive case study research. The case study approach is often discredited as the same yardstick is applied to a general view on case approaches. I find it very important to distinguish between these different approaches, and in the following I differentiate between case reports, case studies and case study research.

Case reports, case studies and case study research

I see the narrative, anecdotal case description or case report as 'helping discipline' (after Nerheim 1995). It is a valuable method in order to elaborate on a clinical description, exemplify a fixed design, describe theoretical principles by illustrating the music therapy work, or functioning as a clarifying example, but it is not an independent scientific method.

The case study is an 'independent' methodology. As a 'study' it follows certain rules of documentation ensuring validity (e.g. audio/video data material, triangulation or member checking), and it develops 'detailed, intensive knowledge about a single 'case', or of a small number of related 'cases' (Robson 2002, p.89)'.

The case study research can be considered as 'basic science', and is seen as:

A well-established research strategy where the focus is on a case (which is interpreted very widely to include the study of an individual person, a group, a setting, an organization, etc) in its own right, and taking its context into account. Typically it involves multiple methods of data collection. Can include quantitative data, though qualitative data are almost invariably collected. (Robson 2002, p.178)

Based on D. Aldridge (2002), criteria that define a case study research might be formulated as follows: A case study research transmits a clear focus and a clear study overview, describes the theoretical framework, background issues, relation to other works or fields, the profile of the case and its context and ethical consideration. It explicates data collection methods and procedures, describes the different components of the data analysis (data reduction, data display, drawing of conclusions and verification) and formulates meta-reflections, policy and practice implications (e.g. generalisation and indications for further research).

Robson describes in short a scientific attitude to research: it must be carried out systematically, sceptically and ethically:

> *Systematically* means giving serious thought to what is done and how and why it is done; in particular, the researcher must be explicit about the nature of the observations that are made, the circumstances in which they are made and the role the researcher takes in making them.

> *Sceptically* means that the researcher subjects his/her ideas to possible disconfirmation, and also subjects his/her observations and conclusions to scrutiny.

> *Ethically* means that the researcher follows a code of conduct for the research, which ensures that the interests and concerns of those taking part in, or possibly being affected by, the research are safeguarded. (Adapted from Robson 2002, p.18)

The point of differentiating categories of case approaches is to make it clear that case study research is a valuable research methodology that is not to be confused with case reports. The boundaries between case studies and case study research are vague and there have been calls for general criteria for the evaluation of qualitative research articles to be established.

> Qualitative research is about exploring particularity and diversity, and there is a plethora of qualitative research approaches around with rather different answers to basic ontological, epistemological, and methodological questions. This diversity creates some problems though in the process of evaluating articles ... (Stige 2002, p.65)

In this sense, it is clear that case study research, and qualitative research in general, are relatively new fields still needing ongoing discussions on guidelines and evaluation.

Pattern-matching

With a background in experimental psychology, Yin (1994) has made an important approach to research in open systems in his book *Case Study Research: Design and Methods*. He describes single-case designs, as well as multiple-case designs, where he stresses that the use of multiple-case designs 'should follow a replication, not a sampling, logic' (p.51). With a sampling logic to all types of research many important topics could not be empirically investigated (Yin 1994, p.48); with the replication logic it is possible to treat each individual case study as a whole study, and then to consider conclusions across cases.

As a method for analysing case study evidence he suggests the technique of *pattern-matching*.

> For case study analysis, one of the most desirable strategies is to use a pattern-matching logic. Such a logic…compares an empirically based pattern with a predicted one (or with several alternative predictions). If the patterns coincide, the results can help a case study strengthen its internal validity. (Yin 1994, p.106)

Simpler patterns with a minimal variety of either dependent or independent variables can be the focus for pattern-matching, as well as non-equivalent dependent variables or rival explanations (see Yin 1994, pp.106–110). In pattern-matching, Yin states that the fundamental comparison between the predicted and the actual pattern may involve no quantitative or statistical criteria, but this implies that future case study research develops more precise techniques when the pattern-matching is used for conclusion drawing (ibid., p.110). These ideas make the case study, or case study research, an important strategy for research fields where the purpose is to develop clinical applicability and not entirely to focus on outcome arguments. Until such improvements in the precision of pattern-matching occur, Yin advises investigators to be cautious not to postulate very subtle patterns. 'One wants to do case studies in which the outcomes are likely to lead to gross matches or mismatches and in which even an 'eyeballing' technique is sufficiently convincing to draw a conclusion' (ibid., p.110).

William Trochim (1985) and Donald Campbell (1966) have written extensively on pattern-matching. Trochim distinguishes between theoretical and observed patterns. 'Pattern matching always involves an attempt to link two patterns where one is a theoretical pattern and the other is an observed or operational one' (Trochim 2002). A theoretical pattern is a hypothesis about what is expected in the data; in the following my focus will be on observed patterns, and I will give examples of these: patterns that were sought in the data *after* the data collection, and that were not theoretically predicted beforehand, but that were matched to theories presented in the first part of the thesis (see Ridder 2003).

> The major differences between pattern matching and more traditional hypothesis testing approaches are that pattern matching encourages the use of more complex or detailed hypotheses and treats the observations from a multivariate rather than a univariate perspective. (Trochim 2002, p.1)

This multivariate perspective is applicable to principles of flexible designs, of observations in open systems and of retrospection. In this sense, I formulated a hypothesis that helped me keep the focus on heartrate throughout the research process, but was worded in such a way that it was open to the emergence of non-predicted patterns.

Case studies and pattern-matching techniques

Mr B participates in 20 music therapy sessions in four weeks. The research was approved by The Ethical Committee of Århus County, and Mr B's wife signed consent, letting me use certain parts of the story, the observations and the video recordings of Mr B. Each music therapy session is based on long-familiar songs that I would sing to Mr B, sitting beside him on a sofa in a small cosy room. The sessions are structured with a greeting song, certain songs that I would sing in the middle of the session and a song that signals the ending of the session. In between these 'structural songs', I sing two to four songs in the first part of the session, and three to four songs in the last part of the session. These are a selection of songs that seem to have a personal meaning to Mr B.

Here I just present small extracts of Mr B's case study and of some of the observations made during music therapy. The music therapy method, main purposes of the clinical setting, details about the songs, singing style, and regulating techniques are described in Ridder 2003.

Profile of Mr B

Mr B, now in his mid-seventies, was born in the 1920s into a family of four in a small town in Denmark. He has been married for more that 50 years and has raised four children. He worked as a truck driver for most of his life, and the first symptoms of dementia started in his sixties when he had retired. With the progressing symptoms, he stayed at home with his wife as long as possible but then moved to a local old people's home and lived there for three years. It became more and more challenging and problematic for staff to carry out personal care. Mr B would push staff away or hit them when they tried to help him dress or bath. He was then moved to a special care unit, and had lived there for one year and five months when he started in music therapy. His diagnosis reads, 'Dementia with Alzheimer's disease without specification'. On the functional assessment staging scale (Reisberg 1988), he is described as being at level 6 (of 7), and on the Mini-mental State Exam cognitive test (MMSE) (Folstein, Folstein and McHugh 1975), he scores 0 out of 30. According to the Cohen-Mansfield Agitation Inventory (Cohen-Mansfield *et al.* 1989), Mr B shows physical aggressive behaviour less than once a day, mainly in personal care situations, and physical non-aggressive behaviour (pacing, ambulating, moving furniture, etc) about three to six times a day. He gets no medical antidepressant or antipsychotic treatment.

Mr B used to play the accordion. According to his wife he liked Swedish ballads (for example, Evert Taube), songs from revues, 'oldies' and folk music. He stopped singing in sing-alongs when he lived in the first old peoples' home, and replaced singing with whistling. At the time he moved in at the unit he had also stopped whistling.

Mr B is very difficult to involve in activities at the unit, as he will mostly get up after a while and walk away, not being able to concentrate on what is going on. All in all, it is questionable if he will benefit from the music therapy, if he will 'understand' what is going on, and 'participate' at any level.

Patterns in the heartrate data

During music therapy Mr B's heartrate is measured with equipment designed for measuring heartrate changes in athletes using a belt with a sensor around his chest that transmits his heartrate data. The researcher wears a wrist receiver to store those signals, which can later be transmitted to a computer. The belt does not disturb him, nor influence his ability to walk about, and is put on during morning care some hours before the music therapy, so that he gets accustomed to the elastic strip with the heartbeat receiver placed around his chest. The bar chart, Figure 9.1, shows the mean heartrate (heartrate) measured in five-second intervals during five music therapy sessions a week for four successive weeks.

This bar chart does not show clear patterns that indicate some kind of change, but shows that, during the majority of sessions (16 sessions), Mr B's heartrate is at a moderate level between 66 and 73 bpm (beats per minute). In the next bar chart, Figure 9.2, I do not look at mean heartrate levels, but focus on what happens to the heartrate in the first part of the session. I define the 'first part' of the session to be the first seven minutes, and with the help of computer calculations that draw tendency lines, I establish if the heartrate level increases or decreases.

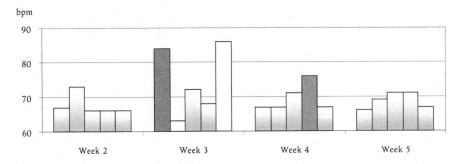

Figure 9.1 Mean heartrate of Mr B during 20 sessions

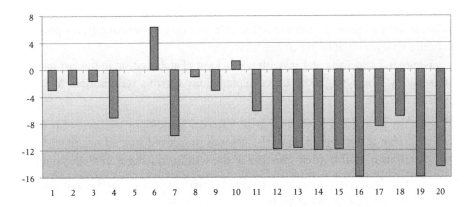

Figure 9.2 Decrease or increase of bpm during first seven minutes of sessions 1 to 20

This bar chart shows a change over time. It shows that Mr B's heartrate decreases (during the first part of a session) to a much greater extent in the last 9 sessions, compared to the first 11 sessions. (No data are calculated for session 5, as the receiver did not register signals in the beginning of the session.) In a further analysis, the increase or decrease in the first part of the session is compared to the average heartrate in order to establish if there is an increase or decrease in relation to the last part of the session. This is defined by four regulation categories: di (decrease – increase), dd (decrease – decrease), id (increase – decrease), and ii (increase – increase). When heartrate decreases in the beginning of a session with an old person suffering from dementia and then increases again (di) it might indicate that the participant is able to sit down and relax, but then participates actively later in the session, in contrast to a session where heartrate continues decreasing (dd). From a general point of view this might indicate that the participant is inactive or even falls asleep. Only twice in Figure 9.2 do we see that heartrate increases at the beginning of a session. This might indicate that Mr B is not able to find rest in these sessions, but when heartrate decreases later in the session (id) it might show that he calms down later on – in contrast to sessions where heartrate continues increasing (ii). Sessions in the ii–category might indicate that the participant is being overstimulated by the music therapy. The four regulation categories are very general and must be used carefully without over-interpreting, but they are useful as they are easily calculated and give clear hints about heartrate data. Table 9.1 shows the regulation category of each of the 20 music therapy sessions with Mr B.

Table 9.1 shows that all the last nine sessions are in regulation category di (decrease – increase). This indicates a certain pattern where Mr B's heartrate decreases in the beginning of the session and then increases again. It seems to be quite a stable pattern in the last half of the 20 music therapy sessions. It is important to notice that no sessions are in the ii-category.

Figure 9.2 and Table 9.1 give hints of a kind of stabilisation in the last half of the sessions. There might be other explanations for this stabilisation. We can hypothesise that:

- the decrease is a result of some 'external' conditions that assist Mr B to relax at the beginning of the sessions (improved state of health, reductions in staff burden, changes in the weather, changes in medication)

- the decrease is a result of 'familiarity with treatment', and is not due to the music therapy as such

- the decrease can be directly related to the influence of music therapy (effects of the relation with the music therapist, of the familiar songs, of the structure of the session, of reminiscence, validation or other therapeutic effects).

In a case study, it is possible to rule out a few of the 'external' aspects that explain why a change happens, and it is possible to include data that register medication, daily routines, number of staff on duty, but still there are variables that are impossible to control. Nevertheless, it is important to describe a certain pattern of changes in a person, as Alzheimer did in the case of Johann F., to include this understanding in further descriptions or in larger outcome measures. In the case of Mr B daily questionnaires, completed by staff, ruled out changes in medication, health, changes in routines or changes in staff members on duty. Nevertheless, the change in heartrate pattern might have other explanations.

Table 9.1 Regulation category in each of the 20 sessions

Session	1	2	3	4	5	6	7	8	9	10	11	12	13	14	15	16	17	18	19	20
Category	di	dd	dd	di		id	di	dd	dd	id	dd	di	di	di	di	di	di	di	di	di

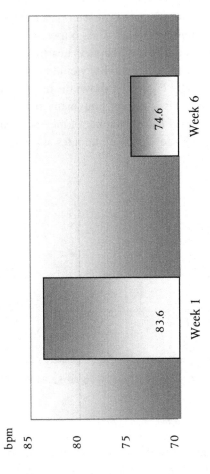

Figure 9.3 Mean heartrate in pre-treatment week and in post-treatment week

To analyse if the heartrate pattern, which shows steep decreases in the beginning of the last sessions, is a result of something more than familiarity with treatment and leads to a change that does not only happen in the music therapy room, but brings changes to daily life as well, we need to look for certain patterns before and after the music therapy treatment.

Mr B's heartrate data were sampled for five days, at the same period of the day as the music therapy, *before* the 'treatment period' and again *after* this period. When mean heartrate data are compared, we see a clear drop in mean heartrate levels from week 1 (pre-treatment week) and week 6 (post-treatment week), see Figure 9.3.

To establish that the drop of 9 bpm in heartrate levels (from 83.6 to 74.6 bpm) is not a random variation, a possibility would be to display the distribution of the bpm values graphically. Figure 9.4 shows the heartrate data on the horizontal axis, and on the vertical axis is shown how many times a certain value occurs. This number is then divided by the number of measurements: as Mr B's heartrate was measured on five days for about 25 minutes at five-second intervals.

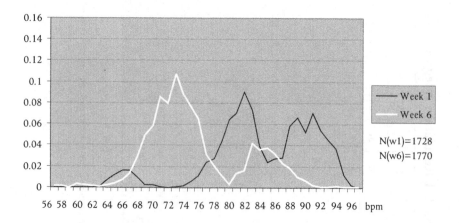

Figure 9.4 Distribution of heartrate values in Mr B

The grey curve in figure 9.4 shows the distribution of bpm values in week 1 (pre-treatment week) and the white curve in week 6 (post-treatment week). The two curves show a very clear parallel shift that indicates a marked change in heartrate levels from before, to after, music therapy. With such a clear parallel shift, there is no doubt that the drop in levels is statistically significant (t-test shows a p-value that is 0.001, see Ridder 2003).

The pre-post-measurements show that Mr B's heartrate levels decrease markedly in the week after the month with daily music therapy sessions. For some persons suffering from dementia, who are difficult to engage in activities and therapy and who are difficult to calm down if they are upset, the music therapy might have a valuable calming function. For other persons suffering from dementia, who are difficult to engage in activities because they seem to be in a burnt-out state (Kitwood 1997), or hypo-aroused state (Ridder 2003), it would be important to see if music therapy results in increases in heartrate levels. By describing different cases, and by combining quantitative measures with in-depth analyses of the process in the music therapy, we might get an understanding of the effects of music therapy – before we try to establish that this effect is due to the music therapy. In the case of Mr B, we see a marked drop in heartrate levels a whole week after the music therapy treatment. If this change is due to the music therapy we need more descriptions of the processes in the sessions, typical features of the relation to the music therapist, of the music itself, the structure of the session, and of music therapy techniques being used, to develop clinical approaches and establish if the music therapy is helpful to more persons with the same problems or symptoms.

Patterns in the video observation data

With the help of processed data, e.g. the examples displaying heartrate data above, we are able to describe the music therapy from a certain angle. By using video observations we are able to describe the sessions from a very different perspective. If some patterns, described from one perspective, can be related to descriptions from another perspective, then we have more views on the phenomena and the internal validity of the argument increases.

In the following examples I looked through the video material and made observations shortly after each session. As both music therapist, observer and researcher, I was part of the process at the time I did the observations, interested in a broad perspective on every session, wanting to describe all the responses that I was able to see from the participant in the music therapy. My interpretations, ideas, thoughts and speculations were noted immediately after the music therapy, and were not part of the video transcripts.

In the video transcript of Mr B, I focused on his responses and noted these together with a precise time indication. The 'raw' videotapes were kept, so it was possible to go back in the material at later stages in the research process. I made notes while I was singing, and these observational data could later be processed in various ways. In the following example, I used the technique of event-coding (Robson 2002, p.334). Mr B never participated by singing in the music therapy but it happened, now and again, that he 'sobbed'. I was interested in this emotional response, or 'event', where Mr B breathed deeply and jerkily, accompanied by a sad facial expression. With the help of the video transcripts, I recorded how many times Mr B sobbed in each session (Table 9.2).

Table 9.2 shows 52 sobs altogether. They all occur during singing, which shows that they are related to this. The table does not show any clear pattern or change over time, but when the sobs are displayed according to the mean heartrate level of the session it shows that most sobs occur when heartrate is low, and that no sobs occur when heartrate is at higher levels. This relationship is shown in Figure 9.5. In one session, session 14, the heartrate level is relatively high, although Mr B sobs twice. This makes a jump on the '1–2 sobs line' and is indicated with the dotted line.

The relationship between a higher frequency of sobs and a lower heartrate level is interesting in the work of developing and refining music therapy techniques. When Mr B sobs, it is my impression that he reacts to the song that I sing to him in a nostalgic way, and that it is possible for him to communicate emotions dealing with longing, or loss, in this way. It is my belief that it is important for Mr B to share these feelings in a structured and secure situation, and that it might have an impact on his quality of life in general. With the information that the sobs occur to a higher extent when his heartrate level is low, it seems important that the music therapy sessions are structured in a way where, in the first part of the session, regulation techniques help Mr B to calm down, and where the next step is to select personal songs that he seems to recognise.

Combination of several data sources

In the last example I show a way of displaying data where different types of data are recorded in one graph. In this example time-scale, heartrate measurements, songs, sobs, etc, are put together. I made similar graphs for each session with Mr B, and the visual impression made it easy for me to recognise certain features of each session long after the end of the music therapy course. These session-graphs show how many songs are sung, the pauses between the songs and possibly specific responses given by the participant. Such a graph is a clear reduction of what happens in a music therapy session, but when dealing with huge amounts of data, as in most flexible designs, the data need to be processed and thereby reduced and selected in order to describe certain meaningful patterns.

Table 9.2 Number of sobs in each session

Session	1	2	3	4	5	6	7	8	9	10	11	12	13	14	15	16	17	18	19	20
Sobs	1	1	2	12	4	0	5	0	5	0	3	1	2	2	6	1	2	2	0	3

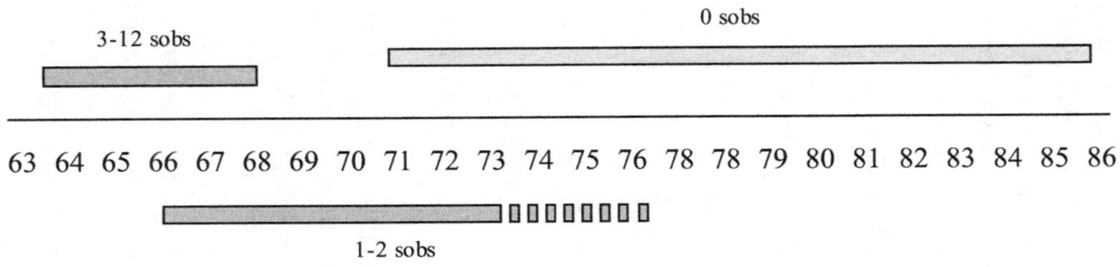

0 sobs

3-12 sobs

1-2 sobs

63 64 65 66 67 68 69 70 71 72 73 74 75 76 78 78 79 80 81 82 83 84 85 86

Figure 9.5 Sobs connected with mean heartrate of the session

Figure 9.6 is an example of a session-graph from the very last session with Mr
B. The time-scale on the horizontal axis shows that the session lasts about half an
hour. Ten songs are sung in this session, which is indicated by the oblong, grey
fields. The vertical axis shows the beat-per-minute values, that vary between 55 to
80 bpm, and show quite big changes. The biggest drops in heartrate occur when
Mr B sits with his eyes closed (- -), indicating that he takes a small nap. Usually, Mr
B does not verbalise very often, but during this session he verbalises several times,
especially before and during the last song. At 10:21 Mr B sobs for the first time. He
sobs again shortly after 10:27, and for the third time at the very beginning of the
last song (when the session-graphs are displayed in colour, it is easier to look for
similarities, differences, changes or patterns).

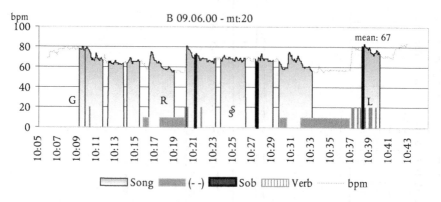

Figure 9.6 Session-graph, Mr B, session 20 (G: greeting song. L: last song)

The pattern that is interesting in this session, and is found in other sessions as well,
shows that Mr B's emotional reactions occur to the familiar songs that I sing in the
last part of the session. The first thing of importance in this session is that Mr B
remains seated instead of ambulating, and his decreasing heartrate indicates that he
apparently calms down. Shortly after song number 4 (about 10:16), Mr B closes
his eyes. When he opens his eyes again, I have a song ready for him. I sing the song
'R' (Roselil og hendes moder), a 'structure song' that I sing in every session after the
first couple of songs. Halfway through the song, Mr B seems to take a nap. When
he wakes up, he verbalises and I start singing the sixth song, a song that he knows
very well, and after some time he sobs.

    Several data from different sources are systematised in the session-graph; after
having worked with several session-graphs with several participants, I am
acquainted with reading the graphs and they give me a lot of information in a short
time. This is necessary when dealing with lots of data and wanting to get an
overview of these data.

Conclusion

Mr B suffers from moderately severe dementia and has problems in understanding and processing environmental information; in communicating linguistically and also has deficits in episodic and semantic memory function. When he sobs, he shows an emotional response to something going on here and now. In the last song, he responds promptly to the song. When I sing to Mr B, I express myself in a structured way by using well known melodic, harmonic and rhythmic features, that he can relate to in a way that is not too demanding for him and fits his capabilities. Mr B shows environmental attention and responds to something going on in the outside reality, that simultaneously resonates with inner feelings or reminiscences that he is not able to explain to me verbally.

Session 20 shows a special pattern that is important when we consider clinical applicability of this case study that was part of a case study research including more cases, as well as more research methodologies. This special pattern indicates that Mr B needs the structure and the cues built up in the music therapy session, in order to calm down – even by having a small nap. After this period of relaxation, Mr B is momentarily lucid (Norman 2001) and shows environmental attention. This brings the therapy to a point where reciprocal communication (in this case expressed by sobs and singing) is possible. Before the therapy with Mr B it was questioned if he would benefit from the music therapy. The fact that he remains seated, calms down and then, in moments, participates actively by communicating emotional responses to certain songs indicates that he benefits from the therapy. When this is related to the fact that his heartrate drops markedly in the week after the music therapy, it might tell us that the music therapy has a calming effect over time on Mr B (not being able to 'prove' this without replication). It is of general clinical relevance that the music therapist in similar situations, with clients with related problems and needs, must integrate regulating techniques in order to help the participant to calm down, as well as techniques that further the communication in the therapy with focus on non-verbal and para-linguistic expressions.

In the above examples I have shown how principles of pattern-matching with inclusion of various data sources can be employed as documentation in a case study design. They are an important foundation for the conclusions that we draw later. Case study designs are mostly related to a narrative tradition, where an in-depth understanding of the person, relationship, context, method and reflections are included. This makes this design very extensive, but has the interesting perspective that the single case might function as an eye-opener when similar or opposing patterns are recognised in the clinical setting. These may lead to new attempts to understand, describe, develop and document what we experience in practice.

CHAPTER 10

Cannabis, Brain Physiology, Changes in States of Consciousness and Music Perception

Jörg Fachner

In this chapter I would like to present an EEG study for physiological measuring of sensory data during music perception influenced by a psychoactive ingredient, namely cannabis.

Early research on music and drugs was published under the rubric of basic research on music perception, production and therapeutic use (Bonny and Pahnke 1972; Eagle 1972). A German research music therapy project by Weber focused on the use of psilocybin, a fungus with psychoactive ingredients (Weber 1974). His work was in the tradition of model psychosis research. The method of a model psychosis was invented to compare psychotic states of hallucinations with drug-induced hallucinations and to discuss its noetic and clinical considerations (Gouzoulis-Mayfrank *et al.* 1998; Leuner 1962). The aims of this approach are to describe pathological states, like states of schizophrenia, which appear to be analogous to some experiences made during psychedelic drug use. In Weber's research, a drug-induced altered music perception served as a model of functional regression to lower levels of cognitive development.

Research with psychoactive substances and music perception help cast some light upon neuro-physiological functions of state-dependent recall and cognition. In the context of pop cultural developments, drugs with euphoric, sedative and psychedelic effects have been discussed to influence life-style and artistic stance of musicians (Boyd 1992; Shapiro 1998; Whiteley 1992). The effect of cannabis on auditory perception and musicians' creativity has been a crucial issue since the early days of jazz (Mezzrow 1946; Musto 1997; Sloman 1998). For Lindsay Buckingham, cannabis seems to work like a refreshing of his listening abilities and a break-down of pre-conceptions (Boyd 1992, p.201), 'If you've been working on something for a few hours and you smoke a joint, it's like hearing it again for the first time.' George Harrison would have agreed with him (Boyd 1992, p.206), 'I think that pot definitely did something for the old ears, like suddenly I could hear more subtle things in the sound.' Not only musicians, but casual listeners also seem to be convinced that cannabis enhances auditory perception (Aldrich 1944; Tart 1971). We will return to this anecdotal conclusion later.

Studies carried out with cannabis and basic auditory perception revealed no significant changes of ear functioning (Caldwell *et al.* 1969; Martz 1972; Thaler, Fass and Fitzpatrick 1973). Investigating selective and divided attention, state-dependent learning and measuring of basic auditory functions under the influence of cannabis suggests that changes seem to be located in brain functions processing auditory information from periphery sensory organs (Globus *et al.* 1978; Moskowitz 1974).

> ... the locus of effect is very likely on attention or the central processing of the input data. There is no evidence to suggest that auditory sensory processes are effected by marihuana. (Moskowitz 1974 p.143)

Further research has not been done in this direction (for a comprehensive overview see Fachner 2000b) and therefore I thought of a small study with a mobile EEG-Brainmapping unit. I was curious to know if the above-mentioned subtle changes in auditory perception could be seen with an EEG brain imager, which visualises the topographic electrophysiological changes in the brain. If these changes were evident, would it then be possible to relate cannabis-induced auditory changes to an altered central processing of sensory data?

Methodological considerations

The physiological measure featured here is a well-known neurological diagnostic tool for measuring spontaneous or evoked changes of ongoing electrical currents in the brain, the electro-encephalogram (EEG). Gained with a set of electrodes applicative on the surface of the scalp, amplified currents can be analysed and rescheduled to the related events. It is possible to analyse the EEG visually or to quantify the EEG traces by computer-aided methods. The quantified EEG (QEEG) can be transformed to a 'brain map' of EEG activity exhibiting topographic variations of amount, percentage and amplitudes of brainwaves (Duffy 1986; Maurer 1989). The QEEG can also be statistically compared by degrees of significance (Duffy, Bartels and Burchfiel 1981).

Results of an EEG experiment are mostly shown in a distinct brainwave pattern exhibiting more or less amount of wave ranges like alpha (α), beta (β), theta (θ) or delta (δ) waves, their amplitude power, changes of frequency and topographic distribution. Such topographic activation patterns differ on frequency ranges. This is an important feature of the EEG, because dominant brainwave frequency ranges represent arousal and vigilance states, which represent different consciousness aspects of the measured experience.

The EEG is used in pharmacological tests as a marker of vigilance states induced by pharmacological agents. In neurology, it serves as a fast indicator of epilepsy, brain cancer and damage of cerebral lobes (Niedermeyer and Lopes de Silva 1993). In psychophysiology, it is sensitive to personality factors, linkable to psychological test batteries and is interpreted as a somatic indicator of psychological processes (Becker-Carus 1971; Empson 1986; Hagemann et al. 1999). Because of the time-locked occurrence of EEG, it has been used to show cerebral changes of music perception and experience compared to rest. Therefore, we have a dynamic indicator that is sensitive to personality, situation and cognitive cerebral strategies and also shows inter- and intra-individual differences to music perception (Petsche 1994).

In psychiatric diagnosis it is not easy to detect abnormalities of the EEG, but there is a long tradition of research that compares results gained in experimental settings (Hughes 1995, 1996). To achieve comparability, the idea of a normative EEG database has been discussed (John et al. 1988). So-called 'normal' subjects are measured at rest with eyes closed and their brainwave patterns compiled and averaged to a Norm-EEG. This 'blueprint of normality' should serve as a comparison to subjects for diagnosis with differing diseases but is, as yet, elusive.

There is a huge amount of EEG research but still no unified theory about origin and generation of the EEG waves. To compare results from associated studies, we have to take a close look at the research setting and methodology.

EEG, sensory data and correlated experience

What are we doing when we try to measure a physiological state of the brain? We know that the brain is an important centre both for processing what goes on in the body and for bringing the body into action, but more than this, we also know that brain activity is central to human cognitive and perceptive functions. By recording synchronised or desynchronised brainwaves through 'brain maps', we represent this relationship graphically.

We could record sensory data from afferent pathways of the auditory system by using auditory evoked potentials (AEP) because those frequency patterns represent mainly auditory data. The real time EEG used here, however, shows its event-related reactions of the subject in its complex ways, including auditory data and other sensory as represented in the ongoing brain activity. This gives us a more or less stable physiological marker of cerebral interaction related to behavioural interventions. But it is only a correlation; the EEG trace only co-relates to the measured experience. The EEG trace is not self-explanatory and says, in effect, 'What you see is a summation of post-dendrite action potentials that belong to the neuron ensembles which only become active when listening to music.'

We have to be aware that the same neuron ensembles firing when listening to music are also active when we look at a picture or eat a steak. Just as there is no such thing as a 'grandmother cell', a certain cell that responds only to a highly complex, specific and meaningful stimulus, such as the image of one's grandmother (Gross 2002), there are no 'music cells' responding particularly to music. Complex stimuli are represented by a pattern of firing across ensembles of neurons transmitting electrophysiologic information patterns, visible with an EEG apparatus. If we compare those event-related patterns with patterns derived during rest then we may see a difference. We hope that our investigated target, the perception of music listening, is revealed by comparing the different states of rest and listening.

We are in the middle, here, of the psycho-physiological measuring problem (Machleidt, Gutjahr and Mügge 1989). On the one hand, we have personal music experience, on the other, an event-related EEG trace exhibiting some describable features like frequency and amplitude. Hans Berger, who invented the EEG, hoped that the EEG would represent 'psychic energy' (see Berger 1991 p.24).

> The problem is that the experience and their phenomenological, that means describable expressions are distinct modalities of perception, that exist together but do not exchange or explain each other. The relationship between the modalities is there, because they exist together in the same time and space related coordination. (Machleidt *et al.* 1989, p.8)

Music in the EEG

Research on music and the EEG reflects the problem of inter-individually different music experiences. EEG coherence analysis shows intra-individually constant EEG-coherence profiles during music perception, but those profiles spread over the whole cortex (Petsche 1994). Music listening seems to involve many different areas but is pragmatically believed to have a right hemispheric dominance (Kolb and Whishaw 1996; Springer and Deutsch 1987) as results in EEG research conveyed (Auzou *et al.* 1995; David *et al.* 1989; Duffy *et al.* 1981; Petsche 1994; Walker 1977). However, in her review of human brain mapping methods of music perception, Sergant insists that there is no real evidence that music seems to be processed dominantly in the right cerebral cortex (Sergant 1996) and that even dichotic listening methods, auditory evoked potentials (AEP) or positron emission tomography (PET) scans vary in the localisation strategies of individual perceptions.

Davidson concludes that variations reflect individual perceptual differences and can be observed in the baseline measures before administering sound bits, music fragments or words (Davidson and Hugdahl 1996). Therefore, we should look closely at structural similarities of rest and music EEG profiles in the visual analysis of brain images.

Cannabis and EEG

Even though it is now possible to link the mechanism of cannabis action to the densities of recently discovered cannabinoid receptors in the brain and immune system (Joy, Watson and Benson 1999), topographic pre- and post-EEG studies of cannabis-induced changes are not available. Transient cannabis-induced EEG changes have been previously reported in laboratory studies. Most EEG studies that exist, however, are oriented toward finding brain damage with casual or long-term use. This was a main target during early investigations without success (Stefanis, Dornbush and Fink 1977).

Quantitative EEG measuring in the 1970s commonly used one or two electrodes attached to the right occipital or parietal areas on the scalp (Hollister, Sherwood and Cavasino 1970; Rodin and Domino 1970; Roth et al. 1973; Volavka et al. 1973; Volavka et al. 1971; Volavka, Fink and Panayiotopoulos 1977). Results of this research are somewhat contradictory. Hanley's quantitative EEG study, done with eight electrodes from frontal to occipital areas, found only decreased amplitudes and percentage over the whole spectrum (Hanley, Tyrrell and Hahn 1976). Others reported an increase in relative alpha (α)-percentages and power, a decrease in main or central frequency and a transition to theta (θ) during contemplation, as well as a decrease of relative theta- or beta (β)-percentage and power (Struve and Straumanis 1990). Measuring procedures took no regard to the interaction of substance, set and setting.

In the work of Hess and Koukkou, however, music has been part of the experimental setting (Hess 1973; Koukkou and Lehmann 1976, 1978). Both reported results that were spread in a certain order corresponding to music over the time-course of drug action. Lukas correlated euphoria and higher alpha-index during the first 20 minutes of cannabis action (Lukas, Mendelson and Benedikt 1995).

These results alerts us to the fact that the psychoactive action of cannabis induces EEG signatures that can be identified, but some frequency ranges seem to be more indicative for the quality of the actual experience.

The setting

As musicians who have recorded music in a studio, we know that it is important to know about the function and possibilities of the recording machines and the instruments used to record your music. The studio is an instrument, too. The different rooms produce differing acoustic profiles, some better for a drum-set, a bass, an orchestra, a voice or guitar. The use of these instruments depends on the idea of sound you want to produce. Similarly, the studio equipment, and the way in which the sound is mixed, influences the sound of the music.

The same happens in a laboratory when trying to record physiological measures. These measures are mostly developed by professionals in hospitals, who need them to establish diagnostic standards. The laboratory is designed as an optimal measuring setting, but here the problem starts. If we want to record what happens in everyday life, then we need to have settings similar to everyday life.

Qualitative research emphasises natural settings and encourages us to collect data, including measurements, in those places where events take place in daily life (G. Aldridge 1998; Haggman Laitila 1999). We try to represent real world situations with as few disturbances as possible.

The influence of the experimental setting in a laboratory is an important issue, particularly when we consider how the subject regards his or her control of the situation: 'Not the objective control, as planned by the investigator, determines the changes of physiological measures but the subjectively experienced influence (control) on the process by the subject' (Lutzenberger *et al.* 1985, p.65). One consequence of these considerations is to fit and adjust the measuring tool first to the situation. In scientific experiments we have to be aware that our wish to correlate behaviour and physiology will only be an approximation of what really happens.

Understanding musical experiences

To understand what makes the musical experience of one composition different from another, musicologists have analysed musical content by using scores. Score analysis, to explain varieties of music experience, has been questioned from the stance of situated performing and listening (Small 1998; Tagg 1982). Being in a concert or listening to music on the radio adds the contextual dimension of personal experience in an ongoing situation onto perceptual processes (Buytendijk 1967; Hall 1996). This influences intention and selection of what has been heard, selected and perceived consciously during perception. Perception and action are basic situations in which people find themselves. *Situationism* refers to

> the inseparability of action and context, the relation between the social and material conditions of action, the need to theorize the 'higher psychological functioning' in relation to situated action and the tension between the emphasis on situation and the scientific ideal of abstraction. (Costall and Leudar 1996, p.101)

We see from the above discussion that issues of identity, place and performance, musical practice and production styles, mediating experience of a certain song or classic composition in a specific listening or even the music production situation, are all necessary for understanding listening to music as an aesthetic experience. (Barber-Kersovan 1991; Frith 1998; Kärki, Leydon and Terho 2002)

Appropriate setting

From what we have read, we can conclude that if we are to understand music perception, as it is influenced by cannabis, then the context of listening must reflect a cultural setting where cannabis is consumed. To do this I adopted an ethnographic approach. Cannabis effects on human behaviour and life-style are complex issues that cannot be easily generated in a time-locked laboratory setting. Furthermore, collection of experimental EEG data about what occurs in the brain while listening to music under the influence of cannabis seems to offer many confounding variables. Results could be caused by differing individual perceptual strategies of listening to music (D. Aldridge 1996) as observed in the topographic EEG, a subjective history of drug experiences and tolerance effects, the varying pharmacokinetics of the substance being used and absorbed (Grinspoon 1971; Julien 1997).

We know that states of consciousness are variable (Tart 1975). There is something like a 'normal state of consciousness', and an 'altered state' after smoking cannabis. We assume, from a scientific perspective, that a comparison of quantitative data of a laboratory experiment will reveal differences in states of consciousness. Such states however, end up as small slices of data, artefact-free epochs of the process in a laboratory setting. What is lost is the timeline of the actual experience, or it may become fragmented in the process of editing comparable data-epochs and eliminating artefacts. Administering the measuring apparatus also causes behavioural discomfort for the sake of optimising data transmission. Cables have to be connected, electrodes adjusted, and posture is restricted. Sometimes the test batteries are inappropriate for a 'normal' condition.

Social scientists criticise these behavioural measuring procedures as the measuring itself has an impact on the quality of the data (Deegener 1978). Humanistic critiques also refer us to the uniqueness, and contextual nature, of the human experience, which is dependent on time and place (Rätsch 1992). Leary too emphasises the importance of set and setting in a research using psychedelic substances (Leary 1997).

The experiment

Aims

The aim of this explorative pre/post study was to examine changes in brain physiology when people smoke cannabis and listen to music in the setting of a living room at home.

Considerations

Cannabis may induce a field-related perceptual style (Dinnerstein 1968). To compensate for the previously described lack of sensitivity to the experimental setting and to reduce the laboratory-setting bias in EEG results, we need to adopt a suitable paradigm (Weil 1998). The topographic changes induced by cannabis while listening to music may well be radically different in the laboratory setting as compared with one in which the subject normally listens to music.

An obvious reason to use the EEG in researching cannabis and music perception is the time-related resolution of the data. We can observe synchronous electrophysiological traces of cognitive activity in the EEG (Petsche 1994). While the synchronous correlation of the EEG is its big advantage, it lacks spatial resolution. We can only observe summations of generating units below the surface of the brain. With the NeuroScience BrainImager®, source information is interpolated and therefore it provides spatial information about the distribution of cerebral changes. Amplitude and significance mapping (Duffy 1986; Maurer 1989) can be used to identify and localise changes of cerebral areas and their functional claims during perceptive states.

Methods

To ensure a minimum of laboratory-setting bias, a non-blind pilot study was conducted with a mobile bedside EEG-brain-mapping system in the consumers' usual setting of a living room at home. Four subjects (three male, one female) smoked a tobacco joint mixed with Nepalese hashish (hereafter phrased as THC) and listened with closed eyes to three pieces of rock music in a comfortable armchair. EEG was recorded through rest and music listening periods (see Box 10.1).

Experimental Schedule

- Baseline state: pre-THC-EEG (music and rest – eyes closed)
- Listening to three rock music pieces (defined order)
- 1-minute silence/rest between the songs
- 30 minutes intermission
- Smoking 0.3 gr. Cannabis (20 mg THC) in tobacco joint
- After 10 minutes EEG starts
- Altered state: post-THC-EEG (music and rest with THC)
- Listening to the same music/same measuring situation and setting

---

Box 10.1 Experimental schedule, four subjects (three male, one female)

The rest-EEG is compared to changes of the EEG induced by the target, in our case music. It is believed that the ongoing spontaneously occurring EEG pattern would exhibit a baseline, which shows the normal rest state of the subject's brain. Averaging the baseline recordings serves as a reference for the comparison. This opens up the possibility of comparing another mode of perceiving music – that is when the psychoactive ingredient is consumed.

Four single cases using a quantitative EEG stored on a mobile recording unit were analysed in epochs of listening in different states of consciousness (Fachner 2002b; Fachner, David and Pfotenhauer 1995).

CLOSED EYES MUSIC LISTENING AND EEG RECORDING

Following Baudelaire's description of cannabis intoxication stages, this study accompanies the second contemplative stage (Baudelaire 1966). This setting of cannabis consumption, which reflects a cannabis culture of music listening, goes back to Chinese drug culture and Harlem Tea Pads of the 1930s (Literary Digest 1934; Jonnes 1999 p.119ff). Nowadays a 'chill-out room' used in modern rave parties has the same setting characteristics. It permits a relaxed contemplative listening to music with closed eyes. Closed eyes EEG recording is a common procedure in pharmacoencephalography (Struve and Straumanis 1990), and the EEG studies reported above were selected on this premise in order to compare results with closed eyes conditions.

TOBACCO JOINT

A guideline of research in an ethnomethodological approach is to accept and describe habits, ritualistic aspects and setting of the consumer life-world as Rätsch has proposed for research on psychedelic substances (Rätsch 1992). One of the habits associated with cannabis consumption in European is to mix hashish with tobacco in a joint. The use of tobacco in this experiment is a crucial aspect, because the hashish-tobacco mixture causes different pharmaco-kinetic and pharmaco-dynamic action of THC compared to smoking only herbal cannabis or hashish. Furthermore, hashish obtained on the black market (subjects brought their own cannabis) cannot be expected to be pure. Qualitative gas chromatography testing of the smoked substance was made a week after measuring. Quality was estimated as 'medium quality', containing approximately 20 mg Δ9-THC in the used 0.3-gram hash ('Black Nepalese'). However, the aim of this study was to find out whether smoking induces changes on the EEG, not to reveal a dose-related THC action profile during music perception.

No specific inhalation technique to ensure a comparable uptake of smoke was used, because this would distract from the naturalistic setting of the experiment. Subjects were sitting in an armchair and smoked at their own pace, as they would customarily do. The subjects obviously attained a cannabis high, said they felt 'stoned' and attributed the experienced altered state of consciousness to be mainly produced by the smoked joint with hashish.

MUSIC AND SUBJECTS

The experiment started as a single case study with a follow-up (Fachner, David and Pfotenhauer 1996; Fachner et al. 1995). All three male subjects chosen for this explorative experiment reported themselves as experienced smokers of cannabis. The one female subject was a frequent smoker of cannabis. All of the four subjects refrained from smoking cannabis previously on the day of the experiment.

None of the subjects was a musician but they regarded themselves as music lovers with a preferred style of alternative rock music. Musicians differ in their perception of music as EEG studies have shown (Altenmüller and Beisteiner 1996; Petsche, Pockberger and Rappelsberger 1987).

The music was chosen by the first subject (see Fachner et al. 1995). As a first piece in the experimental sequence he chose the instrumental 'Prelude' by King Crimson (1974). The next song, 'Obsessed', was a folk-punk number with vocals, acoustic guitars, drums and bass, recorded by Dogbowl (1989). The third piece is a live recording cover version of the Beatles song 'We Can Work It Out' performed by King Missile (1989). Songs were played in the same order during pre- and post-THC conditions for all other subjects.

EEG-BRAINMAPPER

The NeuroScience BrainImager samples 28 EEG traces with a 12-bit analogue/ digital converter. This offers 4096 dots per second within a dynamic range (DR) of 256 Microvolt (μV), providing a sample accuracy of 1/16th μV. Average maps interpolated between the 28 EEG trace sample points are processed every 2.5 seconds. The Imager is equipped with an isolation transformer and shielded pre-amplification to be used for example in an intensive care unit, as well as a notch filter on 50–60 Hz to reduce the influence of electromagnetic fields in hostile environments.

Impedance levels were kept under 11 kohms. Cut-off filters were set to 40 and 0.3 Hz. Electro-oculogram (EOG), electrocardiogram (ECG) or electromyography (EMG) traces for artefact control were not applied to avoid laboratory bias. Artefact control was done visually by a time-coded video protocol of EEG traces and subjects. After removing potential artefact maps, (fronto-polar δ threshold at 105 μV on 256 μV DR) Individual and Group Averages were processed using the statistics software package of the NeuroScience BrainImager®.

Pre- and post-rest and pre- and post-music listening results were averaged and subjected to a T-Test. Therefore each piece of music and one minute of silence before the music was recorded and individually averaged, subsequently. The investigation included one extended single-case study with a follow-up (Fachner et al. 1995, 1996). Research focus for each person was on individual drug and music reactions by comparing the pre- and post-individual averages (IA) and the total group average (GA) of the pre- and post-rest and music sessions over the sample. Amplitude mapping does not provide dynamical changes of the music but represents average electrophysiological activity while listening as reflected in the maps. Furthermore, we are able to name areas of difference in the pre- and post-conditions.

Results

The first illustration shows the T-Probability mapping of the EEG changes from pre- to post-THC listening for the first piece of music for one subject. The reference file was pre-THC listening and it was compared to post-THC music listening. From the upper left to the right we see δ-, θ-, and α-probabilities, below β I+II and the spectral mapping. The view is from above the head. What seems to be of interest for a possible cannabis-induced auditory perception style are the obvious α-changes in the left and especially in the right temporal cortex. The temporal cortex hosts the auditory system and main association areas.

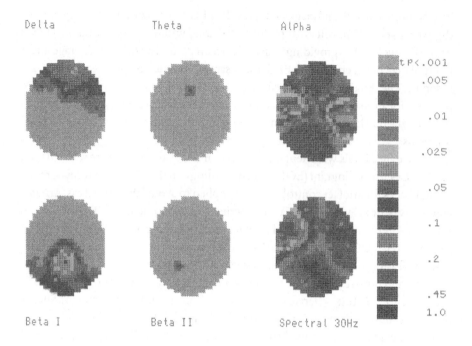

Figure 10.1 Significance mapping T-probabilities pre- and post-EEG changes; first piece of music; n=1

While listening to the first piece of music highly significant changes (p.001) with three subjects in the pre- and post-comparison from pre-THC-music to the first post-THC-music average have been observed. These highly significant changes after ten minutes of smoking mark the first plateau of drug action and a changed listening state. As a proof of Lindsey Buckingham's statement above, it shows that subjects experience and process music in a different way from previously. In all subjects, significance decreased with the second and third song in the sequence (Figure 10.2).

Upon examination of T-Test changes of the second piece of music, we can see δ-, θ- and β-changes, as well as spectral frequency speed changes on the left side of the brain. The left side hosts motor and sensory speech centres, which seem to change more when listening to rock songs with words. This might be of interest for aphasia research.

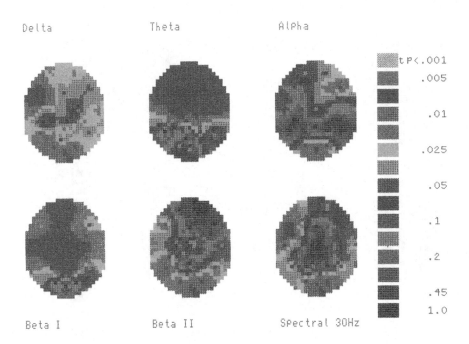

Figure 10.2 Significance mapping T-test pre- and post-EEG changes; second piece of music; n=1

The brain map in Figure 10.3 shows highly significant changes from pre-THC-rest to the post-THC-music EEG of the first piece in the series. As we observed before, this T-Test again shows α-changes over the temporal regions. This might indicate changes in auditory cerebral processing. However, α-mapping showed remarkable changes in amplitude levels, as we observe in Figure 10.4.

Figure 10.4 shows the α-GA over four subjects for the pre/post-rest condition. The 16 colours of the 30 µV Scale represent a 2-µV step on a dynamic range of 256 µV. Comparing pre- and post-rest visually, a decrease of α-percentage and amplitude in the post-THC-rest-EEG was observed with all four subjects. The post-THC-rest amplitude decrease in the parietal areas showed an individual range from 6-10 µV. The GA over four subjects seen here shows a difference of 2 µV. Decrease of amplitudes in rest over the whole frequency range was reported by Hanley *et al.* (1976) and is similarly observed in the present study.

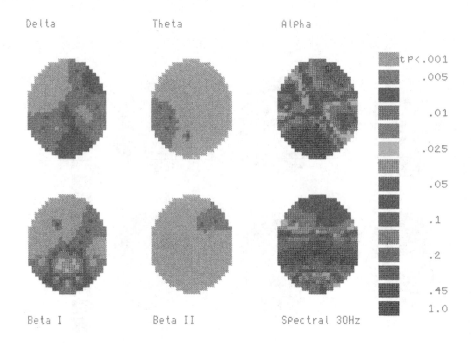

Figure 10.3 Significance mapping T-probabilities EEG-changes from rest to music; n=1

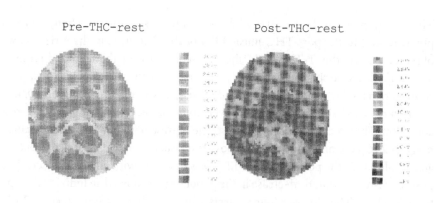

Figure 10.4 Amplitude mapping pre- and post-THC-rest alpha changes; n=4

In Figure 10.5 we see the pre- and post α-GAs of listening to music. An increase of relative α-percentage in parietal regions was observed in the post-THC-music GA for all four subjects. Compared to the pre-THC-music EEG, the individual increase of amplitudes ranged from 2–4 μV. The α-range even indicated changes on higher and lower frequency ranges, mapping of α-standard deviance showed highest deviance in the parietal regions.

Pre-THC-music   Post-THC-music

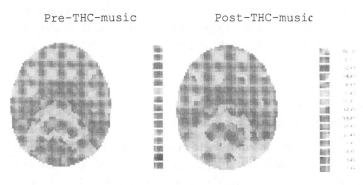

Figure 10.5 Amplitude mapping pre- and post-THC-music alpha changes; n=4

A decrease of α-amplitudes in post-THC-rest and an increase in the post-THC-music EEG has been observed with all subjects, as well as a decrease of percentage and power of the other frequency ranges. Post-THC-decrease of δ-, θ-, and β-amplitudes was a constant observation throughout the individual averages of the four subjects and was observed in GA of the four persons, as well. Higher amplitudes, especially on δ- and θ- range, but also on central parietal β-areas, were observed in the pre-THC-mapping. In temporal areas the θ-decrease is remarkable. Pre-THC-music listening caused an increase of θ-percentage compared to the resting state. In the post-THC-music-maps the percentage decreased in central and frontal regions more than in rest condition, but most decreases appear in both temporal regions.

As seen before, significance mapping of individuals showed highly significant changes (p.001) between pre-THC-rest, pre-THC-music and post-THC-music. Comparing the pre- and post-music listening GA of the four subjects a significance of p.025 on α-range for the left occipital region was detected. Pre-THC-rest compared to post-THC-music showed a small change in the left occipital, as well as the comparison of pre- and post-GA of music listening. This particular region around O1 (left occipital electrode) showed a faster frequency in the spectral map. The occipital region is known to change under the influence of music (Konovalov and Otmakhova 1984; Petsche 1994; Walker 1977). In this context, the change of occipital alpha might indicate changes in visual association linked to music. This region should be investigated with further studies.

A significant change (p.025) at electrode T4 (right temporal lead) was observed in the right temporal cortex. It seems that the Θ-decrease over the temporal lobe reported above is more prominent in the right hemisphere. Comparing post-THC-rest and post-THC-music GA, a small change in this temporal area was also observed on β-1. Alterations in the temporal lobe EEG might represent changes in the hippocampus region as well. The hippocampus is rich in cannabinoid receptors and has a strong impact on memory functions and information selection.

Discussion of results
CHANGES IN TEMPORAL AREAS

During pre-THC-music listening theta-percentage increased but decreased more in post-THC-music than during rest (see Figure 10.6). Comparing pre- and post-THC-music, differences (p.025) were found in the right fronto-temporal cortex on theta, and on alpha in the left occipital cortex (see Figure 10.7). In both temporal lobes, theta-amplitudes decreased during post-THC-music as well. Significant (p.025) changes in temporal and occipital areas and increasing alpha signal strength in parietal association cortex represent a neural correlate of altered music perception and hyperfocusing on the musical time-space.

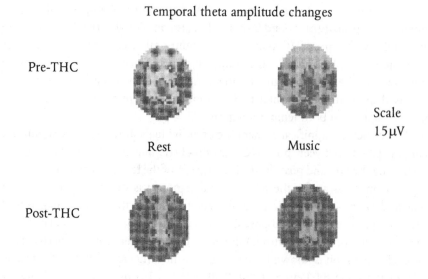

Figure 10.6 Amplitude mapping theta; pre- and post-THC-music and rest; n=4

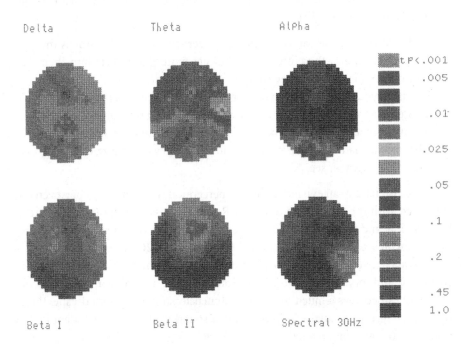

Figure 10.7 Significance mapping T-Test pre- and post-THC-music; temporal and occipital areas (p<0.025); n=4

HOLONOMIC MEMORY FUNCTION, TIME AND A METRIC FRAME OF REFERENCE

Webster claims a 'different manner of retrieval' in memory function during states of cannabis consciousness that are not organised in a sequential linguistic, but a more holonomic order (Webster 2001, p.218) in music, as an aesthetic and Gestalt-oriented manner during music perception. Weakening of hippocampal censorship function and overload competing of neuronal conceptualisations during information selection (Emrich *et al.* 1991) might be connected to cannabis-induced prolonged time estimation and intensity scaling.

Mathew reports a cannabis-induced change of time sense correlated with changes of cerebellum blood flow (Mathew *et al.* 1998). The cerebellum is associated with movement organisation and time-keeping functions. Music is a means of forming time – that is per-forming that exists both 'in' and 'of' time (D. Aldridge 1996).

One Gestalt that might be perceived more intensely in 'cannabis consciousness' (Webster 2001, p.99) is a fundamental element of music, and that is rhythm. A good picture of these processes was given by one of Anslinger's co-workers (in Sloman 1998, pp.146–147):

> ...the chief effect, as far as they were concerned, is that it lengthens the sense of time, and therefore they could get more grace beats into their music than they could if they simply followed a written copy. ... In other words, if you're a musician, you're going to play the thing the way it's printed on a sheet. But if you're using marijuana, you're going to work in about twice as much music between the first note and the second note. That's what made jazz musicians. The idea that they could jazz things up, liven them up, you see.

What we also have in an expanded form of perception is that auditory perspectives are linked with the visual. The drummer Robin Horn said, 'it (pot) does create a larger vision, and if that's the case, then it would apply to your instrument because the more you see, the more you can do' (Boyd 1992, p.205).

Changed left occipital and right temporal EEG activities represent such a change of auditory perspective on musical acoustics. Listening to a record via headphones becomes a much more three-dimensional moving soundscape, there seem to be 'greater spatial relations between sound sources', as Tart identified a characteristic cannabis experience in the state of 'being stoned' (Tart 1971, p.75).

HYPERFOCUSING ON SOUND

A comparison of the individual pre- and post averages subjects showed intra-individual stable EEG-Gestalt, for one subject even in the follow-up. Intra-individual stability of the whole EEG-Gestalt in rest and activation replicated findings on personality and situational sensitivity of the EEG (Davidson and Hugdahl 1996; Hagemann et al. 1999; Koukkou and Lehmann 1978; Machleidt et al. 1989). The α-focus in parietal regions showed individual topographic shapes of receptive activity. This indicates personality factors represented in the EEG, but changes on α-amplitude clearly suggest a functional intensification of individual hearing strategy, as can be observed in Figure 10.8.

Following Jausovec, we can observe more effective information processing. Jausovec associated higher α-scores with a more efficient information processing strategy, less mental workload and flow (Jausovec 1997a, 1997b). Curry also proposes a 'hyperfocusing of attention on sound' as an explanation for changes in the Figure-ground relationship, no. 10 while listening to music (Curry 1968, p.241). This cognitive change of hearing strategy may be mediated via changed time perception for the rhythmical grid and synchronically expanded intensity scaling (Globus et al. 1978) for frequency patterns in acoustic relationships.

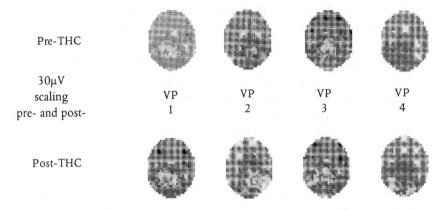

Figure 10.8 Amplitude mapping pre- and post-THC-music alpha Gestalt (VP=Subject 1, 2, etc)

De Souza described a cannabis-induced change of preference for higher frequencies (de Souza, Karniol, and Ventura 1974). High frequencies represent overtone patterns and provide, along with aural time-delay patterns, localisation information about sound sources in acoustic space. This cannabis-induced focusing on higher frequencies might function like an enhancer or exciter in studio technology does by providing a broader acoustic space.

'ARE YOU EXPERIENCED?' – LEARNING AND CEREBRAL LISTENING STRATEGY

Looking at the process of listening, highly significant pre- and post changes ($p<0.001$) occur while listening to the first piece of music but significance decreases for the second and third piece in the experimental sequence. Changes in temporal areas on α-frequency indicate a change in auditory processing.

The experienced user of cannabis effects may be able to use the altered auditory metre and intensity for aesthetic purposes. Becker, in his analysis of jazz musician behaviour, explained how cannabis effects have to be perceived, learned, and domesticated before using them effectively (Becker 1963) including the ability to switch those relational patterns off when needed (Weil 1998; Weil, Zinberg and Nelsen 1968). A skilled and trained musician, however, might benefit from 'losing track' (Webster 2001) during an improvisation and even while playing composed structures. This way of reducing irrelevant information offers spontaneous rearrangement of a piece, a vivid performance with enlarged emotional intensity scaling, and the opening of improvisational possibilities by breaking down preconceptions and restructuring habituated listening and performing patterns (Fachner 2000a, 2002a).

The potential use of cannabis-induced changes in perception can be suggested for medical purposes. Hearing loss could be affected by stimulating the cannabinoid receptor function for retraining purposes, as we know from tinnitus research. Tinnitus patients suffer from continuously present frequency patterns, noise, which can be reduced by systematically ignoring them (Jastreboff, Gray and Gold 1996). The reverse may also be true; it might be useful to investigate cannabis-induced psycho-acoustic enhancing effects for re-training high frequency ranges as a compensatory factor in hearing loss.

CBR ACTIVITY, 'REVERSE ALPHA' AND THE CANNABIS HIGH

Compared to pre-THC-rest and pre-THC-music in the post-THC-music EEG, a rise of alpha percentage and power was observed in the parietal cortex on four subjects, while other frequencies decreased in power. Alpha amplitude changes are similar to 'reverse alpha' findings in studies with gifted individuals (Jausovec 1997a, 1997b, 1998). In these studies, the degree of mental workload and effectiveness of problem solving seemed to be represented by the α-amplitude. An increase marks less mental workload in appropriate brain areas, whereas a decrease represents increased workload. Music seems to be processed more easily with cannabis than without. The rise of average α-amplitudes about 4 μV might be a neurophysiological indicator for the so-called state of 'being high' (Solomon 1966). That auditory information is processed more easily is another argument for using cannabis as a supportive hearing aid.

CANNABIS AS A HEARING ENHANCER?

If we can perceive music much 'better' than before, then maybe using cannabis can help the hearing-impaired. Results reported in the literature, and reflected in this experiment, suggest that cannabis could be used to enhance hearing ability. Acoustic properties of perceived sound are enhanced permitting a more effective spatial distinction between sound sources, which is of importance in hearing loss. Significant changes in temporal and occipital brain areas seem to support this assumption (see Figure 10.7). The changes in these areas represent a changed auditory perspective on musical acoustics, and should be taken into account for further research on cannabis-induced enhanced acoustic perception (Fachner 2002b).

Furthermore, the increased α-percentages over the parietal cortex, which might indicate an intensified perceptual strategy with less mental workload, could be used for training programs with hearing-impaired persons. Acquired hearing loss in high frequency ranges could be compensated throughout reactivating and relearning acoustic memory shapes. Cannabis could be used to intensify the cerebral hearing strategy of the hearing-impaired person. Regarding the discussion about brain plasticity, the cannabis effect might help hearing-impaired persons to compensate for lost abilities.

Thaler's study showed highly significant improvement for a hearing impaired person on an audiological Word-Test (Thaler *et al.* 1973). Others report that prosodic differentiation seems to be enhanced (Rodin and Domino 1970; Tart 1971). In view of the fact that spoken language is based on non-verbal musical elements, and that supra-segmental and prosodic features constitute the sound of the human voice (D. Aldridge 1996) it is possible that it is easier for a hearing-impaired person to catch the meaning of a sentence after having smoked cannabis.

Speech perception enhancement might be of interest for aphasia patients (see Figure 10.2). Further research is needed to explore possible benefits of cannabis for the hearing-impaired.

IMPLICATIONS FOR MUSIC THERAPY

Individual and group significance mapping on alpha-topography exhibited no significant parietal changes from pre-THC to post-THC music listening (see Figures 10.1, 10.2 and 10.7), but all subjects' parietal areas showed enhanced alpha amplitudes (see Figures 10.5 and 10.8). The parietal EEG topographies of music listening exhibited inter-individually different EEG gravity Gestalts (see Figure 10.8) but were in pre- and post-condition stable intra-individually. This means that music is perceived and processed differently inter-individually, but intra-individually the cerebral listening strategy is linked to personality and the way music is perceived is coherent as seen in the brain maps. This might serve as an electrophysiological indicator during the course of individual therapy.

One of the goals of active music therapy is to extend personal expressivity and relationship abilities during improvisation. We know that cannabis has a certain action profile, which has an impact on playing and listening to music. Becker demonstrated that musicians were able to habituate to the cannabis effects (Becker 1963) and used time-expansion issues and emotional enhancement of intensity scaling (Globus *et al.* 1978) for their artistic expression. A reduction of inhibitions can offer a more direct way of emotional expression and this made jazz musicians hot in their playing (Shapiro 1998). Jazz music has promoted improvisational abilities of musicians and created as a tool which music therapists use in active music therapy for their work with clients.

From the stance of modern receptor science, the external agent of cannabis docks on the internal endogenous receptor and stimulates the system more intensively than when it is being activated through endogenous cannabinoid activity.

This shows that cannabis only works as an enhancer of what is already there and does not add something completely new. One will not be suddenly able to play an instrument without learning, but preconceptions about what is possible and ways of perceiving the acoustic field will be changed. But when generations of users report that they can listen to sound more distinctly and that cannabis enhances their appreciation of music, why shouldn't a patient benefit who is consenting to the use in therapy?

Some pioneering work on the use of psychoactive substances during music therapy done by Peter Hess and colleagues has shown that cannabis might also work as an adjunct helper in therapy (Hess 2002). One Alzheimer patient receiving an oral dose was able to concentrate more deeply on sound than before and was attending the therapy process with much more cognitive attendance than before. Cannabis may help to broaden and intensify state-dependent recall of music memory structures and situated cognition of emotional learning.

Conclusion

The study gives promising insights into quantified EEG changes of pre- and post-THC music listening as provided by amplitude and significance mapping over averaged EEG epochs of music. Results are not based on a high number of subjects but on ethnographic EEG correlation of 'stoned' listening to music.

Accompanying this process in the life world provides naturalistic authenticity of tendencies occurring during those processes. Further laboratory research could compare several issues reported and discussed in this ethnographic intervention.

It is possible:

- to combine a qualitatively orientated setting of a single-case study with the quantitative measuring of the target behaviour

- to compare intra-individual epochs of experience statistically

- to compare inter-individual data of epochs by importance related to the adequate setting of the targeted behaviour.

As long as we are trying to measure complex perceptive behaviour, as in music, we must include the context to obtain a result that is close to the real-life situation. Research has to be fitted into real world situations and methods adapted to daily life. Context-derived results have an element of authenticity. It is important to know the technological limitations of a measuring device like a mobile EEG to achieve 'good' quality recordings.

We were able to investigate a single case with a follow-up and compare intra-individual activity of two different recordings in a distance of three years

(Fachner *et al.* 1995, 1996). It was possible to show an intra-individual stable altered music perception indicated by the same topographic activation centres of gravity. Further investigation with four other subjects confirmed topographic activations patterns seen in the single-case study (Fachner 2001).

CHAPTER 11

Guidelines for Case Study Design Research in Music Therapy

David Aldridge

There is a wide range of considerations which need to be made before we begin clinical research. Perhaps the most important question to ask is what the specific guidelines for clinical research are within your own institution or the institution where the research is to take place. Clinicians intending to do research should find sufficient advice to plan a research proposal from the institution where they are working. This will also mean that sufficient advice is given concerning the ethics committee of the institution.

However, one of the first considerations is a matter of attitude. Many of us start out to research with the overwhelming conviction that our work is the greatest idea since sliced bread and widgets in beer cans. As a colleague once reminded me, 'It's a doctoral thesis, not a Nobel Prize entry'. While needing to be self-confident, we also need to be modest in our aims. Rarely do we change the world with a single piece of music therapy research. Those people who have changed the world, have not set out to do so, it is the application of their ideas that has proved their geniality. In addition, we can be so overwhelmed with the brilliance of what we are doing that we keep the project to ourselves and refuse to co-operate with others. I understand the basis of this. Ideas do get stolen. The negative side is that by protecting an idea, we fail to refine it through discussion with others. If you are researching, find a group of trustworthy colleagues who have capabilities that you can use. Most doctoral candidates express the importance of belonging to a group where they can discuss their projects together. The same goes for all of us as researchers; our good ideas can get even better with a little help from our friends. But when we discuss our ideas, it is also a good idea to discuss those ideas with competent critical partners. Researching is not about the justification of your ideas but the refinement of raw ideas through the fire of criticism. In this way we really achieve the nuggets of research gold that we are seeking.

One of the keys to successful planning is to ask crucial questions early in the research process. Here are some considerations which a research methodologist would ask of you.

Motivation

Why are you doing this anyway?

First you need a good idea. The difficulty with good ideas is that they do not always withstand the rigours of questioning. What may seem to be a good idea in the early hours of the morning, while driving home in the afternoon, or particularly after a meal with enthusiastic friends in a restaurant, in the cool light of the next day may not be as world-shattering as you thought.

The next stages of writing the ideas down for colleagues to criticise and making overtures to funding agencies are far more gruelling. It is necessary to develop a tolerance for criticism of your ideas and see how this strengthens them. We need to take a step back and see that criticism of an idea is not necessarily a criticism of us as a person. But the whole process of research is a series of challenges. If that research is to be published, then the work will be challenged by peer reviewers. If it is part of an academic study for the award of a qualification, then the study will be rigorously examined. If it is a study intended to change policy or influence practice, there will be rigorous challenges from vested interests. Research, then, is only for the robust (or thick-skinned). Indeed, many of the traits of a researcher, being indifferent to criticism and single-minded in pursuing a singular aim, are probably not the best assets for maintaining long-term friendships nor winning popularity contests. Like the immune system, challenges can also bring responses that strengthen us. Perhaps the most important step that the researcher can take is to become part of a group where ideas can be stated and discussed constructively. This is also the function of research supervision, in the same way that we have clinical supervision.

If you wish to do research then it is a continuing struggle to maintain that first flush of excitement against what may seem unreasonable odds and what at times seem to be tiresome practical details. These challenges are the ones that curb our worst excesses and in the end facilitate our research. Research takes a great deal of personal motivation. It is important to find some form of personal and professional support which is supportive but critical. In addition, it is possible to work as a group to support each other, share varying skills and to teach each other about research methods. This not only applies to novice researchers. While doctoral qualifications give us the wherewithal to research independently, most of us realise that we need to belong to a supportive group of researchers to maintain our own creativity and help put our ideas into a meaningful context.

For whom are you doing this study?

This is an important question as it ultimately determines the scope of your research and what resources that you bring to the research.

First, if it is a study that will bring you a research qualification then the study is for you. It is part of your training and will give you the basic qualification as a scientific researcher or the platform from which you can do further research. Indeed, as I wrote earlier, my doctoral students are expected to have a burning question that they themselves want to answer. The resources are far more personal and the research is tailored to meet their specific requirements. While we are equal as human beings, our learning needs differ.

Second, it may be that your immediate working group or institution has a research program and this research intends to meet institutional aims. The contents of the study will be debated within a group and they too will be part of bringing resources to bear on what you need.

We have recently completed a series of studies of Qigong for the treatment of chronic complaints like asthma, hypertension and migraine. Although these were doctoral projects for individual candidates, they were supported by a group of medical colleagues who referred patients, offered treatment, suggested questionnaires, developed statistical consultancy skills and criticised ideas.

Not everyone in an institution will want to research, but some may want to do research that is pertinent to the needs of their colleagues and others will offer to help. The ramifications of that research can then be brought into teaching and practice. In a small scale study of music therapy for the treatment of developmentally delayed children, we found that music therapy worked as a short-term intervention. By looking deeper into the statistics we saw that particular improvements were related to the therapy. These aspects were improved relationship, goal-directed listening and hand-eye co-ordination (Aldridge, Gustorff and Neugebauer 1996). As a team, we are still using the results of this study today in our teaching and to guide our further research studies.

Third, there is another group for whom you may be researching, the patients themselves. It is quite possible that a self-help group, or an interested group of patients may wish research to be carried out on their behalf, or they themselves may wish to participate. This too will influence the research study, its objectives and the resources that you can bring to bear. A doctoral study completed here for the treatment of aphasia using a modified form of music therapy was extremely successful. Local self-help groups had supported the music therapist in her ideas and stimulated her to demonstrate that what she had found in practice could be verified formally in a study. Once that study was completed, the challenge was how to teach that particular clinical approach and implement into a regional health care service.

While evidence-based medicine is a vogue movement within music therapy, research has always concentrated on providing applicable results but asks the question 'evidence for whom?' As we see above, the evidence for professional groups, funding agencies, teaching colleagues, patient self-groups, while being of a recognised scientific standard, is multifarious in its forms and intentions.

Resources

How are you going to pay for this research? or Do you have the money?

It is important to bear in mind that research is greedy for resources. A good idea is in itself of little value unless it can be realised in practice. Clinical research can be expensive, particularly if it takes you away from clinical practice. Research grant funding requires time in terms of writing proposals and getting a proposal through both an ethical committee and funding committees. This is where it is advisable to belong to a group of researchers who can advise each other on funding possibilities. Some charities support particular researchers, for example, a charity that supports professional women as the next generation of scientific researchers. It is also important to remember the power of personal persuasion. An art therapist working with me has convinced donors to support her research simply because they support what she is doing clinically, and have asked her what she needs to develop her ideas. That she comes under the umbrella of a university research initiative helps, but the principal initiative came from her. In her search for donations she has split her needs into computing, travelling and living costs, which in turn are supported by differing donors.

Do you have the time to do this research?

It is essential to plan your own time very carefully as a researcher. Before the research and during the progress of the work, even in preparation, it is important to have time to think about what you are doing. It is also vital to read research literature thoroughly and perhaps with a different approach to the one which is used to scan journals for articles of interest. If you are a clinician who wishes to research concurrent with practice, then you may have to consider drastically reducing your clinical practice or working with a restricted range of patients. The activity of research thinking and planned reading, while appearing a luxury to colleagues, may mean a change in attitude to working for the clinician who constantly has to be seen to 'do'. At this stage it is useful to consider how long a period you want to spend on your research project, and then set a target date for the end of that period.

Finally, your immediate family and friends may not quite share your singleminded commitment to advancing the cause of modern scientific endeavour. Apart from research eating into recreation time, those sudden flashes of inspiration of extended thoughts concerning methodological conundrums can occur at weekends or in the evening when you begin to relax. Sometimes spouses do not appreciate the riddle of formulating an algorithm for multiple variables measured over a time series, especially if this occurs over dinner. Children are not always forgiving about postponed trips to their favourite places. After all, a day only has 36 hours.

Do you have help and support?

Research is a serious activity and cannot be tacked on to other activities. We have to find a focus in research and similarly in our working lives. For a study to come to fruition it will require careful planning and expertise.

If possible, find some specialist advice either from a colleague who has researched in the field you are considering, from a known expert in the field or from the funding agency you intend to approach. It is at this stage that statistical, theoretical or methodological advice must be sought, not after data is collected. It is also necessary to find out which colleagues will be willing to co-operate with your work. If we accept the concept of clinical supervision, then we must also consider the possibility of research supervision. The same attitude goes for training; while we train thoroughly as clinicians to be licensed for practice, we forget that we need to also train as researchers.

While we accept in many therapies that we need supervision, it is often forgotten that researchers also need advisors or supervisors. It doesn't matter how experienced we become, we still have blind-spots in our understanding and in our methodological knowledge. Having a supervisor, advisor or supportive experienced colleague is an important resource. Listening to that advice is also an ability that has to be developed.

Will your employer offer support by giving you free time to research/write?

One of the best solutions to research in clinical practice has been a sympathetic employer. With cutbacks in health care funding, those sources of help are sadly missing. What can be negotiated is time to research, to read the relevant literature or to visit symposia. It is possible to convince employers that the service being offered will benefit from your research or that the institution within which you are working will gain from published research. However, it still means that weekends are a luxury and that priorities within personal relationships have to be re-negotiated.

What we attempt is to support researchers by encouraging them to seek stipendia. Not only are employers recompensed but researchers can often make themselves independent for a short period of time. This is of special significance when research needs to be written up for publication. Again, this returns us to the importance of research support that needs to be negotiated. While we may have our own individualised projects, the way forward is to become part of a team or network sharing resources.

Purpose of the inquiry

Are you asking a question or making a clinical statement?

It is important to ask your questions precisely. A question must be clear and simple. This process of clarifying your own emerging question, so that it can be understood by others, is a vital stage for your work and for finding funds. By defining the purpose of the study, you will help define the target audience for your work. This will in turn influence the research methods you use.

If you are making a clinical statement, then the work is not necessarily research, it is more in the direction of clinical audit. The process of research is *re-search*, looking again at what you know. When knowledge is questioned it leads the questioner further, that is the purpose of research. If you want to justify your practice through a series of case examples, this does not necessarily develop anything new, it substantiates what you already know. As writers we do this all the time. We substantiate what we know from our own practice or practice with others with the intention of offering guidelines for practice and it may mean that we gather divergent material together in a new way. What a research approach would do is to take those materials and then assess them for their commonalities of meaning or conflicts in understandings using a rigorous methodology that the reader can follow to discern how conclusions are reached. This is the process that we have seen in the previous chapters.

A colleague of mine is a respected practitioner. His music therapy practice was well known through presentations at conferences and through the visitors that he had to his music therapy centre. He produced many songs that were original and targeted for particular problems with children. He spent a long time in tormenting himself about whether or not to do research, artificially constructing questions that would appear as if he wanted to study. But what he really wanted to do was to write his own book. Once he had a perspective on his own work, that validated his practice without needing to 'research', he found room to say what he wanted to say, and was considerably relieved. Having something important to say is a good reason to write, but it does not automatically mean that this is the basis for a research project.

Who are you trying to convince?

Most clinicians, when they do research, are attempting to convince someone of the validity of their approach. Either they are trying to convince other practitioners, licensing authorities, journal editors, consumers or patients. It is important to be able to see what you are doing and why. In the field of music therapy it is important to state where such practice can be used within a current health care framework, and how such a practice fits in with orthodox practice. In addition it is important to show where the proposed work will improve research expertise, current clinical practice or have an educational component.

In Germany the arts therapies, including music therapy, were threatened with not being recognised as therapies suitable for hospitals through the new health care reforms. By submitting a detailed document about what research had taken place in the arts therapies, we could make sure that the arts therapies were included on the list of recognised therapies. We did not need to produce an evidence-based medicine review, simply an authorised account of the breadth of research that has taken place in acute hospital treatment. This was achieved successfully because we entered into dialogue with the people who wanted the information. They could tell us what we needed.

Aims of the study

The aims of clinical studies are multifarious. The exploration and generation of hypotheses, the refinement of those hypotheses, the discovery of the optimal use of a therapeutic regimen, the safety of that regimen or the active ingredient in a composite therapy are common aims. Similarly music therapists often want to make a definitive demonstration of their therapeutic approach in comparison with another approach or to demonstrate feasibility, or efficacy, in a particular setting.

In the interest of simplicity, it is better to understand what you are attempting and then ask yourself if you are taking on too much. Rather than attempt an overly complex study, that is both explanatory and pragmatic, it may be possible to work as a research group of practitioners satisfying interdependent aims. In this way of working practitioners can work co-operatively with colleagues developing differing sets of answers that answer a common question.

For example, in this book some therapists concentrate on developing method- ologies that show physiological changes during and after the process of therapy as explanatory trials, others are concerned with clinical outcomes as pragmatic trials, and yet others are concerned in the theoretical debate about the nature of musical parameters in therapy. Many of us start out trying to do all three.

One of the most common problems in assessing research proposals is that the researcher aims to do too much. Many researchers want both to investigate their own practice and develop an assessment method. As we have few assessment instruments for music therapy, then suitable studies would develop such instru- ments. We are continually confounded, for example, by lacking a standardised form of videotape analysis. There are instruments in the field of ethnology but until now we have not adapted them for music therapy. The same goes for a qualitative analysis method for analysing videotaped material. It is at this basic level of research that we must also be active to build a platform for further research studies.

It is in the aims section where you will state your hypotheses or ideas to be tested or developed. I am using hypothesis in a loose way here, based on the Greek *hypotithenai*, to put under or suppose where an assumption or concession is made for the sake of argument, or where the interpretation of a practical situation is used as a basis for action. Contained within the notion of hypothesis is that it is a tentative assumption made in order to draw out and test its logical or empirical consequences. It implies that more examination is needed before we can make a firm statement. It is simply a way of saying 'From my experience and what I have read from a theoretical background, with what my colleagues have told me, then I think the situation can be explained like this.' In a clinical project, where a design is fixed, then the project can be expressed as 'If I do A in prescribed circumstances, then I predict that B will happen.' In flexible designs we often only know the con- sequences after the events are analysed. Case studies are often the study of process so that we can retrospectively discover the hypothesis and the consequences as an emerging and completed story. The important thing to remember is that an hypothesis is simply a well-informed explanatory idea that has achieved form and may lead to prediction.

Planning pilot and exploratory studies

It really is important to make exploratory or pilot studies, and not an easy option. By trying out our ideas in practice we see the pitfalls and the possibilities of what we are attempting. Some of these pitfalls can he avoided by asking expert opinion beforehand. Unfortunately the pressure of research sponsors can be for precocious results and evidence that something is being done for their money. Exploratory trials and critical developmental thinking are often sacrificed to such impatience.

Pilot studies are not any easier to construct methodologically. Definitive studies cannot be generated from poorly thought out exploratory studies. As much methodological thinking must go into the pilot studies as the larger study. Data must be carefully evaluated in a series of sequential experiments. These are the platform for the future work. Some doctoral studies are in themselves explanatory studies. We cannot always know what is going to emerge, that is what makes research interesting and such studies pave the way for future investigations.

In a study of Qigong for asthma, we found that it was it was a sub-group of participants who practised regularly where the best results were obtained (Aldridge and Aldridge 2002). From this finding in the pilot study, we could then make firm recommendations for a clinical trial about the structuring of the taught courses and the intervening practice periods.

We can never be sure that the equipment is appropriate or sensitive enough. For those of us that use questionnaires, we can never be sure that the questionnaire will be applicable. Finding case material for a study may depend upon gatekeepers, initially willing to be helpful, but who may get cold feet later. We were to make a retrospective case study in a European clinic renowned for its specialist approach to the treatment of cancer. Central to this treatment was the achievement of a specific body temperature. When we made a pilot study of the records spanning a period of twenty-five years, we found that the measurements were unusable. Temperature had been taken orally, axially and anally, at differing times by differing personnel, and irregularly. Without a pilot study we would not have known that the data was so precarious. We had assumed that the measurement of temperature would be a basic activity if it was central to the therapy.

Setting and contexts

In your preliminary thinking you will have begun to understand the gaps in present knowledge. You will then need to say how your case study will begin to fill these gaps and contribute to that knowledge. This understanding is based on your own clinical knowledge and that of current expertise from other practitioners but is also based on reviewing the available literature. We also have to say why we are choosing a particular location and time. In addition, ideas are located within a culture of ideas, a conceptual ecology. We need to describe where those ideas are coming from and what thinking has influenced them. The early case study work in the social sciences was based upon social ideas and made those ideas apparent.

Literature reviews

A good review will help identify work already done, or in progress, that is relevant to your work and prevent you from duplicating what has already been done. If we read previous studies carefully then we avoid some of the pitfalls and errors of previous research and can design the methodology for our project by identifying the key issues and data collection techniques best suited to the topic. We can also find gaps in existing research, thereby offering an opportunity to find a unique topic. Or, we can find studies that need to be replicated. Replication is unfashionable but establishes validity of earlier findings and a tradition of research work.

Not only will you be finding gaps in knowledge but what you know is located in a set of understandings from other practitioners and researchers. This broader literature provides the context of our own knowledge. Part of this knowledge may be a theoretical perspective and that needs to be made explicit. Case study designs have been seen as contributing to the generation of theories (Eisenhardt 2002) but they are also useful ways of illustrating theoretical perspectives.

Reviewing literature can be a research study in itself. It demands a great deal of application to search, collect and read the relevant material. However it can bring much satisfaction. By reading of other research endeavours over the years we can gain a sense of the community of practitioners who have also been excited by ideas and attempted to demonstrate those ideas in practice.

There are numerous databases available for searching the literature. These searches are made easier and cheaper by your being clear about what categories you wish to search under, in what range of publications, published in which languages and over what period of time. To assist arts therapy researchers we have introduced a free online database under the structured review logo at our website 'musictherapyworld', http://musictherapyworld.net.

A good medical librarian is of invaluable help. Searches usually cost money. A search facility may be available through your professional organisation. Once you have the list of papers it is then important to gather those papers together. Some of them may be in a local medical or university library. More often than not they must be secured through inter-library loans. To do this you will need to make some arrangement with a library. Again, papers cost money and it is important to budget for this. Your professional organisation may have a paper-ordering service which gathers papers at a reduced cost. These facilities are often slower than doing it yourself, and there is usually a limit to the number of papers you can order. It is possible to make an extended search from the reference sections and bibliographies of those collected papers. With the advent of online literature search facilities through internet connections it is possible to access many more databases than ever before. This is in itself a problem as there are potentially too many references and the task of the researcher is to restrict the search and then to make sense of the information he or she has.

Papers also have to be read critically, notes made and a synopsis written up. This is where the researcher often finds that writing skills may have become a little rusty.

Literature, too, can act as a pilot study of ideas where your work builds upon previous studies. It is always an advantage to contact the authors of studies to ask how they would further their work. In journal papers not everything is revealed about the trial in terms of practical details, i.e. it may be an elegant study when reported but difficult to carry out in practice. By looking through the literature with a critical eye it is possible to see exactly what is needed as a next step in your own therapeutic discipline in terms of clinical practice or research methodology. It is also possible to see the mistakes of others and construct a trial which builds upon what has gone before.

Clinical literature is not solely confined to journal articles and books. Some articles quote eminent authors and they are worth contacting particularly for unpublished material which they may be willing to show you. This is the so-called *grey literature.* By contacting authors you may hear how their ideas have developed, particularly when there is some distance in time between the book being written and you reading it. A colleague once challenged a leading child psychologist on the ideas in his book, and the expert replied, 'That was thirteen years ago, my ideas have moved on.'

Location and temporal setting

The geographical or institutional location of the study is important. Where we make our studies influences the type of study that we can make and there are numerous influences, from the nature of the health care delivery in the country where we are working to the tradition of music therapy practices in an institution. Indeed, the introduction of a new practice may be in itself a 'case study'. It is important then to describe where the study is taking place, locating it, perhaps, in a historical context that reflects the ethos of the institutional culture. We often forget that studies are also located in time. Not only do we have to state what the duration of a study is but also understand how that study fits into a particular history.

We can also say why we choose one particular setting, or why we decide to choose a variety of settings. The rationale we choose may simply be that of convenience. It may be that the study is an attempt to provide a new service and the particular location is one that is optimal for introducing new ideas and has a tradition of research studies. We could also choose to introduce a study in several different settings so that comparisons can be made between settings.

Case studies are ideal for studying the life history of particular events like a new service being introduced, or a change in the teaching curriculum. We can set a particular time boundary and see what happens during the process of implementation. It would be possible to introduce music therapy into a school setting, for example, and see what changes occurred over a year, perhaps identifying specific targets for change using identified instruments for assessing change. Other researchers may want to take a flexible design and simply see what happens within the boundaries of time and location, interviewing all the participants involved in the institution, perhaps including parents and members of the board of governors.

Establishing the setting for the study is what gives a case study its boundaries, and it is important to determine these.

Ethics

Music therapy researchers are being asked to have ethical committee approval for their studies. Similarly, journals are also asking for ethical approval of some studies before they will accept them for publication. It is a prerequisite of any research that there will be a detailed discussion of ethical considerations. As we are gathering more and more data through audio- and videotaped material, informed consent is a critical issue. When we also work with people in settings where they cannot give consent themselves through disability, we need to say who is giving consent by proxy and how that consent is achieved.

Before seeking ethical approval it is important to canvas the ethics committee. Not all committees are conversant with qualitative research nor case study designs and there may be differing understandings of what approval is required. I was involved in the early studies of acupuncture for the treatment of asthma when acupuncture was considered to be a form of alternative medicine and few ethics committees had examined research protocols for asthma. Differing ethics committees reacted differently to the proposal, some accepted it, others did not. The *Journal of the Royal Society of Medicine* accepted the study for publication on the same day that the research committee chairman for the project told my boss that it would never be accepted in a medical journal as it was too political (Aldridge and Pietroni 1987a).

Ethical considerations

If your professional group has a code of ethical consideration for research it will be necessary to consider it. Mention such a code of practice in your research application. If you are working with an institution there will be an ethical committee which will need to see your research submission. Your sponsors will want to satisfy themselves that you have obtained approval for your intended research from an ethical committee. While your sponsors may be flexible in their approach, local ethical committees may not be quite as well educated. The onus is on the clinician/researcher to consult with them and explain what he or she intends to do.

As soon as data is collected, and particularly if it is stored on a computer, then that data must be protected and made confidential. Similarly, if the research is to be written as a report, which can potentially be published, arrangements must be made to maintain confidentiality and this must be stated in the application.

The consent of patients and co-operating practitioners must also be obtained. Be clear how you are to obtain this consent, and what information you will give to the patient in the trial. The rights of the patient to refuse to participate in, or withdraw from, the trial must be observed. It is essential that any possible risks to the patient are made clear and harmful consequences removed. If an unorthodox practice is to be used then be prepared for what may seem to be obstructive and awkward questions. As practitioners we take for granted what we do. Our normal decisions and practices can sometimes be misunderstood or misinterpreted. For example, a news programme which juxtaposes concern about the spread of AIDS, highlighting the use of needles by addicts, and the debate about complementary medical practice, notably acupuncture, can indirectly raise issues about risks to the patient from the use of needles. If you are about to embark on an acupuncture trial, and are attempting to recruit patients from referrers who are only marginally convinced about co-operating, such news can have negative consequences.

Any statements about insurance for professional indemnity and the limit of that indemnity can be included here.

Design of the study

In this section you will say what case study strategy is to be used. This is where your methodological musings and debate must leave the heady heights of discussion and appear on paper. It is important to give a detailed account of the research design you intend to use, and some indication of why you are using that design. It is possible to be innovative in designing a study, and that is why Robson's concept of 'flexible designs' is so attractive (Robson 2002).

Data collection

How is the sample of event(s), person(s) or setting(s) selected? (For example, theoretically informed; purposive; convenience; or chosen to explore contrasts.) What are the key characteristics of the sample using identified events and persons, perhaps as explanatory episodes as we saw in Chapter 2?

Are outcome criteria to be used in the study? Then these need to be made explicit. Outcome measures may change during the case study but this needs to be stated, as we saw in Chapter 8.

Whose perspectives are addressed (professional, service, user, carer)? In Chapters 3, 4 and 5, the authors concentrate on the authenticity of the process and the perspective of the patient.

Is there sufficient breadth (e.g. contrast of two or more perspectives) and depth (e.g. insight into a single perspective) to make this a rich case study? As we saw in Hanne Mette Ridder's work with dementia sufferers (Chapter 9), a broad variety of data encouraged a rich interpretation. In Chapter 10 we saw how physiological data were correlated with personal reports. Multiple data collection methods strengthen the grounding of theory.

Qualitative and quantitative data offer complementary understandings.

CHOICE OF DATA

Perhaps the greatest challenge is to sift out what data to collect. There is a temptation to collect masses and masses of data in some mistaken belief that more data is somehow representative of the whole person. It is important to collect multiple data sets that are indicators of therapeutic influence but these data have to be analysed at the end of the trial. The challenge then is to define how the criteria which are used for evaluation are related to the treatment intervention in a clinical case study, and across cases.

The panel which assesses your application will want to know why you have chosen particular measures or indices. Sometimes we can only suggest the areas that may be applicable. The benefit of qualitative studies is that in the progress of the case study we begin to discern other realms of pertinent data. However, in making a research case study proposal, we may be coming across research funding committees that have little understanding of flexible designs and we need to define how the work itself may unfold in its flexibility. Flexibility too has its limits.

It is therefore important to develop instruments for assessing clinical change appropriate to the study. Explanatory studies will seek to find criteria for such instruments. A pragmatic approach will look for a single index which can be used to indicate therapeutic efficacy. As the political climate has changed to accept integrated medical approaches, albeit with drastic changes in terms of health care delivery policy, we often need to include some estimation of economic evaluation. For example, in ethnographic case studies, we see how clinic cultures adapt or change under the influence of music therapy. We saw this in Trygve Aasgard's study as patients, families and hospital staff accommodated the musical initiatives into a broad healing ecology.

Another refinement to a case study design is one that assesses the cost implications of providing such a service. Once we give agencies an idea of how much a successful service will cost in comparison to an existing service, then we can argue in terms of cost benefit analysis and feasibility. It is feasibility analyses that are lacking from evidence-based studies.

If measures are to be used, then it is necessary to say when the measures will be implemented, who will implement them and design a form for data collection. In planning the collection of data allow time for questionnaires to be filled in. If postal questionnaires are used make an allowance for the follow up of unreturned questionnaires, and be prepared to visit if necessary. In a qualitative design, it is necessary to have a defined way for collecting data, transcribing data and managing data as an archive.

Ideally, if data is collected by more than one person, then one person must be placed in a position to collate that data. Research is an obsessive activity. Data collection is tedious: missing data is a calamity. Data managers are only one step removed from angels.

With the advent of modern computing methods it is easy to store and manipulate data. Putting data into a database or spreadsheet is relatively straightforward, getting it out again in a meaningful way is not. The statistical decisions which you made earlier, and your understanding of the relationships between sets of data, will be invaluable at this stage. If data is to be stored on a computer remember that someone has to enter that data and it will be necessary to say who will handle the data, and when they will enter the data. Entering large sets of data at the end of a project leads to error. Data sheets can be lost. Human errors from fatigue are common. It may be possible to consider direct entry of data to a computer with some form of data checking routine built in.

It is important to describe how any specialist laboratory tests will be carried out, the nature of those tests and who will carry them out. Specialist testing is expensive and another potential source of error so it is important to be clear about how valid or necessary such measures are. Some specialist tests can be therapeutic interventions in themselves and it is important to bear this in mind when designing the study.

When we collect narrative material as recordings, or collate various documentary evidence, then the problems compound themselves. We have to record where that data was collected, when and by whom. It is often necessary to transcribe recordings of sessions or interviews. Not only do we have to find a way of transcribing what is transparent to others, but those transcriptions must also be filed and archived. This is where the question 'Have you backed up your work today?', when using a computer, is essential.

Treatment variables

If the case study is of a particular form of treatment, it is important that you say clearly what you will do, when you will do it and why you are doing it. For complementary practitioners working together it is vital that they achieve some standardisation of practice while remaining true to their therapeutic discipline and thereby maintaining their own therapeutic integrity and validity. If your therapeutic discipline contains its own idiosyncratic terms it may be necessary to provide a glossary of terms within the application document.

If you are carrying out a clinical study, it is also necessary to incorporate some time when baseline data can be collected before treatment begins. The time when treatment periods begin and end must be planned and recorded. Criteria must be selected for when the trial period of treatment is to end, and when a 'follow up' assessment is to be made.

It is also important to say what will happen to patients discovered to have new needs during the process of the study. This is possible in a case study approach and is both realistic and authentic to clinical practice. Nevertheless, the change in process must be recorded and justified.

Administration of the study

Analysis of the results

If the data is stored on a computer, and the researchers understand their data, then a statistical package can be used to analyse it. If statistical advice is sought at the beginning of the study and the study designed according to certain principles then the appropriate routines will be clear. With the implementation of statistical analysis packages on microcomputers it is possible to view and analyse the data in a variety of ways. Such retrospective data analysis, sometimes called *post-hoc hypothesising*, is dangerous. While it may suggest new hypotheses and correlations between data, those relationships may be completely spurious. Analyses of data are only spurs to critical thinking, they cannot replace it. Rarely do such post-hoc hypotheses achieve validation in replication studies.

When considering using a statistical package it may be necessary to enlist the help of a statistician to help interpret the results. Many packages also have a graphics capability that will enable the data to be displayed in forms which are sometimes easier to interpret than tables of figures. Again, the appropriate use of tables and graphics is something that can be advised.

When using a qualitative approach we can use a variety of computer software packages for understanding data. This software is really a form of data management and administration by linking codes and categories to text. We still have to do the thinking. What the computer does is to save on a myriad of bits of paper lying around. Some software also allows us to link ideas together graphically as a model using concepts generated from the data. Again, we have to make the conceptual link and state why that link is being made.

Timetable of the study

In the process of making the previous decisions, you will have some idea of how long the study will take. The most common mistake that novice researchers make is to underestimate the amount of time necessary to complete a study. I shall assume that you have contacted the patients, practitioners and referrers to be involved and gained their co-operation. In case studies using a theoretical sample the sample may take some time to collect. Where the case study unfolds itself from one concept to another a decision must be made as to when to stop. Sometimes this is expressed theoretically as being when categories are saturated, which is a very unsatisfactory answer in practice. A nursing researcher told me that after nine years she had discovered her core categories in a Grounded Theory Project and was ready to write up her thesis. Apart from raising questions as to what her supervisor had been doing all this time, it emphasises the need to bring about some pragmatic time boundaries to studies. These can be negotiated with funding agencies, institutions or supervisors.

First, you will need to assess how long it will take to recruit the requisite number of patients. If you are recruiting patients with special characteristics through a seemingly co-operative referrer check the time it will take to recruit a starting sample, assess them and gain their consent. This information will also influence how many patients can be treated in a given period of time. If you are collecting data as well as treating patients then the time you allow for your usual treatment session may be extended. A pilot study will have demonstrated how feasible the recruitment of patients is.

Second, plot the time it will take for all the subjects of the research to be treated and make a definite date for the trial to end. Ensure that any specialist testing will have been carried out by that date and the results received. Allow for any missing questionnaire data to be followed up. In a qualitative study, there will often be further questions and these can be loosely planned for with an estimated time frame.

Third, allow time to analyse the results. Initial data is 'raw data'; it can do nothing by itself, you as researcher must process it. Unlike patients, data is not self-actualising. This is also where we need quality time alone with the data to go through it over and over again undisturbed. It seems to be some variation of Murphy's law that researchers often gather their data while simultaneously trying to raise a family. Grandparents and understanding partners appear to be a valuable research resource rarely factored into research proposals yet are, nevertheless, invaluable. Analyses emerge in case study through iteration, by repeating the steps in a process over time. As human beings we can trust ourselves that we will make sense of complex material but we require time to think once the data is before us.

Fourth, results must be further thought about and then written up in some form for publication, or as a presentation to your target audience. Because we are practitioners does not always mean that we are writers. If we are writing a joint report, then we have to allow time for arguing. A useful tip is to present work at regular intervals to colleagues and to collaborators in the study at the end of the trial. This thinking for a presentation can help your writing, particularly if you record the presentation on audiotape.

Finally, if you are writing and working with colleagues make sure that you have made a decision about who is to be senior author, or at least to have final say on the finished report and who is to be credited in the list of authors.

Costing of the project

As mentioned earlier, research is greedy for resources and particularly for money. In a research submission you will need to justify your needs and also satisfy your potential sponsors that the request is valid. Ask for enough. Do not underestimate your requirements. Find out what is the minimum or maximum trial budget that sponsors will consider. Some research councils will not consider small-scale studies as the administration costs alone are too expensive.

The principal considerations are:

- Staffing costs:
  - the salary of the investigator(s) and the hidden pension and insurance costs over a given period of time, allowing for annual increments
  - secretarial costs
  - specialist services for data handling, transcribing, statistical advice, methodological consultancy, and analysis and research supervision
  - specialist consultancy services for patient assessment.
- Treatment costs: any tests will need to be costed, particularly when carried out by an external agency, and the cost of treatments or medicines will need to be considered.
- Handling charges or overheads: most sponsors will support an institution rather than an individual. Such institutions will often charge a handling cost as a percentage of the funds received.

- Administrative costs: accommodation charges, telephone bills, stationery needs, printing requirements, postage and overheads.

- Travel costs: visits to expert informants, visits to follow-up patients, visits to supervisors and to other research milieu.

- Hardware costs: any specialist equipment which must be rented or bought. If using audio- or videotapes include the cost of the necessary tapes.

- Computing costs: it may be necessary to purchase software for computing or to have that software adapted or written for your trial. If you have access to a computer centre then that centre may charge for such support. Buy a backup hard disk for your own data or save regularly to writeable compact disks.

- Library services: searching for references in the literature, collecting literature and photocopying literature is costly.

Sometimes it is necessary to break these costs down into yearly requirements.

Personnel

For the main personnel working on the project it is important to include curricula vitae, and their appropriate clinical and academic qualifications. Some sponsors require you to nominate a key person to oversee the work. If you are using an external supervisor their qualifications will need to be included.

Research experience can be included in this section. Lack of experience should not preclude the clinician from a research grant providing the sponsor is satisfied that there is adequate research supervision. Otherwise it would be impossible to gain research experience. With the dwindling resources available for research through academic institutions, we are in danger of seriously damaging our research traditions. However, by taking research out of the academic environment we have a chance to promote research training for clinicians within the context of their own practice. This approach is not bound by traditional thinking and should enliven our scientific culture. The only danger is when we limit ourselves by propagating only one form of research as valid or hanging ourselves onto the evidence-based bandwagon as the sole means of validation.

Submitting the research

Send the completed design with a covering letter. It may be that you can submit your design for a preliminary review before a formal submission to a full committee. Be prepared to revise and negotiate a little. Most big committees meet only once or twice a year so it is important to find the final date for submission.

Preliminary submissions to an expert opinion may seem like an unnecessary delay but saves time in the long run, as this is where glaring errors or inconsistencies can be discovered. Modesty, alongside patience, is another research resource.

Conclusion

If you can incorporate all these considerations then the research itself should be easy. Applying for funds is the worst part. It takes a lot of work and organisation with no guarantee of results (see Table 11.1 for a guide).

Remember that research takes time: personal time, reading time, thinking time and time away from your routine practice. It is prudent to negotiate such changes with your friends, colleagues and family.

Be clear about the intended audience for your research.

Research is expensive. It may be worthwhile investing in preliminary research planning which would include a systematic review of the literature and statistical or methodological advice.

For future case study research in music therapy we need a research agency that can offer:

- methodological and statistical advice
- research training
- computer support, with a provision for extended data analysis
- research supervision
- library and literature support
- brokerage with potential sponsors.

As a first step I would recommend setting up a series of single-case research studies. These could then be entered into a database and collected over a given time period. For example, if ten interested practitioners each made five case study designs each year, in five years there would be a central core of research of 250 research papers. These studies could stay close to practice and would be cost effective. There would be fewer ethical problems as the research would be based on daily practice. Given the broad areas of music therapy success in developmental delay and neurological rehabilitation, it should be possible to make the equivalent of multi-centre studies, if we could for once agree upon a basis case study format.

Table 11.1 Checklist of questions and considerations before beginning research

Study overview

Purpose	What are the aims of your study?
Evaluative summary	What are the strengths and weaknesses of your study and theory, and its policy and practice implications?

Study, setting, sample and ethics

Phenomena under study	What is to be studied? What is the nature of the phenomena under study?
Literature review	Are you using a particular theoretical framework to inform your study? How do you locate this study within the existing knowledge as an ecology of ideas?
Context I: Theoretical framework and setting	Where is the study to be carried out? In which setting(s) will you collect data? Why have you chosen this setting? Over what time period will the study be carried out?
Context II: Sample and outcomes	How is the sample (events, persons, times and settings) selected? (For example, theoretically informed, purposive, convenience, chosen to explore contrasts.) What boundaries, or focus, define this as a case study? Are outcome criteria applicable? If so, what are they? Whose perspectives will be addressed (professional, service, user, carer)? Is there sufficient breadth (e.g. contrast of two or more perspectives) and depth (e.g. insight into a single perspective)?
Ethics	Where do I find my ethical committee? Do I need informed consent from participants of the study? Have I adequately addressed the ethical needs of the particpants and the ethical committee?

Data collection, analysis and potential researcher bias

Data collection	What data collection methods am I going to use to obtain and record the data? Is there sufficient detail in my data to provide insight into the meaning and perceptions of informants? Do I need differing sets of data (qualitative and quantitative)? Have I checked out the feasibility of my data collection (interview technique, questionnaire response, recording equipment)? What role do I, as researcher, adopt within the setting? Who will collect the data?

Continued on next page

Table 11.1 continued

	Data collection, analysis and potential researcher bias
Data analysis	How will the data be analysed?
	How will I ensure that my data is not biased, or that I recognise my own bias?
	Will I have enough material to support my analysis? (For example, original data; evidence of searching for negative instances, use of multiple sources, data triangulation; reliability/consistency over researchers, time and settings; checking back with informants over interpretation.)
	Can my findings be interpreted within the context of other studies and theories?
	Costing and grant funding
Costs	How much will it cost to do this research?
	What will it cost for staffing, secretarial support, computer hardware and software, administration costs or handling charges, statistical or methodological advice, travel costs, literature sources, library services and research supervision?
Personnel	Do I have an up-to-date curriculum vitae?
	Do I need this for my co-researchers?
	Have I nominated a research supervisor or a research institution to which I am affiliated?
Grants	What are the criteria of the funding agency?
	Is your study small or large enough?
	Have you tried a preliminary submission to see if your ideas are appropriate?
	When are the submission dates of the institution?
	Implications
Implications	Will my case study findings be generalisable to another setting or population?
	Will my findings have any implications for policy making?
	What will be the implications of my study for practice?
Distribution	Where can I share my findings (journals, presentations, teaching opportunities, conference presentations)?

References

Aasgaard, T. (1999)'Music therapy as milieu in the hospice and pediatric oncology ward.' In D. Aldridge (ed) *Music Therapy and Palliative Care.* London: Jessica Kingsley Publishers.

Aasgaard, T. (2000) '"A Suspiciously Cheerful Lady": A study of a song's life in the paediatric oncology ward, and beyond.' *British Journal of Music Therapy 14,* 2, 70–82.

Alberto, P.A. and Troutman, A.C. (1995) *Applied Behavior Analysis for Teachers,* 5th edn. Upper Saddle River, NJ: Merrill Publishing Company.

Aldrich, C.K. (1944) 'The effect of synthetic marihuana-like compound on musical talent.' *Public Health Report 59,* 431–435.

Aldridge, D. (1985) 'Suicidal behaviour: an ecosystemic approach.' Ph.D., The Open University, Milton Keynes.

Aldridge, D. (1988a) 'The personal implications of change.' *Journal of the Institute of Religion and Medicine 3,* 310–312.

Aldridge, D. (1988b) 'The singe case in clinical research.' In S. Hoskyns (ed) *Proceedings of the Fourth Music Therapy Research Conference.* London: City University.

Aldridge, D. (1989a) 'Music, communication and medicine.' *Royal Society of Medicine 82,* 743–746.

Aldridge, D. (1989b) 'A phenomenological comparison of the organization of music and the self.' *The Arts in Psychotherapy 16,* 91–97.

Aldridge, D. (1990) 'The delivery of health care alternatives.' *Journal of the Royal Society of Medicine 83,* 179–182.

Aldridge, D. (1991) 'Aesthetics and the individual in the practice of medical research: A discussion paper.' *Journal of the Royal Society of Medicine 84,* 147–150.

Aldridge, D. (1994) 'Single-case research designs for the creative art therapist.' *The Arts in Psychotherapy 21,* 5, 333–342.

Aldridge, D. (1996) *Music Therapy Research and Practice in Medicine – From Out of the Silence.* London: Jessica Kingsley Publishers.

Aldridge, D. (1998a) *Suicide. The Tragedy of Hopelessness.* London: Jessica Kingsley Publishers.

Aldridge, D. (1998b) 'A social scientist reflects on 15 years of research in complementary medicine.' *Complementary Therapies in Medicine 6,* 145–151.

Aldridge, D. (2000a) 'The challenge of creativity.' In D. Willows (ed) *The Spiritual Dimension of Pastoral Theology in a Multidisciplinary Context.* London: Jessica Kingsley Publishers.

Aldridge, D. (2000b) *Spirituality, Healing and Medicine: Return to the Silence.* London: Jessica Kingsley Publishers.

Aldridge, D. (2002) 'Philosophical speculations on two therapeutic applications of breath.' *Subtle Energies and Energy Medicine 12,* 2, 107–124.

Aldridge, D. and Aldridge, G. (1992) 'Two epistemologies: music therapy and medicine in the treatment of dementia.' *The Arts in Psychotherapy 19,* 243–255.

Aldridge, D. and Aldridge, G. (1996) 'A personal construct methodology for validating subjectivity in qualitative research.' *The Arts in Psychotherapy 25,* 3, 225–236.

Aldridge, D. and Aldridge, G. (1999) 'Life as jazz: Hope, meaning, and music therapy in the treatment of life-threatening illness.' In C. Dileo (ed) *Music Therapy and Medicine. Theoretical and Clinical Applications.* Silver Spring, Colorado: The American Music Therapy Association.

Aldridge, D. and Aldridge, G. (2002) 'Therapeutic narrative analysis: A methodological proposal for the interpretation of music therapy traces.' *Music Therapy Today* (online), December, available at http://www.musictherapyworld.net

Aldridge, D. and Dallos, R. (1986) 'Distinguishing families where suicidal behavior is present from families where suicidal behavior is absent.' *Journal of Family Therapy 8,* 243–252.

Aldridge, D. and Pietroni, P. (1987a) 'The clinical assessment of acupuncture for asthma therapy.' *Journal of the Royal Society of Medicine 80,* 222–224.

Aldridge, D. and Pietroni, P. (1987b) 'Research trials in general practice: towards a focus on clinical practice.' *Family Practice 4*, 311–315.

Aldridge, D., Gustorff, D. and Neugebauer, L. (1996) 'A preliminary study of creative music therapy in the treatment of children with developmental delay.' *The Arts in Psychotherapy 2*, 3, 189–205.

Aldridge, G. (1993) 'Morbus Crohn – und Colitis ulcerosa Patienten in der Musiktherapie.' *Der Merkurstab 46*, 1, 30–34.

Aldridge, G. (1996) '"A walk through Paris": The development of melodic expression in music therapy with a breast-cancer patient.' *Arts in Psychotherapy 23*, 207–223.

Aldridge, G. (1998) 'Die Entwicklung einer Melodie im Kontext improvisatorischer Musiktherapie.' Ph. D., University of Aalborg.

Aldridge, G. (2000) 'Improvisation as an assessment of potential in early Alzheimer's disease.' In D. Aldridge (ed) *Music Therapy in Dementia Care*. London: Jessica Kingsley Publishers.

Aldridge, G. (2002) 'The development of melody in the context of improvised music therapy with melodic examples "A walk through Paris" and "The farewell melody".' In D. Aldridge and J. Fachner (eds) *Music Therapy World Info CD-ROM IV*. Witten: University of Witten Herdecke.

Alger, H.A. (1984) 'Transitions: Alternatives to manipulative management technique.' *Young Children 39*, 6, 16–25.

Allan, I. (1991) *Rett syndrome: A view on care and management*. Washington, DC: The National Rett Syndrome Association.

Altenmüller, E. and Beisteiner, R. (1996) 'Musiker hören Musik: Großhirnaktivierungsmuster bei der Verarbeitung rhythmischer und melodischer Strukturen.' In *Musikpsychologie – Jahrbuch der Deutschen Gesellschaft für Musikpsychologie*. Wilhelmshaven: Florian Noetzel.

Alvin, J. and Warwick, A. (1991) *Music Therapy for the Autistic Child*, 2nd edn. Oxford: Oxford University Press.

Alzheimer, A. (1907) 'Über eine eigenartige Erkrankung der Hirnvinde.' In E. Schultze and O. Schnell (eds) *Allgemeine Zeitschrift für Psychiatrie und Psychisch-Gerichtliche Medizin 64*, 146–148. Berlin: Georg Rehmer.

Alzheimer, A. (1911) 'Über eigenartige Krankheitsfälle des späteren Alters.' *Zeitschrift für die gesamte Neurologie und Psychiatrie 4*, 356–385.

American Association of Music Therapy (AMTA) (2003) 'Music therapy and individuals with diagnosis on the autism spectrum.' Retrieved 20 February, 2003 from the internet: http://www.musictherapy.org/factsheets/autism.html/

Amir, D. (1990) 'A song is born: Discovering meaning in improvised songs through a phenomenological analysis of two music therapy sessions with a traumatic spinal-cord injured young adult.' *Music Therapy 9*, 1, 62–81.

Andersen, N. (1923) *The Hobo: The Sociology of the Homeless Man*. Chicago: University of Chicago Press.

Auzou, P., Eustache, F., Etevenon, P., Platel, H., Rioux, P., Lambert, J., Lechevalier, B., Zarifian, E. and Baron, J.C. (1995) 'Topographic EEG activations during timbre and pitch discrimination tasks using musical sounds.' *Neuropsychologia 33*, 1, 25–37.

Bacon, F. (1996) quotation no. 5315 in R. Andrews, M. Biggs and M. Sidel (eds). *The Columbia World of Quotation*. New York: Columbia University Press.

Bailey, D.B. (1994) 'Working with families of children with special needs.' In M. Wolery and J. Wilbers (eds) *Including Children with Special Needs in Early Childhood Programs*. Washington, D.C: National Association for the Education of Young Children.

Baker, B.S. (1992) 'The use of music with autistic children.' *Journal of Psychosocial Nursing Mental Health Service 20*, 4, 31–34.

Bambara, L.M., Koger, F., Katzer, T. and Devenport, T.A. (1995) 'Embedding choice in context of daily routine: An experimental case study.' *Journal of the Association for Persons with Severe Mental Handicaps 20*, 3, 185–95.

Barber-Kersovan, A. (1991) 'Turn on, tune in, drop out: Rockmusik zwischen Drogen und Kreativität.' In H. Rösing (ed) *Musik als Droge? Zu Theorie und Praxis bewußtseinsverändernder Wirkungen von Musik*. Mainz: Villa Musica.

Barlow, D. and Hayes, S. (1984) *Single-case Experimental Designs: Strategies for Studying Behavior Change*. New York: Pergamon Press.

Barlow, D.H. and Hersen, M. (1984) *Single Case Experimental Designs*. Massachusetts: Simon and Schuster.

Barney & Friends (1992) 'Clean up.' On *Barney's Favorites Vol. 1.* (CD) Hollywood, CA: Lyons Partnership.

Bateson, G. (1972) *Steps to an Ecology of Mind.* New York: Ballantine.

Bateson, G. (1978) *Mind and Nature.* Glasgow: Fontana.

Baudelaire, C. (1966) 'An excerpt from the seraphic theatre.' In D. Solomon (ed) *The Marihuana Papers.* New York: New American Library.

Baumgartner, G. (1997) 'Bewegungsfundierte Musiktherapie in der Gerontopsychiatrie. Ein Beispiel für die Anwendung der RES-diagnostik in der Praxis.' *Musik-, Tanz- und Kunsttherapie 8,* 105–114.

Beatty, W., Zavadil, K.D. and Bailly, R.C. (1988) 'Preserved musical skill in a severely demented patient.' *International Journal of Clinical Neuropsychology 10,* 4, 158–164.

Becker, H.S. (1963) *Outsiders: Studies in the Sociology of Deviance.* New York: Free Press.

Becker-Carus, C. (1971) 'Relationships between EEG, Personality and vigilance.' *Electroencephalography and Clinical Neurophysiology 30,* 519–526.

Berger, H. (1991) *Das Elektroenkephalogram des Menschen – Kommentierter Reprint des Erstdruckes aus dem Jahre 1938.* Frankfurt am Main: PMI Verlag.

Berglund, U. and Berglund, B. (1970) 'Adaption and recovery in vibrotactile perception.' *Perceptual and Motor Skills 30,* 843–853.

Beutler, L., Moleiro, C. and Talebi, H. (2002) 'How practitioners can systematically use empirical evidence in treatment selection.' *Journal of Clinical Psychology 58,* 10, 1–14.

Bilsbury, C. and Richman, A. (2002) 'A staging approach to measuring patient-centred subjective outcomes.' *Acta Psychiatrica Scandanavia 106,* Suppl. 414, 5–40.

Boakes, M. (1990) 'Vibrotactile stimulation.' Unpublished paper, British Association of Occupational Therapists, London.

Bolger, E.P. and Judson, M.A. (1984) 'The therapeutic value of singing.' *The New England Journal of Medicine,* 311, 1704.

Bondy, A. and Frost, L. (1994) 'The Picture Exchange Communication System (PECS).' *Focus on Autistic Behaviors 9,* 1–19.

Bonny, H. (1976) 'Music and Psychotherapy.' Unpublished doctoral dissertation, Union Graduate School.

Bonny, H. (2002) *Facilitating GIM Sessions.* GIM Monograph no. 1. Baltimore. ICM Books (1978). Reprinted in Bonny, H., *Music Consciousness: The Evolution of Guided Imagery and Music.* Gilsum, NH: Barcelona Publishers.

Bonny, H.L. and Pahnke, W.N. (1972) 'The use of music in psychedelic (LSD) psychotherapy.' *Journal of Music Therapy 9,* Summer, 64–87.

Borling, J.E. (1992) 'Perspectives on growth with a victim of abuse: A Guided Imagery and Music (GIM) case study.' *Journal of the Association for Music and Imagery 1,* 85–97.

Boswell, S. and Gray, D. (2003) 'Applying structured teaching principles to toilet training.' Retrieved 14 January 2003 from the internet: http://www.teacch.com/toilet.htm/

Boyd, J. (1992) *Musicians in Tune.* New York: Fireside (Simon and Schuster).

Bredekamp, S. and Copple, C. (eds) (1997) *Developmentally appropriate practice in early childhood programs,* 2nd edn. Washington, DC: National Association for the Education of Young Children.

Brown, C.J., Chen, A.C.N. and Dworkin, S.F. (1991) 'Music in the control of human pain.' *Music Therapy 8,* 47–60.

Bruder, M.B. (1996) 'Interdisciplinary collaboration in service delivery.' In R.A. McWilliam (ed) *Rethinking Pull-out Services in Early Intervention: A Professional Resource.* Baltimore, MD: Paul H. Brookes.

Bruscia, K. (1991) *Case Studies in Music Therapy.* Phoenixville, PA: Barcelona Publishers.

Bruscia, K.E. (1992) 'Visits from the other side: Healing persons with AIDS through Guided Imagery and Music (GIM).' In D. Campbell (ed) *Music and Miracles.* Wheaton, IL: Quest Books.

Bruscia, K. (1995) 'The process of doing qualitative research: Part II: Procedural steps.' In B. Wheeler (ed) *Music Therapy Research – Quantitative and Qualitative Perspectives.* Phoenixville, PA: Barcelona Publishers.

Bruscia, K. (1998) *Defining Music Therapy,* 2nd edn. Gilsum, NH: Barcelona Publishers.

Bruscia, K.E. and Grocke, D.E. (eds) (2002) *Guided Imagery and Music (GIM): The Bonny Method and Beyond.* Gilsum, NH: Barcelona Publishers.

Brust, J.C.M. (1980) 'Music and Language. Musical Alexia and Agraphia.' *Brain 103*, 357–392.

Bryan, L.C. and Gast, D.L. (2000) 'Teaching on-task and on-schedule behaviors to high-functioning children with autism via picture activity schedules.' *Journal of Autism Development Disorder 30*, 6, 553–567.

Bryan, M. and Tempest, W. (1972) 'Does infrasound make drivers drunk?' *New Scientist 3*, 584–586.

Buell, R. (1999) 'Emerging through music: A journey towards wholeness with Guided Imagery and Music.' In J. Hibben (ed) *Inside Music Therapy: Client Experiences*. Gilsum, NH: Barcelona Publishers.

Bullfinch, T. (1964) [1855] *Bulfinch's Complete Mythology*. London: Spring Books. (Original work published 1855.)

Bush, C.A. (1992) 'Dreams, mandalas and music imagery: Therapeutic uses in a case study.' *Journal of the Association for Music and Imagery 1*, 33–42.

Buysse, V., Schulte, A.C., Pierce, P.P. and Terry, D. (1994) 'Models and styles of consultation: Preferences of professionals in early intervention.' *Journal of Early Intervention 18*, 3, 302–310.

Buytendijk, F.J.J. (1967) *Prolegomena einer anthropologischen Physiologie*. Salzburg: Otto Müller Verlag.

Caldwell, D.F., Myers, S.A., Domino, E.F. and Merriam, P.E. (1969) 'Auditory and visual threshold effects of marihuana in man.' *Perceptual Motor Skills 29*, 3, 755–759.

Campbell, D. (1966) 'Pattern matching as an essential in distal knowing.' In K.R. Hammond (ed) *The Psychology of Egon Brunswik*. New York: Holt, Rinehart and Winston.

Campbell, J. (1968) *The Hero with a Thousand Faces*. Princeton, NJ: Princeton University Press.

Carrington, M.E. (1980) 'Vibration as a training tool for the profoundly multiply handicapped child within the family.' Paper on clinical practice in physiotherapy, Castle Priory College Wallingford, Oxfordshire. Personal communication.

Caughman, J.M. (1999) 'Tools of rediscovery: A year of Guided Imagery and Music.' In J. Hibben (ed) *Inside Music Therapy: Client Experiences*. Gilsum, NH: Barcelona Publishers.

Chapoulie, J.M. (2002) 'Everett C. Hughes and the development of fieldwork in sociology.' In D. Weinberg (ed) *Qualitative Research Methods*. Oxford: Blackwell.

Chesky, K.S. (1992) 'The effects of music and music vibration using the MVTtm on the relief of rheumatoid arthritis pain.' Ph.D. dissertation, University of North Texas. Unpublished.

Chesky, K.S. and Michel, D.E. (1991) 'The music vibration table (MVTtm): developing a technology and conceptual model for pain relief.' *Music Therapy Perspectives 9*, 32–38.

Clair, A. (1991) 'Music therapy for a severely regressed person with a probable diagnosis of Alzheimer's disease. In K.E. Bruscia (ed) *Case Studies in Music Therapy*. Phoenixville, PA: Barcelona Publishers.

Clair, A. and Bernstein, B. (1990) 'A comparison of singing, vibrotactile and nonvibrotactile intrumental playing responses in severely regressed persons with dementia of the Alzheimer's type.' *Journal of Music Therapy 27*, 3, 102–125.

Clark, M. (1991) 'Emergence of the adult self in guided imagery and music (GIM) therapy.' In K. Bruscia (ed) *Case Studies in Music Therapy*. Phoenixville, PA: Barcelona Publishers.

Clark, M.F. (1995) 'The Hero's Myth in GIM therapy.' *Journal of the Association for Music and Imagery 4*, 49–66.

Clark, M. (2002) 'Evolution of the Bonny Method of Guided Imagery and Music (BMGIM).' In K.E. Bruscia and D.E. Grocke (eds) *Guided Imagery and Music (GIM): The Bonny Method and Beyond*. Gilsum, NH: Barcelona Publishers.

Clarkson, G. (1994) 'Learning through mistakes: Guided Imagery and Music with a student in a hypomanic episode.' *Journal of the Association for Music and Imagery 3*, 77–93.

Claussen, J.M. (1997) 'Leken som kultur.' *Bokveunen 4*, 4–11.

Coe, R. (2000) 'What is an "Effect Size"? A guide for users.' http://cem.dur.ac.uk/ebeuk/research/effectsize/ESguide.htm

Cohen-Mansfield, J., Werner, P. and Marx, M. (1989) 'An observational study of agitation in agitated nursing home residents.' *International Psychogeriatrics 1*, 2, 153–165.

Cole-Currens, E. (1993) 'Smooth transitions for a smooth day.' *Texas Child Care 17*, 3, 10–19.

Coleman, K.A. (1987) 'Music therapy in Rett syndrome.' *Educational and Therapeutic Intervention in Rett Syndrome*. Cinton, MD: International Rett Syndrome Association.

Cooper, J.O., Heron, T.E. and Heward, W.L. (1987) *Applied Behavior Analysis.* Colombus, OH: Merrill Publishing.

Costall, A. and Leudar, I. (1996) 'Situating action 1: Truth in the situation.' *Ecological Psychology 8,* 2, 101–110.

Creswell, J.W. (1998) *Qualitative Inquiry and Research Design. Choosing Among Five Traditions.* Thousand Oaks, CA: Sage Publications.

Crystal, H.A., Grober, E. and Masur, D. (1989) 'Preservation of musical memory in Alzheimer's disease.' *Journal of Neurology, Neurosurgery, and Psychiatry 52,* 1415–1416.

Curry, A. (1968) 'Drugs in rock and jazz music.' *Clinical Toxicology 1,* 2, 235–244.

Curtis, S.L. (1986) 'The effect of music on pain relief and relaxation of the terminally ill.' *Journal of Music Therapy 23,* 1, 10–24.

Dallos, R. and Aldridge, D. (1987) 'Handing it on: family constructs, symptoms and choice.' *Journal of Family Therapy 9,* 39–58.

Darrow, A.A. and Gohl, H. (1989) 'The effect of vibrotactile stimuli via the Somatron on the identification of rhythmic concepts by hearing impaired children.' *Journal of Music Therapy 26,* 115–124.

David, E., Pfotenhauer, M., Birken, E. and David, L. (1989) 'Localisation of auditory evoked potentials in man during awakeness and sleep.' *International Journal of Neuroscience 47,* 41–45.

Davidson, R.J. and Hugdahl, K. (1996) 'Baseline asymmetries in brain electrical activity predict dichotic listening performance.' *Neuropsychology 10,* 2, 241–246.

de Souza, M.R., Karniol, I.G. and Ventura, D.F. (1974) 'Human tonal preferences as a function of frequency under delta8-tetrahydrocannabinol.' *Pharmacology, Biochemistry and Behaviour 2,* 5, 607–611.

Decuir, A.A. (1995) 'Statistical methods of analysis.' In B. Wheeler (ed) *Music Therapy Research: Quantitative and Qualitative Perspectives.* Phoenixville, PA: Barcelona Publishers.

Deegener, G. (1978) *Neuropsychologie und Hemisphärendominanz.* Stuttgart: Ferdinand Enke.

Dettmer, S., Simpson, R.L., Myles, B.S. and Ganz, J. B. (2000) 'The use of visual supports to facilitate transitions of students with autism.' *Focus on Autism and Other Developmental Disabilities 15,* 3, 163–169.

Dileo, C. (ed) (1999) *Music Therapy and Medicine: Theoretical and Clinical Applications.* Silver Spring, MD: American Music Therapy Association.

Dinnerstein, A.J. (1968) 'Marijuana and perceptual style: a theoretical note.' *Perceptual Motor Skills 26,* 3, Suppl. 1016–1018.

Dogbowl (1989) 'Obsessed with Girls.' *LP Tits! An Opera* from the Shimmy Disc.

Doyle, P.M., Wolery, M., Gast, D.L., Ault, M.J. and Wiley, K. (1990) 'Comparisons of constant time delay and the system of less prompts in teaching preschoolers with developmental delays.' *Research in Developmental Disabilities II,* 1–22.

Driever, M. (2002) 'Are evidence-based practice and best practice the same?' *Western Journal of Nursing Research 24,* 5, 591–597.

Duffy, F.H. (1986) *Topographic Mapping of Brain Electric Activity.* Boston: Butterworths.

Duffy, F.H., Bartels, P.H. and Burchfiel, J.L. (1981) 'Significance probability mapping: an aid in the topographic analysis of brain electrical activity.' *Electroencephalography and Clinical Neurophysiology 51,* 5, 455–462.

Eagle, C.T. (1972) 'Music and LSD: an empirical study.' *Journal of Music Therapy 9,* Spring, 23–36.

Eeg, S. (2001) *Musikprojektet på Betania. Om musik og demente.* Århus: Lokalcenter Betania.

Eisenhardt, K. (2002) 'Building theories from case study research.' In A. Hubermann and E.W. Miles (eds) *The Qualitative Researcher's Companion.* London: Sage.

Elefant, C. (2001) 'Speechless yet communicative: Revealing the person behind the disability of Rett syndrome through clinical research on songs in music therapy.' In D. Aldridge, G. di Franco, E. Ruud and T. Wigram (eds) *Music Therapy in Europe.* Rome: ISMEZ.

Elefant, C. and Lotan, M. (1998) 'Music and physical therapies in Rett syndrome: A transdisciplinary approach' (in Hebrew). *Issues in Special Education and Rehabilitation Journal 13,* 2, 89–97.

Ellaway, C. and Christodoulou, J. (2001) 'Rett syndrome: Clinical characteristics and recent genetic advances.' *Disability and Rehabilitation 23,* 3/4, 98–106.

Empson, J. (1986) *Human Brainwaves – The Psychological Significance of the Electroencephalogram.* Houndmills: Macmillan Press.

Emrich, H.M., Weber, M.M., Wendl, A., Zihl, J., Von Meyer, L. and Hanish, W. (1991) 'Reduced binocular depth inversion as an indicator of cannabis-induced censorship impairment.' *Pharmacology, Biochemistry & Behaviour 40*, 689–690.

Englund, K., Hagelthorn, G., Hornqvist, S., Lidstrom, I.M., Lindqvist, M., Liszka, L. and Soderberg, L. (1978) 'Infraljudets effeckter pa manniskan.' In Forsvarets Materielverk (eds) *Infrasound. A Summary of Interesting Articles.* Stockholm: Swedish Defence Materiel Administration.

Enoch, A. (2001) 'Let's do it again.' *All Together Now! 7*, 1, 5–7.

Erdonmez, D.E. (1995) 'A journey of transition with Guided Imagery and Music.' In C. Lee (ed) *Lonely Waters. Proceedings of the International Conference: Music Therapy in Palliative Care.* Oxford: Sobell Publications.

Erdonmez Grocke, D.E. (2001) 'A phenomenological study of pivotal moments in Guided Imagery and Music (GIM) therapy.' Ph. D. dissertation, The University of Melbourne (1999). *Music Therapy Info-CD ROM III* Witten: University of Witten-Herdecke.

Fachner, J. (2000a) 'Cannabis, Musik und ein veränderter metrischer Bezugsrahmen.' In H. Rösing and T. Phleps (eds) *Populäre Musik im kulturwissenschaftlichen Diskurs – Beiträge zur Popularmusikforschung.* Karben: CODA.

Fachner, J. (2000b) 'Der musikalische Zeit-Raum, Cannabis, Synästhesie und das Gehirn.' In A. Erben, C. Gresser and A. Stollberg (eds) *Grenzgänge – Übergänge: Musikwissenschaften im Dialog.* Hamburg: von Bockel.

Fachner, J. (2001) 'Veränderte Musikwahrnehmung durch Tetra-Hydro-Cannabinol im Hirnstrombild'. *Music Therapy Info CD-ROM III.* Witten: University of Witten-Herdecke.

Fachner, J. (2002a) 'The space between the notes – Research on cannabis and music perception.' In K. Kärki, R. Leydon and H. Terho (eds) *Looking Back, Looking Ahead – Popular Music Studies 20 Years Later.* Turku, Finland: IASPM-Norden.

Fachner, J. (2002b) 'Topographic EEG changes accompanying cannabis-induced alteration of music perception – Cannabis as a hearing aid?' *Journal of Cannabis Therapeutics 2*, 2, 3–36.

Fachner, J., David, E. and Pfotenhauer, M. (1995) 'EEG-Brainmapping in veränderten Bewußtseinszuständen unter Cannabiseinwirkung beim Hören ausgewählter Musikstücke – ein Fallbeispiel.' *Curare – Journal for EthnoMedicine 18*, 2, 331–358.

Fachner, J., David, E. and Pfotenhauer, M. (1996) *EEG Brain Mapping in Altered States of Consciousness Under the Influence of Cannabis while Listening to Selected Pieces of Music – A Follow Up.* Encino, Los Angeles, California: Society for the Anthropology of Consciousness.

Fanjul, S.D. and Ball, P.M. (1995) *Division of Child Development: Child Day Care Handbook.* North Carolina Department of Human Resources.

Fitzgerald-Cloutier, M.L. (1993) 'The use of music therapy to decrease wandering: An alternative to restraints.' *Music Therapy Perspectives 11*, 32–36.

Fogel, F., de Koeyer, I., Bellagamba, F. and Bell, H. (2002) 'The dialogical self in the first two years of life.' *Theory and Psychology 12*, 2, 191–205.

Folstein, M.F., Folstein, S.E. and McHugh, P.R. (1975) '"Mini-Mental State." A practical method for grading the cognitive state of patients for the clinician.' *Journal of Psychiatric Research 12*, 189–198.

Forsvarets Materielverk (FMV) (1985) *A Summary of Articles on Low Frequency Sound and Infrasound.* Stockholm: Swedish Defence Materiel Administration.

Frith, S. (1998) *Performing Rites.* Oxford: Oxford University Press.

Geertz, C. (1957) 'Ritual and social change.' *American Anthropologist 59*, 32–54.

Gergen, K. (1997) 'Psycho- versus bio-medical therapy.' *Society 35*, 1, 24–27.

Gervin, A.P. (1991) 'Music therapy compensatory techniques utilizing song lyrics during dressing to promote independence in the patient with brain injury.' *Music Therapy Perspectives 9*, 87–90.

Gfeller, K.E. (1983) 'Musical mnemonics as an aid to retention with normal and learning disabled students.' *Journal of Music Therapy 20*, 4, 179–189.

Globus, G.G., Cohen, H.B., Kramer, J.C., Elliot, H.W. and Sharp, R. (1978) 'Effects of marihuana induced altered state of consciousness on auditory perception.' *Journal of Psychedelic Drugs 10*, 1, 71–76.

Goffman, E. (1959a) 'The moral career of the mental patient.' *Psychiatry 22*, 123–142.

Goffman, E. (1959b) *The Presentation of Self in Everyday Life.* Garden City, NY: Doubleday.

Goffman, E. (1961) *Asylums.* New York: Anchor Books, Doubleday & Co.

Goffman, E. (1990) *Stigma. Notes on the management of spoiled identity.* London: Penguin.

Goffman, E. (1997) [1961] 'Role Distance.' In C. Lemert and A. Branaman (eds) *The Goffman Reader.* Oxford: Blackwell Publishers. (Original work published in 1961).

Goldberg, F. (1995) 'The Bonny Method of Guided Imagery and Music.' In T. Wigram, B. Saperston and R. West (eds) *The Art and Science of Music Therapy: A Handbook.* London: Harwood Academic.

Gomm, R., Hammersley, M. and Foster, P. (2000) *Case Study Method.* London: Sage.

Gottschewski, K. (2001) 'Autismus aus der Innenperspektive und Musiktherapie [Autism from an inside-out perspective and music therapy].' In D. Aldridge (ed) *Kairos V: Musiktherapie mit Kindern; Beitraege zur Musiktherapie in der Medizin.* Bern; Goettingen; Toronto; Seattle: Huber.

Gouzoulis-Mayfrank, E., Hermle, L., Thelen, B. and Sass, H. (1998) 'History, rationale and potential of human experimental hallucinogenic drug research in psychiatry.' *Pharmacopsychiatry 31,* Suppl. 2, 63–68.

Graham, J.M. (1995) 'Rett syndrome.' Information packet. Sinai Medical Center.

Gregory, D. (2002) 'Four decades of music therapy behavioral research designs: A content analysis of Journal of Music Therapy articles.' *Journal of Music Therapy 29,* 1, 56–71.

Griffin, M.J. (1983) 'Effects of vibration on humans.' In R. Lawrence (ed) *Proceedings of Internoise 1.* Edinburgh: Institute of Acoustics.

Grimal, P. (1986) *Dictionary of Classical Mythology.* London: Penguin.

Grinspoon, L. (1971) *Marihuana Reconsidered.* Cambridge, MA: Harvard University Press.

Gross, C.G. (2002) 'Genealogy of the "grandmother cell".' *Neuroscientist 8,* 5, 512–518.

Guba, E. and Lincoln, Y.S. (1989) *Fourth Generation Evaluation.* London: Sage.

Guba, E.G. and Lincoln, Y.S. (1998) 'Competing paradigms in qualitative research.' In N. Denzin and Y.S. Lincoln (eds) *The Landscape of Qualitative Research. Theories and Issues.* Thousand Oaks, CA: Sage Publications.

Hadsell, N.A and Coleman, K.A. (1988) 'Rett syndrome: A challenge for music therapists.' *Music Therapy Perspectives 5,* 52– 56.

Hagbarth, K.E. and Eklund, G. (1968) 'The effects of muscle vibration in spasticity, rigidity and cerebellar disorders.' *Journal of Neurology, Neurosurgery and Psychiatry 31,* 207–223.

Hagberg, B. (1985) 'Rett syndrome: Swedish approach to analysis of prevalence and cause.' *Brain and Development 7,* 277–280.

Hagberg, B., Aicardi, J., Dias, K. and Ramos, O. (1983) 'A progressive syndrome of autism, dementia, ataxia, and loss of purposeful hand use in girls: Rett syndrome: report of 35 cases.' *Annals of Neurology 14,* 471–479.

Hagemann, D., Naumann, E., Lurken, A., Becker, G., Maier, S. and Bartussek, D. (1999) 'EEG asymmetry, dispositional mood and personality.' *Personality and Individual Differences 27,* 3, 541–568.

Haggman Laitila, A. (1999) 'The authenticity and ethics of phenomenological research: How to overcome the researcher's own views.' *Nursing Ethics 6,* 1, 12–22.

Haines, J.H. (1989) 'The effects of music therapy on the self-esteem of emotionally-disturbed adolescents' (originally a thesis submitted for the Master of Music Degree in Music Therapy, Temple University). *Music Therapy 8,* 1, 78–91.

Hall, R. (1996) 'Representation as shared activity: Situated cognition and Dewey's cartography of experience.' *Journal of Learning Science 5,* 3, 209–238.

Hammersley, M. and Gomm, R. (2000) 'Introduction.' In R. Gomm, M. Hammersley and P. Foster (eds) *Case Study Method.* London: Sage.

Hanser, S.B. (1995) 'Applied behavior analysis.' In B.L. Wheeler (ed) *Music Therapy Research: Quantitative and Qualitative Perspectives.* Phoenixville, PA: Barcelona Publishers.

Hanley, J., Tyrrell, E.D. and Hahn, P.M. (1976) 'The therapeutic aspects of marihuana: computer analyses of electroencephalographic data from human users of cannabis sativa.' In S. Cohen and R.C. Stillman (eds) *The Therapeutic Potential of Marihuana.* New York: Plenum Medical Book Company.

Handleman, J.S. and Harris, S.L. (eds) (2001) *Preschool Education Programs for Children with Autism, Second Edition.* Austin, TX: Pro-Ed.

Harding, C. and Ballard, K.D. (1982) 'The effectiveness of music as a stimulus and as contingent reward in promoting the spontaneous speech of three physically handicapped preschoolers.' *Journal of Music Therapy 19*, 2, 86–101.

Harms T., Clifford R.M. and Cryer D. (1998) *Early Childhood Environment Rating Scale*, revised edn. New York: Teachers College Press.

Harre, R. and Secord, P. (1971) *The Explanation of Social Behaviour*. London: Basil Blackwell.

Hartman, D.P. (1984) 'Assessment strategies.' In D. Barlow and M. Hersen, *Single Case Experimental Designs*. Massachusetts: Simon and Schuster.

Hess, P. (1973) 'Experimentelle Untersuchung akuter Haschischeinwirkung auf den Menschen.' Inaugural-Dissertation, Ruprecht-Karl-Universität Heidelberg.

Hess, P. (2002) Bedingungen für einen sinnvollen Gebrauch von Cannabinoiden. Europäischen Collegiums für Bewusstseinsstudien (ECBS) Paper presented at a symposium in Frankenthal Germany: 9. 'Dosis, Set und Setting aussergewöhnlicher Bewusstseinszustände'.

Hetzroni, O., Rubin, C. and Konkiol, O. (2002) 'The use of assistive technology for symbol identification by children with Rett syndrome.' *Journal of Intellectual and Developmental Disability 27*, 1, 57–71.

Hetzroni, O. and Schanin, M. (1998) 'Computer as a tool in developing emerging literacy in children with developmental disabilities' (in Hebrew). *Issues in Special Education and Rehabilitation Journal 13*, 1, 15–21.

Hetzroni, O. and Shalem, O. (1998) 'Augmentative and alternative communication: The use of picture symbols in children with autism' (in Hebrew). *Issues in Special Education and Rehabilitation Journal 13*, 1, 33–43SS.

Hibben, J. (ed) (1999) *Inside Music Therapy: Client Experiences*. Gilsum, NH: Barcelona Publishers.

Higgins, R. (1993) *Approaches to Case Study. A Handbook for Those Entering the Field*. London: Jessica Kingsley Publishers.

Hill, S.A. (1997) 'The relevance and value of music therapy for children with Rett syndrome.' *British Journal of Special Education 24*, 3, 124–128.

Hodges, D.A. (1980) 'Appendix A: Physiological responses to music.' *Handbook of Music Psychology*. Washington: National Association of Music Therapy.

Holcombe, A., Wolery, M. and Gast, D.L. (1994) 'Comparative single-subject research: description of designs and discussion of problems.' *Topics in Early Childhood Special Education 14*, 119–145.

Hollister, L.E., Sherwood, S.C. and Cavasino, A. (1970) 'Marihuana and the human electroencephalogram.' *Pharmacological Research Communications 2*, 4, 305–308.

Hooper, J. (2001) 'An introduction to vibroacoustic therapy and an examination of its place in music therapy practice.' *British Journal of Music Therapy 15*, 2, 69–77.

Horn, J. (1998) 'Qualitative researach literature: A bibliographic essay.' *Library Trends 46*, 4, 602–615.

Hughes, C., Pitkin, S.E. and Lorden, S.W. (1998) 'Assessing preferences and choice of persons with severe and profound mental retardation.' *Education and Training in Mental Retardation and Developmental Disabilities 33*, 4, 299–316.

Hughes, J.E., Robbins, B.J., McKenzie, B.A. and Robb, S.S. (1990) 'Integrating exceptional and nonexceptional young children through music play: A pilot program.' *Music Therapy Perspectives 8*, 52–56.

Hughes, J.R. (1995) 'The EEG in Psychiatry: An outline with summarized points and references.' *Clinical Electroencephalography 26*, 2, 92–101.

Hughes, J.R. (1996) 'A review of the usefulness of the Standard EEG in psychiatry.' *Clinical Electroencephalography 27*, 1, 35–39.

International Rett Syndrome Association (IRSA) (1997) Internet site: http://www2. paltech.com/Irsa/what is.htm

International Rett Syndrome Association (IRSA) (2000) *What is Rett syndrome?* (brochure) Clinton, MD: IRSA.

Isenberg-Grzeda, C. (1999) 'Experiencing the music in Guided Imagery and Music.' In J. Hibben (ed) *Inside Music Therapy: Client Experiences*. Gilsum, NH: Barcelona Publishers.

Ishikawa, A., Goto, T., Narasaki, M., Yokochi, K., Kitahara, H. and Fukuyama, Y. (1978) 'A new syndrome of progressive psychomotor deterioration with peculiar stereotyped movement and autistic tendency: A report of three cases.' *Brain and Development 31*, 258.

Jacobsen, K., Viken, A. and von Tetchner, S. (2001) 'Rett syndrome and aging: A case study.' *Disability and Rehabilitation 23*, 3/4, 160–166.

Jastreboff, P.J., Gray, W.C. and Gold, S.L. (1996) 'Neurophysiological approach to tinnitus patients.' *American Journal of Otology 17*, 2, 236–240.

Jausovec, N. (1997a) 'Differences in EEG activity during the solution of closed and open problems.' *Creativity Research Journal 10*, 4, 317–324.

Jausovec, N. (1997b) 'Differences in EEG alpha activity between gifted and non-identified individuals: Insights into problem solving.' *Gifted Child Quarterly 41*, 1, 26–32.

Jausovec, N. (1998) 'Are gifted individuals less chaotic thinkers?' *Personality and Individual Differences 25*, 2, 253–267.

Jellison, J.A. and Miller, N.I. (1982) 'Recall of digit and word sequences by musicians and nonmusicians as a function of spoken and sung input a task.' *Journal of Music Therapy 19*, 4, 102–13.

John, E.R., Prichep, L., Fridman, J. and Easton, P. (1988) 'Neurometrics: Computer-assisted differential diagnosis of brain dysfunctions.' *Science 239*, 162–169.

Johnson, E. (1978) 'The effect of a combined values clarification and songwriting experience on self concept of socially disadvantaged adolescents in a family-oriented group living setting.' Unpublished Master's thesis, University of Kansas.

Johnson, E.R. (1981) 'The role of objective and concrete feedback in self-concept treatment of juvenile delinquents in music therapy.' *Journal of Music Therapy 18*, 3, 137–147.

Jones, M. H. (1975) 'Differential diagnosis and natural history of the cerebral palsied child.' In R. Samilson (ed) *Orthopaedic Aspects of Cerebral Palsy*. London: Heinemann.

Jonnes, J. (1999) *Hep-Cats, Narcs, and Pipe Dreams*. Baltimore: John Hopkins University Press.

Joy, J.E., Watson, S.J. and Benson, J.A. (1999) *Marijuana and Medicine: Assessing the Science Base.* Washington, DC: National Academy Press.

Julien, R.M. (1997) *Drogen und Psychopharmaka: Seventh Edition*. Translated by T.A.S. Hartung. Heidelberg: Spektrum Akademischer Verlag.

Kärki, K., Leydon, R. and Terho, H. (2002) *Looking Back, Looking Ahead – Popular Music Studies 20 Years Later*. Turku, Finland: IASPM Norden.

Kazdin, A.E. (1982) *Single-case Research Design*. Oxford: Oxford University Press.

Kellogg, J. (1978) *Mandala: Path of Beauty*. Lightfoot, VA: MARI.

Kelly, G. (1955) *Principles of Personal Construct Psychology*, vols I and II. New York: Norton.

Kern, P. and Wolery, M. (2001) 'Participation of a preschooler with visual impairments on the playground: Effects of musical adaptations and staff development.' *Journal of Music Therapy 38*, 2, 149–164.

Kern, P., Marlette, S. and Snyder, A. (2002) 'Sounds on the playground.' *All Together Now! 8*, 2, 3–5.

Kerr, A. (1992) 'Communication in Rett syndrome.' Paper available from: Rett Syndrome Association UK.

Kerr, A. and Stephenson, J.B.P. (1986) 'A study of the natural history of Rett syndrome in 23 girls.' *American Journal of Medical Genetics 24*, Suppl. 1, 77–83.

Kerr, A.M. and Stephenson, J.B.P. (1985) 'Rett syndrome in the west of Scotland.' *British Medical Journal 291*, 579–582.

King Crimson (1974) 'Prelude – Song of the Seagulls.' From the LP *Islands*. EG Records.

King Missile (1989) 'We can work it out' (by Lennon/McCartney). From the LP *Live at Knitting Factory*. Shimmy Disc.

Kitwood, T. (1997) *Dementia Reconsidered. The person comes first*. Buckingham: Open University Press.

Kobialka, D. (1982) 'Crystal Caverns' (New Age music cassette). Adapted for Vibroacoustic Therapy by O. Skille, Vibroacoustic AS. Levanger, Norway.

Kolb, B. and Whishaw, I.Q. (1996) *Neuropsychologie*. Heidelberg: Spektrum Verlag.

Konovalov, V.F. and Otmakhova, N.A. (1984) 'EEG manifestations of functional asymmetry of the human cerebral cortex during perception of words and music.' *Human Physiology 9*, 4, 250–255.

Koppenhaver, D., Erickson, K.A., Harris, B., McLellan, J., Skotko, B.G. and Newton, R.A. (2001) 'Storybook-based communication intervention for girls with Rett syndrome and their mothers.' *Disability and Rehabilitation 23*, 3/4, 149–159.

Koukkou, M. and Lehmann, D. (1976) 'Human EEG spectra before and during cannabis hallucinations.' *Biological Psychiatry 11*, 6, 663–677.

Koukkou, M. and Lehmann, D. (1978) 'Correlations between cannabis-induced psychopathology and EEG before and after drug ingestion.' *Pharmakopsychiatrie und Neuropsychopharmakologie 11*, 5, 220–227.

Kozinetz, C., Skender, M.L., MacNaughton, N., Almes, M.J., Schultz, P.A.K. and Glaze, D.G. (1993) 'Epidemiology of Rett syndrome: A population based registry.' *Pediatrics 91*, 445–450.

Kratochwill, T.R. (1992) *Single-Case Research Design and Analysis*. New Jersey: Lawrence Erlbaum Association.

Leary, T. (1997) *Denn sie wußten was sie tun*. Translated by S.G. Seiler. Munich: Heyne. (Original work published as *Flashbacks, an Autobiography* (1983).)

Lehikoinen, P. (1988) 'The Kansa Project: Report from a control study on the effect of vibroacoustical therapy on stress.' Unpublished paper, Sibelius Academy, Helsinki.

Leuner, H.C. (1962) *Die experimentelle Psychose*. Berlin; Göttingen; Heidelberg: Springer.

Lincoln, Y.S. and Guba, E.G. (1985) *Naturalistic Inquiry*. Beverly Hills, CA: Sage.

Lindberg, B. (1991) *Understanding Rett Syndrome*. New York: Hogrefe & Huber.

The Literary Digest (1934) 'Topics of the day – facts and fancies about marihuana.' *The Literary Digest*, 24 October, 7–8.

Lord, C., Rutter, M., DiLavore, P. and Risi, S. (1999) *Autism Diagnostic Observation Schedule (ADOS)*. Los Angeles, CA: Western Psychological Services.

Luborsky, L,. Singer, B. and Luborsky, L. (1975) 'Comparative studies of psychotherapies.' *Archives of General Psychiatry 32*, 995–1008.

Lukas, S.E., Mendelson, J.H. and Benedikt, R. (1995) 'Electroencephalographic correlates of marihuana-induced euphoria.' *Drug Alcohol Dependency 37*, 2, 131–140.

Lutzenberger, W., Elbert, T., Rockstroh, B. and Birbaumer, N. (1985) *Das EEG – Psychophysiologie und Methodik von Spontan-EEG und ereigniskorrellierten Potentialen*. Berlin: Springer.

Machleidt, W., Gutjahr, L. and Mügge, A. (1989) *Grundgefühle: Phänomenologie, Psychodynamik, EEG-Spektralanalytik*. Monographien aus dem Gesamtgebiet der Psychiatrie. Berlin: Springer.

Madsen, C.K., Standley, J.M. and Gregory, D. (1991) 'The effect of a vibrotactile device, Somatron, on physiological and psychological responses: Musicians versus non-musicians.' *Journal of Music Therapy 28*, 120–134.

Manstread, A.S.R. and Semin, G.R. (1988) 'Methodology in social psychology: turning ideas into action.' Cited in C.Robson (2002) *Real World Research*. Oxford: Blackwell Publishers.

Maranto, C.D. (1993) 'Music therapy clinical practice: A global perspective and classification system.' In C.D. Maranto (ed) *Music Therapy: International Perspectives*. Pipersville, PA: Jeffrey Books.

Maranto, C.D. (1994) 'Research in music in medicine: The state of the art.' In R. Spintge and R. Droh. (eds) *Music and Medicine*. St. Louis: Magna Music Baton.

Martz, R. (1972) 'The effect of marihuana on auditory thresholds.' *Journal for Auditory Research 12*, 146–148.

Mason, J. (1998) *Qualitative Researching*. London: Sage Publications.

Mathew, R.J., Wilson, W.H., Turkington, T.G. and Coleman, R.E. (1998) 'Cerebellar activity and disturbed time sense after THC.' *Brain Research 797*, 2, 183–189.

Matthews, G., Jones, D.M. and Chamberlain, A.G. (1990) 'Refining the measurement of mood: the UWIST Mood Adjective Check List.' *British Journal of Psychology 81*, 1–26.

Maurer, K. (1989) *Topographic Mapping of EEG and Evoked Potentials*. Berlin: Springer.

Mayer-Johnson, R. (1981) *The Picture Communication Symbols Combination Book: The Wordless Edition*. Solana Beach, CA: Mayer Johnson.

McGuire, K.M. (2001) 'The use of music on Barney & friends: Implications in music therapy practice and research.' *Journal of Music Therapy 38*, 2, 114–148.

McWilliam, R.A. (1996) *Rethinking Pull-out Services in Early Intervention: A Professional Resource.* Baltimore, MD: Paul H. Brookes Publishing.

Mead, G. (1934) *Mind, Self and Society.* Chicago: Chicago University Press.

Merker, B. and Wallin, N.L. (2001) 'Musical responsiveness in the Rett disorder.' In A. Kerr and I. Witt Engerstrom (eds) *The Rett Disorder and the Developing Brain.* Oxford: Oxford University Press.

Merker, B., Bergstrom-Isacsson, M. and Witt Engerstrom, I. (2001) 'Music and the Rett disorder: The Swedish Rett Center survey.' *Nordic Journal of Music Therapy 10,* 1, 42–53.

Merleau-Ponty, M. (1968) *The Visible and the Invisible.* Evanston, IL: Northwestern University Press.

Merriam, S. (1998) *Qualitative Research and Case Study Applications.* San Francisco: Jossey Bass.

Mezzrow, M. (1946) *Really the Blues,* reprint 1993. London: Flamingo/Harper Collins Publishers.

Miller, R. (1998) 'Epistemology and psychotherapy data: The unspeakable, unbearable, horrible truth.' *Clinical Psychology: Science and Practice 5,* 2, 242–250.

Møller, H. (1984) 'Physiological and psychological effects of infrasound on humans.' *Journal of Low Frequency Noise and Vibration 3,* 1, 1–17.

Montague, J. (1988) *Music Therapy in the Treatment of Rett Syndrome.* Glasgow: UK Rett Syndrome Association.

Moskowitz, H. (1974) 'Effects of marihuana on auditory signal detection.' *Psychopharmacologia 40,* 2, 137–145.

Moustakas, C. (1990) *Heuristic Research.* London: Sage.

Munk-Madsen, N.M. (2000) *Musikterapi til demente med adfærdsforstyrrelser.* Gentofte kommune: Plejehjemmet Kridthuset.

Musto, D. (1997) 'Busted – America's war on Marihuana.' Frontline Online. Retrieved 3 March, 1999 from http://www.pbs.org/wgbh/pages/frontline/shows/dope/interviews/musto.html

Nabors, L., Willoughby, J., Leff, S. and McMenamin, S. (2001) 'Promoting inclusion for your children with special needs on playgrounds.' *Journal of Developmental and Physical Disabilities 13,* 2, 179–190.

National Autistic Society (NAS) (2003) 'Fact Sheet: Music Therapy.' Retrieved 20 February, 2003 from the internet: http://www.nas.org.uk/

National Research Council (2001) *Educating Children with Autism.* Committee on Educational Interventions for Children with Autism. C. Lord and J.P. Mc.Gee (eds) Division of Behavioral and Social Sciences and Education. Washington, DC: National Academy Press.

Nattiez, J.-J. (1990) *Music and Discourse: Toward a Semiology of Music.* Princeton, NJ: Princeton University Press.

Nerheim, H. (1995) *Videnshapog Kommunikasjon (Science and Communication).* Oslo, Norway: Universitetsforlaget.

Newell, A. (1999) 'Dealing with physical illness: Guided Imagery and Music and the search for self.' In J. Hibben (ed) *Inside Music Therapy: Client Experiences.* Gilsum, NH: Barcelona Publishers.

Nicholas, M.J. and Boyle, M.E. (1983) 'An annotated bibliography of single case experimental research in music therapy. Journal of Music Therapy publications 1966–1982.' *Journal of Music Therapy 20,* 3, 156–63.

Niedermeyer, E. and Lopes de Silva, F. (1993) *Electroencephalography.* Baltimore: Williams and Wilkins.

Nordenfelt, L. (1987) *On the Nature of Health. An Action-Theoretic Approach.* Dordrecht: D. Reidel Publishing.

Norman, H.K. (2001) 'Lucidity in people with severe dementia as a consequence of person-centred care.' Umeå University Medical Dissertations. *New series 753.*

Nozaki, K. and Mochizuki, A. (1995) 'Assessing choice making for persons with profound disabilities: A preliminary analysis.' *Journal of the Association for Persons with Severe Handicaps 20,* 3, 196–201.

O'Callaghan, C.C. (1996) 'Lyrical themes in songs written by palliative care patients.' *Journal of Music Therapy 33,* 2, 74–92.

Parker, A. (1981) 'The meaning of attempted suicide to young parasuicides: a repertory grid study.' *British Journal of Psychology 139,* 306–312.

Pearce, W.B., Cronen, V.E. and Conklin, F. (1979) 'On what to look for when analyzing communication: an hierarchical model of actors' meanings.' *Communication 4,* 195–220.

Petsche, H. (1994) 'The EEG while listening to music.' *Eeg-Emg-Z Elektroenz Elektrom 25,* 2, 130–137.

Petsche, H., Pockberger, H. and Rappelsberger, P. (1987) 'EEG-Studies in musical perception and performances.' In R. Spintge and R. Droh (eds) *Musik in der Medizin – Music in Medicine.* Berlin: Springer.

Pickett, E. (1992) 'Using Guided Imagery and Music (GIM) with a dually diagnosed woman having multiple addictions.' *Journal of the Association for Music and Imagery 1*, 56–67.

Polk, M. and Kertesz, A. (1993) 'Music and language in degenerative disease of the brain.' *Brain and Cognition 22*, 98–117.

Pujol, K.K. (1994) 'The effect of vibro-tactile stimulation, instrumentation, and precomposed melodies on physiological and behavioural responses of profoundly retarded children and adults.' *Journal of Music Therapy 31*, 3, 186–205.

Quill, K.A. (2001) *Do-Watch-Listen-Say. Social and Communication Intervention for Children with Autism.* Baltimore, MD: Paul H. Brookes Publishing.

Rätsch, C. (1992) 'Setting – Der Ort der psychedelischen Erfahrung im ethnographischen Kontext.' In H.C. Leuner and M. Schlichting (eds) *Jahrbuch des Europäischen Collegiums für Bewußtseinsstudien 1992.* Berlin: Verlag für Wissenschaft und Bildung.

Raudsik, R. (1997) 'Vibroacoustic therapy in general medicine.' In T. Wigram and C. Dileo (eds) *Music, Vibration and Health.* New Jersey: Jeffrey Books.

Reisberg, B. (1988) 'Functional assesment staging (FAST).' *Psychopharmacology Bulletin 24*, 653–659.

Rett, A. (1966) *Uber ein cerebral atropisches syndrome bei hyper-ammonamie.* Vienna: Bruder Hollinek.

Rett, A. (1982) 'Grundlagen der Musiktherapie und Music-Psychologie.' In *Herausgeber G. Harrer, 2.* Stuttgart: Fischer# Verlag.

Ricciarelli, A. (2003) 'The guitar in palliative music therapy for cancer patients.' In *Music Therapy Today* (online), April, available at http://musictherapyworld.net

Ridder, H.M. (2002) 'Musik og Demens. Musikaktiviteter og musikterapi med demensramte.' Aalborg: Formidlings Center Nord. www.fcnord.dk. ISBN: 87-91082-11-0

Ridder, H.M. (2003) 'Singing dialogue. Music therapy with persons in advanced stages of dementia. A case study research design.' Unpublished Ph.D. thesis. Aalborg University.

Robbins, C. and Nordoff, P. (1962) *Children's Play-songs.* Bryn Mawr, PA: Theodore Press.

Robbins, C. and Robbins, C. (1998) *Healing Heritage: Paul Nordoff Explores the Tonal Language of Music.* Gilsum, NH: Barcelona Publishers.

Robson, C. (2002) *Real World Research: Second Edition.* Oxford: Blackwell.

Rodin, E.A. and Domino, E.F. (1970) 'Effects of acute marijuana smoking on the EEG.' *Electroencephalography and Clinical Neurophysiology 29*, 3, 321.

Rosal, M.L. (1989) 'Master's papers in art therapy: Narrative or research case studies?' *The Arts in Psychotherapy 16*, 71–75.

Roth, W.T., Galanter, M., Weingartner, H., Vaughan, T.B. and Wyatt, R.J. (1973) 'Marijuana and synthetic 9-trans-tetrahydrocannabinol: some effects on the auditory evoked response and background EEG in humans.' *Biological Psychiatry 6*, 3, 221–233.

Rudestam, K.E. and Newton, R.R. (1992) *Surviving your Dissertation.* London: Sage Publishers.

Ruud, E. (1979) 'Musikkterapi.' *Musikkiskolen 4*, 34–35.

Sackett, D., Rosenberg, W. and Haynes, R. (1996) 'Evidence-based medicine: What it is and what it isn't?' *British Medical Journal 312*, 71–72.

Saluveer, E. and Tamm, S. (1989) 'Vibroacoustic therapy with neurotic clients at the Tallinn Pedagogical Institute.' Paper given to the Second International Symposium in Vibroacoustics. Levanger, Norway: ISVA Publications.

Sandal, S., McLean, M.E. and Smith, B.J. (2000) *Division for Early Childhood (DEC): Recommended practices in early intervention/early childhood special education.* Longmont, CO: Sopris West.

Scartelli, J.P. (1982) 'The effect of sedative music on electromyographic bio-feedback assisted relaxation training of spastic cerebral palsied adults.' *Journal of Music Therapy 19*, 210–218.

Schmidt, J.A. (1984) 'Structural analysis of clinial music: An important tool for music therapy and research.' *Journal of Music Therapy 4*, 1, 18–28.

Schopler, E., Reichler, R., Bashford, A., Lansing, M. and Marcus, L. (1990) *Psychoeducational Profile-Revised (PEP-R).* Austin, TX: Pro-ED.

Schulberg, C.H. (1999) 'Out of the ashes: Transforming despair into hope with music and imagery.' In J. Hibben (ed) *Inside Music Therapy: Client Experiences*. Gilsum, NH: Barcelona Publishers.

Sergant, J. (1996) 'Human brain mapping.' In R. Pratt and R. Spintge (eds) *MusicMedicine*, vol. 2. Saint Louis: MMB Music.

Sevcik, R.A., Romski, M.A. and Adamson, L.B. (1999) 'Measuring AAC interventions for individuals with severe developmental disabilities.' *Augmentative and Alternative Communication 15*, 38–44.

Shah, I. (1991) 'The Blind Ones and the Matter of the Elephant'. *World Tales*. London: Octagon Press.

Shapiro, H. (1998) *Sky High – Drogenkultur im Musikbuisiness*. 2 Translated by P. Hiess. St. Andrä-Wördern: Hannibal.

Shaw, C. (1930) *The Jack Roller: A Delinquent Boy's Own Story*. Chicago: University of Chicago Press.

Sigafoos, J. (2000) 'Communication development and aberrant behavior in children with developmental disabilities.' *Education and Training in Mental Retardation and Developmental Disabilities 35*, 2, 168–176.

Sigafoos, J., Laurie, S., and Pennell, D. (1995) 'Preliminary assessment of choice making among children with Rett syndrome.' *Journal of the Association for Persons with Severe Handicaps 20*, 175–184.

Sigafoos, J., Laurie, S. and Pennell, D. (1996) 'Teaching children with Rett syndrome to request preferred objects using aided communication: Two preliminary studies.' *Augmentative and Alternative Communication 12*, 88–96.

Sigafoos, J., Woodyatt, G., Tucker, M., Roberts-Pennell, D. and Pittendreigh, N. (2000a) 'Assessment of potential communication acts in three individuals with Rett syndrome.' *Journal of Developmental and Physical Disabilities 12*, 3, 203–216.

Sigafoos, J., Woodyatt, G., Keen, D., Tait, K., Tucker, M., Roberts-Pennell, D. and Pittendreigh, N. (2000b) 'Identifying potential communicative acts in children with developmental and physical disabilities.' *Communication Disorders Quarterly 21*, 2, 77–86.

Skille, O. (1982) 'Musikkbadat – enn musikk terapeutisk metode.' *Musikk Terapi 6*, 24–27.

Skille, O. (1986) *Manual of Vibroacoustics*. Levanger, Norway: ISVA Publications.

Skille, O. (1989a) 'Vibroacoustic research.' In R. Spintge and R. Droh (eds) *Music Medicine*. St. Louis: Magna Music Baton.

Skille, O. (1989b) 'Vibroacoustic therapy.' *Music Therapy 8*, 61–77.

Skille, O. (1992) 'Vibroacoustic research 1980–1991.' In R. Spintge and R. Droh (eds) *Music and Medicine*. St. Louis: Magna Music Baton.

Skille, O. and Wigram, T. (1995) 'The effects of music, vocalisation and vibration on brain and muscle tissue: studies in vibroacoustic therapy.' In T. Wigram, B. Saperston and R. West (eds) *The Art and Science of Music Therapy: A Handbook*. London: Harwood Academic.

Sloman, L. (1998) *Reefer Madness: The History of Marijuana in America*. New York: St. Martin's, Griffin.

Small, C. (1998) *Musicking. The Meanings of Performing and Listening*. Hanover, NH: Wesleyan University Press.

Smith, M. (1993) 'Merleau-Ponty's aesthetics.' In G. Johnson (eds) *The Merleau-Ponty Aesthetics Reader. Philosophy and Painting*. Evanston, IL: Northwestern University Press.

Solomon, D. (1966) *The Marihuana Papers*. New York: New American Library.

Spintge, R. (1982) 'Psychophysiological surgery preparation with and without anxiolytic music.' In R. Droh and R. Spintge (eds) *Angst, Schmerz, Muzik in der Anasthesie*. Basel: Editiones Roche.

Spintge, R. and Droh, R. (1982) 'The pre-operative condition of 191 patients exposed to anxiolytic music and Rohypnol (Flurazepam) before receiving an epidural anaesthetic.' In R. Droh and R. Spintge (eds) *Angst, Schmerz, Muzik in der Anasthesie*. Basel: Editiones Roche.

Springer, S.P. and Deutsch, G. (1987) *Linkes – Rechtes Gehirn. Funktionelle Asymetrien*. Heidelberg: Spektrum der Wissenschaften.

Stake, R.E. (1995) *The Art of Case Study Research*. London: Sage.

Standley, J. (1991) 'The effect of vibrotactile and auditory stimuli on perception of comfort, heart rate and peripheral finger temperature.' *Journal of Music Therapy 28*, 3, 120–34.

Standley, J. (1995) 'Music as a therapeutic intervention in medical and dental treatment: Research and clinical applications.' In T. Wigram, B. Saperston and R. West. (eds) *The Art and Science of Music Therapy: A Handbook*. London: Harwood Academic.

Stefanis, C., Dornbush, R. and Fink, M. (1977) *Hashish: Studies of Long Term Use.* New York: Raven Press.

Stige, B. (2002) 'Do we need general criteria for the evaluation of qualitative research articles, and if we do, how could such criteria be formulated?' *Nordic Journal of Music Therapy 11*, 1, 65–71.

Stile, S.W. (1988) 'Single-subject research in early childhood special education: A survey of seven selected journals – 1977–1986.' Paper presented at the conference of the Rocky Mountain Education Research Association, La Cruces, NM, 25 October, 1988.

Stillman, B.C. (1970) 'Vibratory motor stimulation: A preliminary report.' *Australian Journal of Physiotherapy 16*, 118–123.

Struve, F.A. and Straumanis, J.J. (1990) 'Electroencephalographic and evoked potential methods in human marihuana research: historical review and future trends.' *Drug Development Research 20*, 369–388.

Tagg, P. (1982) 'Analysing popular music: theory, method and practice.' *Popular Music 2*, 37–67.

Takehisa, K. and Takehisa-Silvestri, G. (n.d.) 'Intermediate results of music therapy in interdisciplinary work with Rett syndrome in institut Haus der barmherzigkeit, Vienna.' Personal communication. Institut Haus der Barmherzigkeit, Vienna.

Tart, C. (1971) *On Being Stoned, A Psychological Study of Marihuana Intoxikation.* Palo Alto: Science and Behaviour Books.

Tart, C.T. (1975) *States of Consciousness.* New York: E.P. Dutton.

Teirich, H.R. (1959) 'On therapeutics through music and vibrations.' In H. Scherchen (ed) *Gravesaner Blatter.* Mainz: Ars Viva.

TelAbility (2003) 'Enhancing the lives of children with disabilities.' Retrieved 7 March, 2003 from the internet: http://www.telability.org/

Thaler, S., Fass, P. and Fitzpatrick, D. (1973) 'Marihuana and hearing.' *Canadian Journal of Otolaryngology 2*, 291–295.

Thaut, M. (1988) 'Measuring musical responsiveness in autistic children: a comparative analyses of improvised musical tone sequences of autistic, normal, and mentally retarded individuals.' *Journal of Autism and Developmental Disorder 28*, 4, 561–571.

Thielst, P. (1994) 'Linet forstås baglœns – menmå leves forlœns.' Cited in Kierkegaards papers: Papirer IV-A 164, 295. Copenhagen: Gyldendal.

Thomas, L. and Harri-Augstein, E. (1985) *Self-organised Learning: Foundations of a Conversational Science for Psychology.* London: Routledge and Kegan Paul.

Tomaino, C.M. (2000) 'Working with images and recollection with elderly patients.' In D. Aldridge (ed) *Music Therapy in Dementia Care.* London: Jessica Kingsley Publishers.

Treatment and Education of Autism and Related Communication Handicapped Children (TEACCH) (2003a) 'Educational approaches.' Retrieved 24 February, 2003 from the internet: http://www.teacch.com/

Treatment and Education of Autism and Related Communication Handicapped Children (TEACCH) (2003b) 'Autism primer: Twenty questions and answers.' Retrieved 20 February, 2003 from the internet: http://www.teacch.com/

Trillingsgaard, A. (1999) 'The script model in relation to autism.' *European Child Adolescent Psychiatry 8*, 1, 45–49.

Trochim, W. (1985) 'Pattern matching, validity, and conceptualization in program evaluation.' *Evaluation Review 9*, 5.

Trochim, W. (2002) *The Research Methods Knowledge Base, 2nd Edition.* Cornell University. http://www.social researchmethods.net/kb/pmconval.htm

U.S. Consumer Product Safety Commission (1997) *Handbook for Public Playground Safety*, publication no. 325. Washington, DC: U.S. Consumer Product Safety Commission.

Volavka, J., Crown, P., Dornbush, R., Feldstein, S. and Fink, M. (1973) 'EEG, heart rate and mood change ("high") after cannabis.' *Psychopharmacologia 32*, 1, 11–25.

Volavka, J., Dornbush, R., Feldstein, S., Clare, G., Zaks, A., Fink, M. and Freedman, A.M. (1971) 'Marijuana, EEG and Behaviour.' *Annals of the New York Academy of Science 191*, 206–215.

Volavka, J., Fink, M. and Panayiotopoulos, C.P. (1977) 'Acute EEG-effects of cannabis preparations in long term hashish users.' In C. Stefanis, R. Dornbush and M. Fink (eds) *Hashish: Studies of Long Term Use.* New York: Raven Press.

Von Gierke, H.E. and Nixon, C.W. (1976) 'Effects of intense infrasound on man.' In W. Tempest (ed) *Infrasound and Low Frequency Vibration*. London: Academic Press.

von Plessen, C. (1995) 'Krankheitserfahrungen von krebskranken Kindern und ihren Familien.' Inaugural-Doctoral Dissertation, University of Witten Herdecke.

Wakeford, L. (2002) 'Telehealth technology for children with special needs.' *Occupational Therapy Practice 7*, 21, 12–16.

Walker, J.L. (1977) 'Subjective reactions to music and brainwave rhythms.' *Physiological Psychology 5*, 4, 483–489.

Warwick, A. (1995) 'Music therapy in the education service: Research with autistic children and their mothers.' In T. Wigram, B. Saperston and R. West (eds) *The Art and Science of Music Therapy*. Chur, Switzerland: Harwood Academic Publishers.

Weber, K. (1974) 'Veränderungen des Musikerlebens in der experimentellen Psychose (Psylocibin) und ihre Bedeutung für die Musikpsychologie.' In G. Revers, W. Simon (eds) *Neue Wege der Musiktherapie*. Düsseldorf, Wien: Econ.

Webster, P. (2001) 'Marijuana and music: A speculative exploration.' *Journal of Cannabis Therapeutics 1*, 2, 105.

Webster's Seventh New Collegiate Dictionary (1976) Springfield, MA: G. & C. Merriam.

Wedell, C.H. and Cummings, S.B. (1938) 'Fatigue of the vibratory sense.' *Journal of Experimental Psychology 22*, 429–438.

Weil, A. (1998) *The Natural Mind*. 3 Boston: Houghton Mifflin.

Weil, A.T., Zinberg, N.E. and Nelsen, J.M. (1968) 'Clinical and psychological effects of marihuana in man.' *Science 162*, 859, 1234–1242.

Weiss, M. (1996) 'Assessment and intervention of hand behaviors.' Paper presented at the International Rett syndrome 12th annual conference. Boston, MA.

Wesecky, A. (1986) 'Music therapy for children with Rett syndrome.' *American Journal of Medical Genetics 24*, Suppl. 1, 253–257.

White, K.E. (1991) *A Guide to the Saints*. New York: Ivy Books.

Whiteley, S. (1992) *The Space Between the Notes – Rock and the Counter Culture*. London: Routledge.

Wigram, A. and Weekes, L. (1989) 'Collaborative approaches in treating the profoundly handicapped.' *Paediatric Physiotherapy Newsletter* 51, 5–9.

Wigram, T. (1991) 'Assessment and treatment of a girl with Rett syndrome.' In K. Bruscia (ed) *Case studies in Music Therapy*. Gilsum, NH: Barcelona Publishers.

Wigram, T. (1993) '"The Feeling of Sound" – The effect of music and low frequency sound in reducing anxiety in challenging behaviour in clients with learning difficulties.' In H. Payne (ed) *Handbook of Enquiry in the Arts Therapies: One River, Many Currents*. London: Jessica Kingsley Publishers.

Wigram, T. (1995) 'Psychological and physiological effects of low frequency sound and music.' *Music Therapy Perspectives – International Edition*. Silver Spring, Maryland: NAMT Publications.

Wigram T. (1996) 'The effect of vibroacoustic therapy on clinical and non-clinical populations.' Ph. D. psychology research thesis, St Georges Medical School, University of London. In D. Aldridge *Music Therapy World Info CD-ROM* II. Witten: University of Witten-Herdecke.

Wigram, T. (1997a) 'The effect of vibroacoustic therapy in the treatment of Rett Syndrome.' In T. Wigram and C. Dileo (eds) *Music, Vibration and Health*. New Jersey: Jeffrey Books.

Wigram, T. (1997b) 'Equipment for vibroacoustic therapy.' In T. Wigram and C. Dileo (eds) *Music, Vibration and Health*. New Jersey: Jeffrey Books.

Wigram, T. and Cass, H. (1985) 'Music therapy within the assessment process of a therapy clinic for people with Rett syndrome.' British Society of Music Therapy Conference. London: BSMT Publications.

Wigram, T. and Cass, H. (1996) 'Music therapy within the assessment process for a therapy clinic for people with Rett syndrome.' Paper presented at the Rett Syndrome World Conference in Sweden.

Wigram, T. and Dileo, C. (1997a) *Music, Vibration and Health*. New Jersey: Jeffrey Books.

Wigram, T. and Dileo, C. (1997b) 'Clinical and ethical considerations.' In T. Wigram and C. Dileo (eds) *Music, Vibration and Health*. New Jersey: Jeffrey Books.

Wigram, T., Pedersen, I.N. and Bonde, L.O. (2002) *A Comprehensive Guide to Music Therapy.* London: Jessica Kingsley Publishers.

Wigram, T., McNaught, J and Cain, J. (1997) 'Vibroacoustic therapy with adult patients with profound learning disability'. In T. Wigram and C. Dileo (eds) *Music, Vibration and Health.* New Jersey: Jeffrey Books.

Wigram, T. and Weekes, L. (1983) 'The use of music in overcoming motor dysfunction in children and adolescents suffering from severe physical and mental handicap – A specific approach.' Unpublished paper, World Congress of Music Therapy, Paris.

Wigram, T. and Weekes, L. (1985) 'A specific approach to overcoming motor dysfunction in children and adolescents with severe physical and mental handicaps using music and movement.' *British Journal of Music Therapy 16,* 1, 2–12.

Wilcox, M.J. and Shannon, M.S. (1996) 'Integrated early intervention practices in speech-language pathology.' In R.A. McWilliam (ed) *Rethinking Pull-out Services in Early Intervention: A Professional Resource.* Baltimore, MD: Paul H. Brookes Publishers.

Williams, D. (1999) *An Inside-Out Approach.* London: Jessica Kingsley Publishers.

Wolcott, H.F. (1994) *Transforming Qualitative Data: Description, Analysis, and Interpretation.* Thousand Oaks, CA: Sage.

Wolery, M. (1992) *Teaching Students with Moderate and Severe Disabilities: Use of response prompting strategies.* White Plains, NY: Longman.

Wolery, M., Anthony, L., Caldwell, N.K., Snyder, E.D. and Morgante, J.D. (2002) 'Embedding and distributing constant time delay in circle time and transitions.' *Topics in Early Childhood Special Education 22,* 1, 14–25.

Wolery, M., Bailey, D.B. and Sugai, G.M. (1988) *Effective Teaching: Principles and Procedures of Applied Behavior Analysis with Exceptional Students.* Boston: Allyn & Bacon.

Wolery, M., Watson, L., Garfinkel, A.N., Marcus, L. and Coburn, J. (2001) 'Replication manual: Center-based early intervention demonstration project for children with autism.' Unpublished manual.

Wolery, M. and Wilbers, J.S. (1994) *Including Children with Special Needs in Early Childhood Programs.* Washington, DC: National Association for the Education of Young Children.

Wolfe, D. and Hom, C. (1993) 'Use of melodies as structural prompts for learning and retention of sequential verbal information by preschool students.' *Journal of Music Therapy 30,* 2, 100–118.

Woodyatt, G. and Ozanne, A. (1993) 'A longitudinal study of cognitive skills and communication behaviors in children with Rett syndrome.' *Journal of Intellectual Disability Research 37,* 419–435.

Woodyatt, G. and Ozanne, A. (1994) 'Intentionality and communication in four children with Rett syndrome.' *Australia and New Zealand Journal of Developmental Disabilities 19,* 173–183.

Yamada, S., Ikugi, M., Fujikata, S., Watanabe, T. and Kosaka, T. (1983) 'Body sensation of low frequency noise of ordinary persons and profoundly deaf persons.' *Journal of Low Frequency Noise and Vibration 2,* 3, 32–36.

Yin, R. (1994) *Case Study Research. Design and Methods.* London: Sage.

Yontef, G.M. and Simkin, J.S. (1989) 'Gestalt therapy.' In R.J. Corsini and D. Wedding *Current Psychotherapies,* 4th edn. Itasca, IL. Peacock Publishers.

Bibliography

I provide here a list of supplementary references for a range of studies that have been published in the music therapy literature. There are databases of literature sources on the website www. musictherapyworld.net under the 'structured review' section and in the 'in-house' library.

Aasgaard, T. (2000) '"A Suspiciously Cheerful Lady": A study of a song's life in the paediatric oncology ward, and beyond.' *British Journal of Music Therapy 14*, 2, 70–82.

Abs, B. (1983) 'Conditions and possibilities for music therapy in psychiatric hospitals.' *Musiktherapeutische Umschau 4*, 4, 265–280.

Abs, B. (1989) 'Activity and coactivity in music therapy treatment.' *Musiktherapeutische Umschau 10*, 1, 33–49.

Agrotou, A. (1988) 'A case study: Lara.' *Journal of British Music Therapy 2*, 1, 17–23.

Agrotou, A. (1994) 'Isolation and the multi-handicapped patient: An analysis of the music therapist-patient affects and processes.' *Arts in Psychotherapy 21*, 5, 359–365.

Aigen, K.S. (2001) 'Popular musical styles in Nordoff-Robbins clinical improvisation.' *Music Therapy Perspectives 19*, 1, 31–44.

Aldridge, D. (1994) 'Single-case research designs for the creative art therapist.' *Arts in Psychotherapy 21*, 5, 333–342.

Aldridge, D. (1995) 'Music therapy and the treatment of Alzheimer's disease.' *Clinical Gerontologist 16*, 1, 41–57.

Aldridge, D. (1998) 'Music therapy and the treatment of Alzheimer's disease.' *Journal of Clinical Geropsychology 4*, 1, 17–30.

Aldridge, D., Brandt, G. and Wohler, D. (1990) 'Toward a common language among the creative art therapies.' *Arts in Psychotherapy 17*, 3, 189–195.

Aldridge, D., Gustorff, D. and Neugebauer, L. (1996) 'A preliminary study of creative music therapy in the treatment of children with developmental delay.' *Arts in Psychotherapy 22*, 3, 189–205.

Aldridge, G. (1996) '"A walk through Paris": The development of melodic expression in music therapy with a breast-cancer patient.' *Arts in Psychotherapy 23*, 3, 207–223.

Anderson, F.E. (1983) 'A critical analysis of "A review of the published research literature in arts for the handicapped: 1971–1981", with special attention to the visual arts.' *Art Therapy 1*, 1, 26–39.

Bean, J. (1995) 'Music therapy and the child with cerebral palsy: Directive and non-directive intervention.' In T. Wigram, B.M. Saperston and R. West (eds) *The Art and Science of Music Therapy: A Handbook.* Chur, Switzerland: Harwood Academic Publishers.

Becker, H. (1984) 'Music therapy with deaf children.' *Musiktherapeutische Umschau 5*, 2, 131–136.

Bergerhoff, P. and Timmermann, T. (1989) 'Music therapy in cases of obesity.' *Musiktherapeutische Umschau 10*, 3, 243–250.

Berruti, G., Del Puente, G., Gatti, R., Manarolo, G. and Vecchiato, C. (1993) 'Description of an experience in music therapy carried out at the Department of Psychiatry of the University of Genoa.' In M.H. Heal and T. Wigram (eds) *Music Therapy in Health and Education.* London: Jessica Kingsley Publishers.

Blasco, S.P. (1978) 'Case study: Art expression as a guide to music therapy.' *American Journal of Art Therapy 17*, 2, 51–56.

Bohnert, K. (1999) 'Meaningful musical experience and the treatment of an individual in psychosis: A case study.' *Music Therapy Perspectives 17*, 2, 69–73.

Boisvert, S. and Benveniste, M.K. (2002) 'Music therapy with children having physical or sensory deficits.' *Canadian Journal of Music Therapy 9*, 1, 65–74.

Bonder, B.R. (1994) 'Psychotherapy for individuals with Alzheimer disease.' *Alzheimer Disease & Associated Disorders 8*, 3, 75–81.

Brotons, M., Koger, S.M. and Pickett-Cooper, P. (1997) 'Music and dementias: A review of literature.' *Journal of Music Therapy 34*, 4, 204–245.

Brown, M.M. (1999) 'Auditory integration training and autism: two case studies.' *British Journal of Occupational Therapy 62*, 1, 13–18.

Brown, S., Goetell, E. and Ekman, S.-L. (2001) '"Music-therapeutic caregiving": The necessity of active music-making in clinical care.' *Arts in Psychotherapy 28*, 2, 125–135.

Brown, S.M.K. (1994) 'Autism and music therapy – is change possible, and why music?' *Journal of British Music Therapy 8*, 1, 15–25.

Brownell, M.D. (2002) 'Musically adapted social stories to modify behaviors in students with autism: Four case studies.' *Journal of Music Therapy 39*, 2, 117–144.

Bruscia, K.E. (1982) 'Music in the assessment of echolalia.' *Music Therapy 2*, 1, 25–41.

Bryan, A. (1989) 'Autistic group case study.' *Journal of British Music Therapy 3*, 1, 16–21.

Burke, M. (1995) 'Music therapy following suctioning: four case studies.' *Neonatal Network Journal of Neonatal Nursing 14*, 7, 41–49.

Burkhardt-Mramor, K.M. (1996) 'Music therapy and attachment disorder: A case study.' *Music Therapy Perspectives 14*, 2, 77–82.

Bush, C.A. (1988) 'Dreams, mandalas, and music imagery: Therapeutic uses in a case study.' *Arts in Psychotherapy 15*, 3, 219–225.

Butterton, M. (1993) 'Music in the pastoral care of emotionally disturbed children.' *Journal of British Music Therapy 7*, 2, 12–22.

Byrne, L.A. (1982) 'Music therapy and reminiscence: A case study.' *Clinical Gerontologist 1*, 2, 76–77.

Cathala, A. (1983) 'Use of music to improve language and communication?' *Pratique des Mots 42*, 19–22.

Celi, S. (1990) 'A case study illustrating the interface of music therapy and analytical psychology.' *Dissertation Abstracts International 50*, 7–A,

Chesky, K.S. and Michel, D.E. (1991) 'The Music Vibration Table (MVT): Developing a technology and conceptual model for pain relief.' *Music Therapy Perspectives 9*, 32–38.

Cirina, C.L. (1994) 'Effects of sedative music on patient preoperative anxiety.' *Todays OR Nurse 16*, 3, 15–18.

Colwell, C.M. (1997) 'Music as distraction and relaxation to reduce chronic pain and narcotic ingestion: A case study.' *Music Therapy Perspectives 15*, 1, 24–31.

Coulter, H. and Loughlin, E. (1999) 'Synergy of verbal and non-verbal therapies in the treatment of mother-infant relationships.' *British Journal of Psychotherapy 16*, 1, 58–73.

Cowan, D.S. (1991) 'Music therapy in the surgical arena.' *Music Therapy Perspectives 9*, 42–45.

Cross, P., McLellan, M., Vomberg, E., Monga, M. and Monga, T.N. (1984) 'Observations on the use of music in rehabilitation of stroke patients.' *Physiotherapy Canada 36*, 4, 197–201.

Curtis, S.L. (2000) 'Singing subversion, singing soul: Women's voices in feminist music therapy.' *Dissertation Abstracts International 60*, 12A, 4240.

Custer, S.L.A. (1996) 'Using music therapy in a clinical setting to lower the levels of anxiety and stress.' *Masters Abstracts International 35*, 2, 0588.

Daveson, B.A. and Kennelly, J. (2000) 'Music therapy in palliative care for hospitalized children and adolescents.' *Journal of Palliative Care 16*, 1, 35–38.

Davis, G. and Magee, W. (2001) 'Clinical improvisation within neurological disease: exploring the effect of structured clinical improvisation on the expressive and interactive responses of a patient with Huntington's disease.' *British Journal of Music Therapy 15*, 2, 51–60.

Davis, K.L. (1998) '"To never surrender": Music therapy in the fight against multiple sclerosis.' *Canadian Journal of Music Therapy 6*, 1, 20–34.

Diaz de Chumaceiro, C.L. and Yaber, O. (1995) 'Serendipity analogues: Approval of modifications of the traditional case study for a psychotherapy research with music.' *Arts in Psychotherapy 22*, 2, 155–159.

Dicamillo, M.P. (2000) 'A bio-psycho-social model of music therapy-assisted childbirth: An integrative approach to working with families.' *Dissertation Abstracts International 60*, 12A, 4329.

Edwards, J. (1999) 'Music therapy with children hospitalised for severe injury and illness.' *British Journal of Music Therapy 13*, 1, 21–27.

Erkkila, J. (1997) 'The meaning levels of music from the point of view of the theory and the clinical practise of music therapy.' *Dissertation Abstracts International 59*, 04C, 0998.

Erkkila, J. (1997) 'From the unconscious to the conscious: Musical improvisation and drawings as tools in the music therapy of children.' *Nordic Journal of Music Therapy 6*, 2, 112–120.

Fagen, T.S. (1982) 'Music therapy in the treatment of anxiety and fear in terminal pediatric patients.' *Music Therapy 2*, 1, 13–23.

Fredrickson, W.E. (2000) 'Perception of tension in music: Musicians versus nonmusicians.' *Journal of Music Therapy 37*, 1, 40–50.

Frohne, I. (1982) 'Music as a form of creative therapy.' *Integrative-Therapie 8*, 4, 325–343.

Gardiner, J.C., Furois, M., Tansley, D.P. and Morgan, B. (2000) 'Music therapy and reading as intervention strategies for disruptive behavior in dementia.' *Clinical Gerontologist 22*, 1, 31–46.

Geissler, M. (1986) 'Music therapy with an epileptic child. A case study using anthroposophically oriented music therapy.' *Musiktherapeutische Umschau 7*, 2, 131–139.

Gerdner, L.A. and Swanson, E.A. (1993) 'Effects of individualized music on confused and agitated elderly patients.' *Archives of Psychiatric Nursing 7*, 5, 284–291.

Glassman, L.R. (1991) 'Music therapy and bibliotherapy in the rehabilitation of traumatic brain injury: A case study.' *Arts in Psychotherapy 18*, 2, 149–156.

Goldberg, F.S., Hoss, T.M. and Chesna, T. (1988) 'Music and imagery as psychotherapy with a brain damaged patient: A case study.' *Music Therapy Perspectives 5*, 41–45.

Goldstein, C. (1964) 'Music and creative arts therapy for an autistic child.' *Journal of Music Therapy 1*, 4, 135–138.

Goldstein, C., Lingas, C. and Sheafor, D. (1965) 'Interpretive or creative movement as a sublimation tool in music therapy.' *Journal of Music Therapy 2*, 1, 11–15.

Goodman, K.D. (1989) 'Music therapy assessment of emotionally disturbed children.' *Arts in Psychotherapy 16*, 3, 179–192.

Gregory, D. (2002) 'Four decades of music therapy behavioral research designs: A content analysis of Journal of Music Therapy articles.' *Journal of Music Therapy 39*, 1, 56–71.

Groene, R.W. (1994) 'Effectiveness of music therapy intervention with individuals having senile dementia of the Alzheimer's type (Alzheimer's Disease).' *Dissertation Abstracts International 53*, 10A, 3468.

Grootaers, F.-G. (1985) 'Group music therapy from a holistic point of view.' *Musiktherapeutische Umschau 6*, 1, 37–67.

Grun, M., Dill-Schmolders, C. and Greulich, W. (1998) 'Creative music therapy and Parkinson's disease.' *Rehabilitacia 31*, 4, 253–255.

Guzzetta, C.E. (1995) 'Music therapy: hearing the melody of the soul.' *Holistic Nursing: A Handbook for Practice 2*, 669–698.

Hadsell, N.A. and Coleman, K.A. (1988) 'Rett syndrome: A challenge for music therapists.' *Music Therapy Perspectives 5*, 52–56.

Hakvoort, L. (2002) 'A music therapy anger management program for forensic offenders.' *Music Therapy Perspectives 20*, 2, 123–132.

Hanser, S.B. and Clair, A.A. (1995) 'Retrieving the losses of Alzheimer's disease for patients and caregivers with the aid of music.' In T. Wigram, B. Saperston and R. West (eds) *The Art and Science of Music Therapy: A Handbook.* Chur, Switzerland: Harwood Academic Publishers.

Hassner, M. (1983) 'Therapy with rock music?' *Musiktherapeutische Umschau 4*, 3, 217–222.

Heal, M. (1991) 'Psychoanalytically oriented music therapy for the mentally retarded. Two case studies.' *Musiktherapeutische Umschau 12*, 2, 110–127.

Hibben, J. (1992) 'Music therapy in the treatment of families with young children.' *Music Therapy 11*, 1, 28–44.

Hilliard, R.E. (2001) 'The use of music therapy in meeting the multidimensional needs of hospice patients and families.' *Journal of Palliative Care 17*, 3, 161–166.

Hoelzley, P.D. (1991) 'Reciprocal inhibition in music therapy: A case study involving wind instrument usage to attenuate fear, anxiety, and avoidance reactivity in a child with pervasive developmental disorder.' *Music Therapy 10*, 1, 58–76.

Hooper, J. (1993) 'Developing interaction through shared musical experiences: A strategy to enhance and validate the descriptive approach.' In M.H. Heal and T. Wigram (eds) *Music Therapy in Health and Education*. London: Jessica Kingsley Publishers.

Hooper, J. (2002) 'Using music to develop peer interaction: an examination of the response of two subjects with a learning disability.' *British Journal of Learning Disabilities 30*, 4, 166–170.

Hooper, J. and Lindsay, B. (1990) 'Music and the mentally handicapped: The effect of music on anxiety.' *Journal of British Music Therapy 4*, 2, 18–26.

Hooper, J., Lindsay, B. and Richardson, I. (1991) 'Recreation and music therapy: An experimental study.' *Journal of British Music Therapy 5*, 2, 10–13.

Howat, R. (1995) 'Elizabeth: A case study of an autistic child in individual music therapy.' In T. Wigram, B. Saperston and R. West (eds) *The Art and Science of Music Therapy: A Handbook*. Chur, Switzerland: Harwood Academic Publishers.

Hsueh, M.Y. (2002) 'The effects of music on behavioral and cognitive skills in an individual with Down syndrome.' Masters thesis, Texas Woman's University.

Hughes, J.R., Fino, J.J. and Melyn, M.A. (1999) 'Is there a chronic change of the "mozart effect" on epileptiform activity? A case study.' *Clinical EEG (Electroencephalography) 30*, 2, 44–45.

Inselmann, U. and Mann, S. (2000) 'Emotional experience, expression and interaction in musical improvisations: A qualitative-quantitative single case study.' *Psychotherapie, Psychosomatik, Medizinische Psychologie 50*, 3–4, 193–198.

Jacavone, J. and Young, J. (1998) 'Use of pulmonary rehabilitation strategies to wean a difficult-to-wean patient: case study.' *Critical Care Nurse 18*, 6, 29–37.

Jackson, M. (1995) 'Music therapy for living: A case study on a woman with breast cancer.' *Canadian Journal of Music Therapy 3*, 1, 19–33.

Jacobowitz, R.M. (1992) 'Music therapy in the short-term pediatric setting: Practical guidelines for the limited time frame.' *Music Therapy 11*, 1, 45–64.

Jakab, I. (1965) '"Scribbling" in art therapy.' *Journal of Music Therapy 2*, 1, 3–7.

James, M.R. and Freed, B.S. (1989) 'A sequential model for developing group cohesion in music therapy.' *Music Therapy Perspectives 7*, 28–34.

Jellison, J.A. and Gainer, E.W. (1995) 'Into the mainstream: A case-study of a child's participation in music education and music therapy.' *Journal of Music Therapy 32*, 4, 228–247.

Jochims, S. (1990) 'Emotional coping with neurological diseases in the acute phase of illness: The possibilities of music therapy as a form of psychotherapy demonstrated by two case studies.' *Psychotherapie, Psychosomatik, Medizinische Psychologie 40*, 3–4, 115–122.

Jochims, S. (1991) 'Coping with illness and free improvisation. On the function of actively creating sounds as exemplified in grief work.' *Musiktherapeutische Umschau 12*, 1, 4–20.

Jochims, S. (1992) 'Depression in old age. A contribution by music therapy to grief work.' *Zeitschrift-fuer-Gerontologie 25*, 6, 391–396.

Johnson, J.K., Cotman, C.W., Tasaki, C.S. and Shaw, G.L. (1998) 'Enhancement of spatial-temporal reasoning after a Mozart listening condition in Alzheimer's disease: A case study.' *Neurological Research 20*, 8, 666–672.

Kehrer, H.-E. (1988) 'The autistic syndrome: Current research into symptoms, causes, and therapy.' *Musiktherapeutische Umschau 9*, 1, 20–28.

Keller, V.E. (1995) 'Management of nausea and vomiting in children.' *Journal of Pediatric Nursing 10*, 5, 280–286.

Kellogg, J., MacRae, M., Bonny, H.L. and di Leo, F. (1977) 'The use of the mandala in psychological evaluation and treatment.' *American Journal of Art Therapy 16*, 4, 123–134.

Kennelly, J. (2001) 'Music therapy in the bone marrow transplant unit: Providing emotional support during adolescence.' *Music Therapy Perspectives 19*, 2, 104–108.

Kortegaard, H.-M. (1993) 'Musikkens funtion i den skizofrene Indre Verden – musikterapi i psykoterapeutisk behandling.' *Nordic Journal of Music Therapy 2*, 1, 18–27.

Kugler, J., Schedlowski, M. and Schulz, K.-H. (1995) Psychoneuroimmunology: How the Brain and the Immune System Communicate with Each Other. Lengerich: Pabst.

Kydd, P. (2001) 'Using music therapy to help a client with Alzheimer's disease adapt to long-term care.' *American Journal of Alzheimer's Disease & Other Dementias 16*, 2, 103–108.

Langenberg, M. (1989) 'Problems and opportunities of music therapy in the treatment of eating disorders.' *Musiktherapeutische Umschau 10*, 3, 183–194.

Langenberg, M., Frommer, J. and Tress, W. (1993) 'A qualitative research approach to analytical music therapy.' *Music Therapy 12*, 1, 59–84.

Langenberg, M., Frommer, J. and Tress, W. (1995) 'Case study in research in music psychotherapy: A qualitative approach.' *Psychotherapie, Psychosomatik, Medizinische Psychologie 45*, 12, 418–426.

Langenberg, M., Frommer, J. and Tress, W. (1995) 'From isolation to bonding: A music therapy case study of a patient with chronic migraines.' *Arts in Psychotherapy 22*, 2, 87–101.

Lehtonen, K. and Shaughnessy, M.F. (1992) 'Projective drawings as an aid to music therapy.' *European Journal of Child & Adolescent Psychiatry: Acta Paedopsychiatrica 55*, 4, 231–233.

Levinge, A. (1993) 'Permission to play: The search for self through music therapy research with children presenting with communication difficulties.' In H. Payne (ed) *Handbook of Inquiry in the Arts Therapies: One River, Many Currents*. London: Jessica Kingsley Publishers.

Link, H.M. (1997) 'Auditory Integration Training (AIT): sound therapy? Case studies of three boys with autism who received AIT.' *British Journal of Learning Disabilities 25*, 3, 106–110.

Lintz, M. (1990) '"I want to be called Mrs. A." The use of a gong in music therapy.' *Musiktherapeutische Umschau 11*, 3, 237–255.

Lipe, A.W. (1991) 'Using music therapy to enhance the quality of life in a client with Alzheimer's dementia: A case study.' *Music Therapy Perspectives 9*, 102–105.

Lipe, A.W. (2002) 'Beyond therapy: Music, spirituality, and health in human experience: A review of literature.' *Journal of Music Therapy 39*, 3, 209–240.

Loos, G. (1975) 'Atypical course of a music therapy treatment: A case study.' *Praxis der Psychotherapie 20*, 3, 109–124.

Loos, G. (1986) 'To listen, to hear, to merge.' *Musiktherapeutische Umschau 7*, 3, 165–179.

Loth, H. (1994) 'Music therapy and forensic psychiatry – choice, denial and the law.' *Journal of British Music Therapy 8*, 2, 10–18.

Ludwig, A.J. and Tyson, F. (1969) 'A song for Michael.' *Journal of Music Therapy 6*, 3, 82–86.

Magee, W. (1995) 'Case studies in Huntington's Disease: music therapy assessment and treatment in the early to advanced stages.' *British Journal of Music Therapy 9*, 2, 13–19.

Magill-Levreault, L. (1993) 'Music therapy in pain and symptom management.' *Journal of Palliative Care 9*, 4, 42–48.

Meyer, C. (1991) 'The search for new ways of music therapy with a 28-year-old psychotic. The view of a female cotherapist.' *Musiktherapeutische Umschau 12*, 1, 52–62.

Moe, T. (1998) 'A schizotypal patient's music therapy process through the use of a modified version of GIM.' *Nordic Journal of Music Therapy 7*, 1, 14–23.

Moreno, J.J. (1985) 'Music play therapy: An integrated approach.' *Arts in Psychotherapy 12*, 1, 17–23.

Morgan, S. (2002) 'This news is for you.' *Hearing Loss 23*, 5, 37–38.

Neugebauer, L., Gustorff, D., Matthiessen, P. and Aldridge, D. (1989) 'Utilizing music in one's own biography. The example of a female musician.' *Musiktherapeutische Umschau 10*, 3, 234–242.

Niedecken, D. (1991) 'Under the influence of music: Case study of music therapy with a prepsychotic adolescent: The function of music in the psychotherapeutic process.' *Psychotherapie, Psychosomatik, Medizinische Psychologie 41*, 2, 77–82.

Nolan, P. (1989) 'Music therapy improvisation techniques with bulimic patients.' In L.M. Hornyak (ed) *Experiential therapies for eating disorders*. London: Guilford Press.

Odell, H. (1988) 'A music therapy approach in mental health.' *Psychology of Music 16*, 1, 52–61.

Odell, H. (1989) 'Case study review: The case study as research, Proceedings of the Fourth Music Therapy Day Conference 1988.' *Journal of British Music Therapy 3*, 2, 27.

Odell-Miller, H. (1995) 'Why provide music therapy in the community for adults with mental health problems?' *British Journal of Music Therapy 9*, 1, 4–10.

Oldfield, A. (1995) 'Communicating through music: The balance between following and initiating.' In T. Wigram, B. Saperston and R. West (eds) *The Art and Science of Music Therapy: A Handbook*. Chur, Switzerland: Harwood Academic Publishers.

Orff, G. (1982) 'The value of acoustic phenomena and of pre-melodic playing in the development of a blind girl.' *Musiktherapeutische Umschau 3*, 4, 283–293.

Pickett, E. (1987) 'Fibroid tumors and response to guided imagery and music: Two case studies.' *Imagination, Cognition & Personality 7*, 2, 165–176.

Pickford, R.W. (1983) 'Music therapy with a Belgian patient: A follow-up.' *British Journal of Projective Psychology & Personality Study 28*, 2, 31–35.

Pilz, W. (1998) 'Creative music therapy in a psychiatric hospital: Case study of a patient diagnosed as suffering from schizophrenia.' *Musik-, Tanz-und-Kunsttherapie 9*, 2, 55–63.

Pilz, W. (2001) 'Life after death. A single-case study of music therapy in child psychiatry.' *Musik-, Tanz-und-Kunsttherapie 12*, 4, 157–165.

Priestley, M. (1980) 'Analytical music therapy and musical response.' *Musiktherapeutische Umschau 1*, 1, 21–36.

Priestley, M. (1986) 'Music therapy and love.' *Musiktherapeutische Umschau 7*, 1, 1–7.

Priestley, M. (1987) 'Music and the shadow.' *Music Therapy 6*, 2, 20–27.

Priestley, M. (1988) 'Music and the listeners.' *Journal of British Music Therapy 2*, 2, 9–13.

Priestley, M. (1995) 'The meaning of music.' *Nordic Journal of Music Therapy 4*, 1, 28–32.

Purdie, H. (1997) 'Music therapy in neurorehabilitation: Recent developments and new challenges.' *Critical Reviews in Physical & Rehabilitation Medicine 9*, 3–4, 205–217.

Purdie, H. (1997) 'Music therapy with adults who have traumatic brain injury and stroke.' *British Journal of Music Therapy 11*, 2, 45–50.

Ramsey, D.W. (2003) 'The restoration of communal experiences during the group music therapy process with non-fluent aphasic patients.' *Dissertation Abstracts International 63*, 07B, 3266.

Rauch, E.U. (1998) 'Improved treatment for the chronic schizophrenic.' *Dissertation Abstracts International 59*, 02B, 0885.

Redinbaugh, E.M. (1988) 'The use of music therapy in developing a communication system in a withdrawn, depressed older adult resident: A case study.' *Music Therapy Perspectives 5*, 82–85.

Ricciarelli, A. (2003) 'The guitar in palliative music therapy for cancer patients.' *Music Therapy Today* (online), available at http://www.musictherapyworld.net

Rider, M.S. (1987) 'Music therapy: Therapy for debilitated musicians.' *Music Therapy Perspectives 4*, 40–43.

Rider, M.S. (1987) 'Treating chronic disease and pain with music-mediated imagery.' *Arts in Psychotherapy 14*, 2, 113–120.

Risch, M., Scherg, H. and Verres, R. (2001) 'Music therapy for chronic headaches. Evaluation of music therapeutic groups for patients suffering from chronic headaches.' *Schmerz 15*, 2, 116–125.

Risch, M. and Verres, R. (2001) '"Music touches my pain": Evaluation of music therapy groups for patients with chronic headache by means of systematic comparison of contrasting individual case studies.' *Musiktherapeutische Umschau 22*, 3, 185–203.

Ritchie, F. (1991) 'Behind closed doors: A case study.' *Journal of British Music Therapy 5*, 2, 4–9.

Ritchie, F. (1993) 'Opening doors: The effects of music therapy with people who have severe learning difficulties and display challenging behaviour.' In M.H. Heal and T. Wigram (eds) *Music Therapy in Health and Education*. London: Jessica Kingsley Publishers.

Ritholz, M.S. and Turry, A. (1994) 'The journey by train: Creative music therapy with a 17-year-old boy.' *Music Therapy 12*, 2, 58–87.

Rittner, S. (1990) 'The role of vocal improvisation in music therapy.' *Musiktherapeutische Umschau 11*, 2, 104–119.

Robb, S.L. and Ebberts, A.G. (2003) 'Songwriting and digital video production interventions for pediatric patients undergoing bone marrow transplantation, part I: An analysis of depression and anxiety levels according to phase of treatment.' *Journal of Pediatric Oncology Nursing 20*, 1, 2–15.

Robb, S.L. and Ebberts, A.G. (2003) 'Songwriting and digital video production interventions for pediatric patients undergoing bone marrow transplantation, part II: An analysis of patient-generated songs and patient perceptions regarding intervention efficacy.' *Journal of Pediatric Oncology Nursing 20*, 1, 16–25.

Robison, D.E. (1969) 'Report on M.' *Journal of Music Therapy 6*, 3, 76–81.

Robson, C. (2002) *Real World Research: Second Edition.* Oxford: Blackwell.

Rock, O.-T.R. (1984) 'The psychotherapeutic effect of music appreciation: The psychology of music therapy.' *Musiktherapeutische Umschau 5*, 3, 189–195.

Rogers, P. (1992) 'Issues in working with sexually abused clients in music therapy.' *Journal of British Music Therapy 6*, 2, 5–15.

Rogers, P. (1993) 'Research in music therapy with sexually abused clients.' In H. Payne (ed) *Handbook of Inquiry in the Arts Therapies: One River, Many Currents.* London: Jessica Kingsley Publishers.

Rolvsjord, R. (2001) 'Sophie learns to play her songs of tears: A case study exploring the dialectics between didactic and psychotherapeutic music therapy practices.' *Nordic Journal of Music Therapy 10*, 1, 77–85.

Rugenstein, L. (1996) 'Wilber's spectrum model of transpersonal psychology and its application to music therapy.' *Music Therapy 14*, 1, 9–28.

Ruppenthal, W. (1965) '"Scribbling" in music therapy.' *Journal of Music Therapy 2*, 1, 8–10.

Saperston, B.M. (1989) 'Music-Based Individualized Relaxation Training (MBIRT): A stress-reduction approach for the behaviorally disturbed mentally retarded.' *Music Therapy Perspectives 6*, 26–33.

Schmidt, G. (1982) 'Music therapy with a compulsive patient.' *Musiktherapeutische Umschau 3*, 2, 119–130.

Seibert, P.S., Fee, L., Basom, J. and Zimmerman, C. (2000) 'Music and the brain: The impact of music on an oboist's fight for recovery.' *Brain Injury 14*, 3, 295–302.

Selman, J. (1988) 'Music therapy with Parkinson's Disease.' *Journal of British Music Therapy 2*, 1, 5–9.

Silliman-French, L., French, R., Sherrill, C. and Gench, B. (1998) 'Auditory feedback and time-on-task of postural alignment of individuals with profound mental retardation.' *Adapted Physical Activity Quarterly 15*, 1, 51–63.

Slivka, H.H. and Magill, L. (1986) 'The conjoint use of social work and music therapy in working with children of cancer patients.' *Music Therapy 6A*, 1, 30–40.

Smeijsters, H. and Hurk, J. (1999) 'Music therapy helping to work through grief and finding a personal identity.' *Journal of Music Therapy 36*, 3, 222–252.

Smith-Marchese, K. (1994) 'The effects of participatory music on the reality orientation and sociability of Alzheimer's residents in a long-term-care setting.' *Activities, Adaptation and Aging 18*, 2, 41–55.

Spitzer, S. (1989) 'Computers and music therapy: An integrated approach: Four case studies.' *Music Therapy Perspectives 7*, 51–54.

Standley, J.M. (1999) 'Music therapy in the NICU: Pacifier-activated-lullabies (PAL) for reinforcement of nonnutritive sucking.' *International Journal of Arts Medicine 6*, 2, 17–21.

Steele, A.L. (1977) 'The application of behavioral research techniques to community music therapy.' *Journal of Music Therapy 14*, 3, 102–115.

Steele, P.H. (1984) 'Aspects of resistance in music therapy: Theory and technique.' *Music Therapy 4*, 1, 64–72.

Streeter, E. (1999) 'Finding a balance between psychological thinking and musical awareness in music therapy theory – a psychoanalytic perspective.' *British Journal of Music Therapy 13*, 1, 5–20.

Strobel, W. (1988) 'Sound, trance, and healing. The archetypal world of sound within music therapy.' *Musiktherapeutische Umschau 9*, 2, 119–139.

Summer, L. (1985) 'Imagery and music.' *Journal of Mental Imagery 9*, 4, 83–90.

Sutton, J.P. (1996) 'Jerry's story: a music therapy case study.' *British Journal of Therapy & Rehabilitation 3*, 4, 215–217.

Taylor, D. (1969) 'Expressive emphasis in the treatment of intropunitive behavior.' *Journal of Music Therapy 6*, 2, 41–43.

Thöni, M. (2002) 'Guided imagery and music in fifty minute sessions. A challenge for both patient and therapist.' *Nordic Journal of Music Therapy 11*, 2, 182–188.

Tomaino, C.M. (1998) 'Music on their minds: A qualitative study of the effects of using familiar music to stimulate preserved memory function in persons with dementia.' *Dissertation Abstracts International 59*, 05A, 1504.

Tsuboi, K., Makino, M. and Tsutsui, S. (1992) 'Music therapy: An application to the treatment for eating disorders.' *Japanese Journal of Psychosomatic Medicine 32*, 2, 121–128.

Tuepker, R. (1983) 'Morphological methods in music therapy.' *Musiktherapeutische Umschau 4*, 4, 247–264.

Tyson, F. (1979) 'Child at the gate: Individual music therapy with a schizophrenic woman.' *Art Psychotherapy 6*, 2, 77–83.

Usher, J. (1998) 'Lighting up the mind – Evolving a model of consciousness and its application to improvisation in music therapy.' *British Journal of Music Therapy 12*, 1, 4–19.

Ventre, M.E. (1994) 'Healing the wounds of childhood abuse: A guided imagery and music case study.' *Music Therapy Perspectives 12*, 2, 98–103.

Ventre, M.E. (1995) '"Healing the wounds of childhood abuse: A guided imagery and music case study": Errata.' *Music Therapy Perspectives 13*, 1, 55.

Waerja, M. (1994) 'Sounds of music through the spiraling path of individuation: A Jungian approach to music psychotherapy.' *Music Therapy Perspectives 12*, 2, 75–83.

Wager, K.M. (2000) 'The effects of music therapy upon an adult male with autism and mental retardation: A four-year case study.' *Music Therapy 18*, 2, 131–140.

Wardle, M. (1984) 'Music therapy with female prisoners.' *Musiktherapeutische Umschau 5*, 3, 233–242.

Weymann, E. (1989) 'Indications of innovations: Improvisation as a means of assessment and evaluation in therapy and as a subject of research – as exemplified in a case study in music therapy.' *Musiktherapeutische Umschau 10*, 4, 275–290.

Wheeler, B.L. (1987) 'The use of paraverbal therapy in treating an abused child.' *Arts in Psychotherapy 14*, 1, 69–76.

Wigram, T. (2002) 'Indications in Music Therapy: Evidence from assessment that can identify the expectations of music therapy as a treatment for Autistic Spectrum Disorder (ASD); meeting the challenge of Evidence Based Practice.' *British Journal of Music Therapy 16*, 1, 11–28.

Wildman, C. (1995) 'Music Therapist as (a) case study: examining counter-transference with a young child.' *Nordic Journal of Music Therapy 4*, 1, 3–10.

Wimpory, D., Chadwick, P. and Nash, S. (1995) 'Brief report: Musical interaction therapy for children with autism: An evaluative case study with two-year follow-up.' *Journal of Autism & Developmental Disorders 25*, 5, 541–552.

Wimpory, D.C. and Nash, S. (1999) 'Musical interaction therapy: Therapeutic play for children with autism.' *Child Language Teaching & Therapy 15*, 1, 17–28.

Wosch, T. (2002) 'Emotional micro-processes in musical interactions. A single case study on improvisations in music therapy.' Doctoral dissertation, University Münster, Germany.

Wylie, M.E. (1996) 'A case study to promote hand use in children with Rett syndrome.' *Music Therapy Perspectives 14*, 2, 83–86.

Zagelbaum, V.N. and Rubino, M.A. (1991) 'Combined dance/movement, art, and music therapies with a developmentally delayed, psychiatric client in a day treatment setting.' *Arts in Psychotherapy 18*, 2, 139–148.

Zallik, S. (1987) 'In search of the face; an approach to mental handicap.' *Journal of British Music Therapy 1*, 1, 13–15.

Zelazny, C.M. (2001) 'Therapeutic instrumental music playing in hand rehabilitation for older adults with osteoarthritis: Four case studies.' *Journal of Music Therapy 38*, 2, 97–113.

Subject Index

281

Author Index

CPSIA information can be obtained at www.ICGtesting.com
Printed in the USA
LVOW03s0154100615

441775LV00022B/116/P